W9-AVZ-503

THEY WEREN'T GRANTED CEASELESS RAPTURE

"Wait. . . ." Like a shipwreck survivor falling into a bottomless void, Anne clung to Tavo in the steamy pool. "I need time."

"Do you?" he coaxed, returning her eager hands to their original destination. "Feel me, Ana. . . . Feel my love. Can you not admit that our time together should never end?"

Even as her lips sought his windburned mouth, Anne grappled with reality. *End,* his careless word tolled.

"I'm leaving tomorrow, Tavo." She longed to escape his embrace, but her limbs postponed her orders, her slim legs winding around his hips.

"You are the one who pretends this is our last night, Ana."

Yet through his ragged breathing, his apparent conviction, Anne sensed disquiet. "But, Tavo, don't you see? In your heart, you're leaving me, too."

WELCOME TO...

HARLEQUIN SUPERROMANCES

A sensational series of modern love stories.

Written by masters of the genre, these long, sensual
and dramatic novels are truly in keeping with today's
changing life-styles. Full of intriguing conflicts
and the heartaches and delights of true love,
HARLEQUIN SUPERROMANCES are absorbing
stories—satisfying and sophisticated reading
that lovers of romance fiction have long been
waiting for.

HARLEQUIN SUPERROMANCES
Contemporary love stories for the woman of today!

Catherine Healy

PRIVATE CORNERS

Harlequin Books

TORONTO • NEW YORK • LONDON
AMSTERDAM • PARIS • SYDNEY • HAMBURG
STOCKHOLM • ATHENS • TOKYO • MILAN

Yo te la he dado y estate satisfecho. Chau.

With particular gratitude to my family—
a close, extended one in the County Kerry way;
Bob Cookingham, Peter Miller, Ann Sausado,
Sergio Maggione, Pasadena Berlitz, Maria Elena and
Enrique Valenzuela Encima and the late David Kuester.

Published April 1984

First printing February 1984

ISBN 0-373-70111-X

Copyright © 1984 by Catherine Healy. All rights reserved.
Philippine copyright 1984. Australian copyright 1984.
Except for use in any review, the reproduction or utilization of
this work in whole or in part in any form by any electronic,
mechanical or other means, now known or hereafter invented,
including xerography, photocopying and recording, or in any
information storage or retrieval system, is forbidden without
the permission of the publisher, Harlequin Enterprises Limited,
225 Duncan Mill Road, Don Mills, Ontario, Canada M3B 3K9.

Grateful acknowledgment is extended to the following:
Dick Dorworth, for the quotation from THE STRAIGHT COURSE.
Copyright © 1970 by Dick Dorworth. Used by permission.

All the characters in this book have no existence outside the
imagination of the author and have no relation whatsoever to
anyone bearing the same name or names. They are not even
distantly inspired by any individual known or unknown to the
author, and all the incidents are pure invention.

The Superromance design trademark consisting of the words
HARLEQUIN SUPERROMANCE and the portrayal of a Harlequin,
and the Superromance trademark consisting of the words
HARLEQUIN SUPERROMANCE are trademarks of Harlequin
Enterprises Limited. The Superromance design trademark
and the portrayal of a Harlequin are registered in the
United States Patent Office.

Printed in Canada

TO THE READER

The story that follows is a fantasy, wrapped in the real drama of the Hotel Portillo, a Chilean ski resort that refuses to be intimidated by the highest, rawest peaks in the western hemisphere, the Andes.

It is true that South America's elite vie for rooms in the limited space, and that they are remarkably cordial to North American strangers. The world's fastest racers do speed down avalanche chutes, setting records, and blazing-hot sunshine does transform a winter holiday at Portillo into a tanning spectacular. Los Techos in San Martin, Argentina exists, as does Bariloche, the spectacular southern route over the Andes, and the German colony in Puerto Montt.

However, within the excitement of truth, I have created characters and events from my imagination.

CHAPTER ONE

HER DREAM HAD NO BEGINNING. It never did, or middle, either. Never once did the memory linger of his familiar palm cradling her cheek, and never upon waking did she recall the long intellectual fingers that held her secure.

Anne Mahoney wrapped her body tighter into the feather pillows on her four-poster bed, squirming unconsciously, trusting the promise his lips vibrated into the hollow beneath her ear.

You are safe now.

Tell me, she enticed mentally.

Mine, his soft baritone vowed.

Her breath slowed. *Tell me.*

I love you.

Anne's closed lids flickered rapidly as she watched herself turn to meet his generous mouth, her sleeping eyes absorbing his features.

But too late. His face was hidden in yellow swirls of smoke and smog. Fire alarms rang, and she fought for air, panicked in the choking acrid stink. The nightmare was upon her again with a different cast, a new setting. Thin fingers clawed at her, frail from the ravages of emphysema.

"Ring the nurse! I'm suffocating. Ring her!" screamed

a wizened woman in a hospital bed, until sirens smothered her hysterics.

The firemen weren't there yet, the television mini-cameras weren't there, the *Times* wasn't there. Anne had first rights on the drama. She clutched her spiral reporter's notebook and hesitated, trapped between duty and decency.

"Help me! Help me, my oxygen tank's going to ex-plode—"

The pink telephone by Anne's bed rang again.

Thick mahogany hair skimmed bare shoulders slick with sweat as she blindly grabbed to shut off the alarm clock. It was silent, not set to buzz the time until 8:30 A.M.

In her mind, the siren sounded once more.

Anne stared at the illuminated digits, disoriented, her eyes swollen. 2:02.

"Damn." Anne's breath was ragged. She propped the pillow against her back and scooped her hair off her clammy neck, the haunting lips and hands lost in night-mare.

Twisting a swatch of damp hair on top of her head, she flexed her tired shoulders. *Be sensible, Mahoney,* she chided herself, impatiently dissipating the smell of fear in her nostrils. Lung stories and smog come every August, smog and fires hot until September. . . .

2:03. The telephone rang a fourth time. This time she recognized it.

It couldn't be the maverick congressman from California's thirty-fifth district on the affluent Westside of Los Angeles, she knew. Although Charles Roderick III was a front-runner in his political ideas, and she loved him for it, the congressman was a Gibraltar in his habits. Charles had called yesterday afternoon, as usual, about three-thirty California time, before he went out to dinner.

The digital clock clicked 2:04.

"Hello?" Her greeting was professionally encouraging.

"Listen, Anne, sorry to wake you." William A. Snider, metro editor of the *Los Angeles Chronicle*, sounded choked. Was he crying? Dread deafened her, even as Anne strained to hear her boss. "It's Clark. The report just came over from the Catalina Island police. Stephanie was in the sailboat that was run down in the channel this afternoon—"

"What boat?" Anne's question begged a denial. Her protesting mind had already linked the *Chronicle*'s newest financial reporter with the water before Snider finished his sentence.

Stephanie had been ecstatic the day before about sailing to Catalina Island with her boyfriend. "And you thought there was no justice in this life, Annie?" Her best friend had gloated about how covering stockholder meetings on Saturdays was a more reasonable way to earn compensatory time off than reporting murders and mayhem.

"Will you listen to me and get off the blood beat?" Steffie had nagged once again in her breezy way, knowing from her own experience how emotionally grueling it was to work general assignment for the *Chronicle*. The Pulitzer-prize-winning newspaper prided itself on personalizing the news. Its reporters were ordered to write from the heart, and it was often tough.

"Hi-ho, Catalina. For three and one-half days Joel

and I will smell air we can't see. No mucking around the City of Industry on Friday with a pollution inspector...." Anne and Steffie had been walking out the door for lunch. "See how sane life is when you stop chasing ambulances?"

"And know for days ahead of time what I'm going to cover?" Anne had shrugged carelessly. "B-O-R-I-N-G! I'd die."

Dead. Die. Dead. The pink of the twenty-five-year-old reporter's face drained ash gray.

"Was Steffie injured, Will?" Anne asked.

Usually Snider's astringent tone pitted his preciseness against the untidy world, a trait cheerful Steph had teased him about until a smile betrayed his sentimental heart. But tonight William A. Snider rambled.

"Some damn drunk—" He cursed. "The cops and the Coast Guard don't know. I'm guessing the bastard was drunk, plowed his yacht into that plastic bathtub Stephanie's boyfriend had. I told her to drop that idiot. Why the hell he took her out in the middle of nowhere.... I thought you said that doctor loved her, Mahoney. What kind of true love didn't make her put on a life jacket? He should have known Steffie was too impetuous to be careful. She's as reckless as you."

"What about—"

The growl rolled over Anne's whisper.

"What the hell's his name? Dr. Joel Enright. Age thirty-three. A Beverly Hills internist." Anne could imagine Snider reading from the wire copy on his computer screen, hunched so his short blocky body appeared even shorter. "The drunk smashed into their Cal-25, threw his twin diesels into reverse and took off for somewhere. A real rip and run."

"Tell me, Will." Anne forced the sight of Steph's blue eyes, dark as spring pansies, out of her mind. "How is she?"

He was silent, and the stillness gave her answer.

"I know you and Stephanie are friends, Anne. Were friends...." He faltered. "I'd have called sooner, but we've been waiting for the I.D. to come down. The Avalon cops wouldn't release it until her parents were notified. It took a while to track them down. Her dad was negotiating a deal for his bank in Sydney, and her mother was with him."

"How did Steph die?" The stunned reporter fell back on the only defense she knew, the total detachment that comes from sifting and sorting facts. Anne already knew when. In the afternoon. Probably when she herself had been pounding hard for the perfectly exact adjectives to describe fear in her emphysema story.

All the patients had used clichés. "Sweating palms. Thumping heart." They had camouflaged their despair and helpless anger in pat phrases. Anne wiped her wet hands across the floral cotton blanket on her bed and blew on them, trying to coax the stiffness from her fingers. There was nothing trite about sweating palms, she thought now.

"Apparently Clark was tangled in the ropes on the front sail and sank with the boat. The details are still sketchy." William A. Snider gruffly harnessed his grief.

"Here's what we know now. Enright was picked up about five-thirty in the afternoon by a couple of yachtsmen from Newport Beach. They anchored in Avalon about eighty-thirty, called an ambulance and the police. American Press says Enright wasn't suffering from exposure. The ocean's about sixty-eight degrees this time of year, and he wasn't in the water long enough. They quote a Coast Guard doc.

"The emergency room at the hospital says he was treated and is being kept overnight. No phone calls allowed until later. What's he look like?"

"About six-foot two. Engaging grin. Exuberant hair."

When Joel took the helm, his curly sandy hair lifted in the sea breeze. Anne could see him as surely as if she was standing on the bow waiting for his next order to jibe. Steph would stretch up, trying to contain the wild mass with her hands, but with all her antics she couldn't reach high enough and they would all three laugh outrageously.

Anne swallowed with a tight cough. Her cold skin felt suffocated in a damp sheath of static electricity. Still she continued talking in an impassive voice. "Enright's lanky. The kind of guy who hasn't filled out his shoulders yet."

"Good imagery."

The click of the computer keys was barely audible. Anne strained to hear, automatically pacing her information so Snider could keep up with her, the way strangers cooperated when she took stories over the phone.

"Legitimate to call Enright her fiancé?"

"Who the hell's business—" Anger penetrated Anne's shock.

"If you don't read news it hasn't happened, right?" Snider snapped.

She curbed a retort, the smooth line of her jaw taut with the effort. The demanding editor hadn't whiplashed Anne's reluctance to expose privacies since her novice days. "They were talking about a small wedding in October or November after the smog clears," she went on. "But nothing was decided. Is—"

Anne couldn't remember what she had planned to ask. A surge of hate, of readiness to fight, to kill for revenge, pushed through her mind. "Who did it? Do they know?" She forgot Snider had told her, and in his forced calm he had, too.

"No idea. The Mexicans are helping run a dragnet from here to Ensenada—"

"But why didn't the cruiser sink?" Anne's wail was subconscious. She believed she was simply collecting more facts. "When two cars collide, if one's totaled, the other doesn't escape."

"Coast Guard dispatch says the only place boats are strong is on the bow. It's almost impossible to break one there. The official speculated the powerboat jammed a V into the midcenter of Enright's vessel, and maybe—" Snider laughed harshly "—maybe scratched his paint job pulling out."

"But why? Who'd watch someone drown?"

"We're working a lead that they might have been running dope and were afraid of the feds. You've got a narc contact, right?" Snider didn't notice her silence. "Give me his—"

"I'll be down in thirty-six minutes."

"Forget it, Mahoney. Take today off—"

"Give me thirty-six minutes." Her voice was a reflex. "If I crank like crazy I can get one, maybe two pieces in for the first run—"

"I don't want to see you until Monday." Snider's anger temporarily settled on Anne, but she had tucked her cordless phone between her ear and shoulder and was already dressing. "Stephanie Clark was your best friend—"

"So it's my story!" Anne reached back to zip up her dress, twisting to grab the bottom of the zipper without dropping the phone. She had no idea which dress she chose, nor that Snider was insisting she take a three-day weekend for her own good.

"Give me your narc contact," he repeated, and Anne ignored him.

"I'll be there in twenty-five minutes."

Snider wasted no more time arguing. "The desk people tell me you didn't finish your emphysema story until ten-thirty. Don't kid me. I know you didn't eat dinner. Drink some milk before you leave your apartment." He hung up.

A grainy scrub soap from Belgium rubbed raw color on her face, and an erase stick disguised the exhaustion under her eyes. Unlike many square-jawed Irish, Anne had high sloped cheekbones in an oval face, a gypsy's Black Irish face. But her skin was peach, not olive, and her eyes were round as copper pennies. Usually wide and slightly surprised, this morning they were two sockets branded into her aching head.

Blowing her runny nose, Anne shut down all thoughts of Stephanie. There wasn't time to collapse. Later, she promised herself. Later, when night returned and she came home, for then no one would know.

"Annie's like cotton candy on a stainless-steel stick," her father, the owner and manager of the family's three hardware stores, had always praised his only daughter's drive. "Once she's made up her mind," her mother always modified.

Those who didn't know their daughter wouldn't believe Anne's parents. They'd be misled by a welcoming, sometimes mischievous smile. The eldest of two Mahoney children, she had always been a striver, like her grandfather, who had founded the chain of stores on the eastern edge of the Los Angeles Basin, near the orange groves at the base of the San Bernardino Mountains.

Snider had read Anne Mahoney accurately and hired the honors graduate from Pomona College. He didn't care that she had no journalism-school background. Her exceptionally perceptive clips from the student newspaper were sufficient persuasion.

"I'm using you, Mahoney," he would warn, giving her increasingly difficult assignments. The more tragic the story, the more likely that an Anne Mahoney by-line would bring tears to the eyes of the *Chronicle*'s readers the next morning.

Frequent emotional letters to the editor commended her sensitivity, and accolades from the L.A. Press Club praised her courage at disasters. It was a heady time. At first Anne cried, too, alone, late at night. She cried until she was wrung dry, so dry in fact that she didn't even notice when she turned off her emotions.

Anne mechanically flipped through the sweaters in her closet. The gold cardigan would protect her from the chilly desert night, Southern California's only respite from ten August days of 103-degree temperatures and Stage II smog alerts.

Her stomach revolted when she approached the refrigerator. She hated orders. It was excuse enough to disobey.

The drive from her apartment in Santa Monica to the *Chronicle* building downtown passed in a verbal onslaught about Stephanie's drowning. Murder, they were calling it on all-news radio. Steffie was the lead story, boosted to notoriety because her father was a financial celebrity.

William A. Snider was scrolling copy on the borrowed computer screen at the city editor's desk when she hurried silently into the carpeted newsroom. Anne had never witnessed the metro editor take over a breaking story. Otherwise, in spite of the craziness of the task ahead, everything was normal.

Snider, as usual, was perfectly groomed. "So you came anyway, Mahoney." He typed on. "Okay. You can write the obit for the early-morning run." Behind his conservative, black plastic glasses, the editor's eyes were red rimmed.

Obit. Anne refused to flinch in the face of reality. Grim truth was her job.

"Her parents are calling in at four. Be careful. You know how nervous Stephanie's mother is. I'm sure she's on tranquilizers now. Your best bets for information are her father and that brother at Yale. What's his name?"

"Richey," answered Anne, and called the sophomore. Robot fingers recorded the Clark family history while the dark California night passed into day at summer school in New Haven, Connecticut. With the onset of dawn, Richard James Clark IV, now the sole heir to his great-grandfather's banking empire, broke down and cried.

Tension tightened Anne's pale face, yet she had scant time to comfort the teenager. Her story was due in twenty minutes.

Green words of light appeared on her video screen, a stranger's thoughts from far away. *Inarticulate,* Anne thought nervously, and erased her lead with the touch of a key. She started over. *Too detached.* Steffie wasn't an elderly statesman who'd lived out a full life. Anne grimly sent those words into the ether. The third time her facts and emotions connected and the story flowed.

"End what you have and begin a new file, Mahoney," Snider shouted. "I need to start editing your copy."

Anne hit the control button and typed "EN." The green words disappeared into the master directory, where Snider retrieved them. With a quick tap of two keys, she was in a new file, flipping through her notes and remembrances without pause. Page by page, she passed bits of the story to Snider.

When the final eight inches had been sent, Anne rotated her stiff neck, longing for one of Charles's shoulder massages. He had masterful strength in his compact fingers.

She glanced at the digital numbers on her wrist: 3:56. Four minutes before Steph's parents were to call. 6:57 A.M. in Washington, time enough to reach Charles and tell him what had happened.

"I'm sorry, the congressman's out jogging," his answering service said. "If you'd like to leave your name and number, he'll return the call."

She did. "And please, say it's urgent—that—"

"Mahoney, call on 238."

"Just tell him that. Thanks." Anne punched a different extension number.

"Anne, are you all right? Stephanie's mother and I have been concerned about you. We know you share in our loss, too." The elder Richard James Clark consoled her. "I've spoken with Will Snider, Anne. He tells me Richard supplied all the Clark background you need. The wire services can pick up your story, so we won't have to repeat to them. . . ." His composure slipped. He knew the press and dreaded the ordeal ahead. "Richard is flying to Los Angeles on our company jet, and I'll be meeting him at Catalina with some divers. . . ."

Anne won another bout with queasiness, rubbed her freezing hands on her cold bare arms and continued typing Richard J. Clark's official statement.

"Mrs. Clark will be in seclusion at an undisclosed place in Southern California. Private funeral arrangements will be made in New York at the Clark estate overlooking the Hudson River after—" his voice caught "—Stephanie's body is recovered. We are devastated by our daughter's death and grateful her fiancé survived."

Anne was hanging up when the banker startled her.

"Have you cried?" he asked, and when she hesitated, he broke through his own preoccupation. "Remember you are alive, Anne. We Clarks love you."

No tears blemished Anne's unnatural calm. She updated Stephanie's obituary for the late-morning final, keeping her mind and fingers on automatic. Already the story of her friend's life had been shortened to make room for news about the search for her killers.

"See what you can get from your narc contact," Snider yelled at her. "Were the feds tracing any drug boats last night?" Then he assigned another interview and a third. In between calls Anne dialed Washington once more.

Charles's office shunted her aside. Congressman Roderick said he would return her calls later, she was informed. An assistant had tried to call, but the reporter's line was busy. Yes, Anne understood an important bill on school lunches was before the House of Representatives at that very moment, 7:15 A.M., California time.

"But if the vote hasn't been called yet, why can't you transfer me down? This is important. No, I don't want to tell you what it's about. This is—" Anne squelched the truthful word, "personal," and hardened her tone into the standard reportorial threat. "I am on deadline. If you want to take responsibility for not informing the congressman that he has a call from the *Los Angeles Chronicle*—"

"We have informed him, Ms Mahoney." The assistant was undaunted. It was common knowledge that Anne and Charles Roderick had been dating for a year. The *Chronicle* would never assign Anne to cover him. "He will be telephoning later this afternoon."

Anne seethed. She had never asked him for anything. Well, almost nothing.

"I miss you," she had said early in their acquaintance before she learned to appreciate the career convenience of a fairly attentive, out-of-town boyfriend.

"It probably would do us both some good to be with each other, but we're not." His tone had been impatient. The subject was closed, and from long distance Anne had imagined the determined Roderick jaw tightening. Yet she had embarrassed herself, anyway. "Don't you miss me?"

Ever a romantic in his political stance, Charles Roderick was sensible with his emotions. "Anne, if I didn't miss you, I wouldn't call."

Well, he hasn't, Anne thought now, stretching wearily, and reached for the phone to call the coroner's office. She needed details about how divers searched for bodies. This was her first ocean drowning.

Other reporters and editors were a shapeless blur. Anne tuned out the occasional sound of weeping and concentrated on the breaking story, unaware of Snider monitoring her actions.

At 1 P.M. the metro editor shouted for her to come into his office. Anne grabbed a notebook and hurried past the city editor's desk into Snider's walnut-paneled quarters.

"I want you out of this town for three weeks," he ordered bluntly before she had crossed over to his desk.

"What're you talking about?" Anne was openly astonished.

"Out of town. Immediately. I don't like what I see going on in your mind. . . ."

"I can't leave," she argued, startled out of her remoteness.

"Nothing's going on in your mind," he finished.

Snider's personal attack sabotaged Anne's ability to fight back. He had been confident it would. He knew very well that under the cocky facade of most journalists lurked a terrifying apprehension: that someday beneath their by-line the world would see a stupidly written story, or read lazily gathered, false information.

"Wasn't my story all right?" Anne protested, concerned. "I thought if I used a less formal tone people would understand that Steph isn't just some dead rich girl. She's—"

Snider angrily pushed back a shock of gray hair. "You damn women reporters are all alike. I've been telling you and Stephanie to get out of this business before it ruins you—peeping through keyholes and calling it First Amendment privileges. What the hell's wrong with your congressman?" He yanked a tissue out of the box on his desk and honked his nose. "Why aren't you home having his babies? Another five years, you'll still be living alone and smelling of kitty litter like every other old female reporter.''

"Margaret Mead. Margaret Mead.'' Anne chanted the feminist fighting words she and Steph used to taunt Snider when he started his children-kitchen-cooking harangue. She turned before the editor spotted her quick tears at the memory, and headed out the door. "I've got to get back to my story.''

"You're leaving today, Anne. For three weeks. Richard Clark and I agree you need time to mourn properly.''

"I need to work this story.'' Anne's smile was unyielding. "*You* need me. What about the killers? Who's going to interview Joel when the hospital lets us through, hmm? Are you planning to send Cindy Berger out on it? Joel thinks she's an idiot, and Nelson puts everyone off with his badgering—including me. I'm not turning my narc contact over to anyone—''

"All my reporters have a narc contact, and if they don't I'll know why!'' Snider exploded. "I had to have you write the obit, but I won't have you collapsing on me tomorrow. It's time you pulled out of the fast lane to destruction.'' He was ranting now, unaware he was ordering Anne to drop into neutral in the same relentless way he had kicked her forward.

"People shared their closest feelings with you because you cared, Annie. You reached out to them. Get that? Past tense. You haven't reached out to a stranger in ten months, maybe a year. You fix your expression in a way that worked before. You're cashing in on the past, and miss, your savings account is bankrupt.''

The blocky editor put his arm around her taut shoulders and sighed. "We need you at your best. Steffie's killers can't escape much longer. There'll be a trial, and we need you to cover it. It's going to be tough reworking the schedule. Half the staff is on summer vacation now. I agreed to give you two weeks off, but Clark convinced the fourth floor you should have three. Who am I to argue with his golfing buddy, our publisher?''

"But if you do need me. . . .''

Snider gently rapped his pudgy knuckles against her chin. "Annie, Annie. We've all got bosses. You like to ski, right? I remember the series you did two winters ago when the chair-lift cable snapped at White Summit in the Sierra, killing, what, twenty-seven people?''

"Twenty-eight," she corrected, wary.

"As I recall, you asked for a couple of comp days to ski the powder, didn't you say? 'Getting your head together.' ''

"That's a cliché, William A. 'Head together.' My head is together. Besides, it's summer.'' Her voice was triumphant. She had scored with a fact.

Snider pounced gleefully. "If you fly far enough south it's winter. Don't you remember your geography?''

A flush pinked Anne's throat, and she fought back that announcement of vulnerability.

"The plane leaves for Chile at 8:30 tonight. You'll have a few hours to get ready, but no more. Clark doesn't want. . . . I don't want you brooding. . . .''

"Chile?''

"What, you'd prefer another laetrille kid story in Tijuana? A driver from Clark's bank will stop by your apartment at six. You don't need any inoculations, and don't worry about clothes. Clark cabled his Santiago office to buy some ski gear.''

"All taken care of, am I?" Anne despised being marched lockstep under someone's commands. "What if I refuse?"

Snider ignored her. "Don't worry about money, Mahoney. You deserve some bonuses. The publisher has signed for a ticket to Santiago and three weeks' leave with pay. The advances are ready in traveler's checks at payroll. Clark pulled a few strings and somehow found space for you in Portillo. He's paying, so it's probably not el broom-o closet."

He brushed a fist under his glasses, shoved them up to rub his eyes. Clearing his throat, he said, "After Portillo you're on your own. I'm told there are half-a-dozen ski areas in Chile and Argentina. You're clever, Annie. Find a few of them."

"Are you all right, Willie?" Anne touched his arm, her eyes shadowed.

"Don't forget to come home, dammit. The hills start burning by mid-September." His phone rang. "Give me a minute," he said, and pushed the hold button before anyone on the other end could have agreed to be kept waiting. "Going home to pack now, Annie?" It wasn't a question, either.

His ungrateful reporter stood on her pride. "No, I'm going home and drink the milk I skipped this morning." She hated herself when she felt petty. "Then I'll pack."

IT MADE MORE SENSE to pack first, everything but her cosmetic bag. After she laid out travel clothes, Anne slipped into the shower, numb, exhausted and apprehensive. She had never been out of the United States before; the beach vacation in Baja, California didn't really count. Her passport was blank, a possession only because it was *Chronicle* policy to have one.

Scalding water drenched her body. Anne groped for the temperature-control handle and turned it, too drastically. Cold water stunned her, cold like the swimming pool in her apartment building, brutally cold like the ocean, blasting her eyes and nose, running into her ears. Dripping, pouring, mingling with the tears standing in her eyes. She was drowning.

She reeled at the wet pain. *Was it awful when you died, Steffie? Was it quick? Before the end did you feel peace? Would you have violently resisted rescue, the way the lifeguards say?*

Anne fled the water and toweled her face until the friction scoured deathly images from her mind. She dried the rest of her body rapidly, oblivious of faded bikini marks, a dim blueprint of overwork and underplay.

The phone shattered her fragile calm. It must be Charles, she thought, her heart beating rapidly.

"Are you okay, Anne?" Her mother sounded worried. "We heard about Steph early this morning, but we didn't want to bother you until your last deadline. The desk said you were out of town for three weeks. What's going on?"

Anne explained briefly.

"Skiing in South America? Is that safe? I don't know—" Jean Mahoney stifled her anxious tone, knowing her daughter would withdraw with a scoff about smothering mothers.

"Let me rephrase that." Smile crinkles warmed Jean Mahoney's blue eyes, the same round, wide-eyed shape, if not color, she shared with her daughter.

"What a terrific opportunity, honey." Anne's mother's words were carefully casual now. What a generous gift, a very good idea. Anne should send a postcard if she had time. Take care.... And then, because Jean Mahoney knew Anne better than anyone, except perhaps Stephanie, she added, "If you need to talk, if you need money, call us collect."

Time was short. The bank's driver was due in a few minutes. Anne looped a silver Navajo belt through her stone-washed jeans and tucked in a creamy silk blouse. Before she could slip on her high-heeled boots, the phone sounded again.

"Despite Schmidt, you're sure of a seven to four majority on the final committee vote?" Charles was on a second line with someone else. Anne walked back to her bedroom, locked her suitcase and finished dressing while Charles concluded his other conversation.

"It's been a long terrible day, Anne. I'm exhausted from pushing that bill through," he complained, finally directing his attention to her. It was the first time in a long while that Anne had listened to Charles's routine opening, and this time his noble fatigue for "the people" infuriated her.

"I'm very sorry to hear about Stephanie," he continued, heedless of her dangerous silence. "I'd have called sooner but I knew you were...."

His condolences came too late.

You knew I was what, Charles, she thought bitterly, and pushed the hang-up button on the cordless receiver, very slowly and very deliberately so he would think they had been cut off. *Did you know I was wishing you would hold me so I could cry. Charles? Did you know I was wishing I would never picture Steph drowning again? And what does that mean? That I stop taking showers? That I sleep with my eyes open?* Unable to cope any more, she plugged in the microphone on her answering machine and began to dictate.

"This is Anne Mahoney. I've been having trouble with my telephone, so I hope you're able to get through for this message." The lie tasted good. "Anyway, I will be skiing for the next three weeks. If you leave your name and number after the beep, I'll call you back September 3."

And then, a spontaneous crack in her ambiguous information. "If you need, uh, want to reach me, I'll be at Hotel Portillo in Chile through Aug. 19. They have a phone, but I don't have the number right now."

The telephone rang again. Anne defiantly picked up her bag. On the second ring, she bolted the door. She could hear the murmur of her taped voice inside her apartment. She had a hope that Charles would track her to the waiting lounge at Los Angeles International, and if he missed her plane, that he would call Portillo the next afternoon.

She would if the situation was reversed.

CHAPTER TWO

ANNE CLOSED HER EYES when she finished the second of three Agatha Christies she had purchased at LAX. Even with her eyes shuttered, they stung with fatigue. She refused to open them, hoping for sleep, and that was when her abused nerves overwhelmed her.

First those in her fingertips crystalized. She was experiencing a frightening paralysis for the first time. Not a numb paralysis. This was different. In an instant her nerves froze up to her cheeks and down to her feet. Then the crystal network shattered. Anne felt herself break, and it hurt. Slivers of glass pierced her through. Blood rushed from her head. She trembled in her cramped economy seat, unable to stop shaking. How long she remained so, Anne didn't know.

With a tremendous effort born of pain, she forced memories of happiness into her mind, and there were many. Her growing up had been happy, she liked her work and was consumed by it, she loved Charles Roderick, loved the way he asked for her opinions now and treated them seriously.

Eventually the sun dispelled the darkness. Anne smelled hot sausages and coffee; with the odor came reality. She looked down at her disgusting wrinkled blouse. For at least five minutes she scrubbed her fuzzy teeth in the tiny bathroom, absentminded in her tidi-

ness. She buttoned on a fresh winter white silk blouse
and stuffed the soiled one in her big leather purse. When
she returned to her seat for breakfast, her digital watch
read 4:17.

"Pretty early sunrise for winter, isn't it?" Anne
asked the stewardess when she arrived with a tray.

The woman's hazel eyes laughed, and a delighted
smile crossed her smooth face. "I love telling passengers
this," she confessed, reaching into a seat pocket for the
in-flight magazine. "The time is about seven-thirty.
You'll have to change your watch ahead three hours."

"To East Coast time? Chile doesn't border the Atlan-
tic."

"No, it's on the Pacific, the same as California. But
look...." The leggy brunette showed Anne a map of
the western hemisphere at the back of the magazine.
"North America and South America don't line up. If
you fly straight down from New York, you'll hit Santiago— Do you want cream and sugar in your coffee?"

The coffee helped, and so did a second glass of
orange juice. Anne picked at a chive omelet, then gave
up. She had no appetite.

The jet dropped its landing gear and cruised over a
steep hogback ridge, past small villages, finally banking
left into a steep brown valley. A few minutes later it
braked near a two-story airport. Three men in open
parkas pushed portable steps out to the plane.

Anne shrugged on her fleece vest halfway to the door,
years of reporting experience propelling her to the head
of the line with charm, so that *she* had the first view of
the eastern horizon.

Mountains were commonplace in Anne's life, for Los
Angeles sprawled among nine-thousand-foot ridges

whose upper reaches were dusted with snow. Salt Lake City and Denver she knew, cities that abutted the fourteen-thousand-foot Rockies. Yet not even the Rockies rivaled the Andes.

Barren foothills backed into a second range of ominous purple, which ended in long wispy clouds. And there, where her North American eye was trained to expect blue sky, still a third wall thrust above the clouds, a jagged, formidable mass far whiter than the feathery streamers below. The grandeur dwarfed Anne's troubles.

Customs passed her through quickly. Waiting at the other end was a wiry man in his fifties, an inch or so shorter than her, dressed in an immaculate, three-piece black suit, shiny in a few spots. His dark brown hair was tightly waved, and his complexion was light olive, although his flat cheekbones were native American. He was the driver from Richard Clark Senior's bank, Carlos Luzzini.

"What do you think of Chile?" he asked, putting her suitcase into the trunk of a silver Mercedes Benz. His wrinkled walnut face smiled, anticipating her approval.

Anne would learn that Luzzini's question was the standard Chilean welcome, evidence of curiosity bred in isolation. She would discover that the driver's friendliness and pride, his knowledge of his small country and his eagerness to tell her about it were typical. However, she only knew when she sank into the leather back seat that she was grateful for his conversation.

Luzzini talked of unconquerable Araucanians and volcanos, of the western hemisphere's four highest peaks and the popularity of the American school in Santiago, of taxes, new South African irrigation techniques and a ski area the French had planned for the wide-open mountains above Santiago.

"We will have the world's longest run when it is built," he claimed, and when asked for an opening date, admitted it might be never. Why? The usual problem. He shrugged. Money.

Rude shacks lining the highway on the outskirts of Santiago disappeared with the miles. As they journeyed north, Luzzini deftly passed other cars, wide buses and weathered wooden wagons drawn by gaunt horses. Strange knobby hills were lush with new grass, and hedgerows of stern poplars halted the wind.

Anne hid in the strange sights. *Keep talking,* she pleaded silently. *Push out the old ugly thoughts. Leave me no room to think.* And so she asked more questions.

Portillo was 165 miles northeast of Santiago, Luzzini told her, about four hours away. British engineers in the early 1900s, building a railroad alongside the old Incan road over the Andes, discovered the special snow of Portillo.

During World War II, the neutral Chilean government constructed grand hotels in the five most beautiful places in the country. Portillo was one. A New Yorker leased it twenty years later, and his nephews had made the resort legendary among the elite skiers of the world, Carlos told her. He shared much more. The lease was for ninety-nine years, and half the guests were millionaires from São Paulo, he'd heard, although of course he'd never stayed there himself. And the sun was very hot.

"When I drive you to Chillán next week, you will have a dark tan." Luzzini glanced in the rearview mirror. "Although your skin is perfect as the peach blossoms we will see in about half an hour."

Anne ignored the compliment. She was uncomfortable with physical praise, for in her experience a rude pass invariably followed. Rather than saying thank-you, she changed the subject.

"Aren't I on my own after you drop me off?"

"We are responsible for you." Determination overrode the nervousness in his statement. Luzzini apparently was not used to giving orders in his job. "I was told to pick you up one week from today, on August 20, and drive you south to ski on some of the volcanos where we have lifts with small refuges where you can stay. Chillán, maybe Villarica, Antillanca. You'll probably want to see Bariloche, Argentina. Everyone has a good party in Bariloche."

Door-to-door delivery sounded marvelous, actually. Anne couldn't rally any energy to make plans of her own. Maybe fresh air would help.

First she searched through her bulging purse for a brush. She pulled it through her thick mane, shook out a middle part, caught the mahogany mass in a twist high on her head and fastened it loosely with a matching barrette. "That's better." She cracked the window open. "Makes me crazy when my hair flies in my nose. Does it take two weeks to reach Ante... Ante...."

"On-tea-yan-ka. No, two days. If you like quiet local areas, we can take our time. If you want diversion, I will take you to Bariloche more rapidly."

Anne stared out the window, far away in a mood, not a location. Orchards spread out from the highway to the base of the foothills. Some of the branches reached bare arms to the sky, while others sought the earth, a convenience for the fruit pickers.

"Apples, peaches, some pear plantations. The peach trees are the ones with the branches growing down," Luzzini answered when she asked. "Gustavo Mohr de la Huerta contracts for most of the fruit along here. Industrias Mohr is one of Chile's ten largest corporations. Perhaps he will be in Portillo and you will meet him. Señor Mohr would be difficult to miss. He raced on the Chilean team in the Olympics. The Chilean women are his. He is very blond."

"Blondes have more fun, they say." Anne rotated her tired neck slowly, unkinking her shoulders and yawning. She was sleepy.

At the crossroads town of Los Andes in the Aconcagua Valley, the driver turned east toward the mountains. Gnarled trees knotted with years of pruning lined the streets. Low stucco buildings sat directly on the edge of the narrow sidewalks.

Carlos pulled up to the curb at a bright blue restaurant on a corner near the central plaza. "Would you like lunch?" he asked rhetorically, opening the car door, waiting for Anne to force her swollen feet back into her boots. "The food here is quite good."

"Thanks, but I'm really not hungry." She didn't mean to be thoughtless. "I'd love some coffee while you eat, though."

When he placed their orders, Luzzini again urged a toasted ham-and-cheese sandwich on Anne. He looked anxious.

She glanced at her digital wristwatch, wondering how to move time forward. It was a stupid triviality, but Charles always took care of daylight-savings changes.

She was a mechanically retarded addict of gadgets. "Really, I've no appetite," she insisted. "It's only 10:05 A.M. in Los Angeles."

Back in the car, she asked once again, "How much farther?"

"About an hour."

The scenery changed rapidly as they climbed into the foothills. The Aconcagua River romped to their right. Across the shallow rapids, mud-and-wooden huts tilted precariously on the sheer dirt banks.

Luzzini shifted to second, and the valley narrowed until suddenly, dead ahead, loomed a massive white wall topped with rough gray peaks, a gothic cathedral spotlighted by the sun. The Pan American highway before them was a washboard of hairpin turns. Bull-dozed walls of snow were banked ten feet higher than the car, creating a snaking white canyon with room for one car and one bus to pass, but only in a few of the wider places.

Luzzini shifted to first gear and began the arduous climb. Anne spontaneously crouched low on the seat to look up through the windows. She had never seen anything like it.

Chairs from a lift to their left carried skiers up, beyond her view. One couple waved at the limousine. The Mercedes twisted and twisted again, up and around through one tunnel, then another. They were peculiar tunnels with roofs angled to the incline of the mountain. The groomed snow on top of the roofs was part of a ski run.

"You can see how steep the mountains are," Luzzini said, rounding the twenty-seventh and final corner. "There is very little room for skiers at Portillo."

Ahead was a curved slice of sunshine, the bright yellow Hotel Portillo. Anne counted six stories. The roof was sky blue. *Change that to plain brilliant blue,* she mentally edited the adjective, for nothing was as blue as the sky.

While porters carried her suitcases inside, Carlos carefully printed his home telephone number on a business card and handed it to Anne. "Expect me at 9 A.M. on Saturday the twentieth, unless a storm blows in. In that case, well, we shall meet again in three weeks or a month. Telephone me whenever you can get through."

His words passed without notice, for Anne, surprised by the heat from the unclouded sun, was unsnapping her vest.

"*Chau,* Señorita Mahoney." Luzzini's farewell sounded like the Italian *ciao*.

"*Adios,*" Anne said, the way they did in L.A.

The lobby of the famous hotel was unexpectedly plain, small and functional with dark linoleum tile floors and low ceilings. There was a little boutique to the right.

"Is there a message for me?" she asked as she registered, hiding her disappointment when the reply was negative. Anne swiftly made an excuse for Charles. *He'll call later when he knows I've arrived.*

Her room on the fourth floor was small, too, but she didn't notice. Anne's mind was outside. She raised the latch on the small Bavarian-style windows on the far wall, threw open the double panes and inhaled the crisp, warm air.

A *petite* lake behind the hotel spread to the triangular end of a tricorn granite wall. To the right of the lake, a single skier wedeled between two constricted rock claws, a blue streak of tight fluid turns, effortlessly controlling the hostile run. Anne watched enviously until the midnight blue disappeared at the bottom. She glanced at her watch: 11:17. It was 2:17 in Washington; 2:17 in Chile, too. Not much time if she wanted to test the slopes.

There were two knobs in the shower, one marked *C*, the other *F*. She wondered vaguely what the *F* stood for and turned on the *C* first to blend cold with hot. A gush of steaming water nearly scalded her hand. Then she remembered her high-school Spanish. *Frío* was "cold," as in "freeze."

The brisk shower eliminated the surface fatigue of eighteen hours' travel—twenty and a half hours if she counted the ride to the airport and the wait for the plane. Feeling renewed, Anne brushed life into her hair, blushed her wan cheeks and shuffled through two new suitcases of clothes, amazed at the choice.

"Thank you, Richard Clark," she murmured, zipping into a copper jump suit of a thin, wind-and-waterproof fabric, elasticized at the waist. She didn't snap on the white vest with its matching blaze of copper.

"What level skier are you?" asked the ruddy attendant in the basement rental shop, measuring Anne's height with practiced eyes, then rolling them suggestively down to her chest. She ignored him. "One seventy-fives are a good length," he went on. "Later in the week we'll put you up to 180s or 185s, but we'll start shorter and easier."

Anne slipped out of her right boot so he could adjust the bindings to her foot size. "You speak awfully good English," she said, thinking the yellow straw color of his hair made the back of his thick red neck look redder; not burned, just a toughened red.

"*¿Por qué no?*" The attendant singsonged an exaggerated Mexican accent. "I'm from Jackson, Wyoming by way of Tahoe City, California. Where're you from?"

"L.A.," she said, chagrined at her erroneous assumption.

"Where in L.A.?" asked the mid-twenties joker, putting down one ski and beginning on the other.

"Santa Monica."

He'd already memorized the basics so didn't look up. "Yeah. You look like you've been living in summer coastal fog. What're you doing after dinner tonight?"

"I'm not really available. I'm going with someone," Anne refused, her glibness polished by experience.

"American girls are all alike," he sighed, theatrically exasperated. "Either they've found a new squeeze and are being faithful, or they've just broken up and can't cope with 'in-tim-acy.'" He imitated a Southern soprano. "Or they're looking but saving themselves." The frank chuckle that followed was enigmatic. "Wait'll you encounter the South American playboys here. Gooood luck!"

The attendant ducked out of the fitting room, opened the door outside and dropped her skis on the snow. Anne stepped into them with a snap.

"Better get moving before the sun drops, L.A. lady." He handed her a pair of poles. "The mountains block the rays early. See you in a couple of hours."

Anne coasted down to the lift, her turns awkward. She had no idea how to shout "single" in Spanish in order to become paired on the chair, so moved silently through the short line. When it was her turn, she sat alone.

The blue blur twisted by. A man, she realized this time, an exceptionally tall man whose face was hidden under a cardinal-red baseball cap. His knees were springs on the moguls, navy blue shock absorbers over and down the bumps. With his sudden slight shift of balance, rooster tails of deliciously light powder arced behind him, impressing Anne and irritating her.

Obnoxious jerk. She was scornful, resolving to ignore his grand slamming and unable to. She glanced back to watch him finish his run. *An idiot Austrian ski instructor.* She'd recognize one of those confident blond giants anywhere.

Two winters ago, a few weeks before the cable-car disaster, Snider had decided it was time for a story with an upbeat ending. He had sent her to the northern Sierra. "Check out the healthy fulfilling life of ski instructors—make that Austrian ski instructors, Mahoney," he'd ordered. "We want a handsome stereotype for the photographer."

It hadn't taken more than three après-ski beers before a group of willing blondes were bragging about their retirement plans.

"Retirement?" Her felt-tip pen waited, ready for their definition.

"To rich American widows," shouted one, lifting his frosted mug.

"Prost drauf!" they chorused.

"That means 'Cheers to that!' " whispered the leader of the ambitious beauties, his unwelcome translation so close to Anne's ear that she scratched the resulting tickle, regretfully missing his nose. Another one across the table slipped his leg between Anne's with a sly wink.

Later, the most persistent was undaunted by her refusals. "How can you deny you want me?" said Hans, trapping her in a corner at the far end of a brightly lit hallway, pressing his aroused body against hers.

Anne had struggled until Hans Whoever realized her cries were not a prelude to ecstasy. The carefully perfect specimen of a man stalked away with a disgusted snort about American teases. Although Anne had stalked to her room equally disgusted on the surface, she was shaken beneath her bravado, for a few minutes. Then she laughed.

She related the incident at once, long distance to Stephanie. The ridiculousness had been too good not to share. "Kiss me with your mouth open," she had mocked the Hans's gutteral accent, and they had giggled. "Excuse me, Steph. I've got to go brush my teeth."

Henceforth the two women referred to any aggressive behavior guaranteed to achieve the opposite effect as "a Hans."

Such memories deflated Anne's temporary elation. This time there would be no exuberant friend to share her South American adventure with, and this time, Anne decided grimly, there would be no repeat Austrian tales. The Hans who had skied by was far better looking than any of the instructors she had interviewed. Doubtless his ego was equally well developed.

Anne slid off the chair lift prudently and turned left, away from the other skiers, away from the Blue Hans. The slope was gradual. As she eased through four inches of untracked snow, she began to remember the sport. She bent her knees, flexed her arms out front and glided, an hourglass of copper, turning occasionally on the plain. At the edge of the rise she paused. The lake was straight below, luminescent as a black pearl.

Anne continued a short distance down the hill and took off her skis. Jamming them deep in the snow for a backrest, she shook her hair free of the wool cap with its copper-and-white pompom and leaned back on her makeshift chair.

The sun to the west beamed across her face. With her mirrored sunglasses in place, Anne closed her eyes, drowsy and content, four years old at Grandma and Grandpa Higginses' ranch in Colorado. It was Christmas, and the cold to a California child was new and exciting.

The wind made gentle swishing sounds as it piled snow into drifts. The girl walked to the old log barn with grandpa, his body reassuringly close when the snow was too deep.

"It is a remarkable sight." The stranger's baritone was ear level, near enough for warm moist breath to torment her right lobe. Anne squelched an alarmed squeak as tiny hairs straightened at the nape of her neck.

"You are an exceptionally wise skier to take time to appreciate what you see, not keep your eyes blinded downward, looking only a few feet ahead."

She didn't need to look to connect the voice with the face. It was the Austrian ski instructor. Who else would intrude with such aplomb, as though he had the right to join her; to step out of his skis, as she could hear him doing, and sit beside her.

"May I join you?"

"No, and you already have."

Anne's full lips pinched together, and irritation played across her mobile features. "The thing I like about you, Mahoney," William A. Snider often said, "is even when you try to be subtle, you aren't."

Her menacing retort didn't discourage the trespasser. A quick side glance caught him disciplining smile dimples from the sharp planes of his tanned face. Although the bill of his red cap shadowed his eyes, his straight nose had a scattering of lighter patches where an earlier burn had peeled and reburned. The flaw pleased her.

"If you'll excuse me...." She tried to rise, but the Hans had cleverly situated himself between her and her poles. She would have to lean over his powerful chest to grab them and hoist herself up.

There was no way she was going to touch his long body. What was he, anyway—six-foot five? Six? A jolly Green Giant? This man wasn't jolly. Stymied, she put an edge in her tone. "Excuse me. Will you please hand me my poles?"

Anne might as well not have spoken.

The Blue Hans took off his cap and ran oversized hands through his blond hair. The sun caught the fairness. The loose waves shone, lustrous silver glints of moonbeams, not sunshine.

"Black is a word with intense emotional properties," he mused, his eyes on the dark pearly lake. He propped an elbow on his left knee to support his angular jaw. His arm brushed Anne's and remained.

Needles of pleasure pierced her feet like fiery sand on bare skin. She wiggled her toes in the hard plastic boots and shifted away from the blue figure as best she could. His arm followed, glued with a featherweight pressure.

"Black moods, black future, black sheep, blackout—"

"Black and blue," she warned.

He laughed heartily. Sun-roughened chiseled lips

parted over straight teeth, and the harsh angles of his face eased.

"Black Irish," snapped the irate Miss Mahoney, unable to resist the verbal bait. "Black rage."

"Black despair," he countered, disarmingly accurate.

"Bleak despair." She nervously straightened the sunglasses on her nose, piqued that she was revealing herself. "Why are your lips so chapped? Do you consider it unmanly to use chapstick?"

"The slightest touch of yours on my lips would—"

"Black bread is delicious." Anne interjected a swift counterpoint. "Black hear— Uh, black hole in a galaxy."

"And consider, a truly black night is not negative. It enfolds you in a comforting void, just as nothingness can be beautiful and consoling. I have faced the black soul of Laguna del Inca on many occasions, for many reasons, and all were essentially the same. The lake down there restores my peace."

A tricky Hans. This rascal acts nice before he jumps you. Anne willed her curiosity still, refusing to question why someone with his looks and confidence needed peace, whether he spent every summer teaching at Portillo, why the lake was black, not blue or green. . . .

"The bottom is one of the three factors that affects the color of a lake." He was invading her thoughts. When she secretly glanced at him, he was waiting. He caught her eyes and held them in a gaze much removed from his erudite discourse. From behind the shield of her sunglasses, Anne knew this man hid more than he ever revealed.

"Light transmits through the water. . .like a stained-glass window," he was saying. "If you have a bottom that is fairly near the surface, say white sand in Tahiti or a swimming pool, the sky reflects off the surface and there is a nice blue color. Laguna del Inca's depth is unknown.''

His intense eyes asked the personal question before his lips. ''Are you like that?''

Anne knew he wanted to probe her depths. She was spellbound, and apparently readable, for he answered himself. ''Like you, yes. The unknown is more appealing. You find it so?''

He pretended she was interested, and despite herself, she was.

''The government has unsuccessfully sounded for the bottom of the lake but has never found it. For such immense blackness, the bottom is probably not of sand, but of rock, like the walls of the canyon.''

Anne fought the lure of his intellect. She counted it a victory not to plug her ears like a spiteful fourth grader to halt his shrewd wooing.

''You are probably wondering what the other determinants of color are.''

Was he playing with her? Anne couldn't tell from his tone, and it was dangerous to look his way again. ''Indubitably.'' There was no mistaking her mockery. For emphasis, she shrugged her shoulders. It was her best parody of boredom. Yet he refused to relinquish control.

''At this elevation, the sky is a darker blue, hence the reflection is darker.'' Anne shifted again, and again he shifted to face her, somehow managing to envelop her in the field of his electricity until her charged flesh was inseparable from his. ''In fact, the sky is so dark this afternoon that the lake appears black.''

"What happens on cloudy days?" The reportorial question slipped out.

He looked at her as though she had captured his inner being. Anne caught her breath, frightened by the force of this fleeting encounter. After a time, like a man drugged, he replied.

"In Portillo, when there's a cloud in the sky, it snows. Usually it's sunny, so we can enjoy the vista and drink in extraordinary views, like the sight of your hair sparking copper at the urging of the sun."

The compliment caught her off guard.

"Although, to be sure, the enchanting color is emphasized by your jump suit. You are to be admired. It is a memorable combination. . . ." He took the collar between his thumb and index finger and drew it out to her silky mass of hair. "The effect is yours alone. No other woman could wear it as you do."

His prey yanked her collar away, flustered. She had never had a man openly analyze the colors she wore.

Anne lifted her sunglasses to more effectively glare up into his eyes, and reeled at their impact. Through the mirrored lenses especially yellowed to deflect snow blindness, she had seen his eyes were blue, and assumed an ordinary blue. But this Hans had Saxon eyes, light blue as a glacier in early morn, yet toasty as Delft blue tiles around a fireplace. Inky blue rings outlined the unusual color.

"Would you leave me alone? If I wanted your rapacious—" she lingered insultingly over the long word "—company, I would have asked for it. Now hand me my poles."

The instructor deflected her anxious snarl. "Black eyes and blue eyes. I see what you were saying. Then there are autumn eyes like yours." He considered at his leisure, while the dreaded telltale pink flushed Anne's throat.

"Not big and brown. No...." He leaned closer, absorbed. "Cinnamon. Yes, that is the color. Cinnamon. But I can only see the blending of gold in moments like this when I feel your breath near on my chest. The gold is subtle. The color of the poplars against the russet of oaks upriver from Vienna in September."

Anne's heart raced. She was enraptured, aquiescent in a trap of sweet words and her wild unaccustomed response.

"Does the color soften and fade as autumn rain before the winter?" He shook his head as though to clear his mind and stood up, a man to match the giant mountains. He pulled Anne to her feet and handed her the poles.

A tall woman who was accustomed to eye-to-eye encounters, Anne felt miniature next to him. The top of her head didn't reach his strapping shoulders. "A yard wide," the fashion editor at the *Chronicle* would enviously describe them. That was how the aging editor had gauged Charles Roderick's football shoulders. The width had balanced their appearance, Anne always thought, for hers and Roderick's brown heads were on a level when she wore heels.

Anne cocked her bindings and stepped in. The snap restored her vigor. She growled the only German skiing expression she knew: *"Hals und Beinbruch."* It literally meant "Break a leg," the Austrians had explained, for good luck. Let him interpret her meaning as he wished.

She would have sped gracefully away if she could have, but to her chagrin she had to mince uphill, sidestepping to reach the run without slipping back down to the Hans. She puffed in the thin air of the two-mile altitude. She coughed for breath. She perspired from the exertion over the minimal distance.

"This is probably giving the Hans his best laugh of the day." Anne unzipped her jumpsuit midway down her chest to cool off, for he was safely behind her. " 'Oh, Mizzz Mahoney, the glow on your face is charming.' " She mimicked his technique, trying to downgrade its effect. " 'The smell of you overwhelms all senses. Is the fragrance Essence of Locker Room?' "

Her derision ceased at the crest of the hill. She was staring straight down a wall of packed snow and swallowed hard. Now she understood why she and the Hans were alone.

Helplessly Anne looked for an escape to an easier route, but it was far away, uphill and on the other side of the chair lift, too distant for walking. Ahead was a twenty-foot outcrop of gray granite, and behind a sharp drop into the lake. The chute below her was narrow and it looked slick, for the fresh cushion of powder on the flats above had fallen away, leaving only hard snow and harder ice.

The acid of fear seared Anne's stomach.

She angled her skis a scant few degrees downhill and coasted across to the other side, leaning into the hill for security, ready to sit if she fell.

The rented French slalom skis skidded on a glazed patch. Anne's shaking knees locked. She wiped her wet face on the shiny copper sleeve, grateful no instructor was with her, barking orders: "Bend those knees! Lean away from the mountain! Keep those shoulders parallel to the fall line!"

Fall line.... A fancy phrase for the way she'd roll if she fell...straight down.

Finally her paralyzed legs responded to her commands. The rigid figure inched on, anxiously seeking a place to turn, and never did until too late. Anne had skied into the granite boundary. To turn, she'd have to back up.

Anne glanced downhill and looked away, dizzy.

The Blue Hans flew by, rotated like a hovering helicopter on the ski closest to Anne, turned with a whir and sidestepped up to her. The sharp edges of his skis braked into the icy face of the mountain. The sharp crunch shattered the silence.

"Wrap your hands tightly around the poles." The deep voice was gentle.

Anne stiffened her backbone. "I'm perfectly...I'm enjoying the view from this side."

"No one enjoys herself stuck on a ledge. I will make you happy again. Do not be afraid. Wrap your pole straps securely—so." He demonstrated.

"Do I have a choice?" She argued even as she obeyed.

The big Austrian ignored her gibe. He reached for the wheels near the ends of her aluminum sticks. Holding the poles low enough to support his unwilling partner at a comfortable height, he stooped effortlessly.

Anne gripped, and the metal became a trembling extension of her arms. He held the poles steady, his strength quieting the quiver. "Put your weight on your downhill ski. Good. Now back up slowly. Lean toward me...."

Her cheeks, which had begun to redden in the sunshine, blanched.

"Everything is all right. You are safe." His words were strangely familiar. "We are not discussing style. No one can learn when she has fear. Later we can practice turns, but not here. For now, trust me. Lean out in my direction. Brace against me, and I will hold you up. You are safe."

Anne tentatively tested the makeshift buttress.

"Harder. All your weight."

He held her easily, and her breathing evened. Thus reassured, she slid backward.

"Good, good. Another foot or two."

Anne complied, hushed by his confidence. Suddenly shy, she fixed her gaze back over her shoulder in the direction she was moving, never meeting his eyes.

"A little more. Enough. We will stop here for the moment."

Anne leaned into the great blue fortress of his body and rested. Only a tooth biting her tense lower lip showed her fear.

"Are you baring your fangs at me?" he teased.

Anne smiled, gratitude overtaking her antipathy.

"We are going to sideslip down this rough part," he continued, as relaxed as if rescues were everyday affairs. Dropping her poles, he slipped another few feet down and reached up to plant his own poles about a yard below Anne, creating a safety nets of sorts.

"Keep your hips aimed toward the rocks but turn your pretty chest to me," he instructed. "Stick your poles about six inches down the hill, far apart. Good, good. If your poles don't hold you. . . ?"

He paused for her name, and Anne denied him an answer.

"I like your spirit." He threw back his head and

laughed. "You will get off the Garganta easily. If your poles don't hold you, miss...?" His voice rose again in a question, then finally continued. "You'll tumble into me, and I will stop you. Now, put your weight on the downhill ski again, so. Fine. Roll your knees on the inside edges of your skis. See how they brake you? Try it again."

Anne obeyed.

"Practice one final time. Excellent. This time let your skis slide a little bit."

Anne's stomach wrenched. *Slide sideways down ice?* "I c-can't."

"You are safe. Slide only an instant, then brake. Trust me."

The word "trust" pierced the deafness of panic. She gripped her poles until her gloved fingers pinched her palms.

"I am here. Do not be afraid."

She rolled the skis downward, inhaling sharply in fright at the free-falling motion. She slammed her weight back into the icy wall and tottered unsteadily, sweating with the effort.

"That was just fine." Long arms maintained the metal fence of poles close to Anne while the practiced athlete slipped a few inches downward, dug in and re-staked the shield.

"Move your poles, too. All right. Slide toward me again."

They proceeded thus down the mountain, inch by painful inch.

Once around the shadow of the rocks, Anne's hopes plummeted. Although the chute was wider, the slope didn't flatten. She looked beyond the Austrian to the distant yellow hotel and sighed, a signal of defeat to her unsteady feet.

Her skis slid out from under her, and she pitched sideways into his sturdy ankles. Hard snow burned her face; her shoulder ached from the impact. Anne lay at his feet in misery, a whimper rising in her throat.

"Your pride is hurt, but you are all right," the Hans insisted, cutting his skis deeper into the ice. Easily picking up her slack body, he settled her on the slope again, brushing snow off her thin suit. His wide palm passed the length of her sore arm, then rubbed her flank. The firm touch tranquilized the shake of her muscles. She panted for breath, her confidence rattled.

"Rest on your poles," her rescuer ordered, shedding his gloves. He resettled his red cap on his head, all the while chatting casually, as a senior might address a freshman at a college mixer.

"Where are you from?"

Anne's answers were winded.

"Los Angeles."

"What do you do?"

"Reporter."

"You are very attractive." He ticked off his analysis on long intellectual fingers. "You have a quick mind and a sharp vocabulary. And you can afford Portillo. Undoubtedly you are on the television news. Are you an anchorwoman?"

"Newspaper."

"An old-fashioned girl?"

Anne went red. The Blue Hans made everything sound intimate. Irritation shot a little strength into her system.

"When did you arrive? It must have been today, because one entire day would not have passed without my noticing the way you tilt your head when you are curious.''

"What time is it now?''

He glanced at his gold wristwatch. "4 P.M.''

"About an hour and a half ago.'' She was breathing normally again.

"When did you arrive in Chile?''

"Ten this morning.''

"You traveled all night on that tedious flight from Los Angeles. You have gone from sea level to two miles in elevation—'' He scowled. "When was the last time you skied? It has obviously been a while, because you are unpracticed, but not too long or you would not have gambled on an unknown slope. Since two winters?''

Anne sulked. She was the one who grilled confessions from strangers by correctly analyzing details. She'd be damned if she'd cooperate with a prying, interfering ski instructor.

"No comment.''

He abruptly charged five lengths backward. For spite, Anne tilted her chin disdainfully and refused to watch. The sound of ice being cut into moved uphill, then closer. What was he engineering now?

Suddenly his broad hands reached under her loose vest and circled her ribs. She felt the force of his hard fingers from her waist to the swell of her breasts.

"What big hands you have, grandma!'' Anne darted away from the wolf.

In an instant she felt rather than heard his chuckle as he pulled her back against him, running her skis through a tunnel he had created in the exaggerated V of his own pair.

Before she could lunge aside, the Blue Hans caught her thighs between the muscular vise of his legs and squeezed her into submission. "Spread your legs...."

"Don't be rude!"

"Way out in a snowplow."

She felt his chuckle once more. Furiously she rammed her elbows into his solar plexus, slamming her funny bones against solid flesh. "Ah." Her bleat was involuntary.

His laughter rang off the gray pinnacles above them. "Now!" he pointed the tops of his skis in a wide plié, directing them both straight down the run.

Anne dragged her skis, to no avail.

"Unhand me, you—" Even in distress, she recognized the ineffectual, Grade-B-movie level of her comeback and censored it. She strained away from him, a futile effort. His body was adhesive, his hands and thighs powerful.

Slowly, slowly they skimmed the incline, flowing left, then sweeping right, using the most elementary of all ski techniques. Anne's involuntary snowplow acted as a double drag on their speed.

Finally, trusting their lazy descent, she relaxed. The sun lighted her face, the blond giant was warm on her back and she floated in a world of white and blue. Together they moved on to the same mental waltz.

His thumbs, massaging a rhythm on her breasts, were only skimpy fabric and a bit of lace away from her skin. Anne had no memory of when he began encroaching. A rising ache trembled beyond the bonds of his cradling hands, and she drifted to her senses' music.

"Stop that, please." Yet outrage had not quite penetrated the orchestra of her dream.

"Tranquillo. Tranquillo."

The waltz slowed when the slope gentled. Passing skiers smiled at the striking couple, her pale darkness a foil for his blond strength. An elderly man called out something in Spanish, and the Hans answered with a wave.

Once freed from one of the lulling thumbs, Anne's music ended in a crescendo of embarrassment. She tried to squirm loose.

"Are you leading again?"

"Me lead, you lewd—"

He threw back his head and yodeled as he cruised to a stop. "A hat is too hot today. It's making your brains boil." He yanked her cap off by its pom-pom and combed her tangled hair with his fingers, lifting the shining strands and letting them drop.

"Lovely," he murmured, holding her steady between his legs, then, after a deliberate pause, liberating her. "You see, sweetheart, you are safe now and can ski happily again. Break a leg," he called over his shoulder as he set off. *"Auf wiedersehen."*

Anne stomped into the equipment check-in room and briskly handed her equipment to the cheeky attendant, petulance in every inch of her stance.

Somehow he seemed amused. "Have a good run?" He ran a hand through his unruly hair. "My name's Hank—"

The similarity to "Hans" grated on Anne's nerves. "Naturally," she interrupted. "Let me guess. You're pretty speedy, too, aren't you?"

"Hey, does it show?" A wide grin broadened his round red face.

"An educated guess. Excuse me, please." With that barely polite cutoff, Anne left.

CHAPTER THREE

SETTING HER TEMPORARY HOME IN PERMANENT ORDER soothed Anne. Empty hangers in her closet were soon draped with new clothes in the colors of daybreak. Colors Snider, of all people, had ordered. The man had unlikely talents.

Tank tops to the right, then lightweight stretch pants and a second jump suit beside the copper one the Hans liked. She rubbed the slick collar between her fingers, remembering the sound of his hard fingers on the fabric. It had been a callused sound. He was not soft or lazy. His hands told her that, and the barrel of his ribs, too.

He had labored for what purpose, she wondered, hanging up two vests and several new dresses. His goal had not been trivial; she knew that from his face. It was too lean, too solid and watchful for someone who had dallied with vanity.

Anne arranged wisps of underwear and heavy wool ski socks in an old walnut secretary, which doubled as a bureau. After sliding her new suitcases under the narrow twin bed nearest the window, she laid a few magazines and paperbacks on the bedside table under the service buzzer and considered her work.

Not quite satisfied, Anne shifted the novel she hadn't finished over to the upholstered reading chair in the corner, a comfortable nook near the framed Indian weaving on the wall. The umber chair was less than a yard away from one of the beds, close enough to use for a footstool.

There was no radio, no television, no telephone. The Spartan room was stripped to beautiful essentials, a man-made echo of the stark black ice, gray rock and flawless blue sky visible through the panes.

Sitting on the arm of the chair, Anne opened the window wide and rested her elbows on the ledge. Although the setting sun had disappeared behind the nearby canyon walls, its continued effect was magical. Rosy shadows flamed the three adjacent peaks behind Laguna del Inca, the hues shrinking as the sun dropped, until dusk dimmed the view.

The air was cold now. Anne latched the windows, composed and for the first time in two days, hungry. Her brief outdoor exercise, frightening as it had been, had revitalized her. *Who told me facing terror is addictive, that surviving death makes you feel more alive,* she wondered, showering again and washing her hair. A diver, wasn't it? In an interview about sharks. She blow-dried her hair with a new 220-voltage dryer provided by Richard Clark Senior's bank.

Anne took the bank's hint about Latin formality and chose a new crepe dress from the closet. The material was a sheer wool apricot, a color she seldom wore, but the blending of pink in the apricot highlighted the sun glow on her cheeks. The draped skirt clung to her hips when she strode confidently to the elevator.

"Dinner, please," Anne said to the jacketed elevator attendant. He grinned with a shrug. He didn't speak English.

"Food." Anne pointed to her mouth, glossed with lipstick.

"Claro."

The elevator dropped to the second floor, and he opened the door for her.

Nearly the entire floor was occupied by a grand, two-story salon with conversational groupings of cozy stuffed couches and chairs. Anne understood then why the lobby on the ground floor had been so functional-looking. *This* was where guests gathered.

Northward, towering windows looked out upon the same view of the lake that Anne had from her room. Wooden booths, gleaming with decades of rigorous polishing, were set at right angles to the glass. Four teenage girls played cards in one, their laughter largely muffled by the high, thick wooden backs.

It was 6:30, and they were the only people in the room.

A fire blazed in a great stone fireplace to the distant left; the dining room was located at the right end of the room. Through the closed double doors Anne could see waiters in red cotton jackets clearing baskets of biscuits and pitchers of orange juice.

Her stomach growled. She tried to open the doors, but they were locked and the waiters ignored her rattling. She didn't understand. It was dinnertime. She hadn't seen a coffee shop off the lobby or she would have left the waiters alone to their cleanup. A hamburger sounded great, maybe a bowl of hot soup. Even a biscuit.

She rapped sharply on the door. The tallest waiter ambled over. He said something in Spanish and pointed to his wristwatch, shaking his head.

"But I'm hungry," pleaded Anne, frustrated by the language barrier. She held her watch up to the glass, then pointed to her mouth. "Hungry. It's 6:30. *Por favor*."

The impassive waiter returned with an authoritative man dressed in black, holding a clipboard in his sturdy, square hand.

"Please, your name."

"Anne Mahoney."

The maître d'hotel scanned the list. "Nine and a half in the night, Señorita Mahoney."

"Nine-thirty!" Anne was dismayed. She was used to eating something by seven or seven-thirty. It had never occurred to her that she would have to follow the Latin custom of late dining. "Is there another restaurant in the hotel?"

"The cafeteria where the instructors eat."

That would never do. Once she'd had food and sleep she could deflect eyes that fixed on her, crystalline blue eyes that understood more than she ever wanted to reveal. But she could not face the Blue Hans now.

"Can I have a little something here? A roll? *Por favor*?"

"No. It is not possible." The maître d' spread his hands in a helpless gesture. "The time for the tea stop thirty minutes ago. We have much work now to prepare for dinner. We are at your service at nine and a half. But the cafeteria. . . ." His smile was friendly.

Anne politely returned his smile and paced across the carpeting to an open arch she suspected led to a bar. Surely they'd have peanuts. She blinked in the dim amber light cast by colonial Spanish sconces and stood still, getting her bearings. A bartender aimlessly wiped a clean wooden counter. He looked grateful for a customer.

"Hey, hey, come join us!" The shout from behind was obviously directed at her. The clownish ski adjustor with the broad grin was sitting at a corner table with a taller, tightly muscled brunet. Both were in conservative blazers and ties.

"Hi, there," said Anne, walking over to them. "Nice to understand someone. Are we the only Americans— North Americans, I should say—here?"

"I dunno. Maybe five other guests besides yourself are from the U.S. of A." The ruddy blond was offhand.

"Where're all the people?"

"What time is it? About six-thirty? Probably taking siestas. They run off the slopes, guzzle orange juice for gawd's sake, then go to bed. They need the sleep to stay up all night at the disco."

"I'm Jonathan Lynch," said the man in the white, button-down shirt, rumpled in proper prep style. He half rose from his leather chair to pull out a similar one for Anne.

"Known as Lunch," quipped the blonde, whose unruly hair had been controlled except for an escaped cowlick in the back. He stood until Anne was seated.

"Lunch, except to my mother. She has pretensions."

"She can afford to," said the stocky partner of the comedy team. "Lunch is naming his first kid Out To. Can't you hear her teachers? 'Susie Laird...Johnny Lasamore...Out To Lunch."

"Rotten name for a boy." Jonathan Lynch touched Anne's arm. "What'll you have?"

She felt only the light pressure of his hand. No tremors weakened her knees, no thumbs pressed an advantage....

"What'll she have?" squawked Hank Purdoe, and the duo began joisting verbally, parlaying innocent remarks into outrageous risqué ones. They were clever smart alecks, and Anne relaxed. She worked with wise-mouthed reporters—sometimes she was one—and in a strange land among strangers, it felt good to laugh as she did at home.

"I'll have a beer." She interrupted the asexual duel of words.

The impassive waiter started to write her order down.

"No white wine? And you're from L.A.?" said Hank, while Lunch, with a hand on her arm, was asking what her name was.

"Listen, Anne Mahoney, Purdoe and I have class," Lunch said after she told him. "We'll buy you a real drink to *salud pesetas amor*—health, wealth and love. We refuse to clink our glasses against a beer can."

"Okay, okay. You and Hank twisted my arm. A vodka martini on the rocks with three olives. I'm starving. Any peanuts?"

"Nope," Lunch discouraged her. He spoke quickly to the patient waiter, his Spanish smooth, his hand gestures expert. Then he was back in English and Anne couldn't stop laughing.

"What's the story on dinner, anyway?" she asked shortly, fishing a couple of tiny salty olives out of her wide glass. She ate them immediately and reached for a paper napkin to wrap the pits. "The maître d' told me I can't eat until 9:30."

"Can't!" Hank plastered a dumbfounded expression across his round face. "People kill for the second-dinner seating. Presidents kill, fabulously wealthy twits and twitesses kill. Who are *you*, Anne Mahoney?"

"What am I? Famished."

"You need more olives." Lunch signaled the waiter. He motioned another round for all of them, then held up four fingers and pointed at Anne. *"Uno y cuatro aceitunas, por favor."*

"No more for me, thanks." She shook her head merrily. "One martini's enough."

"It's already gone. You must have been thirsty. Think of them as juice for your olives." Hank reached for his wallet. "You don't want 'em drying out, do you?"

Lunch inched his chair closer. "Tell us, Anne Mahoney from Los Angeles. Why are you at the Hotel Portillo, where the nearest tree is two miles straight down the mountain?"

"No way, you guys. It's my turn." Anne moved her empty glass to the side. She didn't notice the waiter replace it with another. "Why are you here?"

"Teaching the FRE's, fat rear ends," said Lunch, shoving a lank of brown hair off his narrow forehead.

"That's Vail, Lunch," interrupted Hank. "Not Portillo. Only trim little rich tushes here."

"NT you've got, Anne Mahoney. Curves, not bones," observed Lunch, obviously thinking he had flattered her. Anne cut him dead with a ferocious glare.

Lunch cleverly shifted subjects. "I'll see you tomorrow at ski school. By the way, you're pretty coy about the Latin who pulled the strings for you to get into the 9:30 seating—"

Alcohol pinked Anne's cheeks, and she felt a little muddled. "I don't know any—"

"Uh-uh. No lies to your friends, Annie. But you wait. I've got some clout of my own." Lunch snapped his fingers. "It's as good as done. You're in my class."

"I didn't know I was taking a class."

She drained her glass, catching two olives in her mouth.

"Half a day of group lessons is included with room and board." Lunch gently tapped the bottom of her glass, and she chewed on the remaining two olives. "You've got to pay for your own massages, though."

"But only if you rise to the level of your impotence—" Anne began laughing at the forthcoming Purdoe law. "—and can't snare a fast-fingered Brazilian to relax your tired muscles for free...."

"It's tough competition." Lunch leered. "Now, we've got the fingers—" he popped the knuckles of his left hand, then signaled the waiter for another round "—but it's hard to afford C and C on instructor's wages."

Hank looked morose. "That's what we've learned down here, Annie. You can't speed up an indecent massage without caviar and champagne."

Indecent massage. C and C. No wonder Austrians lurched further out of control south of the equator. "By the way, how many of you instructors are Austrian?" Anne kept her tone casual.

"Have you met Gisela yet?" asked Lunch. "She's Austrian, I think. She's a bloody Pied Piper with an accordion. A whole generation of kiddos learned to ski from Gisela."

"Especially the Brazilians." Hank Purdoe rolled his eyes suggestively. "Following Gisela down the mountain is the fastest way to find a free masseur."

Anne flashed a reckless smile. "I'm slow."

"I'll get you revved up tomorrow," promised Lunch. "Can you two ski as fast as you talk?"

"Lady, we ski faster than a speeding bullet, faster than the speed of sound!" That was Hank.

"C'mon, you guys. You must be exaggerating. But how would I know the difference? All ski instructors ski faster than I do."

"Now this is serious, Annie," said Lunch.

Hank Purdoe and Anne giggled.

"Seriously. After you pass 110 miles per hour, Annie, you pass the sound of your body ripping through space. Purdoe and I live for quiet time."

"One ten! You've got to be kidding."

"Steve McKinney hit 124.7 here in 1978," said Hank. "Six guys have matched that. Record's now 126.230, set by Franz Weber—speaking of Austrians, Annie—in Colorado. We're down here getting ready for winter."

Later, Anne faintly remembered drilling the speedsters for information. How does your body sound when it goes faster than a car? It crackles, like a forest fire, one of them told her. Was it Lunch? Or Hank? At the time the conversation seemed clear.

A dozen or so guests had wandered into the bar by eight-thirty; by nine-fifteen it was full.

"Don't go in yet." Hank tugged on her sleeve. "It's not chic to experience hunger. That's for the poor folks who stuff themselves, the clods."

After a few minutes Anne excused herself. She stood easily and walked straight through a dream, up two wide flights of stairs to her room. She remembered thinking how alive her face was. She needed no blush, nor erase. A few more rolls with the mascara and her round eyes seemed to have an exotic slant. Finally she stuffed a news magazine in her purse for company during dinner.

The maître d' greeted her by name this time. *"Venga, por favor, Señorita Mahoney."* His white teeth were whiter against the olive complexion of his friendly face.

She followed him through the dining room. Like the salon, it reflected the moneyed style of the thirties, Queen Mary first—class with polished pillars—not built of solid wood in the extravagant postwar fashion, but paneled.

Scalloped booths of brown leather fluted the wall opposite high windows overlooking the lake, more private seatings than the round tables for eight and the rectangular tables for two and four in between.

Every table and booth was occupied, and no one was alone. Where was she going to sit, Anne wondered, looking for the waiters' door. Her authoritative guide undoubtedly intended to hide a single woman diner.

When the maître d' stopped unexpectedly in front of a booth near the back wall, Anne, busy scanning in another direction, walked into him. Ordinarily she would have unthinkingly tossed out an apology and gotten on with the business at hand, namely food. But she stopped dead.

The Hans was uncoiling from the booth. He was waiting for her to slip in next to him, his aloof eyes amused at her discomfiture. She felt clumsy and resented him making her feel that way.

A camel-and-golden-brown houndstooth sport coat, obviously tailored for him, hung from the breadth of his shoulders. Yet the cashmere was more...more tapered, more Italian, more exciting. He looked expensive. Anne concluded the Austrian had already signed his retirement contract.

She glanced covertly at the others in the booth,

searching for the rich widow who could afford the Blue Hans. There was no woman, only two men, the space between them, strangely, a trifle wide for comfort. Truths are developed by probing inconsistencies, Anne knew, but she wasn't seeking truth this evening. She was on vacation.

The two rose to meet her, the politeness in their formality embracing her in a genuine welcome. She gratefully responded. One was young, in his late teens, Anne swiftly judged, and cockily handsome, with a dark complexion that was bronzed even darker. The other appeared to be in his late 60s, flat of belly and youthful. His deeply tanned face was unlined from the top of his receded gray hair to his unsagged chin.

It was...yes, Anne recognized him now. The skier who had waved at the Hans when the instructor had snowplowed with her down the mountain.

A deep flush flooded up from the low scoop of her neckline to her pounding temples.

"Our wait for you was well worth the anticipation." The Hans's voice was dangerously charming. There was one place left at that table; Anne couldn't pretend she didn't understand his meaning, so she very nicely refused before he cornered her again.

"I am so terribly sorry to keep you all waiting," she said, including all three men in her contrite gaze. "But I didn't know I was expected. Perhaps we could dine later in the week?" A beguiling expression crossed her face. Anne had used it successfully on other occasions. "Tonight I would prefer boring only myself. I am quite exhausted from my trip down." She turned away, looking for the maître d' with his clipboard, but couldn't find him.

The older man tched. "Has no one told you the pro-
cedure at Portillo? Probably not. The employees are
used to guests who have been coming here for two, three
generations, and they sometimes forget about the odd
stranger."

Anne couldn't place his accent. It was very English,
as were his charcoal-gray blazer and lighter gray slacks.
Except his cadence was slightly different.

In the back of the booth, the young man looked impatient. "Grandfather sometimes forgets to give the
point until he has bored through the history." His
English was clipped Oxford also. "Portillo's like a
cruise ship. We enjoy assigned seating for dinner and
breakfast." He brushed a rebellious wave of luxuriant
dark brown hair off his confident face. "I say 'enjoy,'
because we are privileged to have you join us."

"Intelligence and beauty is far better for the appetite
than the finest wine," added the grandfather, gallantly
bussing her cheek. "Let us add our welcome to Tavo's
for your stay in Portillo."

"Oh. . . ." Anne's intention to flee was softened by a
velvet swaddling cloth of appreciation and compli-
ments. She wished she could sit next to the older man,
but his grandson had apparently been given that position.

She had no choice. Anne slipped by the silent Hans,
carefully avoiding touching his thighs. The memory of
their muscled commands was too disturbing. What did
they call him? Tavo. It must be a nickname for, what?
She didn't know many Germanic names. Gerhardt?
Otto? Adolf? She wouldn't ask.

Anne shook out the heavy linen napkin and waited,
dizzy. Her desire for food had vanished. The next

move was his, because she was having trouble focusing.

"Your nap must have been a sound one." The demanding man at her side solemnly studied the sheen on her face. "Your color is stronger, and the sun has erased the weariness from your smile."

Nap? Anne was entertained. She felt no need to enumerate her activities, not when he had so arrogantly drawn a mistaken conclusion.

"May I present Anne Mahoney to you." Tavo turned to the others. "She flew down from Los Angeles last night." How did he know her name? And where she was from? His provocation added a devilish sparkle to her expression.

"You must be exhausted, Anne," the older man sympathized. "Whenever my wife and I make the trip from Buenos Aires to San Francisco for conventions, we fly to Miami for a couple of days to break the trip into manageable portions. Although Tavo is correct. You are glowing with health."

"Dr. Radámes Ebert Gamen." The blond giant smoothly made the presentation, his Germanic accent more noticeable against the pure British of the other two. "One of Argentina's premier plastic surgeons."

"It's a pleasure to meet you, Dr. Gamen." Anne extended her hand, shifting farther away from Tavo. His troublesome warmth touched her nervous skin from a foot away, penetrating her protective guard, unsettling her. She shifted again. The warmth clung, like a hot, clear March day at the Santa Monica pier.

Ignore him, she thought, and tried valiantly.

"Oh, dear, I mixed up your last names, didn't I?" She beamed at the surgeon, certain he understood the situation was tense, that he would help tame the conversation. "All of us reporters have trouble remembering the Spanish method in our stories, even we women who should appreciate a culture that doesn't discard the mother's maiden name. Dr. Ebert Gamen. Isn't that correct?"

"Tavo told us you were a reporter, Anne. I can see you're very alert about cultural differences. Some of my Anglo-Argentine clients call me Dr. Ebert. You know how stubborn the Saxon mentality is. But please, we're all on holiday. Call me Radámes. And this is my—"

"I am Pascal Larregoite Ebert," interjected the young man eagerly. He caught Anne's fuzzy glance and held it, then reached for her hand to kiss, not shake it.

"Me encantas," she heard distantly through her confusion. "I am enchanted to meet you, Ana, because you are enchanting," he repeated in English, adding flourishes.

"Hello, Pascal." Anne withdrew her hand, flattered and amused by his posturing. "Are you from Argentina, too?"

"My grandfather and I live in Buenos Aires during much of the year, and we have a cabin in Bariloche, so we are able to practice our skiing on occasion. But—" he shrugged "—it's a two-and-a-half-hour flight from Buenos Aires, so it is more difficult for us to attain the speed of Chileans who live next to the mountains."

Where did that complaint come from, Anne wondered, watching Radámes fidget with his knife handle.

"So..." she said, pushing the introductions on to their conclusion. "We are all Americans here except you, Herr...?" Anne turned to her benefactor, unhappily realizing, as soon as he began to speak, that he was somehow playing with her once more.

"Only Americans will be sitting together at our table here in Portillo this week while we have the too-brief pleasure of your company, Anne Mahoney." He enjoyed his torment; she could feel it in the rising electricity between them. What didn't this annoying man know about her. She knew very well how easy it was to obtain information about people. How didn't bother her. She wanted to know why.

"In Los Angeles, we say everyone is a Californian in his heart." Anne was sarcastic. "I gather you in the Old World are eager to be one of us in the New World."

"Stop teasing her, Tavo! She's suffering culture lag," chided Radámes. "May I make what is apparently an overdue presentation? This rascal at your side, Anne, is Gustavo Mohr de la Huerta."

The name was familiar. De la Huerta. Anne ran through the mental index of facts she had filed, but nothing clicked in the haze.

"Tavo played the same joke the entire time he was at the university in Munich," the Argentine surgeon said. "He derives a certain pleasure in exposing the prejudices of Europeans—and forgive me, my dear, North Americans—who are determined that all Chileans are a swarthy little people. Is 'twisted' pleasure too strong a word for your trained economist's mind, Tavo?"

Tavo apparently didn't mind his older friend's joshing, for his laughter was relaxed. Pascal joined in the South American merriment. Anne was embarrassed. She clenched her hands in her lap and sat back stiffly while the waiter served them fresh cold salmon. Each plate had a sprig of dill and a prettily twisted slice of lemon.

"Twisted? Why, Radámes." She slid the tip of her tongue over an imaginary speck on her upper lip as she turned to the surgeon's naive grandson. "Tell me, Pascal. . . ." She cut a wedge of the tender pink fish with her fork. "Are you also not what you appear to be? Are you an artist or an engineer or a physician, too?"

Pascal's dark eyes gleamed. It was plain he believed Anne's pretended elevation of him to adulthood, and she immediately regretted the impulse. Usually she curbed herself better. Why wasn't the kid in school, she wondered. "What? I'm sorry, I didn't hear you." She sluggishly returned to the conversation. Tavo was now leading.

"Radámes is right. I should stop pulling your leg, although I regret that I must cease the pleasure." Tavo's wide-spread hand patted her knee, and large as it was, his thumb lay disturbingly close to the tender parting of her thighs. Then the wayward thumb was gone. Had she imagined it?

Anne felt feverish. She vacillated about making a scene. Was he sleazy or simply burdened with an over-sized reach? "Imagine the octaves you could hit if you were a concert pianist." She tried to laugh away the situation, her voice faintly slurred. Apparently the others didn't notice.

"Tavo, *por favor*. Don't tell her you are the fruit king of Chile," Radámes warned with a chuckle. "You studied in Munich, but I studied in San Francisco. I know the mentality of the North Americans. Anne will be deceived. Tell her you are the emperor of apples or grapes."

"He would prefer being the emperor in his fine new

clothes," she rejoined, struggling for a teasing laugh.
But the flush on her face was a giveaway. Mentally she
was photographing naked shoulders broader than the
stretch of her arms.

Flustered, Anne scooped up her hair on top of her
head, cooling her neck. When she dropped the strands
with an evasive sigh, the blond Chilean fondled her
hand and gently pulled it toward him.

"But the emperor has no clothes. Are you pulling my
hand?"

Anne jerked her own hand back. The men laughed.
Fighting dizziness, Anne laughed, too, through gritted
teeth.

"Do you know, Pascal, that the Irish are the Latins
of the North? Irrational. Passionate...." Tavo placed
his arm along the back of the booth behind Anne, encircling her with the strength of his presence, but not
touching her. "Also bright. Once this O'Mahoney gets
her balance on skis, she will challenge you for speed.
You see how fast her mind works?"

"Cuidado, Tavo," warned Radámes, tugging slightly
at the corner of his right eye with his tapered index finger. "North Americans have different customs. This is
your first visit to South America, is it not, Anne? You
must understand that flirting is our diversion here. Talk
without action—"

"Not always," Pascal objected, giving a cocksure
wink to Anne.

"Nonsense, Pascalito. Our flirting is an entertainment without consequence. It reassures the giver and the
receiver that they are both attractive people."

Anne doubted Dr. Ebert's analysis. "Excuse me,"
she said flatly, reaching for the pepper shaker in the

middle of the table to escape the disturbing arms. "I am quite hungry."

She cut a sliver of lemon and combined it with a bite of salmon. It was delicious, she thought, chewing slowly. Sudden waves of nausea attacked; she swallowed with difficulty.

Radámes took the bottle of white wine from the bucket of ice on the stand and poured some in Anne's tulip. "Care for some Undurraga? It has a lovely dry bouquet."

He didn't wait for her answer, and now her head ached too severely to refuse. She was clammy all over—chilled, perspiring. Her hot skin burned.

"I would like more also, grandfather." Pascal glanced at the gold watch on his thin wrist. "It's 10:48." The information was apropos of nothing. "Tell me about your skiing, Ana." He leaned close. "Are you an amateur medalist from the Cups or the Games, training down here for Aspen next winter?"

"The Cups?" she puzzled, her auburn eyes focusing on Pascal's blurred brown ones.

"What have you been sniffing?" His young tenor was openly curious.

"What do you mean?" Her own voice came from far away.

"You should see your pupils. I know pupil size."

"Pascal, stop professing wisdom in your ignorance," Radámes said, anger ruffling his usual nonjudgmental tones.

"You think I am a child. An innocent nothing," the equally angry teenager hissed back.

Anne heard only a din. Abruptly she felt herself being turned around.

"What is Pascal talking about?" That was the Hans...no, Gustavo. A pair of glacial blue eyes locked onto hers like frozen magnets drawing the fever from her trembling limbs, leaving her colder and weaker. "Yes, I see. Where were you during tea time? Not in the pool. I searched for you there. Tell me about your nap."

"I don't have to—"

"How many hours now without sleep, Anne? One night in the plane. None the night before because you were too excited about your trip. When did you eat last? So you went to the bar for a quick pick-me-up—is that how you say it?"

"You're not my mother. Besides, I tried to eat, but your idiot customs make it impossible to get food at a decent hour." She started to turn back to a pouting Pascal.

"Answer me. Alcohol can be dangerous here." Tavo turned her around again, and to her dismay she swayed. "How many?"

Anne truthfully couldn't recall. Two martinis? Three? Four? No, it was four olives in the second one....

"Surely you stuck to beer or wine? Hotel Portillo is ninety-seven hundred feet in altitude. Almost two miles. You have to acclimate before drinking. No, of course you did not."

Anne defied his chisled scowl and picked up her glass of wine. She took a sip, sending a vague smile across the table. "What kind of wine did you say this was, Radámes?"

She couldn't hear his answer. In the ensuing silence, she leaned her perspiring forehead into the absorptive wool of her sleeve and felt absolutely ill.

Tavo was on his feet, lifting her limp body out of the booth, scolding in a low tone, inaudible unless one was pressed near the growl in his throat. He set Anne down, and she wobbled. He steadied her into the hard wall of his arm and chest, bracing a leg out to guard her from busy waiters. She reeled into the massive shelter, her hip wedged against his powerful thigh.

"Pascal, deme la perfume de Cristina Caravachel— pronto," he said, and the youth bolted for a vial of perfume from a Brazilian who wafted a heady odor in her path. The savory smell of rare steaks passed with each laden tray. Anne clenched her teeth against the combined assault on her senses, afraid she was going to be sick. The sharp pain in her head was unbearable. Black louvers slammed in the howling wind of her mind.

"Can you walk?"

The sour taste of stomach acid stung her tongue. Anne was afraid to open her mouth to answer. She closed her eyes weakly, feeling only the security of the sure body underneath the softest of cashmere as Tavo gathered her into his arms... and then no more.

IT HURT TO BREATHE. Painfully intense perfume burned her nose. Anne coughed, a deep gagging cough from the pit of her stomach, and struggled to sit up.

The sharp smell of gardenias was relentless. Anne pushed away a cut-crystal vial, but it was returned once more and she choked.

"No, Pascal, no luces." The youth moved his hand away from the lamp in the shadows and awkwardly waited by Anne's side. She tried to speak to him, but was racked with gagging coughs again and gave up. She leaned weakly into the security of familiar arms.

"Lo es suficiente perfume." Tavo made one last pass with the scent, then handed the container to Pascal.

"I'm better," Anne gasped.

"She is coming around now." The deep voice switched effortlessly to English. "She must eliminate the poison from her system. It is an embarrassing trial for anyone, Pascal—" the pause was not a question "—as you undoubtedly have learned. You should return downstairs and keep your grandfather company with his dinner. I know his bypass was a success, but I do not force the excitement."

Gustavo lifted Anne to her feet, a Raggedy Ann. Her knees buckled, but he caught her easily. She trusted he would.

"And Pascal, have our waiter send up crackers and something bubbling to settle her stomach—mineral water or tonic. Yes, tonic. The bitter flavor will cleanse the palate."

Afterward, when nothing remained inside her stomach, when involuntary tears streaked her cheeks and her back ached from the convulsions she had forced upon herself, Anne staggered upright.

Tavo was swirling bubbles into water in the bathtub, his hair curling in the damp air. "We will begin with tepid water. Then as you adjust to the temperature, Ana, I will add more hot and many bubbles." With a fluid motion he turned off the faucets. His sleeves were rolled above his elbows. Long muscles in his forearms bulged under smooth skin for the instant it took him to close off the flow.

Anne braced herself against the cool plaster wall, detached from her wretched body.

Gustavo opened the mirrored door on the medicine

cabinet, squeezed striped toothpaste on a brush and handed it to her with a charming grin.

"I am sorry to inflict my germs on you, but I think you would prefer sharing the brush in the hand than waiting for two in the bush."

Anne tried to smile at his joke, and was sick again.

And again his hand was a lifeline to the sink. He lifted the hair off her shoulders, holding it back from the water. Unimpeded, she gratefully scrubbed until her mouth tasted fresh.

Then he spoke, sympathetically. "When I was ski racing, our craziness was astonishing. How we thought we could drink the rivers dry and not suffer was a measure of our adolescent stupidity." He handed her a face towel. "The absolute worst head holding I have ever done was in Bariloche. We drew lots to see who had to stay sober. 'You lose, Tavo,' my friends on the team crowed, but I was the winner...."

Anne's teeth chattered. "I'm so cold." She trembled. "My head won't stop hurting."

Tavo held her tightly against the heat of his body. "We have a choice about your clothes, Ana," he said finally. "Are you too faint to undress and climb in the bath without assistance? I am afraid you will slip on the tile and crack your head open, and it is too late to ring for a maid to aid you. They have gone off duty."

Anne swayed, uncaring, too weak to make any decision. His grip tightened imperceptibly as she clung to him.

"That leaves only me, Ana. Shh...do not worry. I do a great deal of business in California. I know the reputation of California girls and I know the reality. You are not all casual."

Tavo's large hands were already pulling the light-weight dress over her head. Anne buried her face in the swell of his ribs. She raised her hands obediently over her head, then it was off. As he unhooked the lavender brassiere, his deft fingers left a lingering fingerprint on her back.

"I will help you to the bath and seat you on the ledge...you will be okay there," he said gently. "You can unroll your nylons while I find a robe for you in my closet."

"Where am I?"

"My suite. It is easier to make arrangements here."

The feel of the cold porcelain cut through the haze of Anne's mind, a clarity that ended when she slid into the meringue of bubbles. The tub was a big one from the extravagant forties, not one of the cramped modern kind. She didn't need to scoot way down for the bubbles to tickle her chin. She merely lay there, her hair flowing out from her shoulders, and closed her eyes.

Stephanie's face floated in front of her. Anne's temples pounded anxiously. She sat up, choking, and Tavo was there, rapping her back until she could catch her breath.

"Swallow a little water?"

She pretended yes. "Do you have any aspirin... Gustavo?" It was difficult to remember the stranger's name.

"After you get something in your stomach. Come into the other room." He held a ruby terry-cloth robe open for her to step into and turned his head discretely.

The bedraggled woman backed into the whopping robe; the shoulder seams dropped nearly to her elbows. He quickly tied the belt firmly around her narrow waist—too quickly. Anne languidly ran her hands down the deep red cloth, pressing it against her wet skin to dry herself.

Somehow she was surprised when he lifted her hair out from under the collar, his strong thumb scooping up drenched strands with wide sweeps up the relaxed tendon of her neck.

"Come, Ana." He could have been coaxing a sleepy child. "Sit on my lap and let me dry your hair so you do not catch cold."

She sat sideways on a blue-jeaned leg as hard as the porcelain. She squirmed, and her spontaneous rubbing sparked an aroused friction that refused to be still. The quickened rhythm of his heart penetrated the rich fabric of the robe, but he continued patiently brushing her hair. The heat from the dryer blew across her pale cheeks, ruffling the responsive nape of her neck.

And thus gentled, Anne rested.

WHEN SHE AWAKENED, she was propped up in a large bed in a unlit room. Tavo's face was backlighted by the glow from the bathroom. It hurt to look at the blinding halo and see darkness instead of strongly defined features.

She obediently ate two saltines as he insisted she do, washed the dry crumbs down with tonic water, then swallowed two aspirin he handed her.

"What time is it?"

"About eleven-thirty. Now go back to sleep." He tucked her in. "I will leave the door open to the living room. Call me if you need something."

He kissed her cheek, and his sunburned lips sandpapered her sensitive skin.

"I don't understand the bubble bath," she murmured. "Not when you don't use Chapstick."

Through her dolorous trance, she heard him chuckle. "I had my pilot helicopter a bottle up with the mail yesterday. It was to be a surprise for Pascal after his first race...."

Anne didn't hear any more. With a deep sigh, she was asleep.

SHE REMEMBERED NOTHING until she felt herself being cradled and comforted.

"You are safe, sweetheart. Shh. It was a bad dream. You are all right." There was a fiery-hot, wet cloth on Anne's forehead. Her face was damp with tears. She wiped at them with her sleeve and sniffed.

"Here, blow." He had a tissue.

"I can't...I don't remem—"

"Shh. Do not talk now. You are feverish."

She dutifully swallowed more aspirin. A cold towel replaced the hot one, and a gray shroud shuttered her mind once more.

THE NEXT TIME she woke up, there was a fresh cool cloth on her forehead. She held a hand against it in the curtained darkness. The skin burned.

"I have not broken the fever yet," Tavo said. "I have water running in the bath now."

"I think I'll sleep just a little longer." Her voice came from a long distance; her ears ached from fullness.

Strong arms picked her up, and she nestled into the fresh smell of a recently laundered T-shirt. The cold floor felt lovely on her blistering feet when he set her down. Anne blinked in the unexpected light, her eyes wide and unfocused.

"What time is it?"

"About noon. Lean here against the wall."

"Twelve, noon?" Anne's voice was bewildered.

He handed her more aspirin. She swallowed them with orange juice.

"We will talk when we feed your fever. I have remembered correctly, *no cierto?* Starve a cold—" Tavo interrupted himself to call over his shoulder, *"Venga aquí, señorita,"* and a quiet girl in a white maid's uniform ducked into the bathroom and replaced him at Anne's side.

The lukewarm water was cool on her aching muscles. She shivered. From the other room, he sensed the chills striking again.

"Abra lo llave del agua caliente—pronto." The maid, her long black hair caught in a barrette at the back of her neck, silently turned on the hot water. *"Y oye, destape el desaque de la banera."* She opened the drain.

"Better, Ana?"

"Yes, thank you." Was this her meek voice? The girl handed Anne her special Belgium cleansing cream.

"How did you—"

The girl shrugged, uncomprehending.

"I sent the head of housekeeping to your room to collect a few necessities," Tavo called. "She told me it was fortunate you are a very organized person. I never doubted it—" his sudden laugh was hearty "—except when it has been necessary to do the odd rescue."

Anne smiled sheepishly. Her scrubbed face felt alive even if the rest of her body felt like yesterday's lettuce. The maid handed her a towel and then helped her into her own flannel nightgown, palest pink with deep ruffles along the hem.

"I think I owe you a toothbrush," Anne said, walking slowly out of the bathroom, resting against the maid's shoulder.

Sunlight filled the spacious bedroom with cheerful warmth. Drapes of forest green had been pulled open and a matching bedspread folded and laid across an armchair. A plump maid finished changing the bed. Her stubby hands turned down a taut triangle on the right side.

"I'd protest, but I'm too weak," Anne said with a sigh. Her eyes darkened with tears, like russet bark during a rain. "I hate helpless women."

"I do, too, Ana." Vivid eyes continued to watch her steadily from the doorway. The stern planes of his unyielding face showed worry, and that pleased Anne. His actions had matched the occasional expressions that escaped his control. She was learning to trust what she could read in his face.

Tavo picked her up easily and carried her into the living room. She felt small in his powerful arms, and too thin. He placed her on a comfortable chair at a small table set for lunch. When he sat down opposite her, his tan appeared disconcertingly golden against the black T-shirt with its printed white waves and scrolled letters reading: "10K, *Vina del Mar*."

"Indeed, Ana, you cannot imagine how grateful I am that you are a help-more, not help-less woman." His smile begged appreciation for his pun. It spread across the angles of his cheekbones, its warmth replacing a fixed loneliness.

Her eyes blurred with unshed tears at his sarcasm.

Tavo quickly reached for both her hands and held them loosely, untrapped yet secure. "I am making a little joke, Ana. You are extraordinarily—"

"Stupid, then, or foolish."

"Well...." His eyes held on even while he released her hands. "Let us say you are tired."

A waiter moved around the table then, ladling steaming home-made soup from a shiny caldron. Tavo raised his glass of milk in a toast. "Your rest has been a disguised blessing to me. I spent the morning reviewing nectarine contracts for the Saudi Arabians, a task I would have had to postpone in the press of courting you."

Anne did not believe him. *Courting?* She carefully blew on a spoonful of the steaming liquid. It was a rich lentil with a turkey-broth base. "Delicious," she murmured. "I'm so hungry that I'm not hungry." She drank some of her milk and ate part of a hot flat biscuit, four inches in diameter, which Tavo slathered in butter for her.

She licked the crumbs off her lips and settled back. "Are you always so thoughtful?" Her curious eyes explored his. "Pretending I did you a favor by getting sick so you could do your homework? Arranging all of this?" She gestured at the food and her nightgown. "Cooling down my fever all night?"

"I am always thoughtful when it is important to me," he said simply. "Tell me, please, Ana. What happened to you before you left California? You are suffering from more than a hangover."

She clasped her slim fingers and willed calmness into them. Her summary was professionally concise. "My best friend drowned when a drug-running cruiser ran down the sailboat she and her boyfriend were taking to Catalina.''

"That was Stephanie Clark?''

"Yes.'' She nodded, composed within the rising walls of her emotional shell. Nothing he knew surprised her, but still she had an unspoken question, and he answered it.

"I read a brief notice about Stephanie in the newspaper yesterday. Richard Clark is well-known in Chile. We are associates.'' Tavo reached across the table and sheltered Anne's pale cheek in his broad palm. "I am very sorry, Ana. Stephanie was a lovely girl. Now I understand the reason for your nightmares last night.''

Anne stiffened. What nightmares? They were her secret. Her weakness. Quick overstatement was her stock-in-trade, and she used it immediately.

"Did I scream about snakes and great horned toads? Perhaps I was having the D.T.'s.'' She yawned as though bored. "I know more than I ever wanted to know about D.T.'s after that Christmas series in the drunk tank.'' Her lips parted jovially, but the rigid corners proclaimed her frightened reaction.

Tavo's eyebrow shot up skeptically, but he merely said, "I do not take your yawn personally, sweetheart. If you take a nap now, then dress for a late dinner, I suspect you will feel almost normal tomorrow morning.''

"Thank you, Gustavo.'' She covered another yawn, a legitimate one this time, and stretched wearily. "How could eating wear me out?''

He helped Anne to her feet, ready with support but not forcing it. She found the strength to walk alone.

"Good night, good night,'' she said when he drew the

curtains, snuggling down into the pillow in the darkness. "Sleep tight. Don't let the bedbugs bite."

"Excuse me?"

Anne was seconds away from sleep. "My grandfather always kissed us good-night like that."

She absorbed Tavo's kiss into her dream, a brief embrace on the crest of a wave. She was bodysurfing, riding the surge, laughing and sputtering in a tangled heap of powdery sand and endlessly long, bronzed legs.

Clear aqua waves were lapping her toes when the crackling warned her. She glanced over her shoulder. The mountain of chaparral behind was an inferno. Fireballs, in their race to the sea, flew from clusters of eucalyptus to palms and oaks. The crackling was closer; sparks scorched her nostrils. She reeled at the stench of singed hair.

A yowling gray cat with horrifying yellow eyes hurled out of the flames, its claws set to dig into Anne's face. She screamed and ran into the water. She swam desperately and still the fireballs surrounded her. She screamed again and dived to escape, but she couldn't surface.

"Let me up!" She flailed hysterically. "I'm drowning—help. I'm—"

"Hush, Ana, hush. Wake up. You are safe."

In the warmth of her rescuer's comforting arms, in the anonymous security of foreign darkness, Anne finally cried. It seemed she wept forever.

"Tell me about your nightmare." Tavo sat on the bed and rocked her. "It is important to me. Please, Ana. Tell me about this one and tell me about the others."

For the first time, Anne talked about her terrifying nights. She whispered brokenly, then railed at their imposition, and cried again. She talked about fire and pestilence and other "great stories," as reporters and editors called disasters. He listened without judging her.

She cried about stunned priests, in tears, anointing holy oil on bodies in yellow plastic bags after the crash of an airliner. She had covered the story for one dispassionate week of stardom, she told him, and admitted more.

She confessed the ultimate spookiness of her nightmares—how they came true. At the end of that same week, she had dreamed she was inside a strange passenger plane that nose-dived into the ground after takeoff. The pressure of mounting g-forces had crumpled her chest. At the point when she believed she would be crushed on impact, she woke up.

The next morning at work, Anne learned a military transport had stalled and crashed at nearby Riverside Air Force Base, while she had been dreaming.

Two months later, in a dream, she watched a well-marked airliner burst into flames on takeoff. She recognized the company insignia. Superstitiously, she didn't even tell Steffie for fear that speaking her imaginings aloud would make them come true.

Anne stopped speaking now, but her frantic pulse must have told her listener that she was protecting the core of her angst. Tavo shifted her effortlessly, lying down beside her. She wrapped her arms around his neck and nestled against his long chest, her hips at his waist. His great body dominated the bed. No matter how she stretched he was beside her, all of him, and some to spare.

"Tell me, sweetheart." He stroked her hair in the darkness. Lulled to a feeling of safety, she told how five days after her nightmare, a jet marked exactly as she had visualized burst into flames on takeoff.

Anne sought the slow regular pulse of his heart as a baby in the womb would. "Keep talking," he murmured soothingly. "Tell me." And because he didn't say she needed to open her festering wounds to heal, because he only held her and listened, she exposed a part of her soul.

"At first, the nightmares came right away after I covered a story. But now the old ones are all mixed up with the present and future...and everything's a mess.... I never know what's going to haunt me. Like tonight. It was two years ago, or was it three, when I saw a charred cat during the Laurel Canyon fire. Maybe a burning gray cat is going to attack me next month. It'll be fire season then...."

This time Anne's tone didn't lighten with flip amusement as it usually did. "On the other hand, maybe, it'll just be the usual September fire tragedies."

She wiped her face again with her sodden flannel sleeve and touched his closely shaven cheek. "Thank you for listening, Gustavo." Her voice was remote. Nervous embarrassment invaded her tranquility. She shivered, afraid she had given the stranger the dangerous power to comfort her. If he had that key, he also had the power to hurt her.

Silently she sat up, cursing the immediate, dizzy reminder of her hangover and fever. She tried to make out his enigmatic face in the dark. What was he thinking?

"Have you considered writing out your feelings after these assignments? Perhaps in poems where you could shape the images with your conscious mind? Shh...." His cool fingers silenced her lips. "Think about it when

you go back to sleep. We have much time to talk later."
She felt him yawn.

"I'm leaving Saturday." Her voice was very, very
sensible.

"Umm. . . . Ana, I am quite tired and the couch is not
comfortable for someone my size." The voice from the
obscured face was imperturbable. "I am going to sleep
beside you. You will sleep, too. I promise. Come close,
Ana, away from the evil."

Anne crept to him without protest and fell into a
sound sleep, as though she was accustomed to burrow-
ing into a man. She and Charles had never shared that
particular kind of tenderness. . . .

She was not nearly as cool when the sharp knock
awakened them.

"¿Quién es?" Tavo was on his feet, alert.

Anne didn't understand the muffled masculine answer outside the living-room door. Did she hear her
name? She scrambled to her feet, straining to catch the
words. She wished she knew Spanish better. It was
foolish not to have continued the language after high
school. Why had she shifted to Chinese for her under-
graduate requirements? Probably the glamour of use-
lessness had attracted her.

She felt the wall for a switch and turned on the lights.
An extravagant mass of long-stemmed yellow roses
filled a pair of tall, milky-green vases on the dresser.
Crumpled cellophane filled the wastebasket at the side.
The crackling in my dream, Anne mused, sniffing the
fragrance, her nose like a butterfly flitting from one
blossom to another. She loved roses, especially yellow
roses. There were at least three dozen. . . . She inhaled,
absorbed.

"Ana, the boy says you have an urgent telephone call from the United States Congress." Tavo returned to the bedroom. With a monumental yawn, he ran a hand through his rumpled hair. It was embarrassingly apparent he had been deeply asleep. "The overseas operator will call back in fifteen minutes."

The new vulnerable Ana Mahoney unraveled. "Where's the phone? He's not calling me here, is he?" Guilt added a shrill urgency to her voice. She blathered on. "How did they know to find me here? My God, what did they tell Charles? They didn't tell him I was in this room?"

She turned to Tavo, her face flushed, her hair tumbled appealingly around her shoulders. "What did they tell him?"

"Ana—"

"No, I'm Anne Mahoney. Calm, collected Anne Mahoney of the *Los Angeles Chronicle*. One of the world's seven wonders in a disaster. Damn. . . ."

Tavo had the effrontery to look amused. "The paradox of Anne-Ana. . . ." He drew out the words as though he had all the time in the world. *Well, he thought he did, didn't he?* Anne was flustered. *Wasn't that the last thing he had said before they fell asleep?*

"That's my boyfriend on the telephone." She deliberately snapped off thoughts of Tavo, switching on the remaining few lights she could find, her hem flapping around her ankles. "What the hell did they tell Charles? How am I going to explain this? Where're my clothes? Rats. What time is it?"

Tavo beat her to the final lamp. His mussed hair shone silver, though the harsh hollows of his face were in shadow.

Her memory was equally shadowed. Anne stepped back, warily. "Nothing happened, did it?"

She watched in fascination as his hooded eyes hardened to bits of unfeeling glass. "You have insulted me," he said, and she couldn't see if he meant it.

Insulted? She was the one who'd been held a night and a day, and what, another night in his room.

"I beg your pardon," Anne scoffed.

Leaning against the wall, his hands jammed in the pockets of his jeans, he fixed his eyes stubbornly on hers.

She blushed under his scrutiny but refused to flinch away.

"Everything happened. You do not understand, no?" he said finally. "*Bueno,* you will. It is not important at the moment. You had better get dressed. The housekeeper brought a change of clothes for you. Portillo's two telephones are next to the reception desk and we will have to wait for the elevator, so there is not much time."

"Everything. . . ." Anne's face went ashen.

"Everything." His cool eyes were entertained. "Do not bother lighting candles and clicking your beads. Nothing infringed on the politico's rights. I do not need to experience your body to know it. I know your boyfriend has lost you."

"You know nothing about nothing." Anne bit off the words and yanked a dress out of the closet. "Close the door behind you. . . please."

How much time did she have left, Anne worried, hurrying. Minutes later when she crossed the living room to the door, her feelings of embarrassment had left their mark. He seemed to recognize this, for he smiled, and his features softened in a way she didn't understand.

"Thank you for seeing me through my...uh, drunkenness, Gustavo." Anne held out her hand to shake his.

He shook it with an easy laugh, then lightly kissed her cheek. Her jumbled emotions didn't respond lightly, and a blush colored her face. "This is how we say good-bye in Chile, sweetheart. Come on," he said, wresting control of the situation. "Or your politico will have to wait for you."

It would serve Charles right to wait, Anne thought re-belliously. *I've been waiting long enough for his call.* Her pause gave Tavo an advantage. They were halfway to the elevator by the time she protested, "I can manage by myself."

"You are weak from your fever, no? I want you to talk to my rival, to hear his cold voice...."

"What makes you think it's cold?" Anne petulantly tapped her foot, impatient for the elevator to answer their buzz.

He shrugged in the offhand Latin manner. "Most North American men are *machistas.*"

Anne shot him a sarcastic glance. *"Our* men are macho?"

Tavo was still laughing when they entered the eleva-tor. "We Chileans are *macho normal.* Your men are *machista.* They think of themselves first, second, third...." He leisurely traced the oval of her jaw with a persistent finger. "And somewhere toward the end, they think of their women. We Chilean men—"

Anne ducked away. "Charles isn't—"

"Isn't what? Here with you? Too busy with impor-tant matters? What is he, a congressman? California's two senators are old and married. Senators are always

married, *no cierto*? Or the people will think they are—"
he laughed "—either bananas or kings of fruit."

The elevator doors opened. Anne scampered out before Tavo completed his indictment.

"Does it bother you so much that I have a boyfriend?" She switched to the offensive as she dodged into a small telephone room.

Tavo blocked the slamming door with the bulk of his shoulder. The tiny space smelled of his French spice soap, which had cleansed both of them.

"Ana, Ana, of course, you have a boyfriend. You are a lovely woman. Knowing the competition keeps the hunt interesting."

The telephone rang.

"Chau, chau." He kissed her cheek, closed the door quietly, strolled to the boutique and bought a magazine.

"Ana Mahoney? Momentito."

"Anne? Hello, hello, Anne?"

"Charles. Thank you for calling." Anne eagerly reached out through the static for lasting affection. *He* wasn't a stranger.

"Damn hard to find you. I've been trying since yesterday. Where have you been? How's your vacation going?"

Why did he always use his resonant television voice when he talked on the phone. Anne immediately squelched the disloyal thought. "I've had quite a time—" she started to say.

"Terrific. You deserve some relaxation, honey. How's the snow?"

"There's a great base, and—"

"God, I envy you, Anne. Next time the devil wants a sauna, he ought to spend August in Washington. It's hotter then hell here."

"Why don't you come down and join me?" she said impulsively, her willful eyes watching Tavo leaning against the far wall reading his magazine, waiting for her. *I'm not available to be hunted. You'll see, Señor Mohr de la Huerta.* "Really, Charles, come down. I'm going to be skiing here and there until the middle of September. We could go exploring—"

"And have your guys hound us like they did Jerry and Linda in Africa?"

"Nonsense, Charles. Jerry was a potential presidential candidate, and she's a rock star. You're...." From thousands of miles away she sensed she had offended Charles's sense of importance. His silences were subtle, and effective. "Charles, no one cares what I'm up to."

"I care, Anne—and thank you, I'd love to join you. But this damn Congress is backlogged way beyond our Labor Day recess. Tell you what. I'll schedule a visit home to see my favorite constituent, and maybe we can take a couple of days and drive Highway 1."

Travel together up the coast? Anne was provoked. A quickie weekend hadn't been her proposal. She paused, unsure what to say. She needn't have worried.

"God, I'm tired," he said, as usual, and as was her habit, she scolded him for working too hard. "Hmm." He ignored her, routinely, although she knew he was secretly pleased about her concern. "I'm just on my way out to dinner with Jim and Rosemary Sanders. Remember? He controls the rules committee. We have reservations at Sans Soucci. Say, nice to have you on the same time zone, Anne. You about ready to eat?"

"No. I'm on the 9:30 seating."

"Ah. Terribly continental. Gives the Latins time for extended cocktails?"

Her delayed laughter was weak. "Only the Americans here seem to be into cocktails."

"Well. I'm running late, honey. Love you. I'll call in another day or two."

He never even mentioned Stephanie. Anne glared at the unperturbed blonde beyond the glass, annoyed that he had said Charles was uncaring and cold, furious that he was right.

"So, Mahoney, watch out for wooden nickels." Charles's chuckle was confident. "And don't take any Latin lovers."

"It shouldn't be any problem, Charles...." Anne tossed her hair gaily with a laugh, but her audience of one failed to notice her performance. "I'm only at Portillo for another four days."

"GUSTAVO, I'M PERFECTLY CAPABLE of walking myself to my room." Anne trotted up one flight of steps, then another. She didn't want to stop for the elevator because she didn't want to talk. He slowed his long stride to her step.

"Really, you needn't bother." She was panting by the third flight. One more to go. "Please go away," she ordered firmly. Her door was in sight. His arm brushed hers as they strode down the hallway in tandem. Her heart pounded. Did his?

She fumbled with the key, shook her head no to his gesture of help. At last the door swung open. The smell of roses filled the air; she could make out the two tall vases on her secretary. When had he had them brought down?

"Being with you is not a bother." He combed her thick mahogany hair off her nape with his fingers. "If I were not here, I would be looking for you." Anne didn't understand his pensive touch, his pauses. "I think it is better that you are alone now.... Yes, it is better.... I will have food sent up for your dinner."

Curious, Anne thought, puzzled by the distance in his tone and the belying ardor in his eyes. *He thinks he's in control of me with his orders, but he's not in absolute control of himself.*

"Good night, good night...." He licked his rough, chapped lips. "Sleep tight," he whispered, a safe three feet away. "Don't let the bedbugs bite." And in a phrase he had joined the intimate circle of her family. Even as his words touched her, he started to turn away.

Then suddenly he reached for her. Anne watched him lean forward in slow motion, his eyes exhilarated, and cautious. Pent-up days and nights absorbed her desire and demanded more. She raised herself on tiptoe, and still he had to stoop.

It seemed he released the dammed need of weeks, months, years, a need she didn't know, couldn't comprehend. This handsome rangy giant, all sharp angles and private corners, pursued her very heart as if this was their last kiss, not their first. He found it with a fervor that left Anne mesmerized.

Smothering a groan, Tavo wrenched away and, with a beautifully executed, calmly spoken goodbye, left. No explanation. Anne, personally cynical of motives, professionally analytical of behavior, knew she had affected him profoundly.

And that mysterious sincerity of his was the most seductive element of all. The Chilean's mark was on her empty heart as surely as his roses pervaded her room.

CHAPTER FOUR

ANNE BOUNDED OUT OF BED Monday morning, flung open the windows and stretched her fists into the crisp sunny air, a satisfied purr escaping her lips.

Courting. She delicately sniffed Tavo's roses one at a time, choosing this one and that, cosseting the inordinate mass of fragrance. He was courting her, he had said. Had his voice been commanding, or solemn only to tease?

"Courting without consequence," as Radámes claimed their flirting was? His eyes had revealed nothing. Amusement, yes. Admiration, and later, ardor mingled . . . with what? Something intangible. Some mood, some fear or reluctance. What had she unleashed? For surely when his need to kiss her had been irresistible, he had resisted . . . at last.

Exhilarated by the intrigue, drawn to the mystery, Anne felt her spirits rebounding. The intoxicating roses excited her imagination. He had undoubtedly had them helicoptered up with his daily mail. What an incredibly lavish gesture, and it did impress her. Dozens of long-stemmed roses in winter were no mere nosegay. Was this a preview of being courted by a Latin millionaire?

Anne was eager for Tavo's next surprise, eagerly curious about what tactics he would employ in his hunt. He had only four days. The pressure was on. Anne neglected to note that she had fallen asleep obsessed with the idea of him, and had awakened in the same mode.

Anyone could say no for four days, she was thinking. Even the weakest woman could resist the lure of a taut black, extra-large T-shirt, the tug of blue jeans on a runner's legs. And she wasn't weak, just a little heady with a restlessness that bordered on hunger. She didn't feel like eating, yet she was impatient for breakfast.

Anne selected her clothes carefully. Basil bib pants in a firm stretch material rounded her figure like a sculptor's hands. She pulled out a bright mustard tank top and hesitated, then replaced it with a soft yellow turtleneck.

Would he notice she'd dressed to match his roses? Oh, yes, he hadn't missed anything so far. But how would he respond?

Mohr de la Huerta. Where had she heard that name? Economist, Radámes had said. The fruit king of Chile— Wait. What was it the bank's driver had said when they passed the orchards.... Tall, blond....

Anne had it now. Her natural ability for names and details had not been washed away in endless martinis. Mohr de la Huerta owned one of the ten largest corporations in the country, skied on the Olympic team, the women of Chile were his....

"Here you go again, Mahoney," she sighed, cautious now. Thanks to Charles, she knew the aphrodisiacal effect of power and money, even if the possessor looked like a frog. "Life in Washington is like walking through a field of open poppies for someone like me," the good-looking bachelor congressman had observed with nonchalant arrogance early in their acquaintance, and Anne had crossed her legs.

She had pride, too, and sufficient attention from other men. If Charles wanted easy bouquets, he could pick elsewhere. And so could Mohr de la Huerta.

The women of Chile were his? They were welcome to him. Clever devil. Courting? What a fiendishly appealing word.

"Get your running shoes on, mate." Impulsively Anne parted her hair in the middle and caught the two sides up with combs in a sophisticated twist.

Four days.

She could handle it with ease.

RADAMES SAT ALONE in their booth in the dining room. "The sight of you is as warming as the sun, Anne. You looked rested and lovely." He stood, gesturing to the place opposite him, the seat Tavo had occupied during the ill-fated dinner.

"Tavo ate much earlier," Dr. Ebert explained. "He likes to have a bundle of work ready for his pilot to take back to Santiago at ten."

Anne pretended indifference. When would she see him again? She glanced at her watch and counted forward three hours from the Los Angeles time.

"Aren't the lifts running now? It's nine o'clock." She looked around the dining room, puzzled. It was full. "I thought I was late. Did Pascal sleep in?"

Radámes's brow furrowed deeply. He stirred his coffee until Anne thought he'd forgotten her question.

"¿Café o chocolate?" asked the same waiter who had served dinner.

"Café, por favor." Anne waited for him to pour a mugful from one of the two steaming pots on the tray balancing on his shoulder. Instead he pushed a small covered bowl toward her and removed the lid. Powdered coffee? In Portillo? Anne masked her surprise; she didn't want to appear rude.

"It's typical of Chile," said Radámes, understanding the North American custom of a fresh-brewed beginning to the day. "It drives the Brazilians mad also. We add hot milk and hot water. But if you prefer only water...."

"Why not both? *Agua y... leche, por favor.*" Anne gloated as the waiter departed. "I feel like I passed an old Spanish test. *¿Cómo estás?*" She used the familiar tense.

"You have an excellent accent," Radámes encouraged her. "How am I? Very distracted by my grandson. I apologize that I did not answer your question about Pascal immediately, but I find myself in circumstances which are...." He delayed, then smiled unhappily. He tried for irony and failed.

Anne was gifted in encouraging revelations with empathetic silence. She picked an apple out of the basket of fruit on the table and quietly peeled it, looking up to meet his worried blue gray eyes. "Circumstances which are...?"

With another sigh, he finally continued.

"I find myself in an embarrassing situation for a plastic surgeon who is well-practiced, as you can imagine, Anne, in psychology, too. I cannot talk sense into my reckless grandson and I cannot control my own anxiety about his foolishness."

"Radámes, you are too wise a doctor to have unnecessary fears," Anne soothed automatically.

He reached across the table and patted her hands. The backs of his were spotted with faint liver marks.

"Thank you, my dear. My apprehensions are not irrational. Pascal announced this morning that he is going to speed race."

"How speedy?" Anne had already grasped the story. It was a good one, the kind she wrote well. Conceit, pain, anger and danger were potent ingredients, especially when the danger was anticipated. Passions always flared more powerfully before the fact.

"Radámes, you don't mean the 125-mile-an-hour insanity those American ski instructors were telling me about?" she asked. As usual, she slanted her question in favor of the storyteller's bias. Although provoking sensational statements by playing devil's advocate was a useful method, it was not her style.

Radámes laugh was short. "Hank Purdoe and Jonathan Lynch? Don't even bother to tell me. Of course it was those two charming, crazy young men who stupidly insisted on ordering you martinis."

He ran a distracted hand through his iron-gray fringe of hair. "I am so relieved my wife went shopping in Miami rather than coming with us this year. Sofia's heart is not strong. . . ."

"Why don't you tell him he can't do it?" Anne asked, even though she knew it wasn't likely the grandfather would give a quick, practical kick to Pascal's sensibilities. Given a choice between clear-cut decisions and drama, people preferred starring in their own soap operas. Later they'd waffle, "I was only human," not admitting histrionics were the spire in their lives. Their human craving for excitement filled newspapers; it sold newspapers.

What fascinated Anne was how people wrapped their version of their continuing sagas in elaborate rationales.

She leaned forward, eager to hear Radámes's explanation.

"A direct no isn't a viable option." The distressed surgeon met her eyes and continued, his British accent as stiff upper lip as any commander of the Empire. "He is a man. I cannot insult him, but I rage at his insolence."

Radámes buttered dry whole-wheat toast, coating the hot slices precisely to each edge. He made two swift, sure diagonal cuts and dabbed honey on one perfect triangle, then forgot to eat it. "You are a trained observer, Anne. Surely you wondered why a nineteen-year-old is not in school."

"Uh-huh."

"I am certain you did not miss Pascal's name-dropping and elaborate posing with his gold watch and so forth. It is not uncommon in the Argentine. We call such young men *patucos*. Sometimes they have money and sometimes they don't, but they always pretend to be wealthy and elegant. They are the lizards of our society. Talk talk talk. They do nothing."

He clipped the end off his soft-boiled egg contemptuously. Anne suspected what he was going to say next.

"Pascal is the only child of our only child and he is spoiled beyond measure. Pascal behaves as his *patuco* friends do, to the shame of our family." Radámes sighed. "My daughter, Suzanna, and her husband, Enrique, had a wish that if we could separate Pascal from his associates, expose him at length to a fine man like Tavo, get him up in the morning and outside doing something healthy, perhaps we could restore his sense of responsibility." But the surgeon's sharp features dropped.

One hundred twenty-five miles an hour! Speed racing

might not be responsible, yet the mere prospect thrilled Anne to the point of adrenaline rush, the lights-and-siren syndrome, Snider called it.

How rigid was her itinerary? If buttoned-down Lunch and sun-burned Hank Purdoe were going to try to break the official record, Snider might want the story. Hank was originally from Tahoe City—that would give it a California angle. Radámes's terror was a dynamite touch. It would elevate a sports-for-crazies piece into a universal cry of familial anguish.

Anne hid her excitement, careful not to offend Radámes. "Perhaps your grandson's idea isn't serious. How fast can a beginner go? Surely. . . ."

"Yes, I, too, thought facts would help, Anne, so I asked Tavo. He estimated Pascal would start around forty miles per hour, and with practice get up to sixty or seventy. Tavo said Pascal won't go over eighty. It takes too much strength to hold the skis on course." His voice caught. "They apparently jump and careen. . . umm—" he cleared his throat "—rather extensively."

"Did Tavo speed race? That isn't an Olympic sport, is it?" Anne was distracted from the main storyline. It was one of her failings. "Don't get trapped in the sabotage of interesting irrelevancies," Snider had often scolded her and Stephanie.

"Tavo downhill raced on the Chilean team during his youth. He was in Munich at the university when he competed in the Olympics. That's why he didn't go to the Free University of Berlin like his grandfather and father did. Munich was closer—"

Anne blurted out two simultaneous questions. She wanted to know if he'd won a medal and she needed to understand *his* need for speed. "Tavo doesn't seem crazy," she said, her voice questioning. "He seems so...so rational. Downhill racing, speed racing—what's the difference? They all head straight down the mountain."

Radámes signaled the waiter for more hot water and milk, then systematically fielded Anne's barrage of questions.

"Tavo did not win any medals, Anne, although he made a respectable showing—ninth or tenth place, I believe. As for crazy, I think so now, looking back, but...I was less apprehensive then, shall we say. I can remember sitting here twenty years ago with Tavo's grandparents reassuring them, much the same as you are doing with me. We thought then that if Tavo hit sixty and a tree at the same time, well...." His eyes misted. "You can imagine."

"But Tavo didn't, did he?" Anne pointed out. "Doesn't that give you courage about Pascal?"

"No." He was definite. "Tavo had good fortune and he was skilled. He trained with discipline. Downhill racers must negotiate gates and curves. There is an elegant precision to the sport which, frankly, I admire. Speed is simply brute speed, getting into a straight track and as you Americans say, 'Going for it.' Pascal has had this whim since, who knows, yesterday? Five days ago? This morning? And boom—" the surgeon snapped his fingers "—now he is a speed racer."

He speared the sour flesh of a lemon wedge with his fork and squeezed the juice into a glass of water. The prongs of the fork strained the seeds. Radámes drank the lemon water down, puckering his mouth at the bitterness, and changed the subject. "Lemon is a cleanser for the palate. It's very healthy in the morning."

Anne smiled graciously, her mind working the story. Pascal had slipped in something about speed at dinner, something defensive when he introduced himself. She groped for the detail. He had complained that he hadn't a chance to learn to ski fast because Bariloche was too far from Buenos Aires, not close to the mountains, as Santiago was to Portillo.... He must have meant Tavo had had the advantage over him, all those years ago.

"What was Tavo's record?" she asked, suddenly suspicious.

"Seventy-three point seven miles per hour."

"Well—" Anne shrugged sympathetically "—when they have their race—has a date been set?—we know Pascal will hit seventy-four or...." She had blundered and regretted it.

"Or die trying."

Radámes glanced at his watch, his emotions carefully stored away. Surgeons are congenitally cold-hearted bastards, she had been told by at least half a dozen other types of medical specialists. Was it true?

"Our lessons begin in fifteen minutes, Anne. I suggest we prepare to meet our instructors. At my age, I need to make a few stretching exercises."

Anne was sorry she hadn't asked about the upcoming races more directly in the beginning, but her job had made her a veteran of dismissals, and she agreed gracefully.

However, when Radámes reached out of his reserve once more to give her an appreciative thanks, Anne the person began to feel remorseful about her secret reporting. She could have thought of more comforting sentiments for him, couldn't she?

"HEY, HEY, ANNIE, you daffydill. You're a howl of spring in that yellow turtleneck." The straw-haired speedster handed Anne her skis from the rack in the locker room with a distracted glance over her shoulder. "I hope you're feeling better."

Anne's stomach muscles tensed in her excitement. She was on stage. The all-important audience of one had just arrived. "Oh...hello, Gustavo." She was breezy, the way she had rehearsed herself for this moment. Now what would he do?

The unexpected. He laughed. After he watched her fiddle with her bindings, pretending insouciance, he threw back his head and laughed—not at her, with her—as though they had shared a precious moment known only to themselves. His face wasn't shadowed, and when his eyes lingered above the green bib boosting her full high breasts even higher, Anne saw no ambivalence. He apparently had quelled his ghosts. Beneath the snug yellow turtleneck, her self-willed nipples responded.

"So. You rise to spring, Ana."

His play on words caught her unawares. Was this insolence the flowery compliment she had anticipated all morning? Disappointment flashed across her face before she could continue with her predetermined flirtation. She had anticipated he would say something lovely and that she would respond with a compliment of her own. But it didn't happen according to plan.

"Come, *cariña*, let the sun, not your shyness, put a natural bloom on your face," Tavo said before she could regroup. It was what she had hoped to hear, but too late. She wasn't prepared. He kissed her cheek lightly, his sunburned lips raising a sensation that traveled the length of her flushed body. With an easygoing, *"Chau. 'Ta luego,* Jonathan Lynch will be less careless this morning,'' he skied away.

Anne watched the muscled red-clad legs and broadly yoked black shell until she was startled into the present by the repeated shout of her name.

"Earth to Anne Mahoney. Earth to Anne!"

The relatively level ground between her and Laguna del Inca was lined with ski instructors in navy pants and red windbreakers, a rainbow of students dutifully clustered around each. Jonathan Lynch was waving a ski pole, trying to catch her attention. He was alone.

"Over here, Annie, double-time.''

"Lunch—'' she slid over to his instructor's stand with its condor emblem on a pole and a plaque with his name "—you and Hank nearly killed me.''

"Yeah, I heard.'' His lean face creased with mock shame. "You might say we thought we were facing death, too, when the news reached our evil ears.''

Anne lifted her mirrored ski glasses to better pierce him with a skeptical glare.

He grinned impishly. "Well, I wondered whether you should have the third martini, but I figured, what the hell, you're an adult.''

"No, I'm an idiot!'' Anne admitted, settling the glasses back down sheepishly. "Where's the rest of the class?''

"Great luck, Annie. Your LL, Latin Lover, paid for private lessons. I'm bound by some sort of Henry Higgins honor to transform you from a chicken into a swan. Far out!'' he yodeled, and Anne giggled. Lunch was irrepressible; even the lock of brown hair falling out of parted tidiness was irrepressible. It was a spectacular day, and she was ready to ski.

"I've got money," she said. "Don't argue. I'll pay. No...LL's going to have me in his debt."

Lunch washed his hands of the situation. *"No es mi problema.* I'm told you're going to be a *poco* scared, so *por favor*, El A lady, follow me."

Other pupils and their agile instructors were disappearing over a low rise to the left, away from the bottomless black water. Glaciers iced the summits of the Three Brothers at the back of the lake, the same peaks pictured on Bush Bavarian beer cans, someone had told her.

Lunch ignored the other students. He led Anne in the opposite direction, across the flat in front of the hotel to a Poma lift on the uninterrupted valley wall to the right.

A stolid middle-aged attendant waited for Anne to stow her ski poles in her left hand. He pulled a heavy steel pole and base from a metal logjam. Anne slipped the gray saucer Poma seat between her legs.

"Don't sit down. Just let it drag you up," Lunch instructed. Self-conscious still, and scared, too, after her rescue off the Garganta, Anne silenced a smart retort, basically because she couldn't think of one.

A second Poma took them to a gentle meadow. "Follow me," Lunch said. He snaked slowly down, his body an apostrophe cutting S's in a straight line forward, even though he twisted back to look uphill and coach Anne down.

She copied as best she could. The mild slope steepened—not much, just enough to cause Anne's tracks to swing wide. Her S's were sharp, nervous sudden reverses of direction. On her weaker right turns she sprawled into a cowardly snowplow to slow down.

"Whoa, you're making a lot of work for yourself," Lunch said when she joined him. "I know what you're thinking. You're making nice long traverses across the hill, looking around, enjoying the scenery, hmm? Then you stop for the naaasty, little ugly part, the turn, and then you have some fun going across again. We're going to teach you to have fun the whole time."

Anne didn't have faith and said so, which didn't prick Lunch's good cheer. He unzipped his windbreaker and scratched the crocodile logo on his chest.

"Sun's hot, no?" said the wild preppie. "I want you to keep making turns without stopping. You'll find you can control your speed. Roll your skis from side to side, like this."

Anne imitated Lunch's actions as he talked. "Roll your skis so they're flat on the slope, then set your edges into the slope."

"Bullroar, Lunch. C'mon, speak English."

"Scaredy cat claws back? Watch. Setting your edges is like braking into the hill."

Anne rolled from one side to the other. Each time she braked with an exaggerated cut into the snow, the way Lunch had, keeping her knees flexed. Sure enough, she stopped.

"All right!" His enthusiasm was a gold medal in itself.

"'Bout 125 mph's worth, *no cierto*?" Anne fluffed her hair out, pleased with herself. The strands shone burnished copper in the bright sun. It was glorious to be alive.

"See how the ski turns automatically when you roll?"

"Yeah, right." She could be cocky, too.

"This way, all the work is done with your legs. Forget your shoulders. Forget you have a waist...." The thin instructor leered at her slim figure. "I won't, but you forget it. Think of your waist ending at your hips. The work starts in your thighs."

They rolled and braked, rolled and braked down to the second Poma. "Keep those curves fluid and tight," Lunch called ahead as he followed behind on the lift. "Faster next time. Follow close in my tracks." They rode up, rolled down, rode up and rolled down. It was sensational.

"Doesn't that feel better?" Lunch couldn't resist a little I told you so, but Anne didn't care. She freely gave credit for her progress.

"Now we're going to upgrade the fun," Lunch announced.

Anne blanched. *Pride goeth before a fall.* She didn't want to face Garganta again and said so. That's what she and Steffie called being assertive. Aggressive was what Snider called it in his own inimitable growl.

Lunch whooped. "Garganta, the ol' rocky throat today? Get serious, Annie. Your LL would skewer me on his ski pole. We'll head over to Juncalillo. That's were people ski in the morning."

Tavo, too, she wondered, and flattened her stomach muscles, ready to impress him, if not with her skiiing, at least with her presence.

"Juncalillo is a confidence builder," Lunch assured her, and she believed him. Lunch was easy to read.

They skated, gliding first on one ski, then the other, pointing the tips away from their bodies. They passed the hotel, then struggled up a small hill.

"No sweat here," said Lunch, wiping his dripping

face. "This is Conejo. Rabbit run." The chair-lift entrance for Juncalillo was a couple thousand feet below, he explained. "You probably saw it when the bus brought you up to the hotel."

"Chauffeur," Anne corrected.

"Your LL's driver?"

Lunch, used to being a naughty boy, had no urge to stifle his inquisitiveness for the sake of politeness. He should have been a reporter, Anne thought, miffed.

"No, it was my driver," she snapped, heedless of her overreaction, which might have flashed an alert to her inquisitor. "And I told you I'd pay for this private lesson, Lunch. I do not have a Latin lover. My boyfriend is a North American personality, so I would appreciate it if you wouldn't spread false rumors about me down here, thank you very much."

"Just asking." The impish grin reappeared. "Powder River, let 'er buck!" he shouted like a cowboy. "Let's ski!"

Anne effortlessly rolled her skis, keeping her knees bent loosely and her skis together.

"Flex your knees. Tuck your tush—no, *tuck it!* Turn, Turn, turn," Lunch shouted the pace at her when the Conejo run steepened and sane rabbits would have been challenged off. His voice was an insistent metronome. She obeyed, and to her surprise the shorter turns were like an invisible parachute dragging her speed.

Anne's confidence soared, and soared, until they rounded a bend at the end of a trail, when her spirit crashed in the face of a difficult drop. Not as tough as Garganta, but frightening. She stood sideways and slid down slightly, quickly braking into the side of the hill.

The memory of Tavo's deep voice instructing her how

to get out of impossible situations urged her on. She desperately hoped he wouldn't see her acting the fool, a *tonta*, again. Where was he? Anne had been watching, but no graceful red caught her eye.

Lunch wisely held his instructions, seeing Anne's self-assurance take hold, until she was ready to continue downhill. "Remember, tight turns slow you down," Lunch yelled. "Turn, turn...."

A speeding blue ball hurtled by, passing less than a yard away. Waves of wind like the wake of an open-throttled Cigarillo, the fastest of all motorboats, rocked her tentative stability. Anne tripped and fell with a curse, tumbling halfway down the hill. This time there was no Tavo to break her fall.

"Oaf. Rotten jerk," she muttered, lying still, uninjured, furious. "I'd like to knock his tight little tuck off the mountain."

"You okay, Annie?"

"Yeah. No thanks to that noodle." She brushed loose snow from her face and dried her sunglasses with a spare tissue folded in her pocket. She hoisted one ski on her shoulder and stumbled up to the other one, clumsy in her heavy boots. The ski lay buried where it had twisted off when she plummeted face first.

Fortunately she had barely been moving. Otherwise.... Anne rapped packed snow off her soles with a ski pole, poking at recalcitrant patches with the pointed tip.

What if she'd been going faster? Say 40 miles an hour. Or 60 or 73.7. Would her face be smashed or merely bruised? She was glad Pascal wasn't related to her. Radámes was a trifle pompous, but he had a legitimate whine about his grandson. If this speed-racing notion was a whim, what did Pascal the *patuco* know about the basics, like crouching in race position. . . .

Of course. Grimly Anne stepped into her bindings. Now she knew who the brat of the slopes was. Pascal. Damn the guests, torpedo full-speed ahead; it was his practice time. Well, she wasn't his doting grandfather. She'd tell him no, and she'd say it loud and clear. Aggressively.

Outrage overcame fear. Anne passed Lunch in a hurry, too breathless in the high altitude to shout for him to come along. She assumed he would, and he did.

There was no waiting line at the bottom. Pascal had long since made his getaway. "I'll nail that obnoxious, self-centered, useless adolescent at lunch!" Anne raged.

"You're nailing lunch?" teased Lunch, jumping into the chair with her and stretching.

"You heard me. You know I'm referring to your dangerous protégé. That was Pascal Larregoite who nearly bowled me over, wasn't it? Faster than a speeding bullet, dumber than a doorknob."

"R.O.T., Annie."

"What?" She angrily defied her own image in his sunglasses, convinced that behind the visual screen his brown eyes were twinkling.

"Right on Target," laughed her ski instructor. "The kid's rude, thoughtless, pampered, petulant and a pain in the touchus. He's also got a tremendous natural skill for skiing fast."

"And endangering the poor slobs around him who don't have the same skill."

"Right on target again, Annie. Although Pascal was in control coming down that hill—"

"Control? At what, forty miles an hour?"

"Mmm. Maybe forty, forty-five. But Pascal was in control. He should have steered clear of you. I'll lecture him after the lesson—and after you slam into him at lunch. He'll pay attention."

"Why? What's in it for him that's worth giving up the thrill of terrorizing the tourists?"

"But you have to remember he's got a burr under his saddle, as we say in Jackson, about skiing fast. Fast doesn't mean forty or forty-five or fifty, Annie. Pascal wants to outski the sound of his body. He wants to take off and soar on a cushion of air two inches above the ground. . . ."

Lunch's voice drifted. A dusty public bus rattled its way up the zigzag road, enroute to Argentina. Anne could see animated children's faces pressed to the big front windows. They excitedly waved to the skiers.

Anne waved back, but Jonathan Lynch was oblivious. "Pascal wants to get into another space, where the world is peaceful."

"Heaven?"

"You might call it that. You have to pass 110, sometimes 115 before everything slows down."

Anne scrutinized Lunch's altered expression. The familiar excitement of chasing a good story gripped her. She desperately wanted to cover a brinkmanship, the event that would bring the participants to glory or hell. These potential victims taunted tragedy, unlike her usual subjects, who were felled by chance.

"Is there going to be an international speed race here this summer?" She didn't quash the eagerness in her tone.

"Naw. They haven't held one here since '78, when McKinney set his record. Too many TV aggras in Portillo."

jagged granite, leviathan-gray rickrack cut by a monstrous pinking shear, then upended.

Between the terrifying run and her suspended chair, a smaller series of jagged granite fences crowded the precipice. *Garanitas,* "little throats," Tavo had said they were called. The word was an easily remembered variation of gargle.

A startled cry shattered her repose. It came from her.

Tavo had slipped over the top, darting down a *garganita* as narrow as the length of his extra-long slalom skis. The former Chilean champion's tips pointed straight down; his turns were minimal shifts of rigid thighs clamped together. Long muscles dictated to obedient, amazingly flexible knees, and Anne's mind obeyed his exultant challenge.

She, too, gasped in heady pleasure midway down the vertical run, and she, too, felt a surge of excitement when he broke free of the confining boundaries.

Anne was transfixed. Superior men fascinated her. But through her bemusement, she felt rather than heard a warning. This man was too dangerous for her to flirt with. He already knew too much about her. None of her usual controls were operable. Four days. She could avoid him for four days. It wasn't forever.

Anne exited away from the *Gargantas*, planning her defensive. Tavo didn't eat breakfast; no problem there. Lunches were erratically timed. She could—

"Ana, Ana, hello!" Pascal's shout interrupted her thoughts. Stripped to his waist, his blue-and-white suspenders dangling at his sides, he hurried over to help her out of her skis. His dark eyes, eager as a boistrous puppy's, clouded with hurt when Anne, still rattled from her unexpected reaction to Tavo, laid into Pascal for terrorizing the slopes.

"And I'd like to know where you get off thinking you can act like a jerk." Her tone was overly scathing, but it was too late to temper her tongue.

"Lordyanne Jane, there wasn't any problem," protested Pascal, his adopted Wyoming idioms sounding peculiar in his British accent. "I was not going to hit you. I was in control. Who put a burr under your saddle?"

"You and your buddies Lunch and Hank Purdoe," Anne fibbed. "Do me a favor, would you, please, Pascal? Don't tuck so close. You might be in control, but I'm not."

"Okay," he agreed amicably. "How are you feeling, Ana? I haven't seen you since you sobered up. Are you hungry?"

Anne enjoyed his adolescent bluntness. She wondered if her young brother, Ryan, a much-loved afterthought, would be like Pascal when he grew up.

"Hungry?" She inhaled the aroma of wood fires and grilling steaks. "Starving. Bitching builds my appetite." She gave him a mock snarl, and they were pals again.

"Do you want filet, chicken or link sausages—or all three?" asked Pascal, handing her a plate. Chefs in white stood behind the grills. Stainless-steel trays of lettuce, chunks of cold boiled potatoes and sliced tomatoes and onions were arranged from one end of the serving tables to the other.

Anne indulged in a generous pile of onions. "Today onions, tonight garlic, tomorrow the world," she quipped. "Self-protection. I have to sit next to you tonight, remember?"

Pascal stabbed at a higher pile of the raw potency.

Anne didn't miss his competitiveness. The kid would definitely pass Tavo's 73.7 miles per hour.

"You want wine, no, Ana? White like Californians drink? *Un gran vino blanco. Doña Isidora,*" he told a chef. The man reached into the snowbank behind for an icy bottle and opened it for them.

They walked across the wooden platform on the lip of the mountain, carrying their heaped plates to an empty wooden picnic table covered with a cherry-colored tablecloth. It was hot enough for a Fourth of July barbecue. Many of the women sunned in bikini tops, and without exception the men were bare chested. Anne regretted her turtleneck. She longed for the coolness of a tank top.

"Portillo is fabulous," she exclaimed. "Here's to beach skiing in the winter, which is really my summer, anyway."

Pascal clicked his clear pastic glass against hers. "Portillo is Portillo. Perhaps the best snow in the world, but very small. Certainly there's a challenge...." He lit a cigarette with a flick of a gold lighter. "Nothing like the Valle Blanche, though." He tapped the hollow in his cheek. A beautiful smoke ring popped out.

"That's marvelous! You're idiotic to smoke, but what talent!"

Pascal met her eyes with a pleased unaffected smile. Wisps of the ring hovered nearby. "You really thought so?" He tapped another.

"Where's the Valle Blanche?"

"You haven't heard of it?" The disdainful clip in his accent was also astonished.

"No. I'm not much of a skier."

"It's in the French Alps, at Val d'Esere. The Valle Blanche is the longest run in the world. Not difficult once you climb over the ice top, but the guides are skilled. Then it's just a matter of coasting down."

"Weren't you scared?"

"Of course I wouldn't be."

"Wait a minute!" Anne interrupted impatiently. No wonder Radámes was pulling out what little hair he had left. "Haven't you skied the Valle Blanche?"

"Many of my friends have."

"You made it sound like you had."

He shrugged, tapped another ring. "It is unimportant. I have a better idea."

"So I heard." Anne closed her eyes and lifted her face to the sun.

"Who told you?"

"Everyone." Automatically she protected her sources. "When do you start packing a track?"

"This afternoon we're working on the one on this side. We can only work during mornings on the Roca Jack track. That's above the Juncalillo, where you were skiing, Ana. Avalanche danger is too severe in the afternoon."

"When does your equipment arrive?"

"Maybe by the end of this week. I'll look like a Roman centurion in the helmet." Pascal's boundless energy splashed over her. "Did you know the Italians pioneered speed skiing?"

"And you're Italian?"

"Enough for a natural edge."

"Hmm. How fast do you think you'll go by the September races?"

There was no hesitation. "At least 112."

Pascal's perilous naiveté made great story material. "Don't you have to train for a few years to build sufficient strength to keep the skis from bouncing off the track at over eighty miles per hour?"

Eighty was the limit Tavo had projected. Blending suspect information into seemingly spontaneous questions was one method Anne used to develop accurate data. She had found that mistruths often revealed hidden crucial emotions.

Was Tavo deluding himself that the nineteen-year-old couldn't best the near champion's record by up to forty miles an hour, or had Tavo diminished the speed to soothe Radámes's anxieties? Or had he simply stated an obvious truth, that Pascal didn't have the strength to pass eighty?

Pascal stalled. "It'll be rugged breaking eighty. Skis torque like crazy from 80 to 110." Now Anne knew Tavo wasn't devious. "But my legs are strong. I've been playing polo since I was a child. My parents sent a string of ponies along with me when I entered Saint George's."

"Polo not dangerous enough?"

"By trying to protect life too much, you waste it." A grave adult voice interrupted them. It was Tavo's.

Anne was instantly on alert. Her speeding pulse pounded the message: *Yes, this game is too dangerous. Better avoid trouble with unwavering, unresponding cordiality. And distance.*

She opened her eyes, shielding them from the blinding glare of the sun with her hand, and favored Tavo with a teasing glimpse of her warmest smile before directing its force at the young brunet.

"What time did you say it was, Pascal?"

The young man looked pleased by her attention. "2:15."

"I'm terribly sorry, Gustavo. We gave up waiting for you and were just leaving." She indicated his full plate with a regretful gesture. She thought she had timed it well and hoped the thunderous pulse in her temples didn't betray her.

Tavo glanced at her swiftly. "Better get moving then, Pascal. Enjoy yourself, Ana." Behind her, Anne could hear him cheerfully join a lively group who all seemed to know him.

ANNE STEELED HERSELF for the moguls and conquered them as the afternoon wore on. Pascal hovered nearby, protectively, not forcing her slow pace.

Once the concentration of besting the bumps was no longer required, she needed intellectual diversion. "Why do you want to ski twice the speed of the legal limit for cars in the United States?"

"You mean faster than free-falling from a plane with a chute?" said Pascal, upping the dramatization. This was his soap opera. The other actors would have to accommodate his stage-center position...unless his grandfather suffered a heart attack beforehand. Not much surprised her anymore about human behavior—except, sometimes, her own.

"Why ski faster and faster?" Cheeky confidence had returned to his voice. "When your life is on the line, it is worth living."

Anne prodded ruthlessly. She wished she had a notebook. Since she didn't, she visualized the important quotes written on a blackboard so she would remember them accurately.

"Forget your propaganda, Pascal. I want to understand."

He postured arrogantly. "Partly it is a matter of moving into another space—"

"Don't burden me with *Zen and the Art of Archery*, either."

"Okay, Ana. Part of it is because my grandfather is such a little old lady, always nagging me to be a man. Do you think he has ever complimented me on the polo?"

"Yes." She was pushing him and she knew it.

"A few times. So what? Long ago I grew tired of listening to him as he fussed with his stupid lemon water at breakfast. Grandfather isn't the primary reason I want to speed ski."

Pascal swacked the ground with a pole. "I am a well-regarded polo player, Ana. My father spent a lot of money buying the fastest ponies he could for himself and for me. They get me to the ball in a hurry, and I hit it accurately. But when I put my skis in the track, the speed I hit is mine. It doesn't depend on whose stallion my father buys or which cinema star's face my grandfather carves up. It is my achievement."

The intensity of Pascal's determination didn't penetrate the armor of detached friendliness Anne donned when working a story. She recorded another fact. The boy and his grandfather were warring over the same goal: disciplined achievement.

"Yes, I can understand that," she agreed slowly. "I feel that way when I cover a fire. Not just regular fires, but when the hillsides burn and the air is alive with cinders and you don't know where the sparks are going to land next and whether you'll be surrounded, or safe."

Pascal looked at her, his suaveness back in place. "And your parents, they allow you to continue in this danger?"

"It doesn't please them, but what can they say? It's my profession."

"Is it always like that for journalists? Danger? War?" Pascal had the Lights-and-Siren rush in his voice. Anne recognized it. She should; she was hooked on it.

"Not all reporters. Those of us on blood patrol, yes...." Anne paused, distressed at the memory of Steffie's concerned face, her urgings to give up the adrenaline habit. "My best friend changed to business news because she thought she wanted out of the gore."

They moved forward in the short chair-lift line.

"Is she bored now?"

"She died."

"Oh, so that's why Tavo arranged lessons for you with Lunch, even though my friends made you drunk," Pascal guessed, accurately, Anne noted. "Lunch is the best instructor here. Tavo is always taking care of people. I thought he was—"

"In love?" Tavo surprised them again. Where had he come from? Anne had been trying to maintain a lookout for him. "You are absolutely right, Pascal. I am in love." The blond giant smiled happily, as if Anne had played along with his overstated nonsense.

She was nonplussed. His eyes fixed on her sunglasses, gauging her reaction. He noticed before she did when her teenage escort skated ahead and grabbed the next chair.

"Wait for me," Anne called to Pascal.

A smirk teased over Pascal's mouth. "I don't have the courage. *Chau. 'Ta luego.*"

Tavo stopped the next chair with his powerful hand and held it so it didn't slam into the back of her legs. He settled beside her.

"You took the moguls skillfully, Ana, but I think you are still fearful, no? There is no need to endure Plateau. Tomorrow or the next day, soon, you will find it as lovable as me."

Anne was tongue-tied by his frequent, casual use of the word "love."

"So frightened, sweetheart, and brave. Is it any wonder you fascinate me? How can I not suffer away from the sight of your autumn eyes?" He lifted her glasses. She couldn't escape his scrutiny. The most she could manage was to freeze her glare.

He accepted her mood and turned it to his advantage. "Frosty autumn. Nearly wintertime. My favored season, yet...holding the promise of the final blaze of summer."

He released her eyes, but not her. "Come with me, Ana. We will enjoy a small run together." He had sapped her will to resist. A simple ski run. What harm? Anne followed docilely.

Rather than shooting down Plateau, they continued along the upper edge of the snow, near where it banked into pinnacles thousands of feet high. They forged their own trail over the soft snow, past the Pomas and hotel below. Past Pascal tediously sidestepping up the mountain, crossing the speed track he was packing.

"Do not be concerned that we are ruining it," Tavo said. "They need to smooth it all afternoon. The night air will freeze a glaze on the melted surface, and they can practice tomorrow.''

Anne nodded, winded. They rested a short distance beyond. Anne turned around to watch Pascal's trudging progression up the slope.

"How fast will he go tomorrow?" she asked.

"Easily forty. I doubt he will pass fifty the first day."

"What does 73.7 miles an hour feel like?"

"Sticking your arm out of a car window at 73.7 miles an hour."

Anne considered the analogy, openly shifting her interest to the enigma at her side. He stood relaxed, a black suede shirt soft as butter unbuttoned low on his tanned chest, his sleeves casually rolled above the elbows. Iron arms perhaps wouldn't get battered as brutally as hers.

"At fifty-five, my arm feels like the wind is going to rip it off. Is the wind resistance really that strong?"

"It equates. One of the Finnish speedsters trains by strapping himself on his skis to the top of a car. When I was racing, I thought one hundred must be a fatal number. If a man cracked one hundred, the wind could certainly shred his body. Then two Americans hit 106.5 here at Portillo, and another superstition bit the dust, as you say. And now...two hundred? Three hundred?"

He put his gloves back on, tugging the second one on with his teeth, ready to ski. "Who knows? I stopped creating artifcial limits of round numbers."

"Did you give Pascal the money to buy equipment to break one hundred?" Anne knowingly exaggerated the speed, testing facts again.

"He needs it to break sixty," Tavo corrected.

"Why did you?"

"How would you feel if I did?" he countered.

Anne frowned. "What do you mean?"

"I know you, sweetheart. First you ask if I paid for Pascal's special skis. If I answer yes, then you will think of a clever way to ask why I betrayed my grandparents' friendship with Radámes, no? On the other hand, if I tell you I did not buy the equipment, then you will pursue the speculation as to who did, and why he or she did it with me."

"So?" Anne temporized.

"So I am investigating my own questions. You want to know how I express my loyalty. But I—" his sunburned lips smiled, and the effect was formidable "—I cherish you more than any woman I have ever known. I have a right to understand how you regard loyalty."

Anne was intrigued. No interviewee had ever noticed what she was doing. How did Tavo know reporting? Obviously pretense was useless; she was routed.

"I do not intend telling you. Moreover, I am changing the subject." Anne's obstinate chin jutted out.

He welcomed her dismal defense with a satisfied grin.

"And I am paying for my private ski lesson, too."

"Was it worth it?"

"Don't argue. I have sufficient money." She braced herself for his wicked logic.

"Of course you can pay." He amazed her. "What is it worth?"

"Tell me the price."

"It varies according to what exchange you got for your dollars."

"Black market? Another example of black as negative?"

He laughed. "What was the lesson worth to you?"

Now she knew his routine. Foreplay was over; he was ready to play doctor. Her mouth set, she was wary of his next remark, readying her rejection. And all he did was laugh.

"I learned a long time ago. Never offer anything gratis to a German girl, or an American one for that matter. They are always sure you are trying to buy their affections or purchase the use of the body for a night or two."

Anne flushed. She hated her pink skin and its unprincipled reactions.

"Let us negotiate this fairly," he continued easily. She knew he was having fun. "Did you learn anything?"

"Canto y canto." That was how Lunch coached in Spanish. "Edge, edge, edge."

"Bueno. That knowledge is worth, more or less, caviar in the bar at eight-thirty tonight. Is that a fair exchange?"

"Well, at least you didn't bore me with a proposition," said Anne sourly, aiming her belly button down the hill, as taught, and pushing off.

"Sweetheart, I want you, yes, but without mystery?" He was alongside of her. "No time to savor the salty taste of caviar on your lips? Patience, Ana. We will give time to time and see what happens next."

Their descent was superbly easy. The snow was a cushion of delight under her skis, and Anne's face reflected her pleasure. At the bottom she turned to thank him, give credit where it is due, and leave.

"You look fresh as a...daffydill...." Before she could say anything, Tavo slyly reminded her of Hank Purdoe's compliment. "But let us not push your endurance. The pool is warm, and the day beckons. Why should we have necks of white? We are at Portillo.''

More than anything else, his infectious laughter, filled with invincible gusto, persuaded her to meet him at the pool.

ANNE SHOOK OUT A BATH TOWEL and laid it on the webbed chaise longue in a corner, away from the lazy swimmers sitting on a submerged ledge in the pool. She settled back with a sigh.

The sun stroked an indolent warmth along her shoulder blades, and she dozed, lulled by a distant conversation about surplus orange-juice concentrate. A three-hundred mile swath of groves planted twenty years ago in the Sao Paulo region outproduced Florida last year, a Brazilian was explaining to the others.

Orange groves had greened the foothills of Pomona when Anne was young, before bulldozers uprooted the trees for developers to plant suburbs in their place. A fragrant memory of orange-blossom mornings when she walked to school released an elementary security.

She snuggled happily into the lounge. Nothing disturbed her reverie, even minutes later when Tavo's great firm hands, slick with sun lotion, glossed her back.

"We pick our own oranges for juice in the mornings," she murmured, welcoming the gently massaging fingers. "My parents have two trees in the backyard. Do you raise oranges, Gustavo? Will the Brazilian surplus affect your business?"

"Tavo, please, sweetheart." He swept her hair off her nape with one hand, while the other tended to its business in the small of her back.

"On my farm north of Santiago, we have orange trees

for our personal use, but primarily I sell apples, apricots, nectarines, pears and table grapes. Temperate fruits, not tropical. We have a few plantations of papaya, pineapples and bananas on the farm in the north, but they are relatively small."

He squeezed more lotion into one palm, while the other pursued a tense muscle in her increasingly limp neck. She arched like a contented kitten. "An apple a day...Tavo." She tasted the sound of his nickname in her mouth. "Are apples the most popular fruit in the world?"

"Bananas. You do not want a tan mark, do you?" He had already untied the back-string of her plum bikini rippled with silver stripes. She stirred without protest. His tranquilizing hands coated her tapering waist with number-six sun block and moved on down her trim legs. "Bananas are second only to potatoes in worldwide produce sales."

His beguiling strokes were longer now, thoroughly soaking her reddening skin. "It is the middle of August in Los Angeles," he scolded, not hiding the possessiveness in his voice. "Why are you so pale, *ama*?" The tickle of his slippery fingers spreading each toe roused an unexpected flinch of her hips.

"I've been working long hours." Anne tried to pull back into herself, but Tavo's probing fingers now refused to release the building tension.

"On what stories?" Lubricated hands tenderly stroked upward to her restive thighs, her oiled waist.

"The most recent was how stage-two smog affects emphysema victims. Isn't that enough sunscreen, Tavo?" Her sigh pleaded a denial, and he deferred. The bedeviling massage continued.

"The intention of Pascal to speed race is a story in your emotional speciality," he observed, guiding his tireless thumbs into the pliant flesh at the base of her spine, seeking out and destroying the strain. His large hands fanned out, covering her back.

"Mm-mm. Pascal's stupid, understandable intention."

"Tell me. Why do you feel it is stupid?"

"Oh...." Anne muffled a moan low in her throat and buried her head into her elbow. "You have persuasive hands, Tavo."

"Tell me, Ana. I want to understand how you feel. Your prickles of sentiment have ruptured here...." He drew a line down a cord in her neck. She shuddered. "And here." He kneaded her rigid shoulders, forcing his calm into the nucleus of her protective shell.

"Pascal's decision is stupid because it's dangerous. And it's understandable because he wants to crash normal boundaries on his own, without the splendid polo ponies his father buys. And his poor grandfather is pushing him on to destruction, fretting about him becoming a man, holding you and your Olympic 73.7 up to him. And Lunch and Hank Purdoe are tape recordings on the subject of mystical highs beyond 110."

"Do you not feel it is good discipline for Pascal to get up early in the morning to practice? To struggle against the boredom of sidestepping a track?"

"Yes. But considering the kid fancies himself skiing faster than a free-fall from an airplane, when he hasn't even stopped smoking...I think it's a dangerous whim. But it means nothing to me. He's just one of the characters passing briefly through my life." That was too honest. Other reporters would understand her detachment. She was sorry she'd confessed.

"Hmm. Prickles again." Tavo was silent, his hands working. Eventually Anne sensed her reluctant body's quiescence.

"Ana...." The word was an "ah" of moist air against her slippery flesh. "Let us try an experiment. Close your eyes." Tavo circled her temples with lotion. "Picture Pascal coming down the track we saw him building."

She saw a turquoise tuck on the color screen in her mind. Gray cliffs towering behind him, Pascal was a blurred spheroid.

"Describe what you see."

She did.

"Move in for a close-up. What is the expression on his face?"

"Glazed."

She panted anxiously as she watched the boy hurtle through a narrow gray crack in the cliff. Faster he was flying, faster. Suddenly he wobbled. She cried out, a mute, strangling noise. Her chest constricted until the great hands couldn't comfort her. Anne saw the turquoise ball fling high in the air and bounce in slow motion—once, twice and more, and higher and higher. Then it sank, a sprawled paralyzed heap.

"Describe more. How is Pascal?"

"His body is broken. It's in pieces. Bones are sticking out at loathesome angles." Anne's journalistic objectivity came unglued. "I can't tell if he's dead. He has to be. Otherwise it's more dreadful." She blanked the screen. Tears ran unchecked.

"Put his body back together," Tavo ordered quietly, and waited. "Is he together?"

She nodded.

"Put him on the track. Now, follow him all the way to the bottom. His skis don't waver from the track. See how perfect his tuck is? Faster, no. Watch him flash by the finish line, Ana. Describe what happens next."

"He's walking over to Radámes in that cute, cocky way he has. He's grabbed his grandfather and is pounding him on the back. They're hugging and crying."

"And Pascal is fine." Tavo tied the strings on her bikini top and rapped her lightly on the rump. "Enough barbecue for today. You had better turn over."

Anne rolled on to her side, dazed. "How do you know these things?

Tavo spread a bright yellow beach towel out on a neighboring longue, stretched out and put an arm over his closed eyes. "I have had nightmares, too," he finally answered.

Soon he was asleep, ignoring the discomfort of feet and ankles hanging off the recliner. Anne could study him freely. The gold watch on one wrist and a slender copper band on the other shone brightly in the sun. He was at ease, and Anne realized he had accomplished his purpose. She was at his side, stripped of her professional detachment. Naked, armorless. Slowly, as she watched him sleep, Anne rebuilt her defenses.

She would not have a frivolous holiday love affair. If she made love with the intuitive man lying close to her, she would love him. Four frivolous days would haunt her forever.

CHAPTER FIVE

RADAMES PUSHED ASIDE HIS BREAKFAST EGG and empty coffee cup. With a hard flat sweep of his hand, the plastic surgeon folded the yellowing *New York Times Magazine* and creased it sharply.

A physician friend in Manhattan had responded to Ebert Gamen's Sunday telephone plea for information on speed skiing. By Thursday, the lengthy article had been found, messengered down in a courier pouch and bused to Portillo with Tavo's newspapers and mail.

"Listen to this, my ally Anne. Speed racing is as lunatic as we feared."

Radámes adjusted his reading glasses on his haggard face. "This section is about a nineteen-year-old who put his head too low and went off a course in Italy at 105 miles per hour: With incredible force and speed he went end over end, feet and then head hitting the snow and each turn wrenching his body unbelievably. Afterwards, eleven holes were counted in the snow, feet, head, feet, head, feet, head and, at the end, everything. . . ."

A rigid turquoise form cartwheeled end-over-end in Anne's mind like a colored jack tossed in the air by schoolgirls playing onesies on white cement sidewalks. The same vision that had triggered her superstitious fears at the pool Monday.

Feet, head. The phrase was a clever reversal of the expected order of impact, her professional mind noted and admired, but her professional brain was not in control. Her emotions were, and she shared the grandfather's anxiety.

Anne struggled in her mind to put Pascal back on a glazed mental track, using her intellect to give a happy ending to the race. The best she could manage was an upright Little Boy Blue paper-doll image glued on a piece of typing paper.

"What, uh—sorry." Anne had to stop and clear her head. She hadn't heard anything else Radámes had recited. "What happened to the skier?"

Radámes repeated the answer. "He lived a little more than five hours.... He fractured his skull, broke two vertebrae in his neck...and tore himself open from anus to the navel.... Toward the end he went blind...."

"Oh, my God." Anne gripped the edge of the table, nauseated. Radámes's shoulders had an arrogant thrust.

"Why this year, of all years, those two madmen had to be here in Portillo—"

"Talking about my friends again, grandfather?" Pascal sauntered up to their booth, a defiant set to his handsome features. Patches of vigorous red flushed his tanned cheeks.

"Cut your exercises short, Pascal?" Radámes's usual charm vanished. "Did you decide to wait until the sun had softened the air outside?"

"I performed them earlier this morning." The teenager fought sarcastic steel with a blunt sword. "But of course you are always safely asleep when I leave, so you have an excuse for your ignorance."

Anne made a fuss of moving over in the leather booth

to make room for Pascal. It was better that he face his
grandfather, rather than having her get out of the booth
so he could slide into his usual place next to the angry,
fearful older man.

"You are the sunshine announcing a good day,
Ana." Pascal turned his artful, novice appeal in her direction. "How sorry I am that we have not shared the
opening of each day before."

Curious how similar he and his grandfather looked,
Anne thought, studying Pascal even as she returned his
greeting. The two men's eyes held the same fastidious-
ness intensity, and by blurring her vision, Anne could
imagine Pascal's regular features sharpening with age
and a fretful impatience replacing his determined indifference.

"It would have been simple enough for you to have
joined us, Pascal. We have been here every day."
Radámes couldn't seem to resist having the last word.
"But first you slept in all morning from dancing away
the night at the disco. Now you are the big man with the
exercises and the Formula One speed."

Anne looked up to see Tavo walking toward their
table. The driving nature he kept on a tight leash
showed in the governed stride, the rapid way his body
easily maneuvered around other guests and waiters with
heavy trays.

His cool eyes immediately appraised the situation,
then fixed in full force on Anne. She had no idea how
vulnerable she looked trapped between two warring generations, nor how radiantly her face shone when he
joined them.

This was the first time Tavo have shared breakfast
with them, she was thinking, watching him surrep-

titiously. He hadn't shrugged off his executive manner.
Was his mind on the briefings and letters in the pouch,
ready for his pilot to take back tomorrow? No, she
quickly decided. Tavo had gauged the volatile mood
and decided upon a productive course of action. *What is
he going to do?* She shifted around the booth closer to
Radámes, because Pascal made room for Tavo on his
side.

Then, as if Tavo's physical position represented a
vote for him, Pascal poked nastily at the embers of the
fight. "*Mi abuelo* has insinuated that I will not have the
courage to continue my training and compete in the
race," he charged. "*Bueno,* if that is how he chooses to
insul—"

"Speak English or speak Spanish, but you are not to
mix the languages, Pascal. It makes you sound ignorant," Radámes interrupted. His harsh voice was unforgiving.

Anne's stomach wrenched at the stormy atmosphere.
She couldn't wait for Tavo to stop the battle. Hurriedly
she interrupted, offering fruit from the basket.

Tavo refused. He'd eaten a couple of hours earlier, he
said with a relaxed affectionate smile, and called the
waiter over for hot milk in his powdered coffee.
Radámes squeezed a lemon for his sour water. Pascal
peeled four Ecuadorian bananas, mashed them on a
plate, spooned on a generous amount of clover honey
and sprinkled the sticky mound with wheat germ.

Although Anne had no appetite, she picked convinc-
ingly at her scrambled eggs, listening to the three men
talking about this and that—all inconsequential. In this
mode, Tavo had the domineering restraint of a successful businessman. He reminded her of Steffie's

father. What kind of women were men like these attracted to? Steffie's mother was a supposedly fragile creature who had always ruled her husband, her two resentful children and her several homes with a whip of guilt.

Anne glanced up during a lull in the conversation. Tavo's clear eyes were fixed on her, following every gesture. At her side, she felt Pascal tense and start to speak. Why didn't the boy let the subject of racing drop?

Anne invaded Pascal's provocative words, coaxing for peace. "What I like best about Portillo, in addition to the three of you, is the routine," she said, reaching for a neutral subject. Her words were more gracious than six days before, when she had been a *Chronicle* reporter convincing strangers to confide.

"You can imagine with my work how I never thought I would enjoy routine." Anne's smile was beguiling. "I'm a junkie for unexpected excitement—I admit it. Choices are kept to a minimum at Portillo, and to my surprise, I appreciate it. All I have to do is decide if I want both hot milk and water with my powdered coffee at breakfast."

Tavo listened intently. She could feel his concentration eddy around the teenager separating them.

"We ski, eat, swim, drink gallons of orange juice at tea time, Radámes clobbers me at gin rummy, we have dinner, drink espresso. And I don't know what you all do, but I go to bed and sleep without...." She hesitated. "Sleep better than I can remember having done."

"Why else do you enjoy Portillo's structure?" It was Tavo's question, and Anne carefully considered her answer.

"The limits set my mind free." Her round eyes darkened with unspoken thoughts.

"That's why I am a speed skier." Pascal finished the mashed bananas and poured another glass of orange juice. "They say when you force yourself to stay within the confines of a straight, narrow track, your mind sees universal truths."

Tavo gently clapped a warning hand on the younger man's shoulder.

"They say!" exploded Radámes. "They! You are making this trouble to spite me for chastising your *petuco* behavior."

"Speaking Spanglish?" Pascal said rudely.

"That is enough, Pascal," Tavo admonished.

Radámes dabbed his pursed lips with a cloth napkin, folded it on the table and prepared to leave.

Anne's palms were damp with anxious sweat. She had known confrontations, yes, and anger directed at her, but they had come from strangers. Then it had never seemed personal, not when she was carrying her notebook and was flanked by a photographer. She was unaccustomed to open quarrels among friends and family.

"I am going to race, grandfather, regardless of how you pressure me otherwise." Pascal's eyes were alternately pleading and furious. He turned to Anne and caught her hands in his. She could feel new calluses on the toughening skin. "Ana, when does your plane leave for L.A.?"

"The afternoon of September 1."

"We will schedule the races for August 31. You will return from Bariloche in time. Please, Ana. Say yes."

Forgotten was the story she had toyed with writing; gone was the temptation to ask Snider for an extra day or two to cover the race. Anne didn't want to witness Pascal embracing a horrible death, or see him permanently crippled. She longed for the familiar parade of passing names, to be interviewed and remembered from a distance.

"Pascal, I have to be back.... I, uh, can't promise, but I'll...." She couldn't meet Radámes's pathetic eyes. Though he had intended to leave, he couldn't seem to tear himself away from the table. "What color is the speed ski suit you ordered?" She made her question casual.

"Flame orange."

She exhaled. Pascal wasn't the blue boomerang of her ugly imaginings.

"It is symbolic. I will fireball to glory...."

Reckless, silly, endearing Pascal had stolen her heart, Anne was thinking when Radámes slapped the *New York Times Magazine* on the table.

"What ski suit?" he demanded. "What else have you purchased?"

"Skis and a helmet." Pascal had the irritating smart-aleck tone again. "They're due in on the tourist bus today. Now I'll be able to double my time."

"Who paid?" Radámes demanded, dangerously accusing.

"I did." Tavo separated the fighting dogs with a grim calm.

"What?" said the agitated surgeon. "Tavito. After all these years of our family friendship. How could you betray us?"

"You want him to wear a protective helmet, no, Radámes?"

"For what purpose? To scramble his brains against, with the doubled speed of the special skis?"

"Listen to you, Radámes. You push the boy to be a man. So he accepts a challenge to prove himself on the battlefield of your choice. My friend, you chose Portillo, then you accuse him of childishness. I say let Pascal be the best he can be. For that, he needs the equipment."

Radámes's face was gray under his tan. Anne anxiously held her breath, waiting for him to stop the shrill grating of silence. At last he spoke.

"I have no choice, apparently. Excuse me. I must make my stretching exercises before my skiing."

"Thank you, Tavo." Pascal's expression was exultant as he watched his slender grandfather walk slowly and erectly out of the dining room.

Anne saw the ice of Mohr de la Huerta's wrathful eyes before Pascal did. The discussion was not over.

"I have my lesson. . . ." She started to slide out of the booth.

"Ana, Pascal has an apology to make for the manner in which he spoke to his grandfather this morning."

The startled young man flushed.

Tavo's voice was a whiplash. "Pascal has great charm and talent and someday—I think soon, Ana—he will have your gift of empathy. Meanwhile, he is a boy learning his alphabet. *Por favor,* Pascal, make the first of your apologies. After you give the second to your grandfather, I will meet you at Roca Jack, and we will continue the training."

Anne dreaded dinner.

LUNCH PUSHED HER to ski harder and faster when they had their lesson. She could feel her mood rising with each controlled turn, her jangled nerves smoothing with every curve.

"*Canto y canto y canto.* Edge, edge," Lunch shouted.

Anne turned and turned, exhilarated.

"Dog my tracks on this stretch," Lunch ordered, and she did, making the buttoned-down rebel hurry before she skied him down.

"My turn, Lunch. Chase me!" She hung back momentarily as they rounded the bend and hit the toughest face on Juncalillo. But Lunch's skis were on top of her tail and she didn't have a moment to spare, so down she plunged.

"Point your chicken belly button downhill!" he shouted.

Anne obeyed somewhat, dashed around another curve at the bottom and sprayed a grand finale at the chair lift.

Truthfully, she was glad, however, when the halcyon lesson was over and she could drift back to descents alone, immersed in a dreamy lassitude.

As he had done every day, Tavo joined her for the final few runs of the morning. Sometimes they teased and laughed and were silly, pelting each other with snowballs and chasing down the Juncalillo.

Anne was finding him to be a man of action, and of thought. On the chair lift, they talked seriously about books, movies, ideals, music. Tavo liked opera and kept a box seat at the gilded baroque Colón Theatre in Buenos Aires, where the young musician Arturo Toscanni had been called up from the orchestra to substitute for the conductor and had become an instant sensation. Anne was into reggae.

Today they skied quietly, enjoying their uncanny ability to intuitively judge the other's moods.

"Getting hungry?" he finally asked. "I am."

"Starving. It's an easy decision today. I'm going to have every kind of meat they have, and two filets while I'm at it."

AFTER LUNCH they watched Pascal describe his courage for two long-limbed girls, a brunet with saucy black eyes peering out from behind shagged black bangs and a short sunny blonde. When would he stop talking and show *off* his courage?

Anne leaned against Tavo's unclothed torso and closed her eyes. Their backs were one flesh, resting on a spit of mutual spine, and she didn't fight the feeling. She didn't know why, didn't want to analyze what was happening. "Pascal is full of himself this afternoon. What's he up to, Tavo? Have his skis arrived?"

"Pascal will be practicing on his speed skis this afternoon. We can watch him from here in about—" his arm extended as he read his watch, and her responsive muscles tracked his gesture, "—about half an hour."

"Good. We don't have to move for a while." She felt wickedly lazy.

Anne couldn't remember when the jolly accordion music entered her consciousness. It began as part of the talking, laughing background. Then Anne recognized "Cielito Lindo," accompanied by the clomping of ski boots, half a measure slow as a result of the clumsy weight.

She twisted to face the music, refusing to relinquish

the intimate attachment to Tavo. Zestful Gisela, the blond Austrian ski instructor beloved by the children, swung into "Beer Barrel Polka." Two dancers were joined by two more cavorting, exuberant teenagers, then two adults, and another two.

Anne practiced writing leads in her mind, playing with images of wholesome fun in a wholly Gothic setting of gray arches and spires. "Spontaneous hilarity" was a phrase that had to be included, she thought, as more skiers joined the vigorous stomp, wiggling and whooping in singles and partners and trios.

"Let's dance." Tavo diverted her passive entertainment, leaping to his feet and hitching up his suspenders over his bare chest. Anne pulled back bashfully.

"I'm really enjoying watching," she demurred, self-conscious about learning a dance before an audience of strangers, with a man she wanted to impress.

"Come, Ana. You are shy? But no. This cannot be true. Where is the fearless reporter?"

"I need my notebook." Anne attempted a joke, yet it was true. For years she had participated as a professional onlooker. It was a role she liked, even in high school, maybe because she'd never quite gotten over the agony of seventh grade, when she grew inches taller and matured more slowly than anyone else. Or maybe she simply preferred standing back, dissecting the action.

Tavo simply lifted her high in his arms, nuzzled her ribs with a growl and set her down. His strong arms slipped around her waist, and he coached, "Toe, heel, one-two-three."

The big boots made the simple dance hilarious. Anne chuckled along, following the strength of Tavo's rhythm, for he held her close to his side. "Toe, heel, one-two-three. Toe, heel.... This is how we learned at the German school. *Zehe. Ferse, eins-zwei-drei.*"

Anne got the idea quickly. With each ponderous weighted step, her mood lightened until she was attuned to the rollicking tempo. Tavo swung her close, cast her out and twirled her back, circling his long arm around her waist, catching her to him. Anne kicked her foot back as she'd seen Lawrence Welk's partners do on television, and stumbled.

She ventured an embarrassed look around, but no one had noticed. The revelers were shedding boots and dancing on the wooden slats in their wool socks.

Tavo's boots were off in a moment; he knelt to unbuckle Anne's. Her heart raced as she pulled him to his feet. "More," she pleaded. "Let's never stop."

The sun caught the unmasked happiness on his face, and he hugged her to him. The smell of his bare damp chest was as fresh as his spicy French soap. Then he spun her out again.

"Follow me!" Gisela called, and the accordionist paused momentarily while she stepped into her skis. Merry children clambered after her; frolicking adults did likewise. Anne couldn't resist the call. She flowed with the jubilant multitude.

"C'mon, Tavo," she begged. "Hurry."

Down the moguls they flew to the sound of the polka. The crazy, wild Brazilians leaped bumps in the run like miniature ski jumps, yelling "Yaaaaaa-who!" Tropical cowboys on the loose.

The whooping celebrants dominated the mountain. Their triumphant procession engulfed Anne's timidity about the challenging bumps on the mountainside. She thought only of the fierce sun on her face and the indomitable man at her side.

With the courage of relaxation, she found her legs took the moguls easily. She speared each target hill with her pole, pivoted on the crest, sank into each small valley and rose with a lusty jab at her next, very specific, target.

"Bueno, bueno, bueno." Tavo was alongside, and then the run was over. They were at the bottom. Anne, in her joyous, prideful excitement, tried to wrap her arms around his neck, and failed to reach high enough. She wanted to kiss him as she perhaps had never wanted anything more in her life, but her boots anchored her too far away.

Famished for the touch of him, she struggled to break loose. And then he was leaning down to her. Slowly. She ached for their meeting; she shivered when at last he settled his rough lips firmly on hers, demanding, needing, exploring with a perilous intensity, oblivious of the silent whooshes of passing skiers.

A frenzy of desire exploded through Anne. She was blind to all but the taste of him. This was their first kiss since the night Charles Roderick had called and Tavo had walked her to her room. Three confusing days and restless nights. Anne's frustrated memory of an explosive moment had not been false.

She wrapped her arms around his brawny neck, attaining her goal at last, and shuddered into the wall of muscle and bone, of hot breath and cool quickened flesh now alive. She had held back too long. Once gone, her control wouldn't return.

If Tavo had persisted after his passionate good-night that first night she had slept alone in her bed—or asked, begged, tricked, cajoled, or just pounced—Anne would have refused. "No," she had planned to say. "I have a boyfriend. No, I am not casual. No, I am not in love with you." Men in Los Angeles didn't care if you loved them—that had nothing to do with making love, they always argued. But maybe Latin Americans believed in love, not like.

Anne had never found out, neither in that moment, nor in the three days following. Tavo hadn't pursued her in any usual way. She had never had the opportunity to display her reluctance or demonstrate her virtue.

He dutifully walked her to her room every night after they had sipped espresso in the salon after dinner. He wasn't convinced she had sufficiently recovered; she could tell by the protective manner in which he hovered over her. She didn't know where he went afterward. Back to the salon? To his desk for work? To bed? To the disco to dance with other women? She despised the jealousy the idea awakened. Jealousy was a new feeling. She wanted it driven out of her.

Anne knew he was attracted to her. She had never experienced such concentrated attention. She often couldn't read his guarded expressions, but she recognized raw chemistry—she could sense it grab her even if he kept his hands casually in his pockets. What was his game?

By Wednesday, the third day of Tavo's abstinence, Anne was touching him as they talked in the chair lift. A pat on his broad forearm for additional emphasis to a point, a quick pat on his broad boney knee. "Oh! Look at that," she'd say, and that and that. Anne didn't touch strangers. But she couldn't resist. No more than she could eventually resist asking him what was happening.

She had let him unlock the door to her room on the third night—why not—and then impetuously asked why he always left her. Stupid phrasing, she chastised herself when the question popped out. She didn't want to invite him in. She only wanted the tension of mystery to cease.

"I'm courting you," he grated, as though his discipline had cracked. Unthinkingly Anne clutched the wool of his navy blazer. All right, she could accept that he was courting, but why this way?

"I have observed, Ana, that a relationship freezes at the point when a man and a woman have sex." His great warm hand captured her cold one and placed it over his heart. It beat steadily. "We will make love when the time is proper. You know tragedies, no? It would be an inexcusable tragedy if our relationship should be trapped where it is, with you so willing...."

Tavo threaded his hard fingers through hers and traced her dry lips with his fingertips. The resulting tingle itched. Her tingling lips yearned; she yearned. She bit down on her lip to halt the rasping sensation.

"So willing, and yet so fearfully reluctant." He released her hand. "We have time, Ana, *ama*. Let us enjoy the riddle of each other. We will build an atmosphere and then, we will love."

She hadn't asked him to stay, no of course not. For what purpose. They had time? There was no time. It was Wednesday night. She was leaving Saturday morning, early. There was no riddle. Tavo was building for an all-time, Roman candles, one-night stand. Or was he?

But there at the bottom on the hill, after their polka, after their zany run down the mountain, after she tasted the uniqueness of him, finally, Anne no longer cared what his motivations were. Or hers. She joyously kissed Tavo as she had wanted to, finding extraordinary pleasure in the feel of his checked passion flooding the gates until his encircling arms trembled.

This time Anne slowed down the kissing, pulling away from him, enjoying her effect on this man. Suddenly unsure, she lowered her eyes. Her heavy dark lashes fluttered, preparatory to flight.

"Do not retreat from me again behind the shell around your heart. Please, *ama*. Remain out here with me." Tavo traced the oval line of her face and lifted her determined chin. "You are so beautiful when you join life. You enchant me."

The full force of his allure tore at her barriers. The harsh planes of his cheeks relaxed. "Ana, tell me no—that you will not hide again for another moment. Give us this small minute more of happiness, sweetheart. Say it. 'No, I will not run away.' "

Tavo's irresistible logic tickled Anne's cautious heart back out into the sunlight.

"You're remarkable, Gustavo Mohr de la Huerta," was the sole token she granted him. But her instant hug around his waist was the second time she had reached for him, and they both knew their relationship had altered.

Tavo, craftily, didn't press his advantage. Instead he glanced at his watch and suggested, "Let's go back up to the Plateau. Pascal is going to begin his drills in about ten minutes."

"Aren't you going over to the track to time him?"

"Not the first day. Lunch and Hank think he is better off settling into the track, learning to concentrate on getting into position and holding it without becoming discouraged by how much faster he has to go to beat the ambitious limit he has set for himself.''

Anne and Tavo sat down in the chair lift without interrupting their conversation.

''Do you think he'll hit 110 this winter?''

Tavo accepted her question as that of a worried friend, not an eager reporter, and replied thoughtfully. ''Not right away. He is not strong enough. Obviously the odds are against it altogether. But we do not know the extent of Pascal's desire. He has never driven himself before, which is a disadvantage, because he might easily get fed up and quit. It takes practice to push through discouragement. . . .''

''Like toughing out piano exercises—''

''Or having editors yell at you to do the impossible—''

''How did you know that?'' Anne laughed breathlessly. ''Everyone's been deceived by that wonderful teddy bear, Lou Grant.''

He laughed, too. ''I saw *Superman*. Lois Lane had a great set of lungs—is that the idiom? Is that a prerequisite for female reporters?'' Tavo stroked her knee with his oversized hand.

''Watch your roving thumb.'' Blood rushed to Anne's thighs in anticipation, and she licked her thirsty lips.

''How are your lungs, Ana?'' He continued patting, his thumb obediently, disappointingly, on her knee. ''I have heard you cry, but I have never heard you scream.''

''Listen next time my helicopter crashes,'' she said lightly.

"Hopefully you will not have an opportunity tomorrow, when we take my helicopter up to the Cristo."

"Where?"

"The Christ of the Andes on the border of Chile and Argentina. Is is the top of the world. You will be mad for it, Ana. Then we will ski back home."

Anne gaily entwined her arm in his. "Are you sure it's not too difficult for me to ski down?"

"Do not worry; you will be safe."

In the recesses of her subconscious the familiar promise echoed, and she automatically had faith in his words.

PASCAL STRETCHED AND TWISTED as he limbered up, a contorted tangerine exclamation mark in the distance. Even his head was part of a vivid acrobatic flame, for Pascal's shiny brown hair was hooded with the same form-fitting, rubberized plastic tangerine material, to eliminate air pockets at his neck. Even his hands were covered, all to break the wind.

Anne sat on a cleared picnic table next to Radámes, while Tavo stood by her side, resting his arm on her shoulder. She was dismayed by how tense it was. A sideways glance intercepted a brief unguarded look of concern on Tavo's face.

She didn't understand. She wasn't too worried about Pascal's opening attempts. Rationally, she had decided he probably couldn't build up enough speed today to hurt himself.

Her fears centered on the end of the month, when his marked competitive spirit would be directly challenged by Hank and Lunch. Tavo had supported the young man's recklessness. Tio Tavo, a former world-class racer, used to the stress of racing. Why was he upset this early? Maybe he knew something she didn't.... .

Radámes took her clenched hand and kindly unfolded her stiff fingers. "Do not worry, Ana." He tried to reassure her, unconsciously switching to the more intimate Spanish translation of her name. Increasingly Anne felt like family. And like a dutiful granddaughter, she noticed the crepey skin of his hands was cold and damp. Radámes was frightened.

"We'll all feel better when the first practice ends." She smiled sympathetically. "We'll feel like fools, especially at dinner when Pascal will be as proud as...." She searched for the right word. Pascal was putting on a dazzling silver helmet. The tail reached to the end of his neck. "Pascal will be as proud as a Roman conqueror tonight."

Anne toyed with her make-believe. "Heaven knows, he'll probably wear the helmet to the disco. Pascal will be insufferable," she said fondly. "And how he will suffer. That helmet will be blazing hot under the strobe. He'll be dripping; he'll be drenched and pretending he doesn't sweat. He's a *caballero*, you know. He glows."

The anxious trio laughed at the image. It could as easily be truth as fantasy. Tavo smoothed the back of his hand against her cheek.

Lunch and Hank Purdoe were talking to Pascal now, red-faced Hank gesturing extravagantly to emphasize their points. Pascal planted his legs far apart, his hands on his hips, and flopped forward, loosening his trunk, apparently listening through his workout.

"What do you suppose they're telling him?" Anne wondered.

"Keep the tips of your skis down. If the wind gets

under them, it will throw you backward," Tavo guessed.

"We should each put ten pesos in a pot. Pascal can tell us afterward who was right. What do you think they're telling him, Radámes?"

"Maybe they are advising him to stop at the bottom." The fretful surgeon ventured a little joke. Tavo and Anne humored him with bursts of laughter.

"I bet they're saying, 'Get dooown and boogie, baby.'" Anne made her contribution.

A crowd had gathered now. Pascal's two conquests shyly approached the center table.

"It is impossible to think how fast Pascal will be, no, Dr. Ebert?" said the saucy brunet, Paulina. Under her fringe of bangs, adoring eyes shone. "When you think we only crawl along at about 16.7 miles an hour.... Oh...you must be very proud of him."

Before Radámes could reply, the nubile blonde added dreamily, "Pascal says that a Porche 944 accelerates from 0 to 84 miles per hour in 16.2 seconds. A speed skier accelerates to over 126 miles an hour in 15 seconds. Imagine! Is that not wonderful!"

Radámes harrumphed in his most formidable Oxford manner. The girls apparently thought he agreed with them.

Anne turned around and studied the mesmerized blankness on their faces. Later, she would tell Tavo what the sports photographers always said. The more dangerous the sport, the more beautiful the women. Baseball? Tweedledums in snagged polyester pants. Horses? Dogs. Sailing? Sun-wrinkled dogs. Football? Okay. Grand prixs? Nine-point-sevens. Rugby tournaments where ambulances lined the roadways? Tens.

But Tavo had been a downhill racer, a notably dangerous sport. Perhaps the photographers' theory applied to him. Maybe he had already experienced the fact that the scent of blood turned on beautiful women faster than that Oriental aphrodisiac, ground whiskers from a tiger.

Who had tempted him? Why hadn't he married, she wondered.

Tavo set his wristwatch in the stop-watch mode and stood ready. "I want to keep tabs on his progress," he explained easily, unaware of her emotional retreat.

Anne didn't take her eyes away from the slender orange flame. Pascal stepped into his skis. The bindings were similar to those used by downhill racers, but were fitted with heavy-duty springs and weren't screwed down tight, so the ski would release quickly if he fell.

"Tavo, how big are the skis again?" Anne couldn't bear the silence.

"Two hundred and forty centimeters. Nervous?" He leaned into the highly charged zone where their bodies seemed to meet without grazing. Anne felt his distracted tension. His focus was on the boy who was like his baby brother.

Pascal jumped onto the track, crouching like a brilliant Easter egg, his hands in front of him, breaking the air turbulence.

"Keep your rear up a little higher—higher," muttered Tavo, and Pascal might well have been tucked only inches away, for he obeyed instinctively.

The streak of orange passed the quarter mark in a flash. On her right, Radámes was silent. Anne couldn't hear him exhale.

Pascal passed the middle and held his tuck.

"Keep your hands out there cutting the wind," Tavo coached under his breath, and as he said it, the wind jerked Pascal's left arm.

A collective moan went through the spectators. Pascal pulled his arm back into position. Suddenly the blurred orange egg wobbled, then bounced and rolled.

Feet, head, feet pounded against Anne's temples. "Keep tucked!" she yelled.

Pascal bounced to the bottom where he lay still, a cracked Humpty-Dumpty. Anne jumped off the table, heedless of the two screaming girls crying and carrying on. She beat Tavo and Radámes to their skis, clicked hers on and took off.

Later she couldn't remember the run, only that she pushed hard, frantic that Pascal would be paralyzed. Tavo and Radámes must have passed her, for they were already there when she skidded to a stop.

Hank and Lunch were gathered around the limp un-curled body. Two members of the ski patrol were there, and Dr. Humberto Macias arrived with her. He was one of the two Santiago doctors in residence for the week.

Carefully the rescuers shifted Pascal to the stretcher sled.

"Dígame cómo están mis esquís." Pascal tried to see for himself if his new skis had survived the crash.

Tavo held the young man down. *"Tranquillo,* Pascalito. *Cálmate. Todo está bien."*

"¿Mi traje?" Groggily Pascal searched for rips in his new suit.

Tavo removed his hood and unzipped the ski suit a short way down his chest. The colorful latexlike material fit like a surgeon's glove, so thin and so tight that goose bumps prickled through.

Pascal turned drowsily and spotted Anne. She watched his glassy eyes struggle for recognition, and then it came. "What happened to me, Ana?" he pleaded. "I don't remember. Where are Lunch and Hank?" He struggled to sit up. The American speedsters wisely kept their distance.

"I am here, Pascal," said the grandfather, kneeling at the pale young man's side and firmly settling the boy back on the sled. "You will be just fine, Pascalito, but you must lie still."

Radámes was in charge now. There was no fidgeting. Decades of authority resounded in his purposeful orders. Dr. Macías knelt across from the Argentine surgeon. Tavo was at his side. Radámes closed one of Pascal's eyelids and opened it. The three men studied the pupil size, watching its response.

Anne crept in close to Radámes to see, too. She knew if Pascal had a concussion, his closeted brain would believe it was in the dark and his pupils would ignore light. If he was only badly shaken, his pupils would contract to pinpoints.

Both pupils were big as prunes.

Dr. Macías checked his pulse.

"Keep him flat on his back, Ana," Radámes ordered quietly. The three men rose to confer out of earshot. The ski patrol kept the curious at a distance.

"Ana, I feel so foolish." Pascal's confession was agitated. "I'm okay. Just a little headache."

"Shh. Don't talk. And lie flat. That's important." She wondered why. Anne never bothered with concussed victims for interviews; they were too confused.

"What about my skis?" Pascal thrashed against the straps binding him to the sled.

Anne clutched his hand, trying to infuse some calm
energy into him. His new calluses were good calluses,
she thought, the result of sincere work. Now what
would happen? She wished she could listen to the doctors' conversation.

The three men returned and checked Pascal's pupils
and pulse once more. One pupil closed slightly; the
other was in the dark.

"His pulse is sixty-three," she overheard Radámes
say. What did that mean? Their faces were impassive, so
she suspected Pascal's blood pressure had dropped.
They wouldn't be afraid to say so if the news was optimistic.

"Let's get him down to the infirmary," Radámes
ordered.

"Forget it, grandfather. Are you trying to make me a
woman in front of Portillo? Is my new suit all right?
What about my skis? Why won't anyone tell me if my
skis are broken...."

Anne recognized a common, irrelevant sameness to
his babble. Radámes patiently stroked the lank hair off
his grandson's damp forehead. "You have a concussion, Pascalito. Agitation is one of the signs. Excitement, talking, wanting to be standing up and telling
everyone about your mishap. But listen to me, *nieto*. If
you obey my instructions, you will be strong as one of
your polo ponies day after tomorrow. Otherwise, you
will be troubled with severe headaches."

Pascal nodded and groaned from the resulting pain.

Moments later the rescue sled was gone, accompanied
by Tavo, a subdued Lunch and Hank. Anne darted over
to Radámes. He was using his ski pole to pry the packed
spring snow off his boot bottoms. She hugged the

surgeon. "Was that right what you told Pascal?" she said happily.

"More or less." Tension strained his lean unlined face.

Anne's stomach contracted fiercely. "Tell me about the less first." Her voice had a remote tone.

"At this point we cannot tell how severe the concussion is," Radámes said, locking his fingers into a church steeple atop his nose and mouth. "One pupil doesn't answer to the light. A normal pulse at this altitude is eighty. The first time we measured it, it was sixty-nine. It has dropped to sixty-three."

"What is the danger point?"

"At this altitude, when it hits fifty, we know it is serious."

"What happens if it's serious?"

"The patient may seem to be fine, and then three or four days later, develop a subdural hematoma. That is a blood clot. We have to open the skull and take out the clot or clots. Otherwise the patient will die in a few hours."

"And what you're watching for now is—"

"The possibility that we do an operation."

"But it's likely his concussion is mild, isn't it?"

"That is what we hope. Put on your skis, Ana. I'll wait for you. Humberto Macías can persuade Pascal to lie quietly more effectively than I." He grimaced. "I trust Macías. He is an excellent doctor. Board certified in the United States."

Anne found her skis where she'd kicked them free in her mad hurl to Pascal's crumpled body, and they set off.

FOR THE NEXT TWO HOURS, Anne paced in the hallway outside the infirmary. She didn't want to intrude and she didn't want to be far away if Pascal's condition worsened. Her self-enforced march wasn't lonely. Tavo came out regularly and reported the latest pupil and pulse bulletins. They would stroll together for a brief time, Anne hurrying to keep up. Frequently they touched, tender brushings of arms and fingers, touching that passed comfort.

The infirmary was on the ground floor of the hotel. They would pace from Hank's usual area of confinement in the rental shop to the far door of the game room, which in turn was the entrance to the swimming pool. Then Tavo would return to Pascal.

Anne transmitted medical updates to old friends of the two Argentines as the skiers came in or paused on their way to the pool. Paulina and Maria Páz joined her for a while, chattering about the advantages of using cola for a tanning booster and other such diverting ideas. When it became apparent neither would be allowed in to hold Pascal's hand, they vanished to the pool.

For the first hour and a half, Hank and Lunch remained out on the speed track, practicing. Pascal wanted to know what had gone wrong. Tavo thought it was as simple as Pascal catching wind under his skis and as complex as something self-defeating inside Pascal. Anne wanted Lunch's and Hank's opinions, too.

The speedsters finally returned, flushed with a transcendent elation. Hank was carrying Pascal's specially curved poles of steel and his ten-pound, square-tipped skis with their wax for spring snow.

"Hey, Annie, you're going to iron creases between your eyes." By way of saying hello, Lunch rubbed away the worry lines above the bridge of her nose.

"How can I help but be concerned?" she snapped, waspish when faced with their self-absorption.

"The kid's going to be okay." Hank settled the special equipment at the back of the rental shop. "A day on his back and he'll be on track. *No problema.*"

"Radámes says Pascal might need brain surgery."

"You know how surgeons are, Annie," Lunch scoffed. "Always thinking of the next slice of the knife. Everyone gets concussions. They're no BD, big deal."

They were so guilelessly offhand that it confused Anne. She understood Radámes's too-knowledgeable fears. If concussions were common, however, why was Tavo overly concerned? His reaction didn't fit her other observations of the man. He was acting as though Pascal was his only brother, as though some untimely fluke of nature would fell the boy unless Tavo guarded the bedside.

"Hey, you guys...." Anne came back to the present. "What happened? You said Pascal was a natural racer."

Hank was flip. "Purdoe's law applies: Terror trips, and absolute terror trips absolutely."

"Feeling damn superior, aren't you," Anne charged angrily.

Hank shrugged his stocky shoulders. "How would you like me to make it pretty for you, Anne?"

"Never mind." She walked on by.

Eventually Pascal's pulse stabilized at fifty-seven and began to climb to normal. At last one pupil responded perfectly to light, and Pascal asked for Anne. Radámes and Tavo took a short break while she sat quietly by the bed, relieved to see healthy color returning to Pascal's complexion.

"Hank Purdoe and Lunch just got back from the track with your skis and poles," she whispered, leaning close to the bed. She felt like a conspirator. "All your equipment is okay."

"That's good." There was no emotion in his voice.

The next time the doctors opened Pascal's closed eyes, both pupils were normal.

Tavo walked Anne back out to the hall. "Tired?"

"Um. Very." She flexed her strained neck wearily. He massaged her taut muscles, kneading them until they were pliant. He kissed her neck.

"Almost the end," he said, and they continued walking. "We are going to give Pascal another twenty minutes before we take him up to his room. Then I will be ready for a drink. How about you?"

"Orange juice sounds good. It's nearly tea time."

Tavo laughed easily. "Orange juice for me, only if there are a couple of stiff shots of vodka in it. I am in need of your North American customs today."

Anne linked arms, resting against his strength. "Not me. I'm afraid of vodka up here. Two giant orange juices with lots of ice sounds wonderful to me—and Tavo...." She stopped and put her hand on his chest. His heartbeat quickened. "Let's not go to the bar. I need to clear my head outside."

"The pool it is, then, sweetheart. Why not go upstairs and change? I will call for you at your room in half an hour."

"I'd like to see Pascal settled before I'll be at ease. Do

you think Radámes would mind if I tagged along with you to the room?''

PASCAL REMAINED SUBDUED as his grandfather pushed him to the elevator in a wheelchair. The tangerine suit was a brilliant mockery of the regrettable afternoon.

Has he been defeated, Anne wondered. She was worried that he would continue to race, pushing for his goal of 110 mph. Yet she feared even more that he would slip back into the slack, *patuco* life he had pursued before.

She waited outside the Argentines' room while Pascal put on pajamas. Radámes was settling his grandson into bed when she entered. Pascal didn't fight his grandfather's admonitions.

"Good afternoon, Pascal." Anne laughed lightly, kissed him good-night on the cheek and tucked the covers a little tighter. Pascal looked so vulnerable. No wonder his doting parents had spoiled him. He must have been an appealingly delightful child.

"I'll come see you first thing in the morning," she promised. "Is there anything special you want me to bring you? Cigarettes?" Her nose twitched disdainfully at the word.

"Come close," he said weakly. She put her ear near his mouth. "Bananas," he whispered. "A big smashed mound of bananas with gobs of honey. I've got the wheat germ here."

Anne squeezed his hand when she caught his sly wink.

"Bueno," she said. "Until tomorrow. Sleep tight."

"Do not let the bedbugs bite," Tavo said when they left the room, and pinched her round bottom. Anne giggled. Her stretch pants were too tight for him to grab a decent bite.

No one, thankfully, was at the pool when they stepped out into the lengthening shadows, balancing plastic cups of laced and unlaced orange juice. Their mood was exhalted; they were frisky with the relief that follows a crisis.

Anne carried a stick of lip gloss in the pocket of her slim cotton cover-up. "Now mind, this gloss is not medicated, Tavo Mohr de la Huerta, so it won't screw up your screwdriver." She popped off the top of the tube. "So bend way down so I can doctor you properly before you give me a lip burn—"

Tavo tickled her under her arms instead. Anne shrieked in surprise, dropped the gloss stick and scurried after it. She retrieved it bare seconds before it rolled into the pool.

"Tickling is an old Eskimo method of proving a girl's virginity," Tavo chortled, and his long bedeviling fingers needled another explosion of giggles. "They say fathers used to tickle their daughters in front of prospective suitors—"

"Truce, truce, you octopus!" Anne gasped, wildly trying to escape his endlessly pestering hands. She dodged and kicked off her flipflops.

He bedeviled her again, and Anne thought afterward she would probably never witness a more fulsome laugh in her whole life than his. It rippled across the pool and the terrace. It boomeranged off the glass wind fence and met another laugh on its return.

Anne slipped out of his unalert grasp and ran to a snowbank jammed against the glass wind fence. She scooped up a handful of snow and scrubbed it across the hard ripple of muscles on his bare belly.

"Cat." He sucked for air as rivulets of melted ice

dripped under the waistband of the purple briefs slung low on his hips.

Anne's awakened eyes followed the trickles, and her heart stopped for wanting to chart their sinewy route with her hands. Instead she dried her cold hands briskly up the curve of his bronzed chest. "Truce?"

"Truce?"

"Oaf," Anne laughed again, and mildly pushed at him.

"Help! You got me." He staggered backward, grabbing her with him as he fell into the warm pool. They clung to each other, sputtering and snickering.

"Truce?" she insisted.

"Truce."

"Then I'm getting out of this sopping cover-up." Anne struck out for the side.

"And I will unbutton it, for I am a gallant gentleman."

"If you behave," promised Anne. "And that includes your ill-mannered thumbs, too."

His thumbs took liberties, and his fingers and eyes, too. The tantalizing undressing took him yet another small step further into her long-protected core.

But there was time. They relaxed on the sunny north side of the pool, sitting on the submerged ledge. Heated water lapped Anne's plum-and-silver bikini top, gently splashing near the bottom of Tavo's lowest ribs.

"I needed this." Tavo agitated his cup.

"You sound like an L.A. executive, home in San Marino from the wars on Wilshire Boulevard." Anne ruffled the sun-bleached hairs on his arm. The effect was akin to that of a field of ripening wheat on the prairie, tormented by changing winds. She was fascinated.

"What is this bracelet?" Anne fondled a narrow aged copper band. "Do you ever take it off? I've never seen you without it."

"A friend of mine gave it to me many years ago. Her father was Chilean manager of the largest American copper mining company down here."

"Oh?" Anne's voice was noncommittal, but she backed her fingers away from the circlet. "She must have given it to you for a special occasion—" Anne didn't trust herself to add the real part of her question "—if you're still wearing it."

The hooded expression on his golden face caused her to regret her probing. Eventually, to her surprise, he answered. "Liliana gave it to me on my twelfth birthday, a time when I believed all the world was touched with love. Sometimes I need the symbol to remind me."

And when Tavo wrapped Anne's wet hair in his giant fist and drew her to his rough lips for a sentimental kiss, time itself ceased to pass. His prodigal kisses grazed her eyes, her ears, the most tender points on her throat and nape. Anne forgot young Liliana.

She and Tavo sank lower in the heated water, insulating themselves against the oncoming chill of sunset. They slipped into a powerful calm, quiet tributaries flowing inexorably toward union.

Two condors circled above the raw edges of the monumental rocks to their left. The vultures soared on wind drafts, flapping their wings occasionally. They flew far lower than jets, but from the earthbound view, they appeared deceptively larger.

"How big are they, Tavo?"

"I have seen them with four-meter, ah, that is about twelve-foot wing spans. Some have seen condors with a span of fourteen feet."

"Two of you laid head to head, Tavo. Incredible."

"You can feel a condor yourself when we make your ski resort circuit," he promised. "There is a dusty old stuffed bird hanging from the ceiling in the living room at Ski Club de Chile in Farellones, about an hour into the mountains from Santiago. It is a ramshackle old place, but the food is good. A friend of my grandfather's built it in the thirties when the first lift was installed. Before they used to pack up by mule and ski down. . . ."

His opening "we" slipped by Anne's sharp ears, for at that moment one of the behemoths dove into the shadow of the granite wall on their right. She was imagining slashing talons and beaks preparing to dine.

"What do they eat? What animals can survive up there?"

"Mice somehow eek out an existence." He followed the direction of her eyes. Another condor dipped into a crevice a few thousand feet above them. "Last week I think it was, I saw a fox running along the snow rim. Did you see the BBC special about Andean condors?"

She shook her head.

"I remember particularly the footage of a guanaco baby that died in our south—" Tavo paused to explain. "Guanacos are the undomesticated Chilean cousins of llamas, and much more charming for being wild. In the BBC show, the guanaco mother stood guard over her dead baby for three days, while the condors circled overhead waiting for her to leave so they could feed. The sight was profoundly moving."

Anne felt she was drowning in the blue of his concentrated regard.

"Think of the horrors committed in countries which we of the Western world excuse, saying, 'Their culture does not value human life as we do.' Then consider how much further down the scale of moral and emotional values the lower animals are ranked. Yet that grieving mother defended her dead baby for three days."

Shrewdly she remained silent, not thwarting his trust in her with personal questions, and they silently watched the great birds glide. A third condor joined the other two after a time, then a fourth. There were many in the Andes, Tavo said.

Anne knew California had only nineteen endangered survivors. Charles had successfully sponsored legislation to protect them, and to finance hatchlings at the San Diego Zoo. She didn't mention that. The past was not her reality, and she didn't understand the future.

Sunset passed. Their expectations awakened with the twilight.

"Are you going to the cine at seven?" She only sensed that he was looking at her. "Oh, yes, I'm going." Anne watched the rising moon brighten the sky. She had been waiting for days to see the predinner video of *The Thomas Crown Affair*. "I don't want to miss it this time. Everyone told me it features the world's ultimate kiss," she said, although she knew there were better. She had penetrated his control, and nothing could shake her faith that he knew otherwise, too.

Tavo locked eyes with her. Cool blue to warm russet. He persevered in his deliberate, adroit courtship.

"Please, Ana, *ama*, sit with me and we will hold hands."

CHAPTER SIX

CHARLES RODERICK'S SECOND PHONE CALL came in the glowing aftermath of the movie. As had become their nightly ritual before dining, Tavo checked long distance on the day's activities with his managers while Anne and Radámes played fast and furious gin rummy in the salon.

The evenly matched rummy competition was late starting that Thursday night. Radámes had spent an exasperating forty minutes getting through on the semifunctional Buenos Aires telephone system, ineptly installed, he complained, decades ago by the British. He had called his wife about Pascal's accident.

"Naturally Sofia was horrified that Pascalito was on this suicidal course," Anne vaguely heard the plastic surgeon say. She had drifted in late, uncaring, in a romantic haze.

Her senses were heightened; she saw things clearly, but hers was a scattered focus. By holding the cards close to her nose, pretending to study them intently, Anne smelled the faintest trace of French soap on her left hand. Her memory could see in the dark theatre. She could visualize Tavo's insistent thumb stroking the rhythm of the screen kiss into her palm.

Yet Anne could barely hear her opponent, nor remember the cards. She discarded a jack of hearts, and

Radámes pounced. "Gin." He spread his hand on the table. "Tonight I'm going to make up the points you have scored off me for the past two days. You're not concentrating, Ana."

Anne smiled. *Unlucky in cards, lucky in love.* She didn't hear the uniformed young man carrying the telephone-message blackboard at the far end of the room, tinkling a silver bell and calling her name in a hushed voice.

Radámes tugged on each of his gold-cuff-linked sleeves, a real gambling man with an extravagant shuffle. He played accordion with the suspended cards, a waterfall of hearts and clubs hung on an invisible line, before snapping them back in his hand.

"Your cut, Ana." Radámes rubbed the top of his bald head. "For luck." His gray-blue eyes beamed. "We had good luck today, did we not? The mild concussion knocked some sense into Pascal's thick head. I told Sofia we had no worries."

Blissful ignorance tonight, Anne thought, hiding her knowledge. And maybe ignorant bliss tomorrow and tomorrow night, and then she would be gone. Anne wasn't going to tell Radámes his grandson intended to race. That was Pascal's responsibility, and she hoped he would shirk it until Anne departed Portillo. By the time she returned, the war would be over and all that would remain was the dangerous race itself.

But in his gloating relief, Radámes was building himself up to suffer when Pascal broke the news.

"Now that this nonsense is over, Ana, I will tell you the story Humberto Macías told me years ago when they held the first speed races here," he was saying. "None of us had ever seen such a sport. Humberto's good friend, the owner of Portillo, asked him to head the medical team. 'Bring all your equipment,' the man said. 'This is all I need,' Humberto replied, and held up a spoon. 'Listen, if a skier falls while traveling at 125 miles an hour, we will pick him up with a spoon.' "

Speed racing was lunatic, Anne thought once again. Radámes was right. It was suicidal.

"Señorita Anne Mahoney. Señorita Anne Mahoney." This time the telephone boy caught her attention.

"Who is it?"

Radámes translated. The boy didn't know who was calling.

A telephone room was vacant. In the other tiny room, a lively Brazilian acquaintance named Sylvia was talking to Rio de Janeiro, checking on her four teenage daughters at home. Anne wondered where Tavo was. He must have completed his calls early.

"Hello...? Hello...?" Her voice echoed in emptiness. Was it her mother and dad? Snider? "Hello...?"

"Anne?"

Charles! She didn't want to talk to him, not now. "Hello, Charles." *Don't ask how I am, what I've been doing,* she silently prayed. *Nothing has happened—and Tavo was right. Everything has happened.* "How are you?"

When Charles eventually remembered to ask about her, Anne was ready with spontaneous chatter, the kind of diversionary tactic she handled well. She no longer understood her feelings for the congressman. He was a lifetime away. Still, Chile was neither her home nor her future. She needed time and distance to consider if her metamorphosis was real or an unwritten fantasia.

So she temporized. "What a day we've had!"

"Sounds good—"

"Now it's good, Charles, but at first it was *absolutamente horrible*. Pascal crashed on his first run—"

"Pascal?"

"Oh. . .we haven't talked for days, have we? Pascal sits at our table. He and his grandfather, Radámes Ebert Ganem. He's a plastic surgeon."

"Pascal?"

"No, Charles. You're teasing me." Her throaty laugh was appealingly gay. "The grandfather is the surgeon. Pascal's a crazy nineteen-year-old. *Loco lindo*, like they say down here. Good crazy. He's decided to be a speed skier, but he can't just be your normal beginning racer—no, of course not. He's set an impossible goal of 110 miles an hour by the end of August, and—"

"And crashed and burned today?" Charles Roderick's sexy resonant voice was warmer than Anne had heard in many months. In her heightened mood, it never occurred to her that her newly exposed emotions altered the way others responded to her.

"It was horrible. We were so frightened. You know, the awful fear that comes when you know too much, Charles? It was a couple of hours before we knew Pascal wouldn't need surgery."

"How much longer are you going to be down there?" he asked, and the new Anne noticed his practicality. Charles Roderick III didn't know the two Argentines, saw no chance he would, and therefore had no need to waste time learning about them.

"I'll be back September 2." Anne heard pages ruffling. "Let's see, that's two weeks from tomorrow, a Friday. Maybe I can arrange to meet your plane...well, I don't know—"

"Don't worry yet," Anne interjected swiftly. "Wait until you see what happens."

Charles missed her ambiguous meaning. He had just recalled his reason for calling. Stephanie's murderers had been arrested that morning. Half a dozen Colombians. The fools had been making another drug run to Santa Barbara, he told her. A mob man at the wheel had been charged, his navigator booked as an accessory.

Damn them to hell.

Charles's friends in Justice had told him that a couple of big guys were going to topple; those arrests were being made tonight.

Good. Let them hang. I want Steffie back. Living suddenly seemed very important.

"It's turning out to be your kind of story, Anne," he said. "Snider'll have you on the trial for sure. There's speculation some publishers are interested in a book, maybe a screenplay, and you'll be in prime position to—"

Damn them to hell.

"Anne, are you crying?" Charles sounded astonished.

"Yes."

"Don't cry. It's okay. They've caught them." Anne listened to him struggling for words to comfort her, a difficult task for a man who avoided personal emotional scenes. She appreciated his attempt, but it came too late, it took too much effort, it was no longer enough. "Anne...look...."

"Don't worry, Charles. I'll be okay in a minute."

"Great." Relief bounced across the line. "Well. It's

been great talking to you, Anne. I'd better hang up before my bill reads like the national debt."

"Um. They're waiting dinner on me. I'll be back in Portillo on the thirty-first for Pascal's race, if you want to check on my plane reservations." Why had she told him that?

"Where are you going to be before, in between times?"

Strange. His tone had an anxious edge.

"I don't know. The bank's driver is taking me to ski some volcano slopes, and I'll go over to Bariloche. But I don't know when."

"Damn. I don't like having you out of reach." He retreated from the emotion. "I don't think it's safe."

Anne laughed cynically through her drying tears. "My dear, what is safe?"

"WHY WERE YOU CRYING, Ana?" Tavo gently brushed the shadows under her eyes.

She fumbled through her purse for a tissue. "Silly of me. It was good news. Steffie's killers were arrested this morning."

There was no need to say that the bearer of the tidings was Charles, and Tavo didn't ask. He had discounted Charles from the beginning, Anne remembered. His attention was on her.

"Naturally you're troubled." He sheltered her face in his peace-giving hands. In that moment, neither was aware of Radámes sitting quietly across the table from them.

"I should feel like celebrating, Tavo— Like screaming from the balcony in your suite, 'They got the bastards!' But I feel nothing about them. They're faceless monsters who watched the ropes tangle around Steffie's legs and drag her down." She blew her nose. "It's irrelevant whether they hang or they're locked away. Steffie is gone, and I miss her."

"Do not try to cover the pain, sweetheart. It is important that you miss Stephanie. It affirms your friendship." He smoothed tumbled curls off her bare shoulders. "Tonight is an important night for the three of us. We have much to celebrate, but we shall ease into it, for our happiness has risen from despair."

Dinner passed in a candlelit glow of caviar and French champagne. Prudently, Radámes excused himself early. Tavo partially filled Anne's goblet again.

"To life." Crystal touched crystal. His cool clear eyes assessed the soft curls she had set especially for this evening, the undersea-green chiffon with a flowing off-shoulder flounce, and the compliance in the softened line of her determined jaw.

"To life," she responded.

"Dance tango with me in the disco, Ana, *ama*." His hard leg against her hip brooked no denial. But why would she deny the inevitable conclusion of the night?

And so she entered his arms willingly in the intimate darkness of the disco. "Do you dance as well as you ski?" she murmured against the solidity of his chest. The remembrance of supervised thighs conquering a *garganita* electrified her.

"Mmm...." His hand tethered her waist. "Perhaps my guitar playing is a little better...." They glided onto the cozy dance floor, and he slipped his right leg between hers. Through the soft froth of her dress, she felt the flannel of his trousers covering the maddening strength of those same thighs. Anne stretched to settle her fingers into the thick wavy hair on his neck. The tango began, an erotic dance once banned in Buenos Aires, condemned in Boston, but always adored in Paris....

Tavo's provocative leg rubbed the button of her sensuality, and tiny involuntary spasm shuddered the length of her fluid body.

"Are you sure this is how tango is done?" Her dazed question blended into the consuming rhythm.

"Of course. Look at the other couples."

But in the darkness she couldn't see them, and Tavo's leg had pushed her beyond the brink of reason.

CANDLES FLICKERED IN HIS SUITE, across from the couch where they sat. The scent of fresh roses filled the air. The champagne bubbled deliciously in fluted Italian crystal.

Tavo seared Anne's nose, her generous lips, the quivering hollow in her bare shoulder with his knowing index finger. "Ana, Ana, Ana." The ahhna's of his pronunciation flooded over her skin, swamping her rational mind.

He dipped his index finger in his champagne and traced the same tantalizing route. His finger was fire, her nose was fire, her ripe lips were fire. And when he torched the route with fevered lips, Anne exploded, parched kindling, unblessed too long by nourishing moisture.

Tavo's hot damp breath pressed down into the swell of her breasts, and Anne twisted on the long couch, seeking the feel of his body against hers. He pulled the flimsy tiered flounce down under her unbound breasts, reluctantly taking his hands away to enjoy the effect.

Anne's heart thundered at the look in his eyes until she thought she would swoon from his excitement. Hurriedly she began unbuttoning his shirt, her impatient fingers fumbling on the tight buttonholes.

"Cálmate, cálmate." His voice falsely lulled her while his hands were dynamos on her long legs, churning her blood into a frenzy. She felt the quiver of hard muscles in his back. She ached for release, she throbbed for satisfaction—but her plea drowned in the sharp rap on the door. Her cheated cry escaped into a loud, impatient second knock.

"Momentito!" Tavo ran a hand through his rumpled hair, and gradually Anne saw a sense of his surroundings return to him. His jaw tightened in his irritation. *"Momentito!"* he called again, fixing his gaze on Anne's lost, vacant eyes, obviously willing her with all his might to sustain the mood. But it was too late.

His loving words were sounds passing through her ears, and out. "Knowing you, Ana, *ama*, gives me indescribable pleasure." Slowly, ruefully he covered her white breasts, their rosy tips still ready, then buttoned up his shirt and strode to the door.

Agitated Spanish reverberated through the intimacy of the room. Pascal was in the doorway, his hair uncombed, his clothing obviously donned in haste. When he saw Anne on the couch, he looked flustered.

"Oh, I'm sorry. I didn't mean to interrupt. I—"

"Pascal and his grandfather have had a tremendous fight," said Tavo dryly. "You can easily guess why, Ana. Pascal wants to sleep on the couch tonight until he can move into a room of his own in the morning."

With the feel of Tavo's lips still on her breasts, Anne plunged into a magnified practicality. "Since you fought with Radámes, who will pay for the extra room?" she asked, searching for her purse so she could leave.

Pascal shrugged arrogantly. "My father will pay."

"WHAT DO YOU MEAN it is all right?" Tavo argued when he walked Anne to the door. "Of course it is not. We were this close...." He angrily made a small pinch of his finger and thumb. She hadn't realize the depth of his arousal. "We have time. I keep reminding myself of that fact," he ground out, then trailed a stray tendril back from her pounding temple.

To steady himself? Anne couldn't tell. He merely said, "But it is with too much sorrow I leave you tonight, *ama*."

Why didn't she invite him to share her twin bed? Anne didn't know. She only knew their passionate mood had ended, and all they had left tonight was the afterplay.

"We'll leave for the Cristo about ten," Tavo reminded her, disinclined to leave. His hand thrilled her graceful neck, then drew back. "Enough," he said. "The uncharted feel of you is making me crazy."

After a restless, unfulfilled hour, Anne slept, grateful now for Pascal's ridiculous, ill-timed interruption. She finally realized what the consequences of fulfillment would have been. She would have enjoyed only two nights of loving Tavo, two go-for-broke nights, and then suffered terrible loneliness.

THE HELICOPTER ROSE from a flattened mound of snow near the entrance to Hotel Portillo, lifting its tail in an elegant corkscrew turn around the back of the yellow crescent. Anne's and Tavo's skis were locked on the struts above the sled runners on the craft. Anne sat in the copilot's seat for the better view. Tavo had insisted, while he leaned forward from the back seat, resting his arm against Anne's back.

Inwardly she responded, although to all appearances she was calm. She was leaving the next morning and had faith this last day would be a final lovely memory, with no pain.

"Before we take off for the Cristo, do you want a look at the speed course where Pascal will be racing?" Tavo shifted closer, forcing Anne to lean forward out of their mingled, charged body zone.

The pilot pivoted the helicopter down the mountain and hovered above the Juncalillo run. "That's the Roca Jack." Tavo spoke close to her ear so she could hear him above the whine of the rotor.

The ski slope was a wide path clawed straight up the granite cliffs, a vertical river cut by aeons of avalanches. Five skiers rode a special lift up the crack, each with a plastic Poma saucer between his legs. The saucers were connected to a waist-high crossbar that all the skiers gripped. There were no towers on the lift to be knocked down by avalanches. Instead, massive cables were bolted into the mountain about two-thirds of the way up. That was where the skiers cautiously released themselves, one at a time, on an eighty-degree slope.

"They say old Jack Healy, a Chilean *andinesto*, a mountain man, used to hike to those rocks there." Anne followed the direction of Tavo's pointed finger. "See? Where the rocks are too steep to hold snow? Jack sat there waiting for the sun to make the snow perfect, or for courage. That is why it is called Jack's Rock."

"What's the run like?"

"Standing on a soapy window."

They laughed comfortably for the first time that morning, and Anne relaxed. Already she felt nostalgic.

"The speed racing is held two chutes down from Roca Jack. See? To the right. They are higher. That is where Pascal will start helping Lunch and Hank smooth a track tomorrow."

"Is there much danger of avalanches?"

"Always. There were three avalanches during the trials in 1978. One skier would have been swept away if he had not jumped on the back of another contestant. That is why none of us ski the Roca Jack in the afternoon when the sun has weakened the snow. We change to Condor, an avalanche chute above Plateau."

"Why don't the racers go where it's safer?"

"There is no choice. The higher they go, the thinner the oxygen and the easier to slice through the air. Portillo's course is the world's highest at—" His confident grin was appealing. "I do not always have every fact ready. I think Portillo's speed track is 12,601 feet.... You have a course at Velocity Peak, Colorado, where the last record was set. It begins at 12,500 feet."

Tavo tapped the pilot on the shoulder, and they pivoted over the hotel again and up the narrow valley. They floated past gray granite and above it with nary a bump of rough air, nor a rising sensation.

Ten minutes into the wilderness, on a maroon saddle cleared of snow by the wind and the sun, loomed a dark bronze Christ. It had been cast from melted-down cannons when the controversial border between the two countries had at last been fixed in 1904. One hand was raised in a blessing; the other held a cross.

The helicopter set down gently. Tavo and his pilot ferried the ski gear to a nearby snowbank while Anne dodged away from the chopper, her hair whipping sharply into her face from the blade's turbulence.

She had grown so used to the deafening racket of the rotor that when the helicopter departed, the silence was disturbingly loud. The rapid beating of her heart thudded against her constraining ribs. Her breath came in shallow gasps from high in her throat.

"Walk slowly. Take your time." Tavo steadied her arm. "Our elevation is...let's see, estimating that a meter is about a yard.... We are about 13,800 feet altitude." They proceeded slowly over to a notch in a tumble of rocks. "The Aconcagua is to the left. Can you see? The peak behind the big one in front." Aconcagua looked smaller. On her own, Anne would never have guessed its ranking.

They rested against the warm, dark red lava rocks, looking out at the vista. Anne recorded the memory of his body near hers, each crook and indentation, for tomorrow all she would have was the accuracy of her observations.

What would it be like if they had somehow learned to trust each other by the time she returned for the races? What if his pursuit wasn't game playing, what if her riotous feelings were more than infatuation, what if he loved her? What would her life be like if she stayed here with him? Could she leave the United States?

"Our first base camp when I climbed the Aconcagua was about this elevation." Tavo didn't notice her preoccupation. He was saying something about a second base camp at 18,500 feet. "We spent two days walking back and forth between the two camps to acclimate before we went on up.''

"How much higher is Everest?" she asked, listening now.

"Somewhere around twenty-nine thousand feet. I thought about going with a Chilean team when I finished in Munich, but...." He wavered, then clamped his firm lips, making Anne wonder what was censored. "But I had to return home."

"Why?"

"Family reasons."

He had withdrawn from her. She shrugged, pretending she didn't care, and tried a different tack. "Was Aconcagua hard to climb?"

"Not the actual climb. The weather is what creates the danger. What we call white winds come up suddenly. The blowing snow blinds you and cuts any exposed skin. It is a tornado of sharpened icicles. We were turned back twice by white wind."

"I don't want to pry into your personal life, Tavo, but I would like to understand." Anne spoke deliberately. If he could push her to speak her thoughts, she could do likewise. "Why did you want to do it? Why did you persist?"

"Once, through a series of unexpected coincidences—" his derisive laugh had a haunted quality "—I had no particular desire to live. Aconcagua taught me sometimes it is necessary to confront death in order to accept life...." Again he hesitated.

Anne watched the conflict in his eyes. A charitable impulse overcame her natural curiosity. "Never mind. It's okay. Really." Regretfully she got up from her rocky perch and tugged him to his feet. "I don't need to climb a mountain today," she said, "but I have a yen to survey the world from Christ's feet."

Tavo easily boosted her up to the stone back. She inched along the ledge, feeling the hot metal statue against her back. He picked up two weathered coins scattered among many on the base, good-luck tokens from an arid fountain.

"Keepsakes," he said, handing them to her. "One from Chile and one from Argentina."

Anne was delighted. "I'll have them strung on a gold chain when I get home. They will be a—" her words scattered on the breeze "—a very tender memento of our nice week together."

"Nice week?" He gave no ground.

"Well, an exceptionally nice week," she conceded.

"How about an exceptionally nice several weeks?" He looked immeasurably pleased with himself. "I have arranged to go with you on your exploration tomorrow, sweetheart."

Before she could collect her thoughts, Anne blurted grimly, "Won't that give you business complications?"

Tavo scowled, but she didn't ponder his reaction. She had been stunned by her own cold, economic response to his declaration, her Charles Roderick reaction. For months she had believed she could warm up Charles, given time. What an irony. She was as frozen as the politics-first congressman.

"I have made arrangements."

"Ah...it's a generous offer, Tavo, but...." Anne clutched for excuses.

"But what? I want to be with you. Do not tell me you

want this to end, Ana, *ama*, because I will not believe you."

"All this traveling together.... You maybe don't have to worry about your reputation, but what if the press somehow leaks it? Who would understand that we're traveling as...as pals?" Anne was prattling. She and Tavo wouldn't travel platonically; it was impossible. He would set another mood, and she would not resist. She was a hooked trout being played on a very long line, given an illusion of freedom. But she had a fighting chance to escape.

"I can't see sabotaging my relationship with Charles for the hell of it...."

He quirked an amused brow at her. Charles had been discounted from the beginning, his look said. She would have to fight harder.

"I can't see making that kind of trip without a... without a commitment." There, that was good. Commitment was a brutal word to men of the late twentieth century.

To Anne's increasing discomfort, Tavo disciplined a smile.

"So?" His stance was relaxed.

"So?" *So! So to making a commitment? Talk's cheap, Tavito, you who are beloved by the women of Chile.* She struggled to extricate herself from the quagmire of the conversation. "So I can't see destroying my present life without a real commitment...." She stumbled, then recovered her poise and snapped, "A real one—like marriage." *Now there's a strong word. That takes care of that.* The mention of marriage was anathema to professional bachelors in their mid-thirties.

"What is wrong with marriage?" he persisted, outrageously flinging her attack back at her.

"What's wrong?" She cursed the sudden solemnity in his expression. Was he serious? *Don't insult me with mockery, Tavo. Don't ruin it. Don't make stupid hurting remarks just so you can sleep with me for a couple of weeks.*

She teetered on the ledge of the statue. "Nothing's wrong per se. I mean, philosophically I'm not opposed to...." Anne couldn't force the word out.

Calmly he said it for her, "marriage," and smiled with a charm she found almost irresistible. Even his cool eyes smiled, the blue as snuggly as a baby's blanket. "Good. I am not opposed to marriage either philosophically or specifically. You do not have to think about the commitment you proposed now, Ana. You know it is right."

Now she knew he was making a joke. Her jeer sliced the thin air. "If you're so gung ho, Tavo—philosophically, that is—why haven't you married before?"

He threw back his head and laughed. "No one has proposed."

Anne looked scornfully down at the handsome blond. She didn't believe him.

"In Chile, the women do the proposing. We have very strong-minded women here." He reached for her, and despite her protests, lifted her down. She steeled herself not to respond to the feel of him. She held her hands firmly at her sides, refusing to embrace his strong neck to steady herself.

"When you are ready to ask me, Ana, *ama*, I will be coy." His deep chuckle made her feel foolish. "I might vacillate bashfully, but never doubt, sweetheart, I will accept you."

Anne disentangled herself from his grasp. She could think of absolutely nothing to say—and then, to her horror, she laughed.

At first it was a high, nervous giggle, like a coltish fourteen year-old's. But then the preposterousness of no woman ever asking Gustavo Mohr de la Huerta to marry her struck Anne, and her laughter rippled out in irresistible guffaws.

Tavo laughed, too, until they were holding their sides, gasping for oxygen.

"What's so funny?" she asked him before he could ask her.

"You are. Your refreshing naiveté enchants me, Ana."

She wasn't naive. Her problem was the hunter. He used rules she didn't know about, coaxed responses she couldn't control, and he would never know he had succeeded. She was undeniably infatuated.

The quieted pair slogged around the summit of a bowl, then headed for a saddle on the opposite side, using their heavy downhill skis for cross-country walking. From there they would ski ten miles down a curved valley to the hotel.

The gradually descending route was primeval. Rust pinnacles pierced the brilliant blue sky, ultrabright snow was untracked and the solitude divine. Creation surely began here with the basics, Anne thought. On the raw top of the earth, where stubborn rust lichen clung to rocks and survived. Not in overladen jungles below the clouds.

Eventually the valley flattened, and they walked again. It was hard work. The sun burned upon them; the air was parched. Their lungs ached from sucking oxygen from a thin atmosphere.

"An icy beer," Anne croaked. "My life for a beer." She had stripped off her sweater and turtleneck and tied them around her waist. Her lavender tank top showed purple with sweat. "A beer slush."

"*Jugo de melón,*" countered Tavo. "A freshly liqui-fied honeydew melon, freezing cold...."

When the thirsty sopping couple reached Portillo's ski hill, they rested against their poles. It was an easy downhill slide from there.

"What's your helicopter doing back, Tavo?" Anne peered in the direction of the hotel. "Do you think something's wrong?" Maybe he couldn't get away to go traveling, she thought hopefully. Maybe he would say goodbye with no hard feelings and fly away. *Chau* she'd say. *Gracias.*

Tavo shaded his eyes and squinted. "That is not my chopper. It is a helicopter service from Santiago. One of the Brazilians is probably going home and wants a fast ride to the airport. Last one down to the hotel buys the first round."

Anne poled off, tucking as best she could. But her legs weren't strong enough to hold the racing position and she lost, though not by a mile. Tavo had handi-capped his speed for her.

They were stepping out of their skis when Anne was skillfully separated from Tavo's side by a petite blonde. The woman's ashen hair was wrapped in a chignon, a style too severe for everyone except those with perfect features to flaunt. And she had them, and a golden tan, and a honey suede jacket and tightly wrapped suede skirt. A long scarf in shades of golds, greens and a whirl of crimson trailed dramatically.

"*Amo...*" began the throaty burst of Spanish. The woman brushed her hands against Tavo's bare chest, long pink-lacquered fingernails dallying along his ribs, tracing the outline of the copper bracelet. She was possessive in her intimacy, and Anne knew they had been lovers.

Tavo didn't reply in Spanish. Instead, he held the woman's hands in his, leaned down to kiss her on the cheek and said, "Liliana, I would like to present a North American friend, Anne Mahoney from Los Angeles. Ana, this is an old friend of mine, Liliana Peréz de Alut."

"*Mucho gusto,*" said Liliana, the semi-circle of her eyebrows disdainfully arched, emphasized by a beautician's waxing. She looked offside, over Anne's ear, when she spoke, not meeting Anne's eyes. Something Tavo couldn't see, but Anne noticed, and it amused her. The woman wasn't as confident as she posed.

Before Anne could extend a polite, rather damp hand to shake, however, the taut blonde turned her back. Her interest was Tavo. This time her Spanish was a soft caress.

"Liliana is just home from Tahiti," he explained. "She has been recovering from her recent widowhood in French Polynesia."

Liliana, Liliana.... Of course, Anne remembered. The childhood friend of the bracelet gift, Tavo's symbol of freely given love. Anne watched Liliana's hand return not quite casually to the copper band, and again was amused.

She could see what Liliana could not, that although the rigid cord on the side of Tavo's neck protruded, in all other ways he had pulled into himself. The cheerful manner in which he was asking Liliana about her tropical mourning was a fraud.

"We are extremely thirsty," Tavo cut off Liliana's monologue. "Come with us to the dining room for late lunch and share a bottle of wine. How long are you in Portillo?"

"Lo depende."

I'll bet it depends, Anne thought, and then a strange thing happened. Through her smug superiority, she felt a quick jab of jealousy, then another and another like a mutant virus gone amok, until Anne swelled with such acute envy that she could hold no more without bursting.

She didn't envy Liliana; she envied her situation. The tart blonde would stay on. Perhaps she and Tavo would resume their relationship, perhaps marry—more likely not. The merry widow hadn't captured him before. And it was irrelevant. All that mattered was that Anne wouldn't be with him. She would be back in her life, the successful existence that had fit so comfortably until her ambitious world had turned chaotic one week before.

"Goodbye, Tavo," Anne said, and dodged into the hotel. Goodbye. That said everything. She didn't have to look behind her to know his eyes never left her. He had seen the look on her face and knew she had bid him farewell.

ANNE HID in her room. She read a little but couldn't concentrate. She wrote a letter home, saying nothing about Tavo, which meant she had nothing to say.

Occasionally Tavo knocked on her door. His initial raps were accompanied by a question. "Ana, are you there?"

About six, Anne was hungry. By eight the feeling had passed, and Tavo's knocks were sharp and angry. She stopped reading, started to stir, got up, sat down, read a sentence, started to speak and shut up.

Anne had more than enough time to recall a famous psychology experiment she had studied in college. The researchers had put some kind of banana split for rats at the far end of an electric grid. Every time a starving rat ran for the treat, it got a hot foot.

The rodents either ran to the food and ate despite the pain, or they stayed on the safe side, hungry. Some couldn't make up their minds. The frantic indecisive rats pranced in the middle of the grid, running toward the food and running away from it, pitifully enduring both shocks and hunger. Abject failures.

Anne understood the approach-avoidance rat now.

This starving rat is getting off the grid, she decided abruptly, and sneaked out of the shelter of her room. She ran down the enclosed steps to the pool, her rubber flip-flops sounding in the abandoned hallway as she slammed out through the doors, and tossed two towels on an empty sunning cot.

Stars perforated the velvet of an inky sky, bright pinholes that gleamed an infinite backdrop to the full moon silvering the granite walls. Banks of silver snow against the glass wind fence, and silver steam hid the water.

The slim moonstruck figure pulled the coral cover-up over her head and shook her hair free. Bracing air, warmed by the predicted approach of a snow flurry, quickened Anne's steps.

She didn't pause at the edge of the man-made cloud, but blindly dived in. Hot water fired her cold flesh, her anguished muscles, her bones, and it felt wonderfully good. Pressure pounded her ears as she shot to the floor of the pool until it equaled the pounding of her heart. Her hands brushed bottom. Then she scissored upward, wiggling her shoulders, spiraling, reaching for oxygen.

Anne surfaced with a howl of angry laughter, sleeked her hair off her face and paddled exultantly.

Wisps of snow clouds edged over the canyon walls, dampening all sound save the lapping of water. She grasped the side of the pool and thrust back in the other direction with a clean backstroke, unaware she was being watched from a distant corner.

An uncanny chill leaped from the tips of her full breasts covered by scraps of stretchy coral fabric, past shadows glistening over the concave slope of her stomach, across the hipbone peaks, and on down sleek flanks to exposed toes.

Anne submerged her body, forcing its buoyancy into the comfort of the water, and closed her eyes. Suspended patches of faces made drifting a nightmare: Stephanie's dimpled cheeks, Tavo's firm sun-chapped lips moving closer, Liliana's silly disdain.

Anne grimly erased them. *You are floating free,* she told herself. *Tavo will pass in the night. Tomorrow he will be no more than a memory. He was a diversion. Remember the good times.*

She pictured the mossy green of his flannel shirt stretched across his broad shoulders that afternoon when he'd lifted her to the base of the Cristo. "What is wrong with marriage?" he had asked.

Anne flipped over onto her stomach and cut through

the water, still disconcerted. A worthless proposal, considering she was scheduled to be back in the United States in thirteen days. He hadn't meant real marriage, had he? But if he had—

She picked up her speed, frustrated by the multi-angled pool that made it impossible for her to adequately work off her tension. Beaten, she rotated to her back and rested, her mood as clouded as the moon above. At home, north of the equator, it would have been fat and orange with the approach of harvest. Here, at the beginning of spring, there was no North Star to guide her, nor a Big Dipper upon which to reckon place. The Southern Cross was merely a name to a North American.

A splash sounded in the recesses of her despair and passed unnoticed. Later she tried to separate the instant she knew he was beside her, but a clear demarcation never came. One moment she was alone in the mists, and the next, the demanding lips of her imagination were a startling few inches from her own.

Anne flipped over, setting a pace as devastating as she could rally in the small space. The tall trespasser followed. She pushed harder. *Forget him and he'll go away,* she coached herself. Kick, kick, reach, reach, reach. Yet her disobedient heart reached for him. Just one night.... Surely they could share one night before their time together ended.

Her chest ached, and she rolled her head rapidly, gasping for air. She dropped her feet, testing for the bottom in order to stand and catch her breath. But there was only water.

Wearily she lowered her head and reached forward, only to feel two hands grasp her around the waist. She churned in place, for Tavo had the height to stand and the strength to pull her easily to him.

Light snow began to fall.

"We are not in a competition, Ana. Come to me, where you belong."

She struggled to pry his fingers open with her right hand. But his grip was insistent, and she sank, her left arm flailing helplessly.

Tavo's large warm hands lifted her, shivering, high out of the water, facing her away from him as he waded them both to a shallower point. Anne felt a nibble on her buttocks, and the resulting rush of excitement made her tremble as much as the onslaught of chilly air.

"What are you doing!" Emotion constricted her throat.

"I thought I would eat you for dinner," he chuckled quietly, tracing the invisible imprint of his teeth with two prying fingers. "How did you once say it, Ana?" he whispered. "Yes, I have it. Shall I kiss it well?"

His audacious humor always bypassed her resolve. Anne stifled a laugh, sensing rather than seeing the racy amusement in the eyes that studied her twitching shoulder from behind.

"Drop me right now." Her tone lacked conviction. She kicked backward, hard. Empty air and another chuckle greeted her.

"Mmm, Ana, your winter manners are heating up, no?" Tavo murmured, pulling her to him, circling her waist with one arm.

This time her feet made contact. The response was swift. Tavo clamped his other arm a little lower, and prickles of pleasure made her skin flush. Anne squirmed against his muscular chest. She fought the temptation to curve her back around the swell, and lost. *A tiny moment wouldn't hurt,* her traitorous mind urged. She wiggled into a close fit, until his body heat penetrated hers.

His breathing deepened. "You are an enchanting woman, Ana. Even your protestations excite me. You know it, no? You can feel my desire for you grow, sweetheart...."

He freed one hand and combed her wet tresses out under the faint beam of the shadowed moon.

"Black, brown, red, mahogany.... Exquisite, like a Honduras mahogany forest, hiding a neck that is...a siren's call."

Scooping up her hair to the top of her head, he blew softly on the nape, slowly progressing downward. "I want to taste your neck here, under your ear...and here...and down here, Ana. You can feel it, too? Here at the base of your neck." His lips fired an exquisitely tormenting path over her rounded shoulder and down her back to the delicate strings of her bikini top.

Anne arched even farther backward, her yearning cementing a physical decision.

Tavo tugged on the coral strings with his teeth and pulled, one at a time. Lingering close at the bow, he tickled her spine with his relentless tongue. A soft moan escaped her parted lips even as a rush of overwhelming sensation swelled her sensitive breasts. The bow unraveled, and her top fell loose.

"I want to see you," Tavo whispered huskily against her bare flesh. He turned her to him, holding her slightly away as he removed the coral top with his free hand and tucked it securely into the waistband of his swim suit.

The flaming streamer drifted from the black fabric stretched low across his hips and disappeared in the steam. Anne's eyes were magnetized by flat, defined muscles pointing down to the dark water that lapped below his waist. She felt her own muscles tensing.

"Dios mío, eres hermosa," he breathed, his eyes, too, lingering on her beauty. A flurry of snowflakes sprinkled over her breasts like flakes of gleaming mica caught in the nebulous lights of the hotel beyond the vapor.

His finger traced the lips she turned away. . . so lightly, yet the needles of electricity his touch evoked were almost a physical pain. She nipped those fingers to halt their teasing, and was stunned at the force of desire that met her glance.

He refused to allow her eyes, with their telling warmth, to shift away, even if Anne had wanted them to. She was as trapped by his naked expression as she was by the arms that enveloped her.

"You are shy, Ana? That is one of your charms." The usually trim blond wave hugged his brow, its flat wetness emphasizing a square forehead that sloped to severe planes.

Anne's heart pounded as he crushed her against his chest. His heartbeat surged in tandem, and he raised her higher against him, his broad buoyant hands under her arms like water wings.

He touched his tongue to an unmelted snowflake gleaming on her erect left nipple. "No, oh, I. . . ." Her lips began to move against him involuntarily.

His persistent tongue flicked another flake off her right breast, his mouth defrosting her compliant flesh. Recklessly she brushed her lips to the pulse on his neck, her hands exploring with abandon. The broad muscles of his arms grew warm under her touch, putty to be kneaded at her whim.

"Dios, I knew you would be wonderful, Ana. But you are—''

Anne's once reluctant tongue eagerly tickled her response in his ear, flicking words in the shell, inarticulate words meant to be felt, and understood. Gently, gently she sipped out his unspoken answer, while her impatient hips punctured the boundary between them.

Tavo slipped two strong fingers into the triangle of her stretchy bikini bottoms.

''Wait. . . .'' Like a shipwrecked survivor falling into a bottomless void, Anne wrapped her arms around him and clung. ''I've got to think.''

''Stop thinking,'' he coaxed, returning her eager hands to their original destination. ''Feel me, *amada*. . . . Feel my love. You know you want me, Ana. You want me as much as I am starved for you. Say it.'' Tavo's control was ragged. ''Admit it,'' he pleaded, and she reached for him.

''This is a moment that should never end,'' he murmured hoarsely.

Even as her lips sought his windburned mouth once more, Anne's brain grappled with reality. *End*, his careless word tolled. *End. End. End.*

''I'm leaving tomorrow, Tavo.'' She attempted to escape his embrace, but her reluctant limbs postponed her orders. Her slim legs wrapped around his hips.

''You are the one who pretends this is our last night, Ana.''

''You're leaving me, Tavo. . . .'' No, she was leaving, of course. She was the one. No one was granted ceaseless rapture. Living was an ordinary experience—some good, some bad. The most one could hope for was exciting work and calm at home. *I want rapture,* one part of her mind cried, and the other shouted, *You fool.*

Pain cleared her thoughts. Anne slipped out of his unwary hold and swam to the side of the pool in three adrenaline-boosted strokes. Swinging one leg up onto the cold concrete, she rolled out of the warm steam, only to be pulled back into the water and shaken.

Unslaked desire had clearly shifted to rage. "You are driving me mad with your self-deceptions, Ana. You are the one who is determined that we have a holiday romance." A muscle twitched in his rigid jaw.

Anne knew now that he believed she was leaving him. He was furious that he had lost her before he could bed her. Frosty eyes stared at her, hard as tempered steel. But there was something else in the blue. . .something as elusive as the misty steam. Was it fear she saw? No, it couldn't be, could it? Perhaps it was fear she felt. Anne had conquered fear before, so she attacked.

"I live my life as I choose," she snarled, and kicked, hard, scoring one solid goal against his ribs.

The two combatants glared at one another, both refusing to give a point. Only their heavy breathing revealed the depth of their battle. "You have a compulsion to toy with life, Ana. Look at you run from the first love you have known from a man —" the creases around his mouth were parentheses to his scornful words— "if you are to be believed, and I judge from your infant behavior that it must be true."

There was nothing soft about his voice, nor about her unforgiving, haughty pose. Flint sparked against flint.

"What goes on between that congressman and you is

North American nonsense. Two matched robots. He—"

"He is none of your business, and neither am I! Now if you don't mind, let me go."

Tavo shook her shoulders again, not harshly. She laughed her defiance.

"Oh, no, Señorita Mahoney." His breathing was easing, yet his grip signaled a warning. "You are not retreating now, not now when you have come close to real feelings. I will not allow you to douse your fire—"

"*You?*" She jerked suddenly and sank her teeth into the salty flesh of his tough shoulder.

It was his turn to laugh—derisive, determined, enraged. "*I* will not permit you to return to your frozen ways."

Anne mocked his laugh and kicked again, but this time Tavo made certain she missed.

"I will not make love to you tonight. The time for that has passed." She could hear bitter fury in his tone. "But you are mine, despite yourself. When you are back to your keyboard, writing about other people's feelings with this detachment you foolishly cultivate, you will remember this hour."

"Not with pleasure."

The angered giant couldn't miss the boldness of her conviction, but he ignored it; he would force a surrender of her heart.

"And when you are sitting alongside your congressman and he kisses your breasts, so—" he flicked a casual tongue across the darkened peak that greeted his words "—you will still be my love, for he will never cause them to reply as they do for me, *amada*."

"I'm not your love and I'll never be," Anne fought back. But Tavo had clearly seen her future, her body responded to his efforts to make her remember him forever.

Fiercely he demanded she admit her desire, acknowledge the passion she felt for him, her need of him. Pride stilled her, and Tavo redoubled his efforts, as if he knew that if she voiced her feelings, she wouldn't abandon him in the morning. And he was right, though he would never know it.

At last, when Anne thought she could resist no longer, when her only reminder of reality was one, sensible, unpolished thumbnail she dug painfully into the tip of her little finger, Tavo lifted her out of the water. In an uninterrupted motion, he set her on the frigid concrete and vaulted out, picking up her towels from the empty chair as he swept her into the secluded anteroom.

He encased her trembling shoulders in one of her towels, knelt and rubbed her dry with the other. White terry cloth was a welding torch in his unrelenting hands. Her feet and ankles seared even as her left leg was set afire. Higher he rubbed, and higher. A moan escaped her dry lips as he parted her knees, the friction slower now, and more devastating.

"Say it," he rasped as he ignited her right leg.

Shame, reason and finally pride burned away. No sentences remained in the ashes. Still she wouldn't give of herself in this maddened episode. She didn't know why, and yet she didn't flee. She couldn't.

The fluffy material torched a path up her clinging bikini bottoms. She stood rigidly, her arms at her sides, her hands clenched. Soon her bemused body began to shudder with a rhythm as old as time.

"Please, sweetheart, tell me," he coaxed, Anne didn't notice the catch in his voice. If she had opened her eyes, she would have been stunned at the dulled anguish in his expression.

"I am not persuading you, Ana. You are ready, no? You know that. Your resolve is too strong to allow your body to behave without permission, *ama*. Tell me what your body tells me. . . what mine tells you. Say it." His words were a raw croon.

Words boiled in her mind. *Yes, I want you—yes, yes.* "No," she said. "My mind. . . and my body say no."

"No," she repeated. *Yes,* said her hips. *Yes,* said her immobile feet. *Yes, yes, yes,* said eager arms that reached for him—but her arms held only the lonely night air.

Anne tottered precariously. A fist slammed into the opposite wall. Tavo punched it again, his forehead pushed against the wood. His muscles were tense bands across his shoulders.

Anne wrapped her arms around herself, trying in vain to stop the shaking. His radical withdrawal affected her deeply. "Please, Tavo. . . ." She extended a tremulous hand, wary of actual contact.

He faced her with an obvious effort; his glance paused at the rounded curves. The telltale muscle in his jaw twitched at the vulnerability of her flushed face.

He pulled her bikini top from his swimsuit and tossed it back at her as he strode up the steps. "You had better get dressed." He cleared his throat from a distance, never halting in his abrupt exit.

The discarded material was a red flag to the wounded woman at the foot of the stairs. "Are you so frightened of one stranger, just one more woman passing through your life?" she shouted through chattering teeth. "It's not enough the women of Chile are yours. Did you have to prove you could conquer me, too? You call that *macho normal*? If you have to bed someone so desperately, go jump on your little *ama*, Liliana!''

Tremendous self-discipline showed in his immediate stop. He took the stairs down two at a time and swaddled the towel more tightly around her.

"Forget the top, Ana. We are going to my suite to talk."

"No." Anxiety edged her recalcitrance. She couldn't endure more interrupted lovemaking.

"In my living room, which is what we should have done before."

"No."

"We will not discuss this here." He picked her up easily and carried her upstairs.

Only a few more hours, then I'm away from him. She battled an overwhelming wish to snuggle into his arms. "All right, we will talk." She spoke stiffly. "But not in your room. In mine, so I can dress first. Now put me down."

This time he obeyed, keeping a supporting hand on her shoulder in the elevator. They were silent, ignoring the knowing smiles of the other unknowing passengers.

"Sit down. I'll be out in a minute." Anne opened the door to her room and motioned toward the chair, but he had already gained command of her room.

She took her burgundy velvet pants and a sleeveless mohair sweater from the closet and disappeared into the bathroom, determined to dawdle. She yanked the brush through her hair. Blusher on sun-blushed cheekbones, a heavy hand with the mascara. Their fight had left a poisonous aftertaste. She hesitated over her toothbrush, then poured mouthwash on it and scrubbed.

Anne caught her breath. "Well?" Cautiously she sat on the corner of the bed.

Tavo clasped her hands between his. "I apologize. When I saw you in the moonlight, I was enchanted...."

Instinctively she knew he was speaking from the heart; he wasn't mouthing pretty words for future gain. And she knew there was more, some unexplained obstruction. The set of his shoulders told her he had been frightened of losing her, and his eyes declared that he hadn't yet banished his fear.

Anne waited for him to say this, expected this, since he had taught her, and sometimes forced her, to articulate her own feelings. Instead he delayed. "I forgot myself in the moonlight...I came looking for you because you ran away from dinner, also lunch and tea."

She could tell Tavo was close to confession, and this very reticence convinced her that he cared for her. "Tell me," Anne murmured. She wanted to hear that his anger had been understandable fear that she would leave him.

He was close. He dodged. His tone shifted to puzzlement. "Can this all be so new for you? A sudden love that you cannot control in your dispassionate way, and now jealousy."

Jealous? Her eyebrows lifted skeptically, except her expression gave something away, for Anne was startled by how gravely Tavo had misjudged her behavior. Had she, too, misread him?

"I see it is jealousy, or you would not be suffering this tumult. Liliana Peréz was of my youth." The words were soft and precise. "We have talked of her before, no? But jealousy deafens even someone with your intelligence, Ana. You know that intuitively, but you have never learned to trust your feelings.''

''I trust mine.'' Anne withdrew her hands and cupped them around his freshly shaven jaws. Her gaze was unwavering. Crooks she had interviewed had met her stare honestly and lied with practiced ease. ''Why should I trust you?'' she inquired. ''You don't trust me.''

She met his eyes, warm as a summer sky after a thunderstorm, and willingly shifted to his lap when he reached for her.

''Please, Tavo, if you are serious, why haven't you mentioned introducing me to your parents?'' Her tone was strong, her intention clear. ''We know something of Latin customs in Los Angeles.''

''They are dead.'' His expression was guarded.

''Oh, I'm sorry. I....'' Anne fumbled momentarily, hurt by his secrecy. Delving quickly into the hidden feelings of strangers was her forte, and this vital gap in information insulted her pride. Even more, it hurt her.

''Why didn't you tell me before?'' She pulled away, even as her well-trained mind recalculated the evidence. Liliana had given him the bracelet for his twelfth birthday, when he thought love was God given. Before he knew, it could also be taken.

''After your twelfth birthday, wasn't it? How? Did they die together? Did you have brothers or sisters? Who raised you? What happened to you before you climbed the Aconcagua? What about the confidences we've shared about our lives and our feelings?''

Anne slid off his lap and turned her back on him. ''Let me modify that, Gustavo Mohr de la Huerta. All the confidences you have insisted I share.... *Share!*'' Her voice caught.

"Grave watching is your business, Ana. You dig for other people's unhappiness. Why should I expose my sorrows for your professional responses?"

Stung by his wicked assessment, Anne whirled around and struck. "How can you cherish a grave digger? You'll be coy, but you will accept a proposal of marriage if I offer? What kind of ghoul does that make you?"

"Why do women equate intimacy with information, Ana?" he asked, walking slowly toward her.

"I'm not 'women.' " She backed away, and Tavo followed the short distance until her back was pressed to the wall. She could go no farther, but she refused to raise her head. She had never betrayed the people she loved. She was numbed by his distrust. She couldn't challenge him further.

"You are a wellspring of strength, Anne Mahoney, although prickly. You are brave, intelligent, and underneath your pretense that you slide through life unaffected by its storms, you have an endearing tenderness. Occasionally you let it out."

Anne forgot his praise and refused to forgive his deception. Asking questions, needing answers was as much a part of her as the cinnamon of her eyes.

You understand nothing, she thought, shocked because she had come to believe he understood everything.

"Moreover, *mi vida*, I am a skier. I appreciate the approach of winter in your autumn eyes." His free hand followed the curve of her waist. "Your hip fits...." Tavo's voice thickened. "And I desire you. I have wanted you from the moment I saw you sitting below me on Garganta, braced against your skis, with the sun turning your hair to copper and contentment on your face. I want to share your contentment. I want to watch your pleasure with me when I place that look on your face.''

Suddenly he jammed his hands in his pockets and walked to the door. ''Enough. I have time and, who knows why. . . you need time.''

Time? He understands nothing.

''I will dismiss your chauffeur in the morning, as we discussed earlier, and drive you to Chillán myself. When is he due?''

Carlos Luzzini had said he would pick her up at nine, an hour when Tavo usually worked in his suite.

''It's a regular workday for the driver, so he'll be leaving Santiago at eight,'' Anne lied, her eyes innocently wide. An escape plan formed in her mind. ''So he'll be here, when? About eleven-thirty or twelve?''

Tavo ducked his tall head in the doorframe. ''Good night, Ana.'' He paused. ''Dream of me.''

Anne stifled a retort. Thus far he had won every battle. He had destroyed her faith in her ability to control herself. In passing, he had destroyed her trust in him. *He can't win me if he can't find me,* she thought, feeling desolate.

His steps were audible at the distant end of the hall when Anne shut the door and double bolted it. As much to keep her in as to keep him out through the endless night.

Time, she thought before sleep claimed her. *I am running out on time.*

CHAPTER SEVEN

FLEEING EXHILARATED ANNE. The furtiveness of slipping
into Pascal's room early for an undetected farewell was
more stirring than a stakeout. The challenge of convincing
the bank's driver to help her design a fugitive's itinerary
without revealing who she was hiding from rivaled the
rush of a page-one deadline. Or so she told herself.

Carlos Luzzini didn't approve of Anne's egalitarian
decision to ride in the front seat of the Mercedes. However, he complied, and when he closed her car door
Anne felt her life in Portillo close, too. It was a great relief, although not a final one.

Pascal had exacted a promise from her that she would
return for the speed races on August 31.

He remained stretched out on the floor, exercising,
his legs suspended three inches off the carpeting. He insisted he needed her in person, a show of faith. "My
grandfather needs you, too," he gritted. His thighs
trembled from the painful exercise, and his gray sweat
suit was soaked across his belly.

So, unable to deny her friend, Anne promised, but
not until she also wrested a vow of him: her visit was
their secret.

"Why are you running away?" Pascal wanted to
know. "I ruined it when I intruded the other night,
didn't I? I'm sorry—"

"You ruined nothing," she reassured him. "You were a godsend."

"I saw your face. Not quite a godsend. Is it that cat, Liliana?" he guessed. "Listen, don't worry about her. She's—"

"A cat. But no matter."

Pascal lowered his legs to the floor with a grunt and lay still, panting. "Why can't you tell me, Ana? Don't you trust me? You're as secretive as Tavo. Now if only Tavo were Argentine...."

Likewise, Carlos Luzzini was convinced a man was involved. "An Argentine," decided the chauffeur. "Only an Argentine would not know how to appreciate a tender woman like you. This ill-mannered man talk-talk-talked, no?"

Yes...and no.

"Worthless talkers. It is a pity you did not encounter a Chilean man. But that is no problem. It is doubtful there are Argentines in Chillán...."

"Santiago is like a handkerchief," Tavo had said. "One sneeze and everyone knows it." For that reason, Anne allowed Carlos his delusion.

"He's expecting to take me to Chillán himself," she said, explaining that The Talker—it amused her to nickname Tavo—had learned that her grandfather was a Higgins and wanted to show off the birthplace of Bernardo O'Higgins. He was the bastard general who joined forces with Argentina's San Martin to free southern Latin America from Spain.

"Then we cannot go to Chillán," decided Carlos, and when he reached the Pan American highway he turned left, up to the Uspallata Pass and the border.

"We will show this Argentine," he said, the creases in

his face ironed flat by his broad smile. Carlos had joined the challenge. "I do not believe he will lose hope in one day or two, señorita—"

"Anne...Ana. Please call me Ana," she interjected.

"He will not forget you quickly, Ana. You are too lovely to forget. Except we will trick him." He chuckled. "He will waste time looking for you in Chile, and when he realizes you are not with us, he will assume you are in Bariloche, and he will be consumed with jealousy. The life in Bariloche is very *alegre*, you know what I am saying? Bariloche has many hotels and pensions. It will take him days to discover you are not there."

The thought amused both conspirators.

"So where will I be?" Anne cracked open the window.

"Your annoyer intended to take you skiing at the home of our liberator. We will hide you in a town named for him, San Martin de los Andes."

"I like that." Anne patted Carlos's bony shoulder gleefully. "A grand fake-out for The Talker." She was feeling very good, absolutely liberated from problems and decisions. The weeks ahead were going to be fun.

"San Martin is an excellent hideout for a North American. I do not know the town personally, only I am told your famous bandits, Butch Cassidy and the Sundance Kid, were in San Martin." Carlos seemed to know a bit about everything, and as he humbly insisted, not from personal experience.

He talked; Anne questioned. They gaily waved to the guards at the Chilean border, who waved back while the spirited conversation continued.

Three or four minutes later they bounced onto a dirt

road, and the austere gray granite pass vanished in a showy extravaganza of rock walls higher than the Matterhorn, windsculpted and colorful. Rust, brown, white, bright lilac, green, orange, red rock; every color imaginable mingled with black lava.

Carlos's discourse was choked in the dust. Anne rolled up her window, and he talked on through the twenty kilometers of unpaved frontier. Argentine customs checked them through efficiently. The conspirators pressed on.

It was an awesome three hours down the mountains. There were no trees, nor shrubs—only an occasional clump of grass until they were nearly at the eastern base of the Andes. Beyond the mountains, clear to the horizon stretched a treeless brown plain of dormant vineyards. Wine grapes to press into the world's fifth largest production of wine. Table grapes whose winter popularity in Europe during the Argentine summer had inspired the Chileans to begin raising other fruit for export thirty years before, Carlos had heard.

The luxurious car passed another of the many semi-trucks on the barren highway. Then abruptly it entered an urban forest, Mendoza, undoubtedly the most beautiful of all desert cities.

Saplings lined the wide paved streets in the outlying suburbs of the petroleum-rich city, sixteen young trees on each side of every block, watered by shallow irrigation ditches. The woods grew higher and denser as the Mercedes neared the city center. Eventually the vehicle proceeded under ghostly four-lane arches of white sycamores. Over a century old, their bare arms had linked decades earlier.

The people of Mendoza planned wide streets, outlawed buildings over three stories, designed parks every third block and planted a shield of trees for safety more than beauty. Their desperation resulted from their experiences during the Civil War, when the city was destroyed for the third time by a violent earthquake. That was one of the hazards in an area where quakes over seven on the Richter scale were not uncommon, Carlos said. He slowed in the forested commercial zone, looking for a travel agency.

Did their disaster plan work, the California native wanted to know as she studied the freshly painted, clean city of half a million. Carlos thought so. He was certain of his facts, however—that San Juan, a city one hundred miles north of Mendoza, had been leveled by an earthquake in 1944. And of his gossip—that Argentina's notorious, charismatic leaders, Eva and Juan Peron, first met in San Juan at a national benefit for the victims.

Carlos parked by a sidewalk café. The tables were occupied by vivid brunets eating thick rare steaks and sipping glasses of red wine. The men wore vest sweaters, their dark suit jackets unbuttoned in the temperate warmth of the sun. The women were dressed in pleated plaid skirts and cashmere pullovers.

A travel agency was next door. Carlos talked at length with the owner, relaying the information to Anne. A flight south to Neuquèn was leaving in an hour. The travel agent would arrange for a driver to meet the jet and drive her to San Martin.

"Señor Robinson says there is a charming little lodge in the middle of the ski slope, named Los Techos," translated Carlos. "The food is excellent, quite continental, and the owner and his wife are fluent in English, French and German—and Spanish, of course. If this suits you, he will telephone for arrangements.''

"That sounds lovely," Anne said. "Then when I want to go on to Bariloche...?"

Carlos questioned the slender, precise blond owner in the pin-striped suit. Robinson's thin Scottish lips smiled warmly.

Carlos translated. "There is a bus every morning from San Martin to Bariloche. The trip takes four hours. The *señor* says you will find it quite interesting because you will be in Patagonia. It is their Wild West."

Everything was arranged within minutes. Anne paid the bill and put the voucher booklet in her purse with her passport. She agreed to call Carlos two days before she left Bariloche, which would give him time to meet her at the Vincente Peréz Rosales Hotel in Puerto Montt.

"Why the Peréz Rosales, Ana? Because that is the end of the bus line," her chauffeur and conspirator said sensibly. "And it is our finest hotel in the south."

SAN MARTIN nestled in a snug blue valley at the foot of a bluer lake. Gray clouds edged with black were over the high wooded hills when Anne and her expansive Argentine driver arrived.

"Nieve." The man nodded toward the ominous mass.

Anne wasn't sure whether *nieve* meant snow or clouds. *"Es nieve blanco y frio?"* she asked. They had been baby-talking and charading for three hours. *Blanco and frio.* White and cold? But where was the snow? There was none on the ground.

Si, si. Pero no había nieve hasta quince minutos. He pointed at his wristwatch and at the snow cloud.

Passing the village with its small tourist hotels, they began zigzagging through forests of beech, the wet bark yellowed by the winter dampness. Eventually patches of snow spotted the ground on the shady southern sides, and ultimately the mantle of white was complete.

After twenty minutes of twisted driving, they pulled into a plowed parking lot near a restaurant with a soaring roof and an extravagant expanse of glass. Skiers bundled against the oncoming storm rode a chair lift up from the far side of the modern building.

Anne zipped open the one small suitcase she had brought with her, retrieving a dark gold down parka. "Oh, it's freezing." She shivered, snapping the jacket closed clear to her chin, wondering if San Martin was such a good idea, after all.

A horse whinnied behind her, and she jumped, startled, turning to the sound. A stubby gaucho dismounted from a sway-backed, old white horse and, with a crooked smile, walked toward her. His blousy black pants were tucked into black boots. A heavy poncho in natural colors of beige, black and white wool hung to below his knees. Removing his flat black hat, black as his bushy mustache, he asked, "Señorita Ana Mahoney?"

"*Si, pero yo no hablo español.*" Anyone could learn to say, fluently, that they didn't speak Spanish.

"*No, no, señorita. Usted habla muy bien,*" he reassured her, his swarthy weathered face beaming a welcome.

The gaucho strapped her bag onto a sled behind his horse, explained to the driver what she was to do, then climbed back on his horse and rode away through a trail in the woods.

Anne followed her driver to the lodge, where a natural flaxen blonde with a Dutch bob measured Anne for rental boots and skis. The perky girl—from Brazil, she said—picked up her own skis and swung them up on her shoulders.

"What is your name? Mine is Valeria." She led the way. "I will show you to Los Techos."

Valeria's words were smothered in the deadening silence of puffed snow, falling as furiously as a blanket of dandelion seeds tipped over and shaken. The women stepped into their skis and glided easily to the chair lift. Hunched into the onslaught of tickling white, they continued from the first chair lift to a second. Anne could make out light-barked trees, probably more beeches, but she couldn't see much more in the heavy swirl of flakes.

Her ski pants were covered with giant tears of melted snow waiting to cry down her legs, but chilled immobile to the stretch material. The cold metal of the chair numbed her bottom. Snow bit her face.

"It's not far," encouraged her athletic guide, wife of an Argentine skier. They headed down through a wide run in the woods. Anne kept her eye on the tiny pink figure dashing ahead, following her easily. What a difference the week of skiing at Portillo had made. What would have happened if she had arrived there last. Would she have needed rescuing off Garganta? Would she have even met Tavo? By the first of September, when she was due back in L.A., Tavo normally was at his farms organizing contracts.

Garganta had been an unexpected coincidence, or perhaps fate had engineered their meeting. The mystical Swiss analyst, Jung, had written that there was no such thing as coincidence. And during their helicopter ride to the Cristo, Tavo had spoken on the same theme. "History fascinates me," he had said as they flew over the highway the Incas had built. "I am intrigued by steady, predictable trends interrupted by unexpected coincidences."

Anne had turned around in the copilot's seat to face him. She liked looking at his cheerful, guarded handsomeness. "You are unexpected," she had allowed.

His steady eyes had been serious as he replied, "You, Ana, *ama*, are the unpredicted coincidence in my life."

Valeria called to Anne just then, though the wind whipped away her words.

"What?" Anne skied close.

"Can you smell the fireplaces of Los Techos?"

Anne held her glove out a few inches in front of her face to shield her nose from the attacking storm, breathing deeply. It was wonderful: burning logs, warmth, a toasty fire.

"They have fabulous *asado* on their grills—steaks, chicken, fat sausages. My husband and I eat lunch up here every day," the lively blonde said.

"We always had *asado* for lunch at Portillo. I loved it," said Anne.

"A sort of asado," Valeria corrected with a friendly glance. "If you can call it that with Chilean beef. How their poor cows struggle on rocky hilly pastures! This is your first time to Argentina, *no cierto?* Wait until you taste the steaks of the pampas. Then you will know *asado.*"

"I can't wait," Anne admitted. "I didn't have time to eat breakfast. I'm starving."

"Bueno," and they were off, aggressively aimed

directly down the hill, the fall line, Anne had learned. *Turn, turn, turn,* she coached herself as Lunch had, toward the lights.

Then they were there.

A leggy black-haired woman in her early thirties enthusiastically greeted their knock. "Come in at once and get out of that miserable snow. You must be freezing!" Her curly hair flared out in bouncy layers, framing her sunny face and its peekaboo dimples.

"Hola, hola." She kissed Valeria's rosy cheeks. "This snow is delightful, no? And good for business. How is your handsome bridegroom?"

The snowy guide laughed. "Still handsome. He is waiting for me, so I will leave you now, you understand?" With a brushing kiss goodbye on the other woman's cheeks, Valeria disappeared into the snow.

A slim hand, warm as its owner, was extended to Anne. "I am Claudia Leonardo," her hostess said. "Welcome to our lodge. You must be wet and cold and hungry after your journey. Would you like to wring yourself dry?" She didn't wait for Anne's obvious agreement. "I will send the girl with tea and some fresh cakes in, what—would half an hour suit you? More? Less? You have such a pretty figure, Ana. You are probably one of those lucky women who eats constantly and still looks wonderful."

Anne felt safe, at home, not a fugitive stranger. "You're kind, Claudia. But I'm one of those people who believed 'Thin Thighs in 30 Days,' but conveniently forget the rules. Give me half an hour, maximum." Then Anne remembered her Latin manners. Claudia had an exceptional shape, slim and rounded, and she complimented her on it.

"The boredom of diets is universal, no?" Claudia's dimples added charm to her laugh. "Come. I will show you around a bit on the way to your room."

The Leonardos' oddly angled lodge had the clean lines and light birch walls of elegantly simple Scandinavian design. Primitive Indian weavings in earthy tones hung on the walls. Two were twenty-foot masterpieces, suspended alongside uncurtained two-story windows, while others were rugs on the polished floors.

Anne's room, one of eight in the small lodge, was chic and comfortable. There were reading lights on both sides of the bed, as well as smooth birch stands for books. Guests here were obviously readers.

"We usually dine about nine-thirty. Will you join my husband, Luis Alberto, and me?" asked her exuberant hostess, and then was gone.

The gaucho had already set Anne's luggage on a rack by her closet, so she took the time to soak in the tub before hanging her sodden ski clothes on the shower rail.

There was a knock on the door. A young Indian girl was waiting on the other side with a steaming pot of tea and four varieties of sliced cake: thickly buttered pound cake, a fat slice of Black Forest, rolls of chocolate and vanilla and a tart lemon. Anne was boggled by the temptations and resisted only as long as it took to sit down at the small table and spread a blue cloth napkin on her lap.

Anne had learned to take advantage of tea time and late dinners. She napped and read recent French and Italian magazines, and dozed again. Then she was ready to dine; it was nearly ten. Dinner was an animated affair for seven led by Luis Alberto, a jovial dark blonde who was filled with as much fun and conversation as his wife. While they feasted on local rabbit pâté and succulent venison served with tiny potatoes and spicy red cabbage, the Argentine skiers talked passionately about economics, politics, hemlines and Rousseau's eighteenth-century essay on man's inherent goodness emerging when he returns to nature.

"For this reason Claudia and I left Buenos Aires," said Luis Alberto, passing another bottle of Mendozan Beaujolais. "I did not want to run my father's factory. Let my brother do it. I want to raise my children in the character-building air of the mountains...."

Candles flickered late into the night as the Albertos talked with their guests. The glow of the fireplace made sipping espressos and brandies an intimate occasion. With the liquor came truthful reactions to the United States, politely stated so Anne wouldn't be insulted.

"Are you not afraid on the streets?" she was asked. Most of the guests had been to Miami, New York, and several to Los Angeles, too, the three destination cities of Aerolineas Argentinas. They were always afraid in the United States, Anne learned, afraid of dope-addicted muggers and random murderers. Afraid of an imminent world war to rescue faltering economies, a war they were convinced would again devastate the countries north of the equator. Anne discounted their fears even as they puzzled over North American fears to come south.

"It seems to me the reason you— Excuse me. I do not mean you personally, Ana. The reason the North Americans are cold to strangers is that they are sensibly wary," observed the director of sales for the small Buenos Aires branch of a multinational company. He had turned down opportunities to transfer to the San Francisco Bay Area headquarters.

It was an extraordinary discussion, for Anne recognized how naive her assumptions were. If she had ever thought about it, she would have presumed most South Americans were desperate to live in the United States.

Luis Alberto put another log on the fire and poured more brandy. The conversation drifted to the psychological elements of fear, then anxiety, then to a discussion of whether competition was innate. Anne watched the couples lean into one another contentedly, brushing hands to arms, locking eyes when they wanted to make a point. And she envied them.

Some time later, a gust of wind slapping snow against the window signaled an end to the intense conversation.

"What's the weather report for tomorrow?" Anne asked.

"Sunshine and glorious powder!" Claudia responded.

"Bedtime, then," and Anne remembered to add, "I'm certain your slopes are as exciting as the conversation tonight, so I'm eager to experience them."

GLORIOUS WAS AN UNDERSTATEMENT, Anne thought the next morning when she skied alone out of Los Techos and through the beech forest. Long strands of Spanish moss flocked with new-fallen snow swayed as she passed; the color was magical, a pale chartreuse. Then all was still except the soft squeak of her skis.

She came to a rise on the ridge, gaping at the blue view. Her tips crossed, and she nearly tripped over. Fingers of clear blue lakes snaked through the midnight-blue valley below, the blue rising higher than the mountain where she stood, a cobalt line high on the horizon. Two white volcanos interrupted the even edge of the hills; one volcano was jagged like a broken tooth, while the other was a perfect Häagan-Daz vanilla-ice-cream cone.

At the bottom of the run, a friendly architect with a goatee like a Spanish grandee shared her chair lift. He was on holiday with an Argentine tourist company that owned the ski area. His group was staying in a hotel in San Martin, he said, and he encouraged Anne to come down on their bus, swim outdoors with them—"Sometimes we sing under the stars"—and dine and dance.

She smiled. "Maybe," and sat back quietly, listening. Two small creeks, one on each side of them, gurgled stereophonically.

Later in the morning Anne skillfully edged down a hill of moguls, savoring her confidence. All around her skiers tumbled, the soft snow made them giggling snowmen. She rounded a bend of powdery bumps and heard shouts of laughter and encouragement. A log-cabin bar was off to the side of the trail. A couple dozen skiers were sprawled outside on the snow, basking in the sunshine with bottles of cola and orange pop.

Anne joined them, braking with a sharper turn than she had intended. Fresh powder sprayed the happy strangers. She couldn't understand their gibes as they brushed themselves off, but she recognized their friendliness and their gestures to join them.

A freckled law student, a soccer player, he somehow conveyed, wearing a purple sweater that made his blue eyes seem violet, bought her a cold drink. Anne felt sublime. Was hiding out always such fun?

ON THE AFTERNOON OF ANNE'S SECOND DAY in San Martin, after she and Claudia had gorged themselves on charred, rare, three-inch-thick strip sirloins and fresh salad, they sat out in the hot tub and talked of love.

"Tell me your opinion, Ana. I have a belief that a woman, or a man, is different in every relationship. That with one kind of man you behave one way, and with another you have a different temperament."

"I don't think so, Claudia. People are born with a personality." Anne scissored her legs gently, stirring the water. "You get modified by your families when you're little, but I'm with the Jesuits and the psychiatrists. You're solidly who you are by the time you enter school."

"I used to believe that, too, until I met Luis Alberto. My father is quite stern. He is a Yugoslavian Argentine and he disapproved of too much merriment, so we were quiet at home."

"You quiet, Claudia?"

"I tell you, yes, Ana. And at the university I always had very serious boyfriends, usually engineers, and I was serious like them. I remember one—Carlo. His parents had emigrated from Milan. He was too handsome. Claudia and Carlo—it is marvelous, no? I thought we were meant for each other. But I was all the time so with him—" Claudia struck a Vogue pose and raised one carefully waxed eyebrow aristocratically.

Anne laughed. "My dear, you were elegant. I hope Carlo appreciated you."

"Who knows, Ana. You know engineers. They are preoccupied *constantemente*, as we say. Always, always, always *preocupado* with themselves. He constantly talked about this project and that paper, how tired he was from working so much on important things. Phew. When I think I might have married Carlo...."

Anne listened closely. She knew the situation. "What happened? You and Luis Alberto are so ebullient. Both of you."

"What happened proves my hypothesis. I met Luis Alberto in an anthropology course about the Mapuces at the university." At Anne's questioning look, Claudia digressed. "They are the Indians around here, very much like your Plains Indians. Those are Mapuche weavings on our walls. The Chileans call them Araucanians and refer to their language as Mapuche. Have you heard of them?"

Anne laughed and rolled her eyes skyward. "Heard! Only every time the bank's driver mentions the Incas and I hear again how his quote, 'fierce,' unquote Araucanian ancestors stopped the Incas, the Spanish, the Chilean armies dead in their tracks. So, speaking of conquests, what happened when you and Luis Alberto met?"

"We were full of fun immediately. I appreciated how I felt free to express myself with him. I like myself much better now. What is your experience, Ana? What do you think?"

Anne watched a delicate breeze swing the lacy strands of moss. "My boyfriend is a politician, Claudia. You would like Charles's political goals. He cares about the right things." Anne considered. "But I'm not sure you would like him."

"Why not? I like you, and you are in love with him, no?"

"Yes, I'm in love with him...well...." Anne fiddled

with the coral straps on her bikini top, distracted by the memory of the flash of color tucked in the smooth stretch of Tavo's swimsuit.

"Ah...yes. I'm in love with him. Charles is the first man I've met who didn't bore me after a while. He's bright and handsome and exciting when he's back in Los Angeles— I forgot to tell you he's a congressman, Claudia, so he's in Washington most of the time. When he's home, though, we have a great time. He knows good food, places where roasted duck is perfectly crisp yet still juicy, things like that. And we get together with interesting people...."

"This Charles sounds preoccupied with his pleasures."

Anne's laughter was short. A subtle listener could hear distress behind the mirth. "Always. Crazy, isn't it? I thought it was sexy at first—you know, he was busy doing important things, and I was busy writing about important things, and we were on the same energy track."

"How are you with him? As you are now?"

Anne reached out of the round tub, made a snowball from a drift by the side and tossed it at a tree. It hit and shattered.

"No. Charles and I are like you and Carlo were. He never says anything when I'm too emotional, but...."

"He makes silences, and you understand what he is saying."

"Mmm." Anne nodded. "Do you really believe you can be different when you meet someone more... uh...not like Luis Alberto, exactly, Claudia, but more—"

Claudia crowed, and her dimples flashed. "Ana. You

are so intelligent and yet totally refreshing. Who is he? You have met someone wonderful on this holiday, no? He must be Latin and without question he finds you enchanting, because you are, with your compelling eyes and floating hair."

"I'm not in love with him. We just met last week."

"Ana, Ana, who says love is sensible?"

"You sound like Tavo."

"And you sound like a woman in love. So I am going to drive you mad, Ana. No...." She held up her hands in a dramatic gesture. "This is a torture. You cannot tell me a single word about him. How chiseled his features are, how blue his eyes—"

"How do you know they're blue?" Anne interrupted, suspicious.

"Gustavos are supposed to have silvery-blond hair and blue, blue eyes." Claudia side-stepped the question. "Now. We shall be sensible Saxons, even though you are Irish and should know better than to trust your ration. You must have faith in your unrational mind, Ana. But let us consider my theory. Are you the same with Tavo as you are with Charles the congressman?"

"Well, if we're going to be serious...." Anne groped her way around the tub until she faced the laughing Claudia.

"Okay. I'll word associate. When I'm with Tavo I'm safe, happy, giggling, serious, intelligent, secure, surprised, angry, hurt, sometimes.... Intrigued, exhilarated, aroused, pretty.... But don't all Latin men make a woman feel pretty?"

"It depends on the man," Claudia said. "They all try, and some accomplish it. Aroused? Ana, is it rude to inquire? Why are you here alone?"

Anne moved her big toe around like the periscope of an aimless submarine and watched it through teary eyes. "It hurts more when there's so much... everything's so... passionate." She sighed. "Tavo said he loved me and maybe he proposed, but Claudia, I'm sure he didn't because it makes no sense—" Anne caught Claudia's impatient look and smiled wryly. "I know, I know. But feelings that happen this fast are only infatuation."

"How do you know—"

Now it was Anne's turn to gesture "Stop." "Something dreadful happened, Claudia. I finally began trusting Tavo and I opened my heart...."

"You told him that you loved him? No, you would not. You admitted you had a deep attraction for him?"

"No, not that exactly, Claudia. I told him important things about myself that I've never told anyone. And all the time it seemed like we were sharing— I mean, it wasn't a monologue by me. I know it wasn't. *Was it?* And then my last night in Portillo, I learned he'd deliberately kept the most basic factors in his life a secret from me, because I'm—" Anne flinched again from Tavo's nasty attack. She modified his tormenting words. "I'm a reporter."

"Do you realize what you are telling me, Ana? Tavo told you he loved you, that he wants to marry you— okay, maybe wants to marry you— and you are outraged that he shared no intimate details of his life. While you...." Claudia clasped her hands over her heart, exasperated. "You gave him precious secrets and refused to tell him that you love—*por favor*—have an infatuation with him."

Anne considered. "Yes... and no," she insisted, and

set her full lips stubbornly. "It is better to cut it off clean."

Claudia's jolly brown eyes grew somber. "Maybe he meant...."

" 'If wishes were horses, beggars might ride.' I wish, Claudia, that he'd stop haunting me. Every time I see a certain jawline, I look twice and quiver. I get goose bumps, literally, every time I see—" she grinned sheepishly, grabbed a towel dried her face "—silvery blond hair and blue, blue eyes.... Enough."

Anne hoisted herself out of the tub. "The day's too nice to waste. Let's go ski."

THE PINK SKY OF SUNSET had changed to the lavender of dusk when the knock came on the door. Anne started. Her mind was adrift with the evening star rising outside her window.

The servant handed her an insulated box when she opened the door.

"Muchas, gracias. Usted es un gaucho," Anne thanked him. Dinner conversations had alerted her that to be called a gaucho was the highest compliment to an Argentine's generosity. The stubby man looked very pleased with himself. He also looked curious.

No more curious than me, Anne thought, and opened the taped lid. Nestled in a bed of velvet moss was a clump of wild violets.

Anne showed them to the gaucho, her hands trembling eagerly. *"Cómo...?"* She didn't know how to say, "How did Gustavo Mohr de la Huerta find me?" *"Gracias,"* she repeated, and closed her door. She wanted to be alone to read his letter.

You are like a young fox in the spring, Ana, standing alert in a mossy glade, your cinnamon eyes shy and wise, wary and free, and alone. Come to me, please. I am empty without you.

How can a man who knows nothing know? Anne had a terrible longing to see him. Her head felt light. She caught her breath, and then the disturbing realization surfaced. How did Tavo know where she was? Where was he? In San Martin? At Los Techos? How did he know where she was hiding?

"You told him," Anne accused Claudia. The older woman put down the flowers she was arranging in the dining room.

"Told who, what?"

"Gustavo Mohr de la Huerta. You do know him, right? How else could you describe his coloring when we were in the hot tub?" Anne was furious.

Claudia looked guilty. "It did not seem appropriate just then to mention that we know Tavo."

"Why did you tell him I was here?" Anne's tone was bitter. "Couldn't you resist matchmaking? He'll jump out of a cake tonight—surprise! Dessert for me, even if I don't want it? Oh, Claudia, I trusted you."

"Ana, I did not tell Tavo you are here with us. Perhaps he called Luis Alberto." She shrugged. "I don't know. My husband did not say one word—not one to me. As far as I know, Tavo Mohr is nowhere near Argentina. Luis Alberto said nothing about another guest for dinner. Your hideout is safe for tonight."

"But tomorrow?"

"Do you want to see him or not?"

"So much that I don't dare." Anne's clouded eyes cleared. "And don't you tell him that, Claudia! I'd better make my escape tomorrow. What time does the bus leave for Bariloche?"

"Early. I will take you down. At 6:30, Ana. That way Luis Alberto will have no idea what we have done. But truly, I do not think Tavo trespassed on Luis Alberto's friendship. It is not like him."

Claudia picked up the daisies and irises and continued making small bouquets for bud vases on the dining-room tables. Anne watched her quietly for a time and finally asked shyly, "What is Tavo like?"

"Fabuloso." Claudia's graceful fingers with their long lacquered nails waved expressively. "In every way. Tavo Mohr is an extraordinary, loyal friend. We love him."

Do I, Anne wondered the next morning, leaning her forehead against the bus window as she followed dawn spreading across the buttes and plains of Patagonia. Shrubs similar to Colorado greasewood and sagebrush, merged from the gloom of late night into the sunshine of day.

She had no answer. She didn't know how to label the turmoil she felt.

"But you care for him, Ana. Please, do not hurt him unnecessarily." Claudia had surprised her that morning when she drove her to the bus depot. "You have a strong heart, and he is—"

"He's not weak, Claudia," Anne had protested. "That's what I mean," she added impatiently. "I don't know anything about him. How is Tavo weak?"

"Not in usual ways. Tavo has mind strength, which is

why, if he wants you, Ana, I am convinced he will win eventually."

She turned a radiant smile on Anne. "And that will be wonderful for us, because we are very taken with you, and our friendship can continue. But I am afraid about hurt and pain in the meanwhile, for your heart is strong and his is like a spiderweb of cracks on a porcelain vase."

Anne was listening intently, so Claudia went on. "When I first met Tavo, I was a bride; his paternal grandmother had recently died—from cancer, I think. Tavo stopped in Buenos Aires after the funeral on his way back to the university in Munich and stayed with us. The suffering in his eyes, those blue, blue eyes you spoke of, Ana, was terrible. The señora Mohr was a mother for him after his parents and brother died in the earthquake.

"Ana, if you do not love him, and if, as he told you, he loves you, protect him from yourself. Keep away. Do not always believe what he displays. A few years ago, when his grandfather, Don Jacobo Mohr, had his heart attack, Tavo's eyes showed nothing. . . ."

TELEPHONE POLES merged in the light of day and blurred through the windows of the short speeding bus. Anne counted distractedly. Nine, ten. . . . The poles looked like they marched south to the Antarctic, hundreds, thousands of poles. Twenty, twenty-one. . . thirty-five. . . . Tavo would be thirty-six on the twenty-fifth of November. . . thirty-seven.

How old was Tavo when the earthquake hit? Twelve? How soon did the ground split apart after Liliana's birthday, when she gave him the bracelet. Anne felt the copper on her lips again, warm with the heat of his eagerness the ill-fated night that their passion had swept toward conclusion, only to be swept away.

Anne wiped the bus window clean with her sleeve and pressed her mouth against the chilly glass. Her lips cooled instantly, but her memories were not as easily numbed.

The blue Patagonian sky was less vivid than the blue of his eyes. Were the de la Huertas blue-eyed Spaniards or brown? Who were the Mohrs? Was Tavo a sternly raised eldest son, or the coddled youngest? Why did he study in Germany? Why couldn't she order her mind still? When Stephanie died she could.

Now tears stung Anne's eyes. She dreaded going home.

Four bleak hours later the bus rounded the far end of a lake and drove into a town of hand-planted pines, steeply gabled roofs and carved Tyrolean balconies. Behind the homes and hotels were snowy upthrusts of rock reminiscent of the Grand Tetons or the Alps. The bus headed through a gray stone arch in a Teutonic city center with a six-story clock tower at one end. They could have been anywhere in Germany.

"San Carlos de Bariloche," announced the driver, and parallel parked.

Window-shoppers in ski parkas glanced at the disembarking passengers. Anne didn't notice. She bundled into her parka, settled her oversized purse on one shoulder and slung her small suitcase over the other. Outside, she paused on the sidewalk and sniffed in surprise. The air was heavy with the rich smell of chocolate.

"Thank you for coming."

There was no mistaking Tavo's formal, slightly accented baritone.

CHAPTER EIGHT

HE WAS SMILING his cheerful, proud smile, his very best smile. The force of his unbounded welcome captivated Anne; she had forgotten its power. He was larger than she had remembered—taller, broader in the shoulders, his tan more golden, his thickly waved hair more blond. Only the clear intelligent blue of his eyes had held steadfast against her memory's efforts to diminish all things about him.

Anne wanted him as she had never wanted another man. She had to touch him, to press against the familiar warmth of his chest, her arms squeezing around his waist so he could never go. She fiercely needed to absorb him into her body, yet when that happened, Anne knew with terrible certainty, that she would share a part of herself. Share? She would in part be "we," one. She wanted that, oh, yes, surely she had always wanted the most tender results of union. And just as surely she held back.

Tavo transferred her heavy bags from her rigid shoulders to one of his.

Vehement desire clashed with a reckless last-ditch fear. Anne fought for her self. "Did it take you three days to find me?" Her tone was disparaging even as she wedged her hands in the pockets of her brown corduroy pants, truculently controlling their impulse to stroke the welcome of his mouth.

Then, irrationally patient, she waited to see in which direction they were supposed to walk. Anne had no doubt Tavo had arranged one lovely room with perfect ambience. Neither did she doubt he wouldn't answer the essence of her question: if he wanted her, what had taken him so long? And so the forthrightness of his response startled her, for she had also forgotten his disarming frankness.

"It did not take three days to find you." He set out along the flagstone sidewalk calmly, expecting her to follow. "It took me two days to decide whether I wanted to. I expect jealousy in love, and passion and willing participation and occasional anger. But I did not like the senseless fury you roused in me."

"Doesn't fit your regulated self-image?" Anne goaded, and although she regretted her snipe she couldn't help her scowl. "How did you find me? Did your friend Luis Alberto squeal?"

Her acute peripheral vision caught his genuine smile set, but his big hand rested casually on her neck, his index finger curled intimately under the collar of her parka. "I did not involve the Leonardos in our personal affairs, Ana. It is my confidentiality how I found you. I do not—" his sudden laughter teased "—reveal my sources. You did like Luis Alberto and Claudia, no, sweetheart?" Was his tone slightly anxious? If so, it was a minute lapse.

"I hope you look forward to our encounters as much as the three of us do," he went on. "They will be over to stay with us in the middle of November, a couple of weeks before we begin the craziness of nectarine harvest."

Stay with us? Another oblique proposal?

"Luis Alberto has dragged me away from work to play ever since he began coming over for summer holidays with his aunt and uncle. They lived next door to my grandparents in Santiago."

So that was where the two men met. Tavo had revealed a personal detail as easily as The Talker she had created. Yes. No. Was she supposed to decide? Panic closed her windpipe. *I can't.* Anne coughed—shallow desperate coughs. November. That was only three months away.

It would be fun to see Claudia and Luis Alberto again, to cook them a very California dinner and repay their hospitality. What would she serve? Broiled chicken and artichokes with a lemony butter sauce. Did they sell artichokes in Chile? *No, no. I've got to go home.*

With her tongue Anne battled for emotional distance. "Why don't you leave me alone, Gustavo Mohr?" She refused to walk any further with him. "Obviously I do not wish to continue our . . . our acquaintance."

"Come, come, Ana O'Mahoney. Say it. Our relationship. Our anticipated affair."

She balked. "No, I won't say it. I do not anticipate an affair." *Your nose is going to grow long with that lie, Mahoney,* she thought. *An Irish Pinocchio. He likes subterfuge,* she justified the fib. *Well, that's mine.*

"And I am not shy, either," she added.

To Anne's chagrin, she blushed. Two of his wild violets were preserved in her passport wallet like purple hearts, a memory of . . . no, not cowardice. A symbol of the courage to escape temporary hormonal insanity.

If you are not shy, Ana, it will be simple for you to

tell me what passed through your mind just now that caused your muscles to tense. I can feel them." Stubbornly he hadn't loosened his hold on her neck. He maintained the physical contact as if it was the most comfortable, natural thing in the world for him.

"Demonstrate your bravery, for me. Come, we will have a cup of hot chocolate, and you will tell me what made your eyes shine."

He guided her into a quaint café, ornate as a cuckoo clock with merry red-and-green trim. Inside, tables were covered with green tablecloths, which were layered in turn in red cloths set at diamond angles. A fire crackled in a shiny copper fireplace, a popping background syncopation to the lilting tape of Viennese violins. No one, least of all Anne, could remain unmoved by the holiday atmosphere.

"Remember how rude I was when I thought you were an Austrian ski instructor?" Anne's mobile features were pensive. The demure soft rose of her turtleneck sweater contrasted vividly with the dark rosy tan of her cheeks.

"Oh, how you delighted in your German insults. 'Break a leg'!" Tavo shed his suede bomber jacket and stretched his long legs out their full length. He grinned, a wholesome North American grin.

His face looked younger when he was amused, as he was now. Almost carefree and nearly open, if you knew the signs to watch for, thought Anne, studying him.

"I remember the look on your face, Ana, when you pretended you were standing on Garganta's headwall enjoying the view and would take your own pleasurable time coming down— *'Auf Wiedersehen.'*"

They shared a smile, and the poignant moment, lit by the embers of the fire, tarried.

Anne reached across the vivid tablecloths to settle her right hand on Tavo's. "Warm hands, cold heart." Her mind was meandering.

"You were wrong about my nationality," Tavo's banter shifted abruptly. "Do you also delude yourself that my heart is cold?"

Anne's index finger absentmindedly circled each weathered, fifty-cent-sized knuckle. "All right, Tavo," she said at last, not raising her eyes from his hands. "No. I think your hands are warm and your heart is hot...." *And cracked. Protect him.* She heeded Claudia's warning and attempted a little humor. "Sometimes your hands are even hotter. And all right, I have enjoyed them. But Tavo, that is not the point."

A round waitress poured steaming cocoa into two translucent china cups from a copper pot with a short fat spout. Anne pretended a quiet serenity. *Give me time,* she pleaded, scooping a demitasse spoon into the frothy chocolate. She pursed her lips and blew on the rich liquid to cool it sufficiently to sip. The delay gave her time to think. She had no idea what her answer was. Had he even asked the question?

Tavo didn't ease her way. He, too, remained quiet.

"I've never tasted better cocoa," she said. Next a neutral question. "Why do I smell chocolate everywhere?"

"Bariloche has six or seven small chocolate factories. But Ana, I am not easily deterred. What is the point, Ana? Please." His keen eyes held hers. "This is important to me. The point is that you love me, no?"

His directness never failed to unsettle her. "Love?

Affection...." Tavo's remonstrative stare stiffened her vocabulary. "Listen, stop leaning on me. Okay." She accelerated. "The point is I'm terribly attracted to you, and—"

"Terribly?"

"Okay, terrifically." Her resolve began crumbling. "Okay, okay—you already know, Tavo. I'm insanely attracted to you." She snapped out her final admission. "Does that satisfy you?"

Anne didn't have to ask. He exhaled with a boyish grin. What a pretense. Anne didn't believe for an instant that doubt had entered his mind. She felt unilaterally vulnerable. "No" was always easier to say—damn the consequences—and thus cornered, she battled him.

"And...." Her voice was cool. He leaned back, relaxed, with his hands behind his head, challenging her to pop his balloon. She sharpened her stiletto. "Love...." She repeated the word to show she was unafraid of it. "Love has nothing to do with anything. The hunt is over, Tavo. You have kept your armor secure around your secrets. I am totally exposed. You won."

Then by-line Anne Mahoney, page-one star, stabbed a fatal wound for victory. She didn't wait to see the effects of her charge, to notice whether Tavo had resolved to allow her into his private corners. After all, he had told her about Luis Alberto, but she ignored the clues. Fear of an unknown future prevailed.

"I will miss you, yes, Tavo, when I return to Los Angeles to my boyfr—my fiancé in...what's today, the twenty-third? In nine days. But I *shall* return to him."

To her astonished dismay, Tavo's pupils glazed in pain, swelled and threatened to overtake the irises, then withered to black specks. Students of psychology would know the Chilean giant had seen a problem and solved it. Anne, a political-science major, saw only disinterest.

He reached for her hands and kissed each palm. "I release you, *mi ama*." With a profound sigh he abandoned her hands. "We have both lost. *Bueno*." His tone was flat. He paid the bill and, rising from the table, said, "I have reservations for two rooms overlooking the lake, Anne. Shall we take your bag there?"

"Two?" Sudden inexplicable tears fringed her dusky lashes. Anne pulled a tissue out of her purse to blow her nose.

Tavo laughed with a glimmer of his careless charm and ruffled her hair. "Arrangements can be made for one, if you prefer," he said, holding her chair.

"That wasn't what I meant. I was just surprised, after all your efforts to track me down, that you reserved rooms for two."

"Anne, I have a certain hunger for you, but it is manageable."

"Look how you change the subject," she snapped, feeling the fool when faced with his contained reactions. "You aren't telling me why two rooms, are you? Two rooms are...were...another seduction trick no, Tavo? You make me crazy with your secrets."

He ridiculed her. "Secrets? There is no mystery. We share a suite, Anne. You can lock your door or you can leave it unlocked. And—" his icy blue eyes were bland "—I have the same privilege."

THE HOTEL WAS MODERN—marble floors in the lobby, chrome chairs padded with real leather. Glass in the living room of their suite began at the carpeting and ended at the ceiling, two stories of windows overlooking a lake with no far shore in sight.

"The name of the lake is Nahuel Huapí." Tavo answered Anne's reasonable question in kind after the porter had deposited his luggage in the downstairs bedroom. They followed the athletic stride of the husky young man through the two-story living room and up the wide stairs to one of two bedrooms on the second floor, where the porter set down Anne's leather bag.

Tavo stared out the glass wall in Anne's room, his back to her, and repeated the word. "Naw-well Wah-pee. It is Mapuche."

So what.

She joined him at the window. Sunshine sparkled on the crest of small waves lapping the pebbled shore below. Dense green hills to the north reached into the deep water, dark brawny arms of impermeable green fjords.

Anne questioned him for details—the depth of the lake, the length, the vegetation—feigning interest. Tavo was the consummate tour guide, and she hated him for his dispassionate replies.

When he glanced at his gold wristwatch and suggested she call the bank's driver with their itinerary so they could go on to the slopes, Anne refused.

"*We're* leaving tomorrow?" She was as contrary as possible. "Are *you* leaving tomorrow? I intend staying a few more days."

"Pascal's race has been set next week to suit your schedule. You want to be back in Portillo for that, do you not?" Tavo's indifference was solid. "Radámes is expecting you. You seem to be one of the few, perhaps the only one, who bridges the worry of the grandfather

and the rebellion of the grandson. Of course, Anne...
this situation is really—what is your expression, no skin
off your bottom—''

"Nose—"

"Oh, yes, nose." Veiled eyes revealed nothing.

"Naturally I'm going to be in Portillo for the races,"
she said. She didn't add that she probably would have
been there even if they hadn't moved the date forward,
even if Pascal hadn't begged a promise from her. She
would have called Snider and taken another couple of
vacation days. In truth, she wouldn't have given up her
last chance to gaze upon this fascinating man. Unconsciously, she flicked her tongue over her dry lips, moist-
ening them back to softness.

"What?" She started. His voice had ended on a question. "I'm sorry. I was thinking about the view."

"Wear layers. The summit at Bariloche is lower in altitude than the lowest slope at Portillo, but winds come
up quickly down here. I will call for you in twenty
minutes."

And he was gone. Without a friendly kiss on the
cheek, or one of his devastating backward glances that
caught hers and held the instant for an eternity, or a
smile or anything. Anne strode to the door leading to
the hallway in the suite and locked it with a defiant
snap.

Carlos Luzzini muffled his surprise when Anne informed him over the phone that there would be two passengers waiting for him on August 26 at the Hotel Peréz
Rosales in Puerto Montt. Peréz. Like Liliana Peréz. Undoubtedly the brittle widow lurked somewhere, ready to
pick up the pieces of Tavo. Except he didn't look shattered.

Anne refused to fill in the blank of Luzzini's inquisitive silence. Perhaps that desperately wanted, unwanted other passenger would depart as suddenly as he had come, and no one would ever know his identity, nor his intention.

"*Chau, chau, Carlos. 'Ta luego.* See you later." Anne ended the conversation.

She rummaged through the few ski clothes she'd culled from the many to bring along—something special. *Eat your heart out, Tavo Mohr.* Why wasn't he more upset? She felt awful. She stepped into a clinging lightweight raspberry one-piece suit. Her skin flushed rose with the color. The Italian design refined the distinct dips and swells of her body, and she was satisfied with the effect.

Tavo's footsteps on the carpeted stairs within the suite were deliberate. There was no rattle to her locked doorknob when he tried to enter. He turned it once. His muffled retreat into the other bedroom on her floor was unrushed. Then, silence. Why hadn't he humbled himself and knocked? It irritated her. Where had he gone?

Deliberately she unzipped the raspberry suit midway down the rounded cleft of her breasts. She wrapped a dreamy silk scarf around her throat, flinging the extravagant long streamers over her shoulders. *And that to you, Liliana,* she thought, flawlessly prepared for the next encounter.

This time Tavo knocked on the hallway door. The rap was quiet, but the boldness in his eyes when he saw her provocative attire was not. Anne affected nonchalance.

"Ready?" She asked.

"Occasionally."

She glanced at him quickly. His demeanor was innocent, while Anne was embarrassed by her unruly lustfulness. She wanted to stare at Tavo, to devour the effect of black racing pants stretched tight and a black hand-knit sweater with its subtle design of deer in a misty forest. Mourning black. The effect was sinful against the moonlight of his hair. She longed to run her tongue greedily into his ear. It always made him gasp, made him mortal.

He understood her brazen hunger; she could tell. Was he now going to warn her that she'd better zip a little higher or catch a chest cold, his deep voice caressing the word "chest"?

Tavo closed the door behind her and reverted to the remoteness of information. "Hummel deer are scarce now. You probably ate a type of European red deer at the Leonardos."

Anne flagrantly eyed him, but he was already striding down the hotel hallway. Hurriedly she joined him.

"They were plentiful on the Argentine pampas and on our wetter side of the Andes, too, but no more. They—"

"Who?" Disappointment seeped through her breathlessness.

"Hummel deer." Tavo didn't wait for the elevator. He briskly took the steps, and Anne doggedly stuck by his side.

"What about them?" *Deer? Who wanted to talk about deer?*

"You were scrutinizing the design on my sweater, so I assumed that you wanted to know about the deer." He was admirably guileless. Anne felt like a naughty girl caught with her hand in the cookie jar, and was mute.

"I bought the sweater in Bariloche last June." He unlocked the door on a black Japanese rental car and held it open for her. "There are many expert knitters in Bariloche, a hundred or more. This one was made by a gifted woman who typically wins the prizes. When we come back from the ski area tonight, Anne, we can visit her shop. You might find presents for your family."

Anne braced herself for a gibe about what size Charles Roderick wore. Instead Tavo concentrated on pulling out into the busy two-lane highway rimming the lake. "If you have any brothers and sisters who are chocolate fanatics, you are in fat city." His grin was angelic.

"My little brother is an addict," Anne told him, sorry that Tavo had no family to buy gifts for. She didn't want him to know she had pried elsewhere, so she pretended ignorance and asked if he had any brothers or sisters. She expected a bristly no followed by a measured, boring discourse on the depth of Nahuel Huapí.

"My brother, Alvaro, died nearly twenty years ago with my parents during a 7.4 earthquake in Puerto Montt. They were in a new concrete building in the center of town, visiting a lawyer who handled my grandmother's farm. The structure collapsed. Twenty-two people were killed."

Anne felt his aged pain as though it were her own. She blocked mental images of deadly clouds, of concrete dust and broken bodies, seeing the disaster with the bruised vision of a professional. She touched his arm. Her sympathy apparently surprised him, for the knotted muscle jerked.

Vermont, and I have observed that a skier dictates to his feet with his character. Gustavo Mohr did not want to die on the slalom course. He was compelled to win. That is entirely different.''

Janko pinched his mirrored sunglasses back up right against the bridge of his nose, a nervous habit, for his mind was elsewhere.

"We were held back by our own temperaments," he continued. "In our envious ignorance, we perceived him as reckless. But no, he was precise. He was single-minded. I have heard stories how the man trained, pushing himself beyond physical barriers, concentrating solely on his studies and his sport.''

Was there no social life, Anne wondered, hesitating to probe in a way by-line Anne Mahoney never would have—only she couldn't resist asking.

Janko hedged. "The boy is the man. Tavo has made time for you, no? Or did you meet on the slopes today and do not know the future? You saw how carefully he protected your reputation. I know nothing. However—" he cast his eyes to the sky "—in my speculations. . . .''

Anne laughed. "There is nothing much to know. We met in Portillo and reconnoitered here.'' Reconnoitered. Good word, she thought, and wisely didn't tag on the ridiculous phrase, "by chance.'' "Tavo loves mysteries. It's his game in life.''

Janko proved no fool with words. "And your profession is solving mysteries. If it were not for your beauty, for your intense eyes that scandalously absorb a man, I would think you and Tavo were drawn together through sheer instinct, like a Geiger counter to uranium, the detectee and the detector.''

Anne seized the piece of puzzle. Of course she'd been

drawn to Tavo. Yin-yang. Hot-cold. A teeter-totter. Now she understood the attraction. Simple opposites. A simple solution. She was armed against his deadly allure. Except she wasn't. She had lost track of why she was protesting. All that lingered was her remembrance that it was vital to leave.

Lunch on the sunny decks developed into a lengthy *asado* with grilled strip sirloins, crisp lettuce and tomato salad loaded with slivers of onion.

Janko poured olive oil into an empty water glass. "Remember how surprised we were in Europe, Tavo, to discover the waiters mixed the dressing?" He squeezed a lemon into the glass, added salt and pepper, whipped it with a fork and poured the dressing over the communal bowl of salad.

"How old were we the first time we competed there, Tavo? Seventeen? Yes. The next year you were in Munich at the university."

Tavo poured red wine into the short-stemmed green glasses. His movements were easy in a way Anne had not noticed before. As she watched, she realized she had never seen him with a friend his age. "Or what of the races in the United States, where the waitresses presented us with bottles of salad dressing?" Tavo grinned.

"That horrible orange syrup they call French!" Janko chuckled. "It almost was not worth having to play guitar for our suppers. French, Thousand Island, Blue Cheese. Coffee and tea and—"

Abruptly Janko raised his glass to Anne. "Suddenly it occurs to me how boorish I must sound. To North America." Then one at a time, he saluted the splendid fjords and lake, the distant patches of fertile grazing land and the volcanic peaks behind them. His eyes returned to

Anne and Tavo. "To us, together in Bariloche. Will we 'reconnoiter' soon?"

"Excellent wine," Anne stalled.

"Anne says they now have light wine in the United States." Tavo helped her sidestep Janko's inquisitiveness, but his aid had a stinging price. "Light beer. Light pop. Light love. *Salud.*"

"*Salud.*" Janko drank heartily.

Anne tossed her head with defiance. Sunlight caught the fired mahogany sparks, and if she had lifted her glasses the men would have witnessed similar sparks in her eyes.

"Light beer tastes better, and it's healthier, and you can drink more." The strain of the afternoon's jousting was having an effect. She didn't have a ready retort. "Our love in the United States isn't light. It's honest," she said simply. It never occurred to Anne that her lie about going home to Charles, her supposed fiancé, belied her protest.

Tavo's eyes were unfathomable torches of blue when she finished. He changed the subject. Anne played with her food after her outburst, her appetite gone.

The time came to wave goodbye to Janko, but when she and Tavo snapped back into their skis, she chose to concentrate on her technique in frustrated silence. Tavo sloughed off her moody message in a preoccupied silence of his own. Eventually, back in town, he freed her for shopping.

Alone, with a task to accomplish, Anne's barometric emotions stabilized. Tavo had said he would call for her at nine to take her for dinner and tango. Back at the hotel, Anne napped restlessly. She awakened clutching a pillow, but her wistful dream was forgotten. At first she downplayed the evening by dressing in jeans, worn leather boots and a navy wool turtleneck. The color muddied her complexion. Good.

Ten minutes passed before she could raise herself from her wallow of unhappiness. Light love, indeed. Who was the one who gave up at the slightest obstacle? *Just try and ignore me, Señor Talker,* she thought, and danced back on the approach-avoidance rat grid.

Thus inspired, Anne pulled a brilliant cayenne jersey out of the closet, a hot-pepper dress she'd been saving. The sensual wool fired her skin; it swirled in a blaze around her slim calves. She tossed a matching felt shawl artfully over her shoulder. Sitting on her bed then, facing the unlocked door that opened into their two-story suite, she was ready to scorch her tormenter.

Tavo's knock came instead at the hallway entrance, a minor disturbance, yet a preview of the evening ahead. For nothing proceeded as Anne had anticipated. Tavo checkmated her every reaction with consistently polite charm. She couldn't tell if he was resigned or unmoved, so she tried harder, unsure of what she was trying for.

They ate Italian food, not Swiss fondue, nor more steaks. Anne rebelliously chewed the scalding-hot, fresh-baked bread drenched in garlic butter, licking butter off her fingers, one at a time for extra garlic.

"They bake wonderful bread here," Tavo said, urging another slice on her, then another. He ate none.

Anne was amused. *Wait until he dances with me,* she thought, eating all her clam linguini with satisfaction. More garlic. She wasn't sure whether his ravioli was rife with the potent bulb, but she knew her breath was knock-out.

It wasn't until 10:37, when she drained the last of her espresso, that qualms penetrated her glee. Why hadn't Tavo eaten garlic? What was he up to? It couldn't be *nothing*, could it? Nothing was crueler even than hate or anger or love.

"Is the place where we're dancing tango near here?" She asked, succeeding, with effort, to maintain an equally detached, diffident facade for a brief moment. She cocooned herself in the flaming felt shawl before he could snuggle it around her ready shoulders, and steeled herself for the challenge of the tango. She could manage calm when he drew her into his arms. Hadn't she poked her hands through incubator portholes and touched a five-month-old premature baby hooked to life-maintaining machines through every orifice? A sexy dance once banned for its lewdness would be a minor event.

She faked an exaggerated yawn to hide her tension.

"Argentines sing tango." Tavo stood up, too, his reaction camouflaged by the concrete of his charming expression.

Sing? Anne denied her disappointment. "Believe me," she fibbed, and knew he knew. "I'd love to hear tango, but I'm very tired. I had to get up at four-thirty this morning to leave San Martin. Perhaps some other time."

And Tavo agreed, unruffled. The hurt Anne had glimpsed in his eyes that morning when she'd told him she was returning to Charles must have been her imagination. Speaking of light love—the hell with him, she resolved, reversing herself.

At her door, Anne forgot the garlic and turned her cheek for a friendly Chilean kiss good night.

"Wie man in den Wald ruft, so kommt's zurück." He shook her hand with a slight click to his heels and a formal bow.

His head was bent. Anne couldn't see if he was making a joke. Regardless, she felt he was making fun of her. She wavered, denying him the pleasure of asking for a translation. "So. What does that mean?" Her dratted curiosity.

"As you shout into the woods, so it returns. Good night, Anne."

She paced, then wrote a cheerful note to Charles and sealed it with a flourish as if it were a talisman, then spent a restless night kicking her bedcovers into a twisted, scrambled mess.

She had shouted, Tavo had listened, and as he'd predicted, they were both losers.

IT WAS MIDMORNING by the time their double-decked steamer nuzzled its white prow into the mist. The weeping sky disappeared into the leaden waters of Nahuel Huapí. Fog shrouded ominous granite cliffs. All was gray and white, from the gulls shrieking the steamer's passage to ruptured waterfalls foaming over mossy precipices. All was gray save the cheery red sweater that miraculously sufficed to keep Tavo warm.

There was something impatient about him this morning, now that their two-day journey over the southern Andes was underway. Some indefinable eagerness.

They would sail nearly forty miles up Nahuel Huapí for lunch at a log hotel named as if it was a town: Puerto Blest, a soggy anchorage overblessed by 156 inches of rain a year—more than double the rainfull of the Amazon. They would bus to the next lake, boat to the next shore—bus, sleep, boat—then bus around yet a fourth lake to Puerto Montt, a city of one hundred twenty thousand rimming a bay on the Pacific, at the end of the world.

Mist caressed Anne's cheeks until she couldn't tell if she was weeping or if the rivulets slowly descending her pinched face were indeed rain. Soon winter winds of late August hurled the mist, stinging Anne's numb cheeks until the gale blew itself out. She didn't notice.

Ashore at Puerto Blest; plump cannelloni laden with rich mild cheeses and three other courses she neither tasted nor remembered passed her lips. The eerie neon green of the second lake, a ten-minute bus ride from the shores of Nahuel Huapí, flowed by merely an iridescent bottom to her despair. Why had she insisted on finish, when all she wanted was time to consider how and why and what next? Her answer to Tavo was yes, not no. But now it was too late.

Tavo strode the decks talking to the other seventy passengers on their excursion. He surveyed elusive views of clouded volcanic peaks from the pilot's cabin. Ashore at the customs station, he analyzed with the Argentine forest rangers a cyclic, fifty-year bamboo blight due in another twenty-six years. He stooped to rub pebbly black lava soil between his fingers. He looked happy.

Anne grieved in the seat she shared with him on the bus. He had offered the window, and she had refused, contentiously forcing him to cramp his long legs in the space built for normal-sized passengers. She sat close to the aisle, at least a few inches away from the charged, unpredictable electric zone between them. A safe few inches, she thought.

With the eternal sleepiness of depression, Anne soon closed her eyes and escaped consciousness. She awakened sometime later, nestled into the long broad curve of Tavo's chest. He had shed his red sweater. She lay still against the dampness of his cotton shirt, her heart beating with his heart. *Did he gather me to him, or did I seek him, unashamed in sleep of admitting my dreadful mistake? Is he untouched by my touch?*

Unwilling to move, Anne continued the slow, rhythmic, trusting breath of sleep; half-closed eyes stared out the large window of the tourist bus. Outside was a Lord of the Rings jungle in a snowfield, a weird rain forest of towering bamboo and giant ferns. Plowed snow banked alongside the narrow black lava road. The bus jounced in an unplowed rut. Anne closed her eyes quickly. She felt Tavo's right arm hold her steady against him. She didn't dare open her eyes again for fear of being caught, and soon her pretense of sleep was unfeigned.

THE THREE-STORY HOTEL PEULLA was situated in a grassy clearing near the eastern shore of Lake Todos Los Santos. They were registered by the great-great nephew of the Chilean Swiss family that had pioneered the lake route over the southern Andes and founded Bariloche. Their rooms were side by side.

"Would you walk with me before dinner, please?" Tavo asked, carrying Anne's bag into her room. He set it down on a stand by the twin beds, pushed together. Perky pink cotton sheets were folded over bright flowered quilts of rose, chartreuse and dark green. Pink-cased pillows marched the length of the joint bedsteads. Anne's gloom disappeared.

A walk, together. She'd like that. "Give me a couple minutes to wash my face," she said. Her hair still dripped; her face was wet from the rain outside. Then she laughed for the first time in two days. "Give me a minute to dry my face, and I'll be ready."

Tavo laughed easily, too, and the sharp tension lines in Anne's face eased.

"It is a good idea to get dry before getting wet," he agreed impishly, as if what he'd said reminded him of a private joke. "I am going to change out of my soaked clothes, as well. *Chau*." For a second Anne thought Tavo was going to kiss her cheek; certainly he hesitated before he left.

Their two showers ran simultaneously, the steaming-hot water thawing Anne's chilled flesh. She heard Tavo shut off the water, and she moved in tandem. She rubbed her face, then her shoulders, then her chest, waist and hips briskly with the towel. Was he drying his legs now, too?

The thought excited her.

They opened their doors coincidentally, yet it wasn't by simple chance, Anne thought, matching his stride down the stairs with a hurried effort. She and Tavo were linked in a chain of coincidences as natural as the breath they drew.

It seemed equally natural that the sun had bullied its way through the shroud of clouds, tumbling them into great puffs of fleecy white.

Anne broad jumped a mud puddle in the graveled road and giggled mischievously. Tavo jumped another. They leaned over the small concrete bridge and watched the churning creek drop swiftly toward the lake. They sauntered past a dozen small frame houses with streaks of green moss on fish-scale shingles of faded aqua, turquoise and pink.

Anne's wet head bobbed below the edge of his shoulder when she took an occasional skip. She was exhilarated without really knowing why. She sensed a conclusion.

They passed a beautifully tended rock garden wall with patches of purple iris and yellow tulips, afterward cutting off on a trail through the dark forest, scrambling down a steep incline. Tavo stepped ahead and held out his hand to help Anne down the roughest part. She considered protesting that she was perfectly capable of walking on her own, but both her fingers and her protest were swallowed up by his warm hands. El Grande. Single-minded, all-star El Grande, who by reputation, willingly sacrificed for what he wanted.

They came upon the falls so abruptly that Anne failed to notice the deceptive quiet in the glade came from the deafening boom of the falling torrents. Rainbow sprays soaked them. It wasn't until Anne relinquished her view of the man she loved that she glimpsed violets nestled under dripping ferns.

Tavo squatted on the edge of the falls. His long arms made cupping water from the cascade effortless. He dipped and drank the icy liquid three times before wiping his mouth on his sleeve.

"Come, Anne, you must be thirsty." Tavo had to shout to be heard.

He held out his hand, and she took it, walking without fear, not caring when the spray became a maelstrom of freezing water and furious winds. She rocked on her heels at the falls, staggered by the force. Tavo grabbed her by the scruff of her trousers so she could bend over safely, almost perpendicular, and bob for water. The melted snow tasted more delicious than anything she could remember. She drank greedily again. Water ran down her chin.

"Once more for luck." Tavo tightened his grip.

"Here's to luck. *Salud*." Choking, she raised a wet happy face to him. Wet hair stuck to her scalp.

He combed the strands back with his fingers, and she realized something important had returned to his eyes. "There is a legend about these falls," he continued, smoothing back her long hair. "Anyone who drinks from them will be married within the year. The point is, Ana. . . that love is the point."

"You're right," she said, sitting back on her heels, drenched in the mist of the raging waterfall. "Yes, of course. Love is the point." She reached for his hand, her face serene now. "Come sit with me and watch the rainbows, Tavo."

It could have been that simple. At first it seemed it was. They walked slowly back to the hotel—or were they running—and not soon enough they were pausing briefly before their two doors. In whose room would they be together? Quickly Anne insisted on hers. "I was the reluctant one. I must welcome you."

And she did.

She welcomed his arms around her trembling body. She welcomed his kisses, chapped dry kisses that reassured her the moment was equally momentous for him, and that he, too, was a trifle fearful. They both had squeezed themselves dry of all hope. They had rushed together and torn themselves apart, endured days of hopeless dreams and nights of wishes. Their pretense of polite indifference for the past two days had taken its toll.

Finally, his moister kisses in the sensitive hollows of her shoulders exploded Anne's cautious responses. Fired blood surged up from her center, an uncoiled burning from her thighs to her throat.

They scrambled to shed their soaked, muddy cold clothes. A hot shower to halt her chattering teeth was his idea, yet it was Anne who impatiently welcomed Tavo into her shower. His soapy hands slicked over her body; no part of her escaped his leisurely exploration. He coaxed and coddled. He toweled her dry and kissed her wet until, an age later, she arched on the pink sheets in a shameless frenzy.

"I want you," she gasped over and over. She didn't say, "I love you." He had not. She trusted him, yet she didn't. "I want you, Tavo." It didn't matter. She didn't know him, though she would soon know him completely. And when he could wait no more, when his now tender, now relentless lovemaking also plunged him beyond the threshold of reason, she did.

She watched the protective way he tucked the cheery quilt around her later when they napped. She responded when he cherished her with his murmured words of glad appreciation, stirring eagerly under his demanding hands and lips as they loved far into the night. A gentle wind rapped rain against the dormer window. Never again would Anne hear rain without recalling two cries of ecstasy, cloven from two hearts that had lost control....

Tavo stepped forward courageously the next day and began to share himself. Busing past tidy pastures and grazing Holsteins, their udders swollen with milk for all Chile, he spoke of the lure of free land at a time when the industrial revolution was forcing German peasants off their farms.

Nothing personal, Anne noted. But she would give him time to unpeel his protective wrappings.

He spoke of the potato famine that had devastated Germany as well as Ireland by 1850, of his family's choice of Chile over Ohio, because the young Chilean government promised they could preserve their language and Lutheran culture. He detailed the awesome desperation when his great-grandparents arrived at the tail end of the world—Tavo had read his great-grandmother's journal. In his condominium in Vina del Mar, Tavo had the family Bible, in which thirteen births were recorded in his great-grandfather's spidery script. Ten of the babies died before the age of four.

Distant disasters. Come closer, sweetheart, Anne coaxed silently. *Trust me.* Brushing her fingers over the familiar strong features, Anne murmured, "Tell me," as he had so often encouraged her. His jaw jutted, heroic with family pride. Rain forest had been cleared but a far worse enemy to conquer was loneliness. For to the north were the unmerciful Mapuche, and to the south, beyond the glaciated, shattered end of the continent, lay Antarctica.

Anne's mind compiled the lonely history even as the family Bible had. She knew now of dead grandparents, dead parents, a dead brother. When would he forsake the ancestors to examine his isolated present?

Not until dinnertime did Tavo mention the family he remembered. The couple had checked into two rooms at the Peréz Rosales, perhaps because it was none of Carlos Luzzini's business what their relationship was.

Perhaps because each continued to need a sense of their separate identity.

Luzzini masked his surprise when he discovered who Anne's companion was. Decades of driving for bankers had taught him discretion. He greeted them, asked for his orders and left them alone until the next morning, when he was to drive them to the Mohr farm.

Their hotel sat on the esplanade circling the seawall enclosing the bay. Cars passed, mostly recent Japanese models, as well as joggers and weathered gray wagons drawn by blindered horses. Men in ponchos drove them, slumped under the heavy damp wool that never seemed to dry in the intermittent rains.

Thunderheads blustered in from the south, squalled and blew on, leaving cold sunshine. Although sunset was drenched in a downpour, when Anne and Tavo strolled toward the lights of a restaurant on a distant pier, the rain and wind had ceased. The lights of Puerto Montt rose up an escarpment as steep as any San Francisco hill, disappearing at the top into the twinkling dust of billions of stars.

Theirs was a window table in the seafood restaurant. From her seat Anne could see the unending chain of snow-capped peaks proceeding to the Strait of Magallanes, open to the onslaught of the sea.

Over tiny fresh shrimp, lightly battered and served like popcorn, she prodded him about his brother, Alvaro. He was smart, Tavo told her. Handsome, clever in books, a natural athlete.

"Blond?"

"Brunet, but his skin was fair, like yours, not olive like Pascal's."

Anne listened as a lover, she mentally recorded details

as a reporter, habitually suspending judgement and remaining alert to the nuances. Alvaro sounded perfect, superior in everything his brother had excelled in. As a reporter, Anne wondered—and assumed upon brief consideration—that Tavo was jealous of the deceased Alvaro. As a lover, Anne asked him instead about his de la Huerta grandparents. They were prideful, elegant. He remembered his grandfather seemed exceptionally clever with management and benevolent toward his workers. But Alvaro de la Huerta died when Tavo was seven. The widow de la Huerta henceforth wore black and attended daily mass at 6 A.M.

"She sounds cold."

He agreed. " 'Disciplined' was the word my family preferred."

"What about your parents? Did they have a happy marriage?"

"Did yours?" He called the waiter over to take their order, and Anne knew the answer. Not the details, no, but the fact.

"My parents really are suited," she answered him. "They don't get along perfectly, but you never wonder if they love each other. Wait until you see how they look at one another when one has something to say, as though the other can't wait to hear." Of course he would meet them soon. The logistics of how and when were future details.

"My grandmother and grandfather Mohr were like that." He seemed eager to expose himself now in an overflowing dam of moods, a festering boil that needed lancing.

Anne listened as she never had before. She absorbed the feelings that showed in his unguarded eyes. She laughed with envious joy when he described the wild blackberry kuchen his Grandmother Mohr served his German School friends, the school being part of the Chilean government's effort to preserve a transplanted Lutheran culture.

Anne loved hearing how the same blackberry kuchen, piled high with fresh thick cream, had attracted the wealthy Jacobo Mohr Wendt to the farm home of the petite Imme Schultz, a flaxen-haired beauty. It was obvious as Tavo related the tale that he loved it, too. Grandfather Mohr Wendt had inherited his grandfather's shipping business in Valparaiso—then, before the Panama Canal opened, one of the world's busiest seaports. He was in his thirties, a stern ambitious man, when he had sailed to Puerto Montt on business and was reluctantly convinced by his client, Schultz, to ride all the way out to the farm for tea. And his daughter's *kuchen*.

"My grandfather was struck the moment he saw her. He described to me that it was a lightning from which he never disconnected."

Anne felt the joy she saw in his very pleased expression. She wanted to take his face in her hands and ask softly, her lips a kiss away from his, "And how did your grandmother feel?" A table separated them—no matter; they were attuned. She had no need to ask. He told her. Imme Schultz de Mohr had died with multitudes of admirers and so-called friends, but she loved only a few, and them she unfailingly adored.

Pouring the first bottle of crisp dry, white Doña Isidora, he told her all she needed to know about his family, with occasional interruptions to find out about hers.

They ate a local bouillabaise of fresh mussels, abalone, halibut and crab claws, dipping fat crusty fresh bread into the thin, flavorful creamy broth, rich with butter. They tasted the seafood stew at leisure and hurried their conversation. There was so much to share, daily details of their future life, routines and decisions that were erotic in their newness.

How could Anne learn to make kuchen? Tavo's grandmother's maid still lived in the apartment in downtown Santiago, she would gladly teach Anne. They would headquarter in that apartment, it wasn't cramped, like most North American ones. It occupied part of the top two floors in his office building. During fall and winter shipping season he had to be near the docks at Valparaiso, so he lived in a new apartment overlooking the ocean in nearby Vina del Mar, about an hour's drive from inland Santiago.

"You will be very happy in Vina, Ana." Flocks of pelicans would fly by their balconies. She would hear sea lions barking and smell eucalyptus. It was California without the ravages of overpopulation.

Tavo talked without restraint, and Anne responded to the honest excitement he displayed. Her eyes brightened with trust that fed his trust, which fed hers.

Their future absorbed them through coffee and cognac. "We should probably buy a larger apartment this spring for the two of us. Mine is suitable for a bachelor, not a married man. I will look into it when I return from Europe." He made a note in a small ringed notebook he carried in his jacket pocket.

"When do you leave?"

He traced a large finger across a minicalender. "I have to be in Lima the thirteenth of September, then back for the nectarine buyers at the end of the month. The trees will be in blossom by then, and we will know our production. I am leaving for Holland, Germany, France and so forth in October. The trip will not take long. I need to confirm a few things, then be back here by the middle of the month, when the apples and pears bloom.''

Her separated, bicoastal life with Charles Roderick was beginning to sound like togetherness when compared to the multinational dealings of Industrias Mohr, S.A. Familiar feelings of neglect crept in.

Before Anne completely identified her subtle disappointment, Tavo was saying. "There will be time for us to enjoy Europe briefly, however, before we return next May. We can fly together, or—"

"But I can't go—"

"This time," Tavo interjected.

Her appreciative smile would have pleasured anyone's heart.

"Why not?"

"I need to return to Los Angeles and close down one life—"

"No, sweetheart, I implore you." Tavo raised his hand in a signal to halt, and picking up her left hand, he kissed her fingers. "Do not think 'close down,' or you will frighten yourself again. You are merely shifting things around. We...." The sound of joint plans seemed to taste good to him, too. "We will be back and forth to California."

She squeaked softly when he caught the tip of her ring finger between his teeth. His tight lips nursed her nerves, until at last, when he continued, her mind remained behind at the playground of his mouth.

"My scientists work closely with your university at Davis. I spend time there every year studying their experiments. We work through many of the same distributors as the California fruit growers. You will return to Los Angeles to make arrangements with your family and for your work. That is all."

"That is all! What arrangements?" Anne retreated. She had worked too hard to scuttle her career now. "I can't just watch the pelicans fly by." Frustrated tears shone close to the surface. She wasn't thinking clearly.

"Why, won't you write?"

Anne loved and was loved, yes. She vibrated with the nearness of her new life, but she knew her business, and she knew she couldn't be a news reporter in his part of the world. "AP and UPI would require Spanish and hard-hitting political stories. That might prove difficult for you," she said. "If I were a stringer for *Time* or *Newsweek*, we'd have the same problem."

Tavo shrugged, obviously unworried. Slipping her down jacket onto her shoulders, he said, "Do not worry about it now, Ana. The answer will come to you, and it will be very different from what your logic is considering. I think you were not satisfied with reporting, except you were too caught up in the daily excitement of your job to consider changing."

He held the restaurant door for her.

"It's hard not to worry," she began, bowing her head into the gale.

"What is this surprise? Am I in love with a worrying Radámes?"

Her teasing response to that blew north. Hunching together, they walked, at times trotted, toward the distant hotel, saving their breath. A taxi came in view, but the driver didn't see Tavo's signal and turned left, up one block to the main street.

They trotted until Anne's lungs screamed. Without a sound he knew, and she gratefully tucked into her suddenly immobile wind break. Murmured words made her look up to lip-read the affection Tavo was speaking. Amber streetlights softened his stern features, and he appeared more content than she had ever seen him.

Poor Charles, she thought. *Will he mind?* No one likes change, and she was part of his routine. He hadn't been pleased that she was unavailable at his convenience the last time he'd called. Probably only his ego would mind, Anne hoped, feeling guilty. Then the feeling was gone.

"The point is, Tavo, I love you," she said happily.

Without speaking they picked up their pace, hurrying back to their hotel room, hurrying to undress, each dallying, deliciously torturing the other with tortoise fingers on buttons and snaps. And most exquisitely, slowly of all, Anne's teasing fingers on his zipper....

Her eager lips were on his first. Her fingers first drew out sensations of pleasure in the most secretive parts of his body, and her lips refused to let his bursting sensations burst. First. He struggled to excite her; she slipped from his grasp and set about driving him mad with desire, driving him further than he had ever experienced, branding herself on his very soul. That was her gift to herself.

And when he allowed her to do so, when he twisted involuntarily, when he trusted enough to shout for release, even while denying it to himself, Anne detonated with unrivaled excitement.

"I want you," he groaned anew. "You are a witch." He writhed under her wicked mouth. "I love you," he cried, and sprang free of the bounds she set.

Catching her face then in his great hands, he bore into her frenzied mind, into her welcoming heart, with his eyes. Anne could no more stop trembling than school her desirous hips.

"This is the first time," he said. "We know only each other."

They joined now without restraint. Together they mounted a plateau and climbed higher, then higher. Together they remained on their secret ledge of sublimity. Linked fingers, linked legs, stirring tongues and again, contentment.

SOFT RAIN CALMED THE DAWN. Occasionally the muffled clop of a horse sounded along the esplanade. Anne's lover was standing beside the window, still naked, gauging the weather, finding an excuse to call her driver, Luzzini, and tell him he wasn't needed until late morning to take them to the Mohr farm.

Our farm. Anne Mahoney de Mohr. She played with the sound of the name in her mind, never taking her eyes from the dimly lit, imposing man approaching her, ready for love, her love.

Afterward, when tears of ecstasy were still damp on her cheeks, Tavo wanted to know when she had realized she loved him.

"Admitted," she corrected, eventually. A great time lapse separated her comprehension and her speech. They lay side by side contemplatively. He waited for her answer, faithful she had one.

"When you didn't tell Janko more than was necessary about me in Bariloche, but you did it cleverly, so he didn't resent being held at a distance."

Tavo was openly puzzled. "You will have to explain more, Ana. I am very curious now."

"The way you used to hold back private information was...well, it was painful to me." Anne smiled and turned her head to look at him. Her eyes shone with an all-encompassing pride. "I never met anyone who aroused me so deeply. Your only fault I could clutch to protect myself was your overworked sense of privacy."

Tavo moved his leg close to hers, the blue of his eyes dominated by black pupils. "So?" He prompted, no longer drowsy.

"So suddenly, when you introduced me to Janko, I realized I would never have shared my secrets with a blabbermouth. You were the first person I trusted absolutely. I never even told Steffie about my nightmares before, yet I told you. Why? I was drunk, I was hung over, you were a stranger, I was lonely. Name an excuse, and I probably used it."

Anne rolled over to him, laying her tousled head against his heart. She would have reached the shoulder of an ordinary man.

"Except I never thought of the one excuse that was true. Instinctively I knew you wouldn't betray me. You were too private." His heart imperceptibly kicked up its beat. "Funny, isn't it, Tavo? Privacy. The very character trait I raged against."

Tavo had wanted her from the moment he saw her, he told her once more, as he had the foul night of their fight in Portillo. Remembering the unbelievable aftermath, he slipped his arm around her, allowing no distance to creep between them. "You were irresistible lying back looking at Laguna del Inca—"

"Irresistible?" The word was lovely in its permanence.

"It was not your looks that won me, Ana," Tavo reassured her, as a man does who understands that a beautiful woman of worth must be desired for her character. "You were compelling because you were sitting alone, absolutely at peace in solitude, and I loved you at once for that. The madder you were at my intrusion, the tighter you bound me to you, for I knew you were a treasure."

Solitude. Privacy. A quiet chuckle escaped Anne's lips, warmed with days and nights of kisses, and then she laughed. Those were twined characteristics, not opposites.

"Only you're more of a mystery than me," she said, raising herself up on his chest with her elbow, gently leaning into him. The dim light of a rainy day shadowed her breasts. In places, it was impossible to see where the curve of her ribs stopped and his began.

She went on. "For instance, you claim proudly that you're a farmer in the Mohr tradition, even though it turns out the Mohrs had a shipping line. You're a farmer, which sounds like steady, predictable work, except for weather surprises. Then you pull out your calendar—today Lima, tomorrow Amsterdam, until the apples are in blossom. Meanwhile I drive to Huntington Beach for a biker-gang killing, big deal. My job takes me here and there, too."

Sitting up, she tucked her feet under his broad warm back. Leaning her legs against his torso, she wrapped her arms around her knees.

Tavo listened with his natural absorption as she continued to test her theory of similarities.

"We both probe the armor of others to shield our own," she said. When he didn't confirm her hypothesis, for the habit of confession was too new to him, Anne announced that no denial was an affirmation, and wiggled her toes, tickling him. . . .

THUS THE RAINY FRIDAY MORNING PASSED. Only the promise of late-morning sunshine and Tavo's tenants awaiting their arrival interrupted their peaceful sloth.

Everything about Tavo's tenant, Osvaldo, was round: his cautious blue eyes, his wind-pinked cheeks, his stomach and his stocky legs. Yet Tavo's tenant was not fat. The round was well-fed muscle. Anne judged him to be about forty.

Osvaldo was waiting for them in the late Señora Mohr's gabled, cream-and-brown frame house, where he lived with his wife, Marta, and five children.

Freshly laundered lace curtains hung at the living-room windows, although the furniture was standard modern. Outside a bay window Anne could see the long dirt lane coming up to the house, recently furrowed dark loam fields, too. Tiny radishes and string beans had already popped forth in the sizable vegetable garden at the side of the house. No infant flowers were out of place; no weed dared rear its head.

Marta, skinny as Jack Spratt who ate no fat, came hurrying in from feeding the chickens.

Both were unabashed in their admiration of Tavo, and Anne watched why, concentrating on body language, for she couldn't understand German. Tavo was comfortable with the couple. They responded in kind. He listened intently when they answered his questions, and when he dispensed praise their faces beamed.

"Our experimental plots of raspberries are going very well," Tavo explained to Anne. "I have built a more efficient freezing factory for the berries, so we are going to plant two hectares—this is about, hmm, five acres more of raspberries and put in—" he converted measurements quickly "—four acres of blackberries."

"Enough for a kuchen or two," said Anne softly, stretching up for her whisper to reach his ear, her brown eyes warm as a glass of tea held up to the sun. Tavo settled his hand in its usual place on her shoulder. She rubbed her neck against the two fingers he had slipped inside her turtleneck.

"We are going out to stake the pasture and look at the animals. Will you come with us?" he asked her. Marta was staying behind to prepare lunch, so Anne could borrow her rubber boots. "Otherwise your shoes will be ruined by mud."

Luzzini remained behind. His watchful manner was easing with Tavo's continued concern for Anne. The lovers' joint stance announced the seriousness with which they regarded their coupling.

Tavo and Anne walked side by side, his hand still on her shoulder. They inspected the spotless dairy barns, slogged along muddy tractor paths on the perimeter of barley and sugar-beet fields. Lastly, they made the final decision as to which pasture lands would be converted to berries.

Afterward, energetic round Osvaldo went about his chores while Anne and Tavo walked through fenced pasture to the lake. The grass was a brilliant early-spring green; the air was fresh. Lake Llanquihue, a timorous blue under the changeable sky, extended to the horizon.

The raspberry bushes had budded, but their vicious thorns weren't yet hidden, thorns that eliminated competition on the international fruit export market, because only a few ambitious poor countries had populaces desperate enough to endure the pain of harvesting the berries. Rumania, Hungary, Czechoslovakia and Chile.

"We must find goods to export other than copper and timber," Tavo explained.

Exploitation, thought Anne, searching for a less conflagrant label. The memory of raspberries and French vanilla ice cream sickened her. How could she love an exploiter of the poor?

"The first world has successfully eliminated poverty, no?" Tavo said calmly, sensing her condemnation.

"No, but—"

Chile needed more jobs of any kind, Tavo went on to say, arguing that the berries created work for families to gather enough money for the children to go to school. Anne countered that he should provide his workers with tuition and uniforms if such were necessary for their children's schooling; that education was an unalienable right as surely as life, liberty and the pursuit of happiness.

His hand remained relaxed on her tense neck muscles. Her buried fear of a foreign life jumped to attention. "Is this your country versus mine?" She wanted to flee from her own question.

He continued walking by her side. "There is no versus. You must maintain your ethics, Ana. Please, suspend your judgement while you collect facts, and I will listen without mental blocks, for Chile needs solutions to its problems."

Tavo halted then, and lifting her hands to his chapped lips, said in a voice most somber, "But remember, too, we need our solutions appreciated. You will in fairness find we have created much with our small country."

The notion of fairness soothed Anne once again.

Stepping on the bottom rung of a barbed-wire fence, he stretched the next strand up for her to slip through. He half climbed, half vaulted the barrier, and they continued toward the shore of Llanquihue, stumbling occasionally on hidden clods in the rough pasture.

Swiss brown calves gamboled in the new grass. They stopped to laugh at the youngsters' bow-legged antics. Their bovine mothers grazed, ignoring their children and the watching couple. Anne and Tavo could have been in a pasture of European milk cows anywhere.

"The pioneers' urge to remain German must have worked, Tavo. Look at you." Anne traced his Teutonic features with her fingers. "What will your children be?" It was a careful question.

"Mohr Mahoneys. Chilean-Irish, like our liberator, only they will not be illegitimate as he was—if you hurry and propose to me."

Anne smiled indulgently.

Tavo ran his hands through her luxuriant hair, letting the strands settle in electrified sparks of mahogany. "My children will have fire in their hair like their mother—"

"And eyes of blue like their father. . . and their grandmother Mahoney and their great-grandmother Imme Mohr. . . ."

"No. I want my daughter to have cinnamon eyes that

retain their vitality no matter how cold she pretends to feel."

Anne reached up and clasped her arms around his neck. "Then I insist she have wavy hair that shines like the moon under sunny skies." It wasn't as poetic as Tavo's phrases, but she wasn't practiced in verbal caresses.

They didn't discuss children again until after lunch that same afternoon. Luzzini passed tidy hillside farms in black forests to the north. He had reentered the primal rainforest and finally corkscrewed through permanently damp woods of lichen-sheathed beech to a few mountain cabins. They had arrived at Antillanca Volcano, the weekend ski area for the people of Osorno, a coastal city ninety minutes away.

One lodge belonged to the German School, Tavo told her, another to the French School. The rambling two-story building to their right had been funded through profits in the national football lottery, aimed at bringing sports to those who couldn't otherwise afford them.

"Will our children attend German School, Tavo?"

"Depends on their mother," he said pragmatically. "The American school is the most popular in Santiago at the moment. We can speak English at home, and they can learn Spanish from their friends."

"What about the German?" she pressed. "All those sacrifices."

"Change is the nature of immigration. Our children must speak the language of their grandparents, and that is English," he said generously.

"Thank you," she whispered. "And then our children can do as their father did with English, become fluent in a third language." She was firm. "Of course it will be German. I can study with them."

To THEIR CHILDREN, the strangeness Anne found in the supernatural scenery of Chile would be commonplace. She decided this the next morning when she and Tavo shared a series of T-bars from the back stoop of their comfortable lodge up a perfect snow cone. Antillanca Volcano was out of view, but the remains of its last eruption had formed a brilliant white moonscape of monster dunes, like a frozen, aggrandized Sahara.

The untracked snow beneath their skis was fresh-fallen. Rain had followed the snow, a routine phenomenon, transforming the base to sponge. "Virgin slush," Tavo called it.

"Bliss," said Anne, braver than she had ever hoped to be on the giving waves of snow.

However, Chillán Volcano, a day's drive north, announced its presence emphatically. From the top of the chair lift, up the side of the caldron, they could see one of the three cones smoking. Below, spouts of steam from blowholes punctuated the air like Indian smoke signals on a busy party line.

Private rooms with hot tubs for two lined the hallway on the ground floor of the renovated Hotel Chillán. The isolated summer health spa renowned for its sulfur springs was nearly deserted, but an attendant filled a tub of the naturally hot water, smelling of rotten eggs, for Anne and Tavo. The same smelly water heated the old building.

"Healthy water," Tavo insisted, picking up the pitcherful the attendant had left them, pouring a glass for himself. "It cures this and that. Sure you don't want a drink?"

"I'd rather have a Pisco sour, actually," said Anne, who had begun to fancy the local rum. He splashed her for her reluctance. She kicked a faceful back, and they played like wayward kids until they had drenched themselves and the floor.

"How were you as a child, Ana?" Tavo tossed her a face towel.

"Craved excitement."

But when Tavo tried to give her some, the mineral water sabotaged him. All passion had been relaxed out. Excitement came later in their room, when the humid odor of sulfur from the radiator was only a little distracting...eventually.

By Tuesday, when they had dismissed Luzzini and helicoptered back to Portillo, the curious seemed normal. Even the sight of Holstein bullocks plowing muddy fields below them made sense after Tavo cited eight reasons why oxen were superior to tractors in some situations. He ended with the point that after twelve years, they could be sold for food, not junked.

CHAPTER NINE

THE PORTER HELD THE ELEVATOR DOOR open for Anne and Tavo at the fifth floor, site of the top-of-the-line suites at Hotel Portillo. The designation was left over from an era when the sixth floor was dormitory space, before the space had been gutted and suites built.

Tavo unlocked the door to his suite; he had kept his key throughout his search for Anne. She walked straight across the living room and opened the door onto the balcony. Laguna del Inca glowed black. The peaks of Bush Bavarian's Tres Hermanos shone golden white. Outside, the noon air smelled crisp, while back inside she breathed deeply of familiar smells: Tavo and Portillo. Anne had spent too many hours in these rooms not to react.

She was home.

Home wasn't yet the renovated Santiago apartment where skylights welcomed the sunshine. Anne had only heard about this and her new office, the two-story library with cozy fires stoked by Tavo's handyman, Jose. She could imagine the Oriental carpets and the massive colonial desk of the de la Huertas, beautifully carved in the baroque Spanish style, soon to be her desk.

She would see her new home day after tomorrow when Tavo flew her down the mountain to catch her plane to L.A. They still had to coordinate their schedules afterward. Thus far, joint planning had proven too erotic for the necessary concentration.

Anne didn't unpack many things. Ski pants and two tank tops, one for today, one for the race tomorrow. Her swimming suit. Her plain French blue bathrobe with its manly lapels—why hadn't she thought to bring a prettier one? Something for dinner. She couldn't make up her mind. Would they go dancing? Then the sea-green chiffon, or the lavender.... She would decide later. It wasn't important. She'd ring for the maid to press her last-minute choice.

Tavo was an early riser, Anne had learned, and now she found out he also lived in a frugally organized manner. His toiletries remained in a leather bag, stowed in the cabinet, to be retrieved whenever necessary. A season's worth of sweaters were to the far left of his closet, then shirts, sports jackets, suits and ski wear. Two bulging briefcases Tavo's pilot had brought with him were stashed in the narrow space between the desk and the wall, nearly out of sight.

Unpacking was intimate. They had never actually shared a room. Mingling bodies was different; this was mingling lives.

Her few books were on the coffee table in the living room, next to a stack of *El Mercurio*s, last week's *Der Stern*, *Forbes*, international editions of *Time* and *Newsweek*, and for Anne, the Sunday *New York Times*. Newspapers from Los Angeles weren't sent regularly to Chile, Tavo told her.

Tavo completed his tasks, Anne fidgeting. Her digital watch read 9:03. Rush hour was almost over. She'd be leaving her apartment now, headed for the Santa

Monica freeway. The *Chronicle* was roughly forty minutes away at that time of day.

"Can you please change my watch?" she asked, her smile anxious. "I know I'm about to leave, but it's about time I was on Chile time."

She slipped it off, and Tavo picked it out of her hand.

"Your hands are freezing, sweetheart," he said, rubbing them briskly between his. "Come warm them here." He unbuttoned his suit vest, then his shirt. Anne was surprisingly shy. He put her hands on the bare skin of his chest, and they burned, ice on fire, and the ice began to melt. It was a moment for greater intimacy.

But Tavo, a romantic in business garb, demanded courtship. "Let's ski awhile and sit in the sun. I want to feel you next to me in silence, without the blast of the helicopter blade."

They skied Juncalillo together. It was deserted now. This time when Tavo drew up behind her and clamped her between his legs in a snowplow, she settled into him, her blood stirring.

Lunch passed without memory, for Anne's appetite was solely for the man at her side. She ate a bite or two of filet, toyed with sliced tomatoes, cut her sausage in half. Then Tavo said something profound, which she didn't hear for the hungry look in his eyes, and she forgot eating altogether. She sipped her wine. White, she'd requested, ignoring the niceties of red with red meat. She didn't like red. Too many histamines.

And they were quiet.

Tavo shed his shirt; she had on the skimpiest of tanning tops, they sat back-to-back. Her eyes closed in the sun. Waiting. Her emptiness inside passed outward until she was consumed with wanting him. And still she sat quietly, flushed and ripe for love.

Their moment ended with a whoop. Pascal sprang out of the lunch line, telling two new "chickies"—the word he was currently using—to save his place, and ran over to their table. "Ana, you are back! Wait until you see, tomorrow morning, the all-time fabulous performance. Hey, hey, Tavo." His greeting was North American, but the bear hug for the older man, his idol, the uncle of his affection if not his blood, was South American.

They talked of inconsequentials, none speaking of the momentous events facing them all in the coming days. Marriage, 110 mph glory, life—or death. Tavo opened another bottle of Anne's favorite, Doña Isidora.

"None for me," said Pascal, and with a glance at Anne's happy face, saluted them. "*Chau, amigos.* See you at dinner. We have made sure you are at our table. Tonight, Ana, you have to sit between grandfather and me. Things are, as you can imagine, t-e-n-s-e!"

"Hmm," she murmured, selfishly unwilling to worry about that problem until she had to. "Come closer, Tavo," she whispered in their aloneness. "Come close until you're inside my skin, my bones...."

"I want to be in your heart. Feel." He held his wrist to her throat; she felt his pulse against hers. "They beat as one because our hearts are one." His unreleased passion heated the copper bracelet lightly pressing her skin, a yoke of love. They were bound together in one circle.

Radámes came off two hours of pounding runs down the avalanche chute called Condor, which Portillo's expert skiers challenged in the afternoons, after they conquered Roca Jack in the mornings.

His relief at their return was as apparent as Pascal's.

Unlike his grandson, Radámes talked only of tomorrow's race, couching his remarks in the camouflage of facts: snow conditions, weather report, equipment and so forth. Every fact had a worrisome side. The ski suits, he'd learned, were banned for all other kinds of racing—"sane racing," he called it—and told them gruesome reasons why before they could ask. The thin material was too slick, he said. It greased a fallen skier's way down the mountain.

"We were fortunate when Pascal crashed that we worried only about a concussion." Radámes's voice was rising in agitation. Anne braced for the next blow.

"How were we fortunate?" Tavo did him the favor of asking.

"If he had been going faster, the friction would have burned the latex into his flesh," Radámes said. Anne suspected the surgeon hadn't forgiven his friend for buying Pascal the equipment, but still, what was Radámes to say? He was dependent upon Tavo's support.

In truth, she was relieved when the surgeon joined his old friend, Dr. Humberto Macías. The lovers could ignore his unhelpful facts then, for their own sanity. At least Anne blocked them as rapidly as she could bury them. She couldn't tell what Tavo thought. Perhaps he already knew everything Radámes had discovered.

Once his grandfather departed, Pascal returned, drawing on Tavo's calm strength, even though the young Argentine pretended unshakable confidence. Anne wondered about Tavo's tranquility. His eyes were shuttered. No uncalculated emotions leaked through, and yet . . . he missed nothing.

Just as Anne was thinking she could no longer

tolerate their public restraint, when the urge to possess and be possessed devoured her shyness, Tavo said, "Let's go home."

As ALWAYS, he took his time, stretching her craving to the breaking point, slowly, excruciatingly slowly, until a high, vacant voice Anne barely recognized as hers cried for him. And when at last he entered her, a common groan arose, a primitive surge of primitive release.

They didn't lay back against the bolster thereafter, nor snuggle together, for his eyes refused to surrender her mind, as surely as his body quickly reclaimed hers.

Anne talked with her hips now, and her arms, and her mouth, and nothing except sensation ruled her. They napped and woke, then loved, and finally, hours later in the dark of night, Tavo lit a candle by the bedside. The solitary light flicked across their relaxed bodies, his naked and golden, hers gleaming a pinked brown. She stretched, contented.

Tavo slipped out of bed. Anne watched his body hungrily as he padded across the carpeting to one of the briefcases and returned with one hand hidden behind his back.

Anne waited, her eyes shining at his approach. There was no mistaking her vulnerable message: she loved totally.

"*Mi amor,* you are lovely," he said with a catch in his voice. Anne glanced up through her lashes, and was shocked by his fleeting look of raw torment. It vanished even as she wondered if she had imagined it. She reached for his hand to ask what hurt him, but forgot her question when he touched her so tenderly that it brought tears to her eyes.

"I remember when you said yes for the first time."
He brushed her lips with his hard fingers. "We drank
from the pot of gold at the end of the rainbow. Surely it
was a lucky omen. One we should remember, *ama*, so
please, for me, turn around."

She did so, and lowered her head as he bade. Her
abundant hair fell forward over her breasts. Two gentle
hands fastened a linked band of gold around her neck,
his fingers fastening the delicate clasp. Anne touched
her throat. At the very center of the band was a heart-
shaped stone, the same width as the gold.

"Tavo," she gasped. "You—"

"Should have, Ana, *ama*, come look."

She stood in front of the bureau by his side. The top
of her head didn't reach his shoulders. But despite the
difference in height and coloring, Anne found there was
something very similar about their long limbs and
torsos.

At the base of her slim graceful neck was a brilliant
green *malaquita* heart, a polished copper stone from the
north of Chile. The same neon green of Lago Frio,
when she had been cold with remorse at leaving him.
The iridescent copper green of the waterfall at Peulla,
where she had found her courage. The green of Lago
Todos Los Santos the morning after, where she had
begun to enjoy her happiness.

The two images in the mirror looked out at the
originals without pretense, naked before truth. Love
was the point.

TAVO SLEPT RESTLESSLY. Early in the morning when he
left their bed, Anne was sleeping soundly. She didn't
hear him dress in the bathroom, nor pace in the living

room and leave. A few hours later she surfaced. He had a thermos of hot coffee and cold orange juice ready for her.

"Doing our part to ease the Brazilian orange-concentrate crisis here," said Anne, drinking the glassful in two swallows. She was thirsty.

Tavo waited patiently until she was fully awake before drilling her on how she felt about the upcoming races. Fine, she said. He pressed. Was she nervous; was she worried? Did she have confidence in Pascal? She wasn't negative, but Tavo was deadly serious.

Anne answered all questions serenely, for she had slept well. "I'm worried, but I'm fatalistic. I'm hopeful. I want Pascal to succeed." Tavo's expression hadn't changed. Rather, his lack of expression didn't indicate what he was thinking. "I'm tough," she added. "Is that good enough for whatever is on your mind?"

"Pascal is in shape," he mused, almost to himself. "Speed racing is ninety percent mental. No negative thinking can distract him. It would be dangerous."

Anne tried in vain to read his mind. His recently exposed emotions were bundled away somewhere. *Do you keep your emotions in a separate package, Tavito? Easily wrapped and tied to be set aside?*

He was talking about Radámes. He'd been to see his grandparents' dear fretful friend and ordered him to stay away from Pascal. There were to be no words, no gestures, no glimpses or audible sighs until the final race was completed.

"Can I see Pascal?" Anne asked, battling resentment. Was Tavo going to order her away, too? But she had passed muster, and he needed her help.

"After you come down to the workroom, go up to the dining room and guard Radámes," he said. "I worry about his heart.'' But he didn't look worried. He didn't look anything.

Anne reacted empathetically. ''The timing will work just right,'' she said, like a sensible partner. ''Come sit by me, Tavo. I have a habit,'' she admitted, blushing prettily, because it sounded like it was something perverse, when it wasn't really. ''At home I usually take baths, not showers, and while I'm addicted to showers with you, a bath sounds really good to me now. You'll probably want to get back to Pascal, and I can soak in the tub for a while.''

She slipped up his chest for a very worthwhile kiss, and in an instant regretted her generous offer to release him to Pascal. ''We have enough time, don't you think?''

Tavo hesitated, tempted, then said staunchly, ''I ought to be helping with the waxing in five minutes.'' He gave her a quick kiss and started to get up.

Anne was so ready that the most seductive of wiles came at once to her aid, until Tavo was powerless to resist. Laughing, delighted with their truancy, they gloried in a fast, furious satisfaction. And finally, long after Tavo had gone to help prepare the racers, Anne rose from their bed.

The warm bath water relaxed her further.

Indeed she was so wonderfully relaxed, leaning against the wall in the ski preparation room later, that it took at least six or seven minutes for the tension to permeate her blissful nonchalance.

Hank and Lunch were subdued. Other than an occasional request for a screwdriver or more wax, there was no conversation while they tinkered with final adjustments. Each man's concentration centered on himself.

It was no joke to tweek the devil's nose. The joke came only in talking about doing it.

Tavo worked alongside the three men already dressed in their suits—tangerine, cherry and lemon garb. They were scouring newly waxed bottoms with wire brushes, cutting microscopic channels the length of each ski, miniature rivers for the water that forms between the snow and the ski. Another technique to hasten their speed.

Anne watched quietly. Tavo's pace was that of a determined bull, churning a pace so steady it appeared slow. He drew her increasing fright like a magnet and held her doubts to himself without flinching. Anne could almost see the fear leave the three lollipop men and attach itself to the powerful calm of the former racer.

Did any of them even notice when she left? Anne had the grace to admit it was a minimal oversight if they didn't.

In the dining room, Radámes was having partial success in controlling his fears, rigidly following every detail of his morning ritual: he squeezed lemon in water, and his hand only shook a little when he had to fish out a seed with a fork; he cut his toast in triangles; he stirred boiling milk and sugar in his powdered coffee. Then he worked carefully through his stretching exercises.

Anne joined him, realizing he needed her desperately. By protecting his wife, Sofia, from the strain of the race, Radámes had cut himself off from the emotional support he required.

Tavo came for them after he had dug a foxhole of snow near the speed trap. Radámes and Dr. Macías loaded up backpacks of emergency medical equipment.

Tavo hoisted a bigger share of supplies, leaving the small pack of four Swiss binoculars for Anne to carry, a gift to them all from Radámes.

Anne had never ridden the complicated five-saucered lift on Roca Jack. As she grabbed the crossbar they all held, her own fears cancelled out her apprehension about the races. Somehow she disentangled herself at the top, her technique shot to hell. It was like standing on a soapy window, just as Tavo had said.

He hovered nearby, not criticizing her rigid knees, nor the way she leaned into the hill to be closer to the ground in case she fell, rather than leaning out for balance. Anne was grateful.

They crossed Jack's avalanche chute and headed down the valley, skiing along the crest, where snow ended abruptly at granite walls. On the third chute, the privileged group of observers followed Tavo to their safety hole.

He picked up a short-handled shovel he'd left in the snow and began digging out more room for the medical equipment. The muscles under his flat-woven sweater worked gracefully.

Anne reluctantly turned from the pleasure of watching him to speak to Radámes. "We'll be very proud of Pascal today." She was striving for peace, and Radámes responded by resting his hand on her shoulder. "We really will. He'll be okay." *How feeble that sounds.*

Radámes smiled without hearing. She knew it mattered only that her voice was concerned, and confident.

A crowd had gathered on the Juncalillo run below. From her elevated vantage point, Anne understood what Lunch meant when he said Portillo's speed track was good for stopping. It ran down the snow-filled crack in the mountain, crossed the flats of Juncalillo fifteen hundred feet below and continued up on a gradual bordering hill that provided a natural brake.

Anne scanned the vista with the binoculars. Electric eyes were buried on each side of the track about three hundred yards above them. A green yarn across the track where Tavo was digging marked the second set of timers. The timing section was stationary. To increase their speed, the racers would move their starting position higher up the steep couloir, fifty feet each time. Higher, where the oxygen was thinner so they could slice through it more quickly. Higher, so when they shot down, they would rocket through the timers.

The dazzling trio exercised about them, Pascal in the famous tangerine. Anne didn't have to fine tune the binoculars' focus to recognize him. Lunch was in yellow; Hank in red. She could tell only by the shape of their bodies, for with their matching latex hoods attached, it was impossible to differentiate features.

Lean Jonathan Lynch was first up, donning a matching lemon-yellow centurion helmet. He maneuvered himself sideways across the crossbar on the "T" of the track. With perfect control he raised and lowered himself, flexing his knees for the launch.

"We had better bury ourselves," said Tavo.

"Countdown," came the American voice on Tavo's walkie-talkie.

Lunch sank as broad jumpers do. He rose with a strong leap and turned in the air, his skis landing straight on the track. He thrust forward with three skating steps, and tucked.

The four observers knelt in the snow hole, out of the way of danger to themselves and the skier. Tension gripped the crowded space. Anne crawled closer to Tavo. When she shut her eyes, she could imagine his heart beating. She drifted. A distant roar came from the cheering guests.

Then the eerie unsettling shriek reached her ears, a scream of a body hurtling through the air. A roar, a crackle, a horrible sound that raised her hackles and made her stomach wrench. The scream shrilled closer and closer, ripping the constraining fabric of air, and then it passed.

Anne bobbed up from the foxhole. The yellow egg flew past the spectators and up the lip, rising slowly from the crouch until Jonathan Lynch was human once more.

"Ninety-seven point zero three point twelve," Tavo announced into the walkie-talkie.

"Ninety-seven point zero three point twelve. Ten-four."

The squat cherry bomb leaped into position. The observers dodged down, and Anne's nervousness increased. Would the whine never cease? It roared at them. It blistered their eardrums. It made their bones ache.

Don't fall, she thought selfishly, fearing for Tavo, for herself and the doctors, for a body slingshotted into their makeshift protection was no protection at all. She envied the spectators standing in safety at the base. She fought not to cover her ears.

The sound faded and passed.

"Ninety-six point two."

"Roger. Looks like a good day."

"Fast track. Good timing," Tavo observed to the foursome. Beads of sweat glinted on his forehead. He wiped them with his sleeve and stripped out of his sweater.

Anne was damp all over. It was Pascal's turn.

The four climbed out of their hole and stretched cramped legs while they waited. "He is putting on his helmet." Radámes followed his grandson's actions with the binos.

Anne watched two condors circling overhead. The vultures were waiting for easy pickings—cherry, lemon and tangerine Lifesavers rolling down the mountain.

During Tavo's and Anne's absence, the tangerine bomb had learned not to waver nor wipe out with negative thoughts. His tight tuck shrilled along perfectly for the seconds that they watched before dodging down into their shelter. Anne was really proud of Pascal. She felt exhilarated. Tavo studied the digits flashing on the small black plastic box in his hand. How fast was Pascal going? The only clue was his grip. It was too tight. Calm fingers didn't tense white at the tips. Radámes's eyes were noticeably wet.

The sound passed. The quartet stood.

"Sixty-seven point one point twenty-two." Tavo's voice was matter of fact.

Pascal slowed stylishly to a standing position, an arduous skill.

"All right, Pascal!" Anne cheered, cupping her hands like a megaphone. "Good for Pascal," she repeated to her companions. "Aren't you proud of him?"

Her answer was drowned out in a hideous roar. Lunch had boosted his speed to 105.027. Hank Purdoe couldn't push it past one hundred.

Anne had her binoculars ready. She could see the increased speed buffet Pascal's body, the tangerine bullet wasn't as steady this time. His skis torqued and twisted. He was pitting human strength against the elements, and the battle was fierce. The natural reaction for Pascal to regain his balance was to put out his hands, but in this sport, breaking his aerodynamic position would knock him backward to disaster.

"Adelantate! Adelantate!" Tavo coached, the timer box forgotten.

"What?" Anne couldn't understand his shout.

Pascal flew up the lip and stopped safely.

"Eighty point zero five point zero six."

"What were you saying?" Anne asked Tavo.

He looked at her, puzzled. "When?"

"Now. *Adelantate.*"

"Oh." He was distracted. " 'Get forward.' Pascal was losing his tuck." Anne had never seen Tavo so grave, so held back. Deep shadows of worry ringed his eyes.

"You wanted him to go faster than your record?" Anne said softly so Radámes couldn't hear and think she was rude.

"Of course." Tavo shrugged. "He needed to pass me. My ego is not involved. Speed racing, downhill racing—they are different sports. Besides, many people have beat my time. The long list ought to include friends."

She scooped her hair off her neck. The sun was hot. "Now we can relax. Pascal surpassed you. That's enough." She turned to pick up her jacket. The harsh sound assailed her ears again, and she ducked back into the shelter. Lunch roared by.

"One hundred ten point zero one point thirty-seven."

"Startin' to soar," came the walkie-talkie reply.

Purdoe hit 115 exactly. Then Pascal jumped on the track, skating once, twice—good God—four times to boost his speed.

"Fool," muttered Tavo, and clamped his mouth shut. Radámes cursed.

Anne crossed the fingers on both her hands for luck, an effort, because they didn't cross easily in the thick, clumsy goose-down gloves. Anything for distraction. Surely her sacrificial discomfort would aid him, she thought, a superstitious believer in iodine. If medicine didn't hurt, how could it kill the bad germs?

"Ninety-two point zero twelve." The charm worked. She should help Lunch and Purdoe, too. Her fingers cramped. Lunch passed 117; Purdoe stalled at 111.

Halfway down, they had seen Hank's arm begin to float out. His loud scream had reverberated off the cliffs, and Anne very nearly threw up. He had wobbled, pulling himself back into the egg shape with super-human effort, beating the wind.

Anne said something to Tavo, some time-wasting remark, and he didn't hear. He had withdrawn.

Pascal dropped to 91.972, even though he'd climbed another fifty feet above the stationery speed trap. Would the cry of the banshee, come to predict death, cease? Lunch hit 120. Purdue passed him at 121. Pascal passed 100 by one-sixteenth of a second and returned to the lift.

"To my regret, he is going to keep pushing for 110." Radámes was banked-down British now, terribly and all that.

Anne instinctively knew it was vital for Radámes to witness the sublime after-effect of his grandson's defiance of death. The surgeon had to understand. Just as

Pascal had to learn politeness, if not obedience, in the face of age, the challenge for Radámes was to accept the decisions of youth. The older man had tried with facts, but he needed to see the emotions at work.

"Let's watch from below," she urged. "I want to see Pascal come all the way down the slope. "Hurry, Radámes. We have time. Call up to them, Tavo. Tell them to wait a couple minutes."

Offside from the track, the avalanche chute was as brutally steep as the speed track itself. Anne heard Tavo yelling at her to be careful. He wasn't able to discipline the fear out of his voice as he had out of his face. The race was affecting him badly. "Slip slide when you get scared," he called, and she did. "Take your time, Ana. They will wait."

Bravely Anne slipped and skied down. She maneuvered Radámes and herself to the front of the line.

On his next pass, Lunch slowed to a stop near them. Anne waved, and he looked in her direction, his eyes glazed. "I'm close," he mumbled.

Anne assumed he meant to McKinney's Portillo record of 125.

"My head's still back up there," said Hank when he came down, a florid-faced cherry cough drop melting in the heat of the sun. He skied back to the lift.

Soon Pascal stopped nearby. " '*Cerca.*' " He'd forgotten English in his daze. He removed his silver helmet, took off his orange latex hood and ran his hands through his sopping brown hair.

Radámes hesitated, then reached for the helmet. He held it proudly, but Anne could see the helmet quiver in his usually nerveless surgeon's hands. His beloved grandson had undermined a lifetime of restraint.

"Now I glimpse the understanding," said Pascal, looking directly at Radámes.

"What *nieto*?" asked his grandfather.

"I understand time." The young man's glassy eyes cleared. "I understand why after your heart surgery you wanted to drag time to a crawl, grandfather. When life passes in a furious rush, you see things very clearly."

The two men were alone with one another, their English a gesture for Anne, even though she was a forgotten bystander.

"And what do you see?" Radámes pressed, unnoticed tears wetting his cheeks.

"That you want to live."

Pascal embraced his grandfather; they hugged for a long time. Finally Radámes voiced his elemental fear. "Are you addicted, Pascalito? Will you forever need this thrill of imminent destruction?"

The young Argentine looked squarely at his grandfather. He wavered. He almost spoke, then cleared his throat. At last he answered truthfully. "I do not know."

"Aren't you going back up, Pascal?" Anne asked, her binoculars focused on the red egg streaking toward them.

"Not this year. My legs are rubber from holding the skis on course." Pascal's voice was confident. "I did what I set out to do."

Anne gave him a great smile. He'd grown up. Wisely, she said nothing. How well she knew that maturity was fragile.

When Tavo skied down with the equipment in two packs, one slung over each arm, he confirmed the final results: Lunch couldn't push himself past 123.017; Hank peaked at 122.68, and Pascal clocked 106.001 on his last run.

Tavo's expression was prideful as he grabbed the younger man in an affectionate hug. "You outreached my prediction by a long shot. You really grabbed hold inside and pushed yourself."

Pascal puffed up like a penguin on parade. "Yeah, well. . . ." His Americanism slipped out. "Thank you, Tavo," he said formally.

Only Anne saw that behind Tavo's smile lurked some shadow she didn't understand, the same grim shadow she'd witnessed up at the speed trap. She felt a tremor of an unnamed fright. Even when his hand immediately squeezed Anne's, even after they lost Pascal and his grandfather to a crowd of celebrating guests and were alone, she couldn't shake her trepidation. Not knowing what else to do, she ignored it.

"I'm going to shower and change for lunch," she began. Her tan flushing with anticipation, she added, needlessly, "Will you join me?"

THE CALL FROM CHARLES RODERICK came late in the afternoon when Anne and Tavo were napping at the pool. Neither the United States nor tomorrow's flight to Los Angeles were real, let alone the forgotten congressman. Reality was here, wondering when Claudia and Luis Alberto would arrive. What the guest-room situation in the Santiago apartment was, how one treated the old family maid, what they'd do for wedding arrangements.

She had been about to ask Tavo about the ceremony. Not what kind. It would be small, and in Pomona, she hoped, at the traditional, ivy-covered church on the Pomona College campus. Her question was when. When would they have the free days necessary, with the fruit business set to begin its season of overtime?

"Hello, Anne? My God, I've missed you." Charles's voice startled her. His confession was exuberant. Why? She was guilty and wary. He never said he missed her. She couldn't very well act the hypocrite and pretend she'd missed him, too.

"Hello, Charles." The purr of contentment in her voice embarrassed her. She sought neutrality.

"This three-week separation has been a killer for me.... *Five weeks,* Anne mentally corrected. She hadn't seen Charles since July, when he'd flown back to L.A. for a fund-raising dinner. He laughed warmly. "I'm having separation anxiety." Anne was out of the habit of psychoanalyzing every emotion, so she floundered now. *I'll deal with this when I get home,* she thought.

"A lot has happened while you've been chasing around down there," he went on. That was standard. The man had a fabulously exciting life. She remained silent. "I announced for the Senate seat yesterday."

Tavo's warning that senatorial candidates needed wives resounded from far back in her memory.

"And I'll meet your flight at LAX on the second," Charles was saying. He hadn't paused for her reaction; he was on campaign time. "Day after tomorrow. Seems too long to wait. Things are moving fast, honey. Lace up your roller skates."

Had he written her into his schedule, too? Nervously Anne changed the subject. "How did the *Chronicle* and the *Times* react to your announcement?" Charles was pleased with their initial response, and Anne also listened to details of the editorials in the *LA Basin*—basically, they were pleased, he had announced. Meanwhile, the *San Francisco Chronicle* and *Examiner* called him an unknown. They had their own candidate, a good family man, although that wasn't so important up north. Charles wasn't worried. Southern California had the population....

"Good family man." Anne was increasingly uncomfortable. She didn't want Charles meeting her plane, not with the feel of Tavo still on her skin. Not the way he was talking. It wasn't as if they'd been committed to each other. Charles had never proposed, never said he loved her, sort of but not really.

"Obviously now, with everyone watching me, we can't take that long weekend up Highway 1, so I've scheduled a couple dinners for us and a few important supporters and their wives. Friday and Saturday nights...."

She was in the timetable. Still Anne hesitated to tell him goodbye over the telephone. That didn't seem fair. She'd rather wait. Wait! She had no time to wait. Those supporters and their wives would assume she was the faithful fiancée.

"You're rested after your holiday, aren't you, Anne? No party-girl circles under your eyes?" He chuckled. "Your first public pictures should be pretty." He took her silence for concern about photographic effects of her all-night flight. "If I could have postponed Friday until Saturday I would have."

Sure Charles—if it was convenient for you.

"But you've got stamina out the yin-yang, Anne. That flight won't bother you—"

"Charles, this is difficult to say." She equivocated, fair versus unfair. But public appearances were public announcements. Why not cut the problem over the telephone? After all, that was where their courtship had taken place. She took a breath. "Charles, I'm not going to either of the dinners with you. I value our friendship, but people will make assumptions about us if—"

"Lace up your roller skates, I said." He laughed intimately. She'd always enjoyed the way he laughed. He did it so artlessly, so genuinely that everyone around him felt clever. "There are some things better said in person—"

"Charles, you have a habit of making assumptions about me. Things are different now."

"I know." The low laugh was meaningful.

Anne faltered. She didn't have to burn her bridges.... What was this indecisiveness? She had one love; she had only had one love. Anne lit the match.

"I'm marrying a Chilean—"

Charles laughed, relief very evident. "I'm sorry I couldn't get away to enjoy your amorous mood."

Anne was incredulous. His indulgent sophistication was offensive. "Hold on to your mood on the way home," he was actually saying. "I'll be at the airport."

"Charles," she said. "I'm in love."

"You were discreet, weren't you? Of course," he answered himself. "You love with your head. That's one of your charms, sweetheart."

His careless use of Tavo's endearment triggered the assurance of a convert. Once she had loved only with her head, but no longer was she cheating herself.

"Love does exist, Charles. Neither of us had to settle

for sensible...what a pitiful word that is.... Charles, we didn't have to—''

"I was not settling." Charles was obviously irritated. Didn't he realize he should be furious? If he loved her, he would be hurt, bitter, jealous, fighting for her. She could only believe her desertion had inconvenienced him. Maybe that was her anger and guilt talking.

"Latins are notorious for loving and leaving, Anne. I'll call you this weekend when you've had time to recover your senses. Meanwhile, I'll make an excuse for you at the dinners."

What utter civilized baloney.

"Goodbye, Charles." This time Anne's voice didn't waver. "Thank you for your friendship."

She felt great relief. The deed was done.

"I *will* call, Anne," he said, and she knew she had bungled the whole scene. She should have—she didn't know what she should have done.

"Goodbye," she finally said. Whether Charles called or not was irrelevant. Whether he chose to believe her now or later was his problem. But she felt bad after they hung up. Charles had not been off base in his assumptions. A few weeks ago she would have been blushing and thrilled at his including her in his campaign schedule. If he'd proposed, as he was surely preparing to do, she would gladly have accepted. And why not? She hadn't known any different a few weeks ago.

ANNE AND TAVO PACKED before dinner so they would be ready for the helicopter to ferry them down in the morning. His skiing was over for another year. He had some work to finish up at the office in the morning; Anne would accompany him. At two o'clock, the businessmen's lunch hour, his maid would have a meal ready for them at the apartment. Anne's plane would take off at 6 P.M.

She was restless and moody that night, unhappy about the coming separation. He was edgy. Neither of them slept well.

The savage howl of wind, the continual deafening roar, obliterated the distressing cries of her nightmare. A fragile pink egg was shuddering high on a snowy cliff. Anne moaned as the wind tore at the egg, smashing it from side to side, cracking it into a jigsaw of fractures. The windows of the suite rattled until the rising scream of the wind awakened Anne.

She had crept up Tavo's length, her arms clutched around his neck, and she lay there, curled into him, afraid to sleep again. "I love you," she whispered when the unease of her dream passed.

There was no reply. Why couldn't she trust herself to believe he was asleep? It must be the shrill gale with its shifting levels of force that taunted her composure. Like fingernails on blackboards, or an indignant Siamese. Anne hated wind. The hot Santa Anas blowing off the desert stirred the citizens of L.A. to deeds of dreadful violence—negative ions or something. A legal excuse for murder as surely as cabin fever.

Outside, she could see nothing, not even when she touched her nose to the icy window and looked out. Only a whirl of snow. A freight train of wind thundered by. The old stone building shuddered slightly at its punch.

Too jittery to return to bed, Anne rummaged through a suitcase until she felt sheer flannel. It was her long comfortable nightgown. She pulled it on and settled in a chair near the window, staring out into the turbulent darkness.

"No."

The word was a sigh pounded into silence by the racket. "No! No!" Anne glanced over to the bed. She could hear Tavo thrashing. She hurried to his side and peered closely so she could see without turning on the nightlight and startling him.

His eyelids flickered rapidly, a mental projector relaying his nightmare. "No!" His jaw clenched.

Tavo reached out to the warm hollow where she'd been sleeping. Anne watched his arm fumble blindly at emptiness. She slipped back into place and wrapped her arms around him, whispering comforting words to fight the evil attack of the wind on his subconscious. His breathing gradually returned to normal, and he slept quietly. Eventually the raging howl became background noise as Anne, too, slept.

The bed was empty when she awakened. Her head ached from the inconstant clatter outside—now quiet, now screaming. Sometimes the scream was so continuous that she was startled when silence returned.

Tavo was in the living room surrounded by piles of neatly stacked papers. He was working numbers on his hand calculator. Anne yawned and stretched in the doorway. Every lamp in the room was on, but not all of them combined had the power to lighten the sullen mood outside, murky white as a cloud seen from the window of a jet.

"Good morning." She stepped over the perimeter of papers and embraced him. Tavo smelled of elegant soap, and when she nuzzled her cheek against his, the firm skin was clean-shaven. How could she have missed the sound of the shower? A pity, wasting all that soap and water on only one.

"Mmm. Just a minute." Tavo's long intellectual fingers finished tallying a column. He recorded the red digital answer on a ledger sheet, then turned to the glowing woman. He kissed her, a disappointing, perfunctory kiss, a husbandly breakfast kiss. So soon?

Anne rationalized his distracted behavior as quickly as it occurred. Saying goodbye would be at best difficult, even if was only for a short period of time. She forgave him for expressing a prodigious reluctance. The storm was blowing demons up the mountains. The little devils were biting her, too.

She settled her hand on his strong neck, resting her fingertips fondly under his starched cotton collar. "Your pilot's probably having a tough time getting up here, judging by the storm out the window."

"Better unpack, Ana. He won't be up for a couple weeks."

Anne's innocent laughter gurgled. "Wouldn't that be wonderful, Tavo? Snowbound for weeks. Huddled together, wrapped in our wolf skins until at last, down to our last barrel of sourdough, we eat until stuffed—"

"And drunk...." Tavo's strained formality faded.

"Yes, yes." Her eyes devoured the rising humor on his tired face. "Drunk, and we stagger out into the Arctic—"

"Antarctic—"

"Antarctic blast." Anne clutched him, playacting a lurching walk through a blizzard. "We reel from the storm. We plunge into thigh-high—" She interrupted herself to study him, and with a wicked leer, lowered the snow depth. "Your knees, my thighs. That's a little safer. We don't want you to freeze. Finally, when we're near death, two Russian wolfhounds come bounding through the blizzard—''

"Russian wolfhounds?"

"This is a chic rescue." Anne's eyes danced. "We've fallen. The snow is burying us, and they scratch the snow off. Their breath is hot—"

"Their halitosis penetrates our stupor, and we—"

"They lick our faces with gigantic sloppy kisses—"

"And we say 'Down Prince, down....'"

"And turn into Antarctic snow frogs. We bound away and live happily ever after."

An agonized, guilty look passed over his face before he shuttered the expression. He cemented a relaxed smile so thoroughly onto his face this Anne thought it would crack.

"You look busy, Tavo." She pretended gaiety. "Why don't you finish what you're doing. I'll get the rest of my things ready, and then we can get some breakfast."

"We are snowbound, Ana." Tavo walked over to her bulging suitcases and carried them back to the bedroom. "This storm will not end for three or four days. It will be another two or three days before my helicopter can land up here—"

"But that's a week!"

"With a helicopter. The highway crews will not be able to plow the highway open for two or three weeks."

"Three weeks?" Anne was incredulous. "That's impossible. At Portillo? People don't get stranded forever in world-class resorts."

"Depends. Last year people were trapped below for six weeks. The heavy storms came early, even before the ski instructors moved up. What a bill they ran up in downtown Santiago!''

"But you have to be in Lima in thirteen days, Tavo. And I have to have things settled in Los Angeles. We haven't talked about our wedding at all. If—if you don't get to Lima on time, you'll be late for Europe...." Wide-eyed with unnamed fear, Anne let her words stumble nowhere.

"Down Prince." Tavo rallied some of his teasing calm. Laughter again eased the stern parentheses around his mouth. Mischievous fingers mussed her hair, and when the time came, when he could no longer tolerate the separation between them, he clasped her loving face in his firm hands and lowered his lips to hers.

This kiss was different from all the others. The intensity of some strange pained longing was so heartbreaking. Anne's startled eyes opened; she glimpsed blue, blue longing. Then he blinked, and his naked soul was hidden. He blinked again under her relentless stare, his extraordinary eyes polite and very private.

"Why?" she asked bravely, not guessing.

"Why what, Ana?" he deflected smoothly. "My helicopter cannot land until the avalanches stop and my pilot has a soft spot to set down."

And dear God, she didn't have the courage to insist he tell her what was really happening. To his feelings.

"Avalanches?" Her constricted voice was husky.

"These mountains hold snow like hot chimneys."

"So the soonest we're out of here is?" She was repeating herself like a dummy.

"Is five or six days. The way to prevent claustropho-

bia is to accept an idle week inside, sweetheart. . . ." He
paused thoughtfully after his verbal caress.

He's scared, she realized, scared himself. *He's got
cold feet. It's normal. Don't mention the wedding. Act
casual. Don't push.*

"But I've got lots to do," she said. "Snider needs me
at least through the fires. I have to—"

The windows rattled.

"Damn the wind. I hate wind!" Anne exploded with
frustration. "I've always hated it. How can you be so
calm? Doesn't this set your teeth on edge?"

"I have been through this before. The first time is the
worst. You can have calls made back to the United
States. Portillo contacts its Santiago office on the shortwave."

"You look busy." She leisurely began unzipping her
suitcases. Only her cold, trembling hands betrayed a
fear too important to be revealed. "I'll unpack. Shall I
unpack for you, too? It won't take long. Then I'll send
a message to Snider." She hurried on. "See you later."

Tavo smiled a vague thanks.

Anne disappeared into the bedroom before he saw
tears fill her eyes. When she reemerged and left, with a
light touch on his sleeve, Anne was outwardly as detached and composed as he, giving him plenty of room
to roam, as best she could.

THE MESSAGE TO SNIDER WAS SHORT. "Snowbound. Expect me in one week. Please call my parents."

"Better make that two weeks," warned the tired secretary, stacks of messages on her desk. "You never
know."

"My boss'll never believe it."

"Hope it isn't six, then," said the girl, shrugging her shoulders wearily. "At least you only have one person to contact."

Videos dubbed in Spanish had been running since early in the morning. The small theater was near the office, so it was natural that Anne hid there. She didn't care that the Western was half over. She only wanted conversation, any conversation, and music to drown out the irritating whine of the storm.

In that, she was successful. The Western was followed by a science-fiction thriller. An Argentine contractor on her right filled in on top of the noise between sound tracks. Portillo storms frequently featured winds over one hundred miles an hour, he told her, hurricanes dumping six or seven feet of snow in their vicious path from the Pacific over the Andes.

That was simply one more reality Anne didn't want to face. Disasters were interesting only when they happened to some other victim. Meanwhile, on the screen, good guys battled monster geeks.

Lunch passed with an Ingrid Bergman classic. The small theater room was crowded. Restless guests leaned against the walls and sat in corners on the floor.

"My eyes are dead," Anne admitted to a lawyer and his wife from San Felipe, the center of fruit production north of Santiago. The couple knew Tavo well. Their own small vineyard was a few miles from one of his farms. From time to time the two couples had shared espresso during long Portillo evenings.

The lawyer's wife admitted eye strain, too. She planned to sweat her headache away. Did Anne want to join her in the sauna?

Anne really didn't. Without the distraction of celluloid fantasy, she felt threatened by her anxiety. How much time alone did Tavo need? Had her absence been missed? She sniffed her wrist. His scent, from the soap they shared. In an instant she was as ready for love as if he'd spent the afternoon exciting her.

Tavo looked up from his work when she entered. She didn't know if he'd even left the room all day. Anne couldn't resist. So was the candle drawn to the firefly.

"Making progress?" Her greeting was breathless. She touched his forearms gently, and compelled to have more, slowly ran her hands up his shoulders and began massaging his neck muscles. They knotted at her contact. Inwardly she recoiled from his involuntary rejection and yet she compulsively kneaded the tight cords.

"Decisions are trying," he said. "I am studying my farms, deciding where to renovate."

"What does that mean?" Anne kept up her massage. With concentrated effort his muscles were relaxing.

"Different types of fruit are like cars. New varieties are popular every few years. Jonathans' apples used to be. Now people want all one color, either red or green. Jonathans were part red and part green and too small. Big is the potato right now."

"The potato?" She feathered kisses down his neck.

"The fad, the Hula-Hoop."

"Big and green is the potato for apples. Sounds like an Irish football team. Must be the O'Higgins influence." She laughed.

"You have the picture." He smiled.

"I don't have the picture clearly," she teased. "Three and three-fourths cines in one day blinded me. I think I'll take a nap before dinner." She hoped he would leap to his feet, discard his work and confess he'd been waiting for her return all day. Instead, she sensed him pulling away from her again.

"Wake me in time to change for dinner," she said, fighting for a casual tone.

There was no need for him to wake her. She couldn't sleep in the too-empty bed. The pleasure of having a big man in bed, she had learned, was that no matter how she tossed and turned, she was always in contact with some part of his warm body.

She lay still with her eyes closed, feeling more lonely than ever before in her life. The wind never gave her jangled nerves a moment's peace for repair.

DINNER, TO HER GRATEFUL SURPRISE, WAS FUN. Caviar and iced vodka in the bar before dinner, huge slabs of pink salmon steaks, souffléd potatoes and *al dente* beans helped raise the spirits of the marooned guests. Chilean wines and champagnes flowed, and to hear the established regulars talk, Portillo's storms were marvelous adventures.

Pascal was divinely pleased to escape returning home for an interminable stretch of time. He had things to do, women to chase, tales of heroism to exploit. Radámes was at his most captivating. And Tavo lightened his wary seriousness now that he and Anne were part of a friendly crowd.

Brandy was sniffed and consumed with espresso after dinner. The stories continued. Anne laughed until she developed a stitch in her side.

"Remember the second year after the Americans bought the lease on Portillo?" said Radámes, warming his brandy in his hands. "One of the partners had a daughter making her debut, I think in August. The father chartered a plane and flew her party down to Portillo for a weekend of skiing. Very dramatic, no? The debutantes, their dates, their parents—what a gathering. But on the second day, a storm blew in, and they could not get out for two weeks. That was before they had the shortwave.''

Anne giggled. The liquor was having an effect. "Imagine a hotel full of New York businessmen trapped without a telephone—"

"To say nothing of the parking bill for the jet at the airport." That was Pascal, who never had worried before about money, especially someone else's.

Tavo poured another round of brandy for the expanding group. The milling crowd had sensed where the liveliest conversation was taking place.

Tavo addressed the gathering. "Were you here the year the stranded Florida woman was expecting the president of the United States for a dinner party at her house the next week? She eventually hired two strong boys from the hotel to put on snowshoes and carry her out piggyback."

Anne and Tavo were quiet when they returned to their suite, very late. He was pensive, and she was afraid to be eager. He was slower getting into bed than she was. She nearly wept when he didn't reach for her.

This time it was his turn to make the first move, she thought, hunched on her side of the bed, hating the wind, hating the darkness, hating the fear and her evaporating hope.

"Asleep, Ana?" he finally asked, very quietly.

She heard the twinge of wish in his question.

"Hmm?" She pretended sleepiness.

"Nothing," he said.

Hours later, when he thrashed in his sleep, muttering unhappily, Anne woke him.

"What is it, please," she urged, her voice soothing. She slid over to him and held him close. "You taught me to speak my feelings," she whispered. "Tell me." She brushed hair off his damp forehead, leaning closer to his mouth to hear. He flinched from her nearness. Panic flushed her blood; her stroking fingers on his chest felt panic.

"I do love you, Ana...."

But.... A wail stuck in her throat. Uncomprehending pain ballooned inside her, then burst.

"I love you, too." Her promise was hurried to hush the dread of what was to come. She rested her head against his heart, and it kicked up its tempo.

The wind shrieked.

"But no...I am not capable of love—"

Anne silenced his horrible words with a kiss. She was demanding; she was desperate. She played with his desires, tempting him beyond the detachment of his mind, chasing his arousal when it ran away. She had no inhibitions. She had no doubt, no shame, nor pride. "Love me," she begged.

"I cannot, sweetheart..." he gasped, trying to pull away from her. "Not the way you deserve."

She pleaded. "Love me any way you can. Please."

Her incautious lips swayed him, tormented him, and when his withdrawn resolve ruptured, they moved together in great shuddering thrusts, their union as anguished as the frenzied wind pounding the shutters. Until at long last, they were both spent.

CHAPTER TEN

DAWN PASSED UNNOTICED in the smothering mass of snow. When Anne awakened at last in the gray light of a buried day, she had no sense of time. She was alone in the large bed. Twisted sheets and blankets were the sole reminder of the seduction she had shamelessly perpetrated the previous night.

Dim stormy light hid Anne's discomfiture, but no degree of darkness in the room could camouflage the disintegration she felt. Honestly awake now, she knew her need for reassurance had been so great that she had pretended sex was the same as loving. Pretended? She had been grateful he hadn't turned away.

Anne didn't understand why Tavo said he wasn't capable of loving. He had loved her through her fears of intimacy. He had loved Pascal through his obnoxiousness, and he had loved Radámes even at his most fretting. Maybe she had misinterpreted.

But no. When she walked gingerly into the living room and saw the reserved, polite expression on Tavo's face, she was bludgeoned with the reality. Guilt lurked in the set of his mouth, and before he completely hid it, severe guilt made him shy away from meeting her eyes. *Damn him.*

"Was it only bed talk, Tavo?" She coughed, upset. "Everything?"

Tavo put down the calculator he'd been holding and paced. The creases in his gray flannel slacks were as sharp as the jaw he rubbed. "No," he answered eventually. "I meant what I told you, at the time I said it."

"You love me."

"I...."

Don't say "did." Don't say did. Don't say it. Anne dug her fingernails into her palms.

Tavo said nothing. He stopped by the window, staring out into white. Soft blackberry wool stretched across his shoulders. Blackberry. Would she ever learn to make his grandmother's kuchen? Would he ever again care if she learned? She thought she might die from the pain.

"I admire you, Ana. I appreciate you.... It's just that...." His voice trailed off.

"But you are waiting to see who the next one will be—maybe a little better, a little prettier, a little more challenging," she gritted.

"The next one?" He met her hurt, angry gaze for the first time. She could see he was genuinely surprised. "I have no expectations that I will ever again be as enchanted." He made a move to come to her, dropped his arm to his side and turned away, staring into the swirling void.

His inability to explain infuriated Anne. Her rage imploded, not exploded, and in a tight constrained voice, she asked, "Please, Gustavo, what is the problem? Help me understand."

His short laugh was harsh. "You are clever, Ana. Behavior is your business. Surely in your cynical detachment you knew there were strong reasons why a thirty-seven-year-old man has never married."

She forced herself to continue to be as openly naive as she'd been the day before, when everything seemed happily in order. Sometimes, she was learning, humbleness was the greater part of valor. "I thought you'd never really been in love," she told him truthfully.

Tavo put his hand up against the wooden window frame, his head bowed. "So did I." Then he slammed his fist against the frame. "*Pucha.* I am trapped in this existence. I did love you." This time the laugh was scornful. "That and fifty-pesos will buy you a coffee."

Anne's stomach contracted violently. She remembered Claudia's warning. "Maybe you are too frightened of losing me..." she ventured. "Did something happen yesterday during the races? You were afraid—"

His voice was unforgiving. "The cracked-heart theory of psychoanalysis?"

Anne stood her ground. "Sarcasm doesn't eliminate the problem. If it's not that, what is it?"

"A long story. It is complicated, and I do not really care to talk about it. *Bueno.*" He strode back to his desk, dismissal in his demeanor, a cordial finality in his voice. Anne could imagine he used the same tone in *el patrón* dealings with recalcitrant employees.

"Baloney, too complicated!" she snapped. "We all say that, and editors always retaliate by ordering a one-sentence summary lead. Ultimately, you see, Gustavo Mohr, nothing is complicated."

Tavo lifted his shoulders carelessly. The discussion had ended.

"I'll give you the lead," Anne charged, refusing to allow him the last nonword. " 'Multimillionaire Gustavo Mohr de la Huerta, thirty-seven-year-old strategist behind Chile's two-hundred-million dollar fruit industry, ran away today. 'I cannot love,' said the former Olympic downhill racer, generally credited with singlehandedly pushing the resistant Japanese toward a favorable trade agreement for the burgeoning industry.' "

Tavo faced her coldly, danger in his glacial eyes. Anne fought on, her fury rising like peroxide bubbles on a foul wound.

"A close friend, former *petuco* Pascal Larregoite, summarized Mohr's problem as follows—"

"You always hurt the one you love."

His snide rebuttal knocked the wind from her as surely as a doubled-up fist in her stomach. She gasped out her point regardless. "Said Larregoite: 'Why do we sabotage what we want?' "

The two combatants locked fierce glares. Anne's eyes burned; they teared. She refused to blink first. "Why is it?"

"I am truly sorry, Anne," he said finally. And then he insulted her. "What," he asked, "did your boyfriend say when he called yesterday?"

Anne knew that wasn't what Tavo was actually asking. He wanted to know if she'd torched her bridges, hoping, naturally, that she hadn't, and thus his guilt would be lessened. A charming holiday romance, he could think, looking back on their time together in years to come.

She refused to give him the immediate answer he sought.

"Oh. . .let's see. He announced for senator the day before yesterday. . . ."

*Is that relief in his cloaked eyes? "To hell with him,"
as Grandfather Mahoney would say.*

"Your politico will need a wife." A flat statement.

"You said that before," Anne pointed out nicely. "But not really. Not now, in California. Some dates, a few rumors both directions, and he'll win everyone's vote." She shrugged, not Latin style, but like the old Anne, unshockable-reporter fashion.

"Although..." Anne lowered her voice. Tavo studied her, plainly leery of the confiding tone. "Charles agrees with you, apparently. About a wife, that is. But I trust"—she deliberately didn't use trusted, past tense"—your wisdom, Tavo. You taught me the pleasure of speaking my feelings...."

Her eyes followed the pulsing cord in his rigid neck, and she reveled in the response. Some small part had escaped his discipline.

"So I told him I was marrying a Chilean."

Please don't deny it. Please. The curve of her lips belied the airy, bitter tone in her voice. She looked like a wounded fox cub, bewildered but fighting for its life.

The butcher made a quick, killing slice. "What are you going to do now?" he said.

Her eyes rolled back; she was stunned beyond pain. And then the spark of fire, the stainless-steel spine her father bragged about, the gutsy poise Snider praised, flickered to life. Her resolve blasted adrenaline through her veins, and a deliciously wicked grin flashed.

"What am I going to do? Fight for you."

She had the satisfaction of seeing she'd slipped by his defenses. "Excuse me," she concluded. "But you'll have to pack now."

He arched a quizzical eyebrow. "You're welcome to stay with me, Ana."

"I never doubted it." Confidently she tightened the

belt on her French blue robe. She knew her figure was provocative despite the manly wool. *What's a four-letter word that begins in L,* she thought, her eyes like coiled copperheads. *Lust.*

"I want you to miss me in your bed." She was brazen. "I want you to remember the feel of your hand between my legs. I want you to wake alone and know it is your choice. I want you to feel sorry for yourself. So... as I see it, either you move in with Pascal, or—" she was breezy "—I do."

It was the last satisfaction she was to have.

He arranged a room for her. Alone. Curious; she didn't think there were any to spare. Wasn't that why they had shared one room and gone public with their affair?

The wretched storm blasted on.

"My strategy is not to play hard to get," she told Tavo at lunch, before Radámes and Pascal joined them. "When I act hard to get, it's not an act. I'm not available." He looked amused, which was better than his guilty shut-out air. She continued, expecting his reluctance to pass with the blizzard.

"You know and I know that I want you, Tavo. What you've forgotten is that you want me."

She sincerely believed in the truth of her words. She plunged on. "In the United States the men do the proposing, but you can be sure that when *you* do, I'll say yes."

She laughed happily until she saw the embarrassed expression on his face, and her smile wilted.

ANNE AVOIDED TAVO for the next two days. If she'd had real courage she would have switched tables as well as rooms. Tavo remained friendly during lunch and dinner, but no more, and certainly he never initiated any encounters.

Her head ached from the strain of pretending everything was fine, from smiling when she wanted to weep, from forcing herself to sit still in the cozy leather booth, feeling neither his body, nor his magnetized field. Both his energy and his flesh were drawn tightly away from her interference.

Yet she continued to hope.

Circles shadowed both their eyes, and hollows were appearing in their haunted faces.

As for Tavo, nearly as Anne could determine from his daily conversations with the Argentines, he was working ahead into the business of summer and fall. For her, an escape into marathon movie going made her suffering endurable.

On the third day of the endless storm, a Saturday, Anne played gin rummy in the saloon with Radámes until her fingers were sore from shuffling cards. The surgeon politely didn't ask what had happened, and Anne, longing for Tavo to reach deep inside himself and push beyond his self-imposed barriers, the very accomplishment he had praised Pascal for, kept their problems to herself.

It was no secret, she knew. Every strained look, each reluctant smile—or worse, laughter that was too hearty—told their story.

She gloried in the storm now, counting on time to work its effect on Tavo. But it wasn't until the end of the third confined day that she realized he was unfeeling in his shell, working productively, while she was wasting time.

No, it was more than that. She was bored. She missed writing, not the writing she'd been doing, but what? She didn't know. Something safe, she thought. No tragedies. But now, not when she had become a Job, a Jonah, a King Midas of personal trauma. She'd lost Steffie. She'd lost Tavo. She'd lost Charles— No, it had been time to fish or cut bait on that one....

Something safe. She paced in her room. Pure information. A memory of yoked pairs of oxen pulling plows came to her mind. Oxen seemed so old-fashioned to a computer-trained mind used to a mouse popping around on a screen and jumping on garbage cans to trash an item. A rodent changing numbers, pronto, to line graphs and pie graphs with a noiseless hop.

Someday soon the mouse would be trashed, too, while the oxen plodded on, as they had through time immemorial. They plowed when Hammurabi wrote his laws, and Rome was built and fell. They razed woods in America, and probably, when humans shuttled to orbiting homes, oxen would continue preparing the earth to feed the populace.

Anne kneaded the idea, playing with the concept until her concentration overwhelmed her grieving senses. She didn't hear the air still, nor notice the clouds had passed. Only the stunning rays of sunshine filling her room caught her attention.

She was dismayed. September 4. Sunday. Tavo would be leaving by Tuesday or Wednesday, as quickly as the avalanches subsided and a landing pad was flattened.

Forget him, Anne railed at herself, and wished with all her might that she could. *Give him room, don't push, he'll come around.* Surely he was as punished as she physically. No amount of work substituted for the physical cravings wracking her and destroying her sleep. Could he sleep? Was she in his mind constantly upon waking, as he was in hers? She would do a series on junkies for the *Chronicle* in a couple weeks. She understood withdrawal now—sweaty, obsessed withdrawal.

No more. Anne stiffened her resolve, once again. All she had left was her career, and blast him, he'd made her dissatisfied with what she was doing. She had to create something new. Now. Immediately. Anne grabbed desperately at her life preserver of words and thoughts and emotions.

She borrowed an old typewriter from the office and began writing about oxen. Lovely, castrated beasts. Long-suffering beasts.

The touch of typewriter keys was unwieldy after the ease of a computer keyboard. The garble of strokes slashed across discarded words irritated her more severely than the wind had. She was used to clean copy. Wadded leads piled around the wastebasket were messy. Anne gave up on the typewriter.

A pen was too permanent. Scratched-out words made her thinking look scrambled. Sometimes it was, but in her shaky emotional state, she needed to remember that sometimes her words flowed swift and clear.

Finally, with an electronic-age need for instant elimination of error, she reverted to a pencil with an eraser. She set a cheap green plastic sharpener on the desk, and began. Eight hundred fifty words, she had already decided. Column length. Maybe the *Chronicle* would be interested in a slice of life from South America.

After a while she got stuck on the usefulness of oxen as compared to tractors. How many years did Tavo say the animals could be worked? Anne was afraid to bother him, afraid to face his sophisticated politeness before their next go-around of indifference at dinner.

Picking up her notebook was like picking up a badge of courage. She was a reporter again. No one ever intimidated her when she was reporting.

Not until after she'd knocked on Tavo's door did it occur to her that he might have a woman in his room. There was no response. She rapped again, nervously, and turned to leave.

He opened the door. With relief she saw the piles of paper, and beyond, through to the bedroom, a tidy bed.

She hurriedly explained her question.

"Twelve years. Some oxen keep their strength for thirteen." He was cordial. Was there something more? His face was thinner, a bit more haggard than at lunch, or perhaps that was only wishful thinking. Where was her pride?

Anne blurted out, "I've missed you. Have you—"

"Ana," he interrupted. "Why do you continue with this futile exercise? I am being as pleasant—" *pleasant!* "—as I can. I have apologized and I have spoken frankly. I cannot give you what you want."

Niceness evaporated along with any tatters of hope.

"You are perfectly willing to take love, *no cierto*, Gustavo Mohr de la Huerta! You just can't spare any yourself. You're selfish—"

The frigid silence was so brutal it stopped Anne's outburst.

"What am I to you?" she began again.

His answer was not immediate. The pause gave it potent credibility. "You are a friend."

"A friend?" Her voice was deathly quiet. "Not even a special friend?"

His expression was closed. "No. You are a friend."

"You lie!" she cried wildly, grabbing his arms. "You've lied all along, and this is a lie too, you know—"

He pulled away abruptly. "I am sorry. I cannot deal with this." He strode rapidly toward the bedroom.

Anne's fists balled. He couldn't deal with an honest burst of emotions? She wanted to hit him. "How dare you outsuffer me! How dare you! You hypocrite."

He had closed the bedroom door before she'd finished.

"You fool, wearing that copper bracelet all these years!" she raged at the offending door. "There never was a time when love was yours. Deep down you are not lovable."

An avalanche whistled outside the open windows. It sounded like a distant jet. She shivered. How was she going to escape Portillo and get home? It was unlikely she could, or would, ride with Tavo the next afternoon when his helicopter flew in.

THE WIND RETURNED FIRST. Snow began to blow gently, six feet of fresh-fallen snow swirling merrily. Then the biting wind blew harder and faster until the lonesome cry reminiscent of a locomotive thundering on tracks to nowhere again battered the hotel.

Light dimmed in the salon, where Anne was playing cards with Radámes and tempers were noticeably frayed. This storm was not expected. Guests had hoped to leave in another few days. The fun of an adventure was over. Now they were trapped in mounting hotel bills and neglected business.

Stale air pressed in on Anne; her thoughts were stale and her mood was rancid.

"We won't be out of here for weeks," she griped to Radámes. "I can't stand it. I'm due back. If this storm lasts another three days...that's Tuesday, Wednesday, Thursday...." She began counting with an irritated jerk of her thumb. "September 8. One week late. Then figure two days or three for the avalanches to stop and helicopters to land.... Friday, Saturday, Sunday...." Her voice began to rise. "Another week in this lousy hotel."

She wiped her hands on her comfortable corduroys and smoothed her hair back. "How can you sit there so calmly, Radámes?" She laughed wryly. "I understand Pascal's cheerfulness. It's a good excuse to lay back and chase girls. But aren't you anxious to get home? What if another storm blows in, and another, and—"

"Ana—"

"And how many helicopters are available to take people out, anyway? Say there are ten available, or twenty which I doubt—"

"Ana!" Radámes spoke sharply. "Concentrate on remaining calm," he ordered. "At the San Francisco hospital where I did my speciality, they lectured us on the Alcoholics Anonymous philosophy: compartmentalize each day. I am looking forward to having Pascal join me for stretching exercises in my room in half an hour, and I'm grateful for that. Then we'll have a sauna." He stopped. By now he could judge Anne's reactions.

"Ana, nothing is forever—not the good things, nor the bad."

Tears clung to her thick lashes. "I liked me better when I could control my misery."

"Control is an illusion. Have you not learned that, Ana?"

"But your AA trick—"

"They are all tools. Merely a means to an end."

"And control is the end," she stated flatly, swallowing the observation that she'd been more successful at life before she'd come south and been tempted into exposing her passions.

"Control?" Radámes raised his voice over the sudden, shriller blast of wind. "No, Ana. The end is to appreciate life as it flows."

Anne couldn't resist. The wind was shredding her civilized chatter. "You certainly suffered over Pascal's racing. Projecting ahead. Thinking the worst, biting your lip not to order him to stop." Then she remembered Pascal's outraged, ill-timed arrival at Tavo's door. "And the times you didn't bite your tongue."

Radámes smiled kindly and put the cards away. He stood up. His gray angora turtleneck imparted a stonegray cast to his blue eyes, emphasized by the taut, tanned skin of his face. Radámes might fret, Anne thought, but he was not a doddering old man.

"Sometimes I fail." The surgeon put a carefully tended hand on her sagged shoulder. "But I always feel."

"A Latin solution," she scoffed.

"Irish are—"

"I know, I know. Latins of the North. IRA thugs who put bombs in baby carriages."

"Don't insult yourself or me." His voice was as sharp as Tavo's had been when he'd corrected Pascal's pouting. "If you could have crammed your feelings back into your velvet coffin by now, Ana, you would have. It will take you a while. Unfortunately, you will accomplish your goal if you stick to it with your usual determination. Meanwhile, until you can cripple yourself, why do you not use your feelings?"

"Why?"

He scowled impatiently. Anne backed down. "How?"

"You are an artist. Be one."

"I'm a reporter."

"You write. That is an artist."

"I write what I report. That's different."

"Why are you afraid to say you are an artist?"

"It. . .it sounds so emotional." Anne was as surprised as Radámes at the way her confession popped out, like peas poked out of a pod.

"Yes?" he encouraged.

She dug in her heels.

"Too emotional?" he prodded.

"You know—morose, drunk, depressed, occasional blinding moments of ecstatic happiness. . . ."

"That sounds too Irish. You need some Latin tempering."

Anne laughed, tears in her eyes. Radámes was such a good friend. "Okay, I'll tell you," she said. "I wrote a column this morning."

"Wonderful. Columns are personal, are they not? On what subject did you expose your prejudices?"

"Oxen." Anne looked sheepish.

Radámes laughed. "I hoped, naturally, it would be a repudiation of that rude misconception that Latins are lousy lovers." He put his right index finger by the side of his eye and gently tugged the skin. *Watch out,* he was signaling. "Why not write a real column, Ana?"

"It's none of the world's business how I feel. I like the anonymity of reporting."

Radámes was undaunted. "Why does it have to be made public? Right now all you are doing is considering your feelings. You have nothing else to do...." He nodded toward the window and shrewdly dropped the topic. "Would you like to come exercise with Pascal and me?"

Anne started to refuse politely, then changed her mind. "I'd appreciate it."

STRETCHING GAVE ANNE A NEW FOCUS. She concentrated on a specific task that, thankfully, had nothing to do with her psyche. By the time they finished, her mind was clear.

"Please don't be offended, but I'll be changing tables," she said to her two sweating friends, wiping her dripping face with a towel. "It's too uncomfortable for me to continue...when...."

They understood.

"But breakfast, my dear," Radámes protested. "Please continue to have breakfast with me. You have been an important addition to my day."

Back in her room, she switched on every light in a futile attempt to cheer up the dullness.

The subject today, she decided, was the difference between male and female assumptions. She analyzed, she polished, enjoying the mental exercise. Her reflections were personal, but not about her personally. When she'd finished a goodly portion of her thoughts, Anne realized she had no conclusions, merely vivid verbs and clever phrasing. Thus far, her second column was worthless.

The subject had evolved into male-female attitudes about courtship. She had described the need for sacrifice before fulfillment. Her college psychology professor had talked of experiments proving that the tougher the initiation—read "sacrifice," the professor had said—the stronger the commitment afterward.

Tavo had struggled through her reluctance. He had to track her down when she ran away to San Martin and Bariloche. How much more sacrificing was he required to do before he was committed? What had gone wrong? Had the crucial factor been the challenge of the hunt, not a sacrifice?

Anne yawned, stretching her arms back until her shoulder blades nearly met. It felt good to stretch her mind, too. Abstracting "the romance...." Not "our romance" or "my romance," but *the* romance—set it aside, a dead body to be autopsied dispassionately.

Sacrifice wasn't the element, she decided, sharpening her pencil. The eraser end was worn flat. She nearly tore the paper eliminating the word "sacrifice." The operative word was "faith." It required tremendous faith in the other person to leap into the darkness of the unknown, where lovers might smash on the shoals of rejection, or abandonment. She wrote rapidly now.

Anne was pleased with the essay when she finished. Essay, not column. The latter was too confining. Columns had to fit on the editorial pages. She didn't know where her piece fit, and it didn't matter. She had been misled by dozens of roses and rainbows in a lovers' waterfall, and crashed on the shoals.

She fingered the gold necklace with its coppery-green reminder of the moment when she'd taken her leap of faith and said, "Yes." Why hadn't Tavo? She thought he had.

A memory came to her. Her ninth-grade class had had a graduation "sneak" day. They'd taken school buses to a park in the hills, and before the picnic, gone swimming in the pool. A clowning tomboy had climbed up for the high dive and jumped. At the last instant the supposedly fearless girl had changed her mind and tried to jump back on the board, but too late. Her too-late terror had left her on the concrete at the edge of the pool, bruised, broken, but alive and mendable.

Pascal's too-late terror had catapulted him into a concussion. Tavo had sabotaged himself, too.

Anne didn't know if the class clown ever dove again, but Pascal put his skis back on and bested one hundred mph. Surely Tavo, with his greater strength of character, his firmer grip on priorities, would regain his faith. Given enough time, he'd return; Anne was convinced of it, at the moment.

She left the necklace on and dressed for dinner in a dress that showed it off, silk with a faint gold pattern and a low neckline echoing the curve of the jewelry. A fanny wrap in the same rich fabric flicked her carefree message with every energetic step.

Anne's new place setting was ready at a table of Brazilians. The wine had already been poured. She glanced over at Tavo when she sat down and caught him studying her. He looked away. Neither anger, nor hunger, nor any emotion cracked his pleasant expression.

Resolutely she turned to her new dinner companions, all of them Italian Brazilians from Sao Paulo whom she had met before. Except for one couple from Búzios, the fishing village that sophisticated artists from Rio de

Janeiro had converted into a charming playground of sandy coves and gentle unpolluted waters.

Anne was long past being amazed at how friendly strangers here were to her. Tonight was no exception.

"You still plodding along with the oxen?" teased one of the men. "Have you read Pablo Neruda, Chile's Nobel poet?" The Paulista native mispronounced it "noble." "Neruda wrote odes to the mud you saw the oxen plowing near Temuco."

With a promise to read his copy, Anne stepped out of the mud into her current subject, love and faith. It was much closer to the hearts of the Brazilians. Indeed, if she'd wanted to switch to a more relevant subject, say the orange-juice crisis, it couldn't have deterred them from swapping wisdoms about love. Easily earned knowledge. What else gave such pleasure in life?

They flamboyantly argued that she should forget faith. Too Saxon, they dismissed the concept immediately. They approved of sacrifice, but it fell short, for they believed passionately in passion. Actually, Anne would later summarize the Brazilian position as faith in passion.

The only subject capable of diverting their philosophizing at that point was the weather. By the time dessert came they were despairing over the new storm. There was a shortage of helicopters, they heard. Even after the sun returned and the avalanches stopped booming and helicopters could land, it would take several days to ferry all the guests down the mountain.

"How much does it cost to ride to the airport?" Anne asked, conceding it might be wise to look for alternatives to Tavo's chopper.

The answer shocked her. A helicopter ticket was far more than she could afford. It was a month's rent, plus gas, electricity and the telephone. It was.... How badly did the *Chronicle* want her home? The paper could afford it. A cable to William A. Snider....

TAVO DANCED in the disco that night until three in the morning, Anne knew, for so did she. Their backs nearly grazed on several occasions, and still they pretended distance, and purported interest in their changing partners.

Only an intuitive, obsessively familiar observer like Anne could sense Tavo's dancing was not intimate. Yet she envied his partners. She begrudged them his nearness and his attention.

She was jealous, yes. She hadn't tried jealousy to break through his resistance. She had been honest; she had been patient, humble, understanding. She had angrily flailed with her tongue.... There were few recourses left.

Anne bumped hips with her Venezuelan oil-man partner and smiled, overly delighted with his flirtatious reaction. She snuggled into the arms of a Chilean dentist for a slow beat and disappeared for a walk in the corridor with a virile American retiree, age forty-two, from the Virgin Islands. She refused to notice whether Tavo witnessed her departure, or his reaction.

By three in the morning she was exhausted. Her feet hurt from dancing in sling pumps; her heart was empty. She didn't know whether Tavo was jealous. She only knew she wanted to rest her head against him and feel the music.

Ironically, they left at the same time, each alone.

Nothing in his brisk demeanor invited a smile or a hello. The hallway echoed their silence, the same corridor they had paced worrying about Pascal. When the elevator door opened on her floor, Anne said over her shoulder, "As you shout in the woods, so it returns." The door closed too quickly for her to hear his reply. It didn't matter. She knew there was none; that was her return.

THE HOTEL MANAGEMENT scheduled an amateur show the next night, a circus to appease the restless natives, Anne thought, joining Radámes in the temporarily converted disco. He had saved her a front-row seat. She kissed a hello on his cheeks and settled into the folding chair.

"I like this tweed." She fingered the British heather jacket. "The color does nice things for your eyes. Where's Pascal?"

"He promised me that he and your crazy countrymen are the stars of the show."

"Batten the hatches," Anne groaned. "Surf's up. Did he give you any clues to his sudden dramatic ability?"

The sun-toasted corners of the surgeon's eyes crinkled. "This time it's a surprise."

Before Anne had time to turn Pascal's unexpected secretiveness into a joke, the lights were lowered. Chairs scraped the floor as the audience settled in for a long session. Here and there throats were cleared. After six days of confinement the guests were danced out, movied out, backgammoned out, drinked out and just plain bored. No entertainer could have asked for a more receptive audience.

Brahms by an adolescent pianist brought a crescendo of *Otra, otra, otra,* and a nervous, plump girl did her best on "Flight of the Bumblebee." The audience cheered her.

A pimply juggler brought down the house when one of the ping-pong balls ponged him in the head, and the Venezuelan oilman tap-danced, a Fred Astaire with a ski-pole cane.

"I don't hear you volunteering to be Ginger Rogers," Radámes whispered.

"*Por favor!* I only tango," teased Anne, appealing to his Argentine pride. "We could show— Holy Moly...."

Pascal, Hank Purdoe and Lunch marched onstage, gallant Three Musketeers. Feather dusters stuck on their speed helmets transformed the plastic into dramatic chapeaus; shower curtains safety-pinned at their necks became sweeping capes.

A young boy beat out a drumroll on the low wooden stage with his hands. Anne had seen him tagging after Lunch between ski classes.

"Laaaa-dies and gentlemen. *Señoras y señores....*" Hank leered into the darkness.

"*Señoritas...*" piped up Pascal.

The three bowed, removing their helmets with synchronized grandeur. When they straightened up the drumming began again. Lunch swigged a clear liquid and held it in his mouth while he passed a glass to Hank, who drank without swallowing and passed the glass to Pascal.

"What the—" Radámes muttered.

The drummer stopped. Simultaneously the trio extended their right hands, flicked on cigarette lighters and spit the liquid. Flames shot back to their mouths.

Several women screamed. Even as the shrieks pierced the air, the flames died.

The fire-eaters bowed into the stunned silence and exited. Radámes's sudden laughter broke out. "It was lighter fluid," he chuckled, applauding heartily. The crowd recovered its wits and roared; they clapped. The musketeers clowned through three bows, the audience stomped their feet. "Bravo," they shouted, rising to their feet, shouting, *"Otra, otra, otra"* in vain.

Then the lights were turned off. The audience felt for their chairs and sat down. A single spotlight played over the dark walls and ceilings, and as the tension grew, swung directly to the center of the makeshift stage.

Tavo sat in the blackness, alone, the black of his turtleneck and his pants throwing into relief the glow of his moonbeam hair, the deep gold of his tanned face and the palest of gold of the simple Spanish guitar on his lap.

For Anne, the audience disappeared in the darkness. She saw only the face she loved and the softly rounded instrument he held patiently as he demanded, and received, absolute attention. Then he sprang from total silence—not even the scraping sound of a chair—to a pulsating rhythm, a raucous, comical *yacare*, a rousing song people in the audience knew as well as their names.

Four, maybe five hundred voices shouted the song. Tavo strummed harder to be heard until Anne thought surely the metal strings would snap under the strumming of his fingers.

The song never really ended, for it blended into

another, and another. Tavo, like a professional performer, molded the emotions of his audience—now sorrow, now hope, now torrid love with a Brazilian samba that brought the crowd to its feet, clapping the rhythm, undulating their hips. Grinding, fervid movements.

How long ago it seemed that Tavo had insisted she polka on the plateau. How foreign to be a bystander. Anne snaked to her feet, unable to resist the insistent pull of the samba. She felt freed from the sidelines and from an observer's by-lines. She gyrated as the others were doing into the darkness.

"Tropicals," Tavo had once described Brazilians. "Tropicals draw no line between conscience and desire. Their attitude is simple: how can you prevent what passion dictated you do. Why try." Understandably, Anne lost herself in Brazilian rhythm.

Time was banished from the room, along with light. Only mood survived, a mood of heartache and passion. Even Mexican favorites well-known in Los Angeles, such as "Guadalajara" and "El Rancho Grande," were passionate. Radámes sang with tears in his eyes and hoarseness in his throat. Tens of dozens of others in the room cried and loved with Tavo, including Anne, although she knew only the music, not the words.

Tavo cradled the guitar, his cheek pressed against the curve of the instrument, even as he'd held her at the curve of her waist, nestled in his lap.

The crowd hushed when at last he slowed to a clear melody. *"Si me dejas ahora,"* his strong baritone mourned.

"If you abandon me now. . . ." translated Radámes in a whisper.

The amateur singers quieted until only Tavo's voice

could be heard. They breathed as one until the final note, when the magic ended and each was abandoned, blinking and befuddled, to the startling glare of lights, leaving behind the spent performer. They pushed out, the show over, headed up to the bar for champagne.

"You were wonderful," Anne said when she reached his side, absorbing the way the natural waves in Tavo's hair had tightened in the dampness. In her imagination she felt his cheek against her hip, just as it had pressed against the guitar. She ignored the instrument separating them and the publicness of the stage. Her appetite for the man overwhelmed her resolve, and her lips parted eagerly as she leaned toward him.

He took her mouth, possessed it and demanded more. There was no soft response this time. His kiss was hard from hunger. She would have given more with no thought, no protest, no pride. For six days without his touch, six days of withdrawal had left her as weak as an addict. She craved him.

"What do you call this technique?" he asked, pulling away. For the first time Anne saw his eyes. They were bold and frosty.

She shivered. "Someone just walked over my grave."

"A seduction technique? Are you going to fight for me and win by remaining 'unavailable,' as you insisted last week, or is this a temporary lapse in your unilateral battle?"

His attack astonished Anne. She shook her head to clear it, a mild no in the puzzled movement.

"A case of snowbound lust?"

He was making no sense. She stared at him, bewildered. Somehow her restraint goaded him.

"Why can't you give up decently?" he said. "Make love, have a little fun, or—"

"*Te dejos*. . . . Abandon you, no?" Anne spit out the words of his song. Anger shredded the spell, and he seemed to relish their confrontation.

He quirked an equally angry eyebrow at her. "Abandon?" he scoffed. "What do you know about abandonment."

It wasn't a question. She knew that for this cold bastard she had ditched Charles Roderick III, possibly the next senator of California and a perfectly decent boyfriend, as boyfriends go. She had been ready to abandon her career, her country, her family. . . .

Civility departed as quickly as her sexual desires.

"You are a savage child." She enunciated each word. Anne wanted them branded on his soul. "You have never forgiven your mommy and your daddy for abandoning you, *no cierto?* You understand me, Gustavo Mohr?" Her face was white with rage.

"Any shrink could tell you your problem, even the dumb ones who flunked out of school. Somewhere in your twelve-year-old mind you decided it was your fault they died—if only you'd done *this* differently or *that* differently. And you're still mad that they were in the wrong building at the wrong time in Puerto Montt—" She caught her breath and rushed on before he could interrupt. She didn't care that his hands were rapping the side of the guitar in fury.

"And what was the story about your brother? You never quite got around to telling me if Alvaro was older. He was, wasn't he? Just enough that you always competed against him and you never, ever had a chance to beat him, because he abandoned the race before you had a chance."

Anne was horrified at the accusations coming out of her mouth. She had thought them, she believed them, but she had never intended to say them like this. "Your Olympic near victories were mere dog dung for you, the survivor, no? Your brother would have won a medal—"

"I do not intend to listen to your hysterics, Señorita Anne Mahoney." He walked away.

"The gullible Miss Anne Mahoney, who believed you, you rotten coward," Anne snarled at his broad back. It was a cheap shot, and she immediately regretted it.

Tavo spun around. "You begged me."

She burst into tears, appalled by this disastrous turn their encounter had taken, and still she couldn't stop herself. "You seduced me," she accused.

"You would have returned the favor tonight if you could have." His coldness had turned brutal.

"That's different." Her voice was pleading.

"So is death."

"Damn you to hell!" she shouted at the door that closed behind him and crying. "You fool." She was trembling with humiliation. "You don't have to marry me. Just love me." She couldn't stop the sobs. She crouched in a dark corner of the empty room and cried until she had no more tears, and still the sobs continued. Dry sobs that racked her chest and sent aching shots of pain down her arms.

Later she crept up to her room. Dawn was hidden in the relentless snow. Anne drew the curtains. She wanted to ignore the coming day. There was no reason to wake.

What do I know about death, she thought indignantly, her head on the peculiar Chilean pillow, wide as the bed. It was narrower than the ones she was used to and too hard to sleep on, even if she could have. *I know as much as any living person does. Nothing.*

A SHARP KNOCK AWAKENED HER in the darkness of her room. Her digital wristwatch glowed 1:07.

"Who's there?" she called. Her words sounded thick with the hangover of agonized sleep. Her heart pounded. Dared she hope for an apology?

"It's Pascal."

Anne kept the disappointment out of her voice. "Just a minute," she called loudly, sitting up on the side of the bed. Her head ached. She felt fluish from fighting, fragile from her slumped shoulders to her queasy stomach. "Give me another minute," she called again.

Pascal rapped a samba beat on her door. *"Andele arriba!"* he shouted with an exaggerated Mexican accent. *"Arriba, arriba."* The cheerful knocking on her door continued. Anne slipped on her robe and, running her fingers through her tangled hair, opened the door.

Pascal pretended amusement at her sleepyhead appearance, but under liveliness Anne knew he was concerned about her.

"You have precisely—" the accent was as British as his grandfather's "—41.089 minutes to get ready for lunch."

Anne's determined chin announced "No" before she did. She couldn't sit at Tavo's table again. The matchmakers and patcher-uppers had better understand right now that the relationship had been bombed into oblivion.

Pascal quickly patted her shoulder. "We're eating in the cafeteria with the instructors, Ana," he said. "I miss you at our table, and so does grandfather...." He hesitated. "Tavo has been impossible to be around. He has never behaved like this before, so I know he misses you...."

Anne blinked back tears. "I deluded myself he did, too, Pascal, but after last night I know it's irrelevant whether he misses me or not. He's determined—" She stopped. Further revelations would be indiscreet. Moreover, they were useless. "Thank you for fetching me, Pascal, and for worrying about me." Her smile was tremulous.

She hugged him and gave a farewell kiss on his scratchy cheek. "What's this?" she teased, rubbing her fingers over the tanned sandpaper.

"Today's idea. We'll be here at least two more weeks, possibly three. One of the girls in the beauty shop told me she can trim a beard any shape I want. What do you think of a goatee like Don Diego de Garcia?"

"Say, who?" Anne rasped out a good Hank Purdoe.

"You know—Zorro, Ana." Pascal pinched an imaginary tuft of hair on his chin.

"I know you. If I don't lead in the lunch line, there won't be any food left." Anne gently pushed him along. "See you shortly."

"Personally, I like you in that silk blouse with jeans and the Navajo belt," Pascal thought to call back as Anne was closing the door. "Silver on your round little hips—"

"You're bad, Pascalito."

Under the shower, however, she grew serious. Pascal's concern demonstrated a generosity of spirit she would never have suspected when she first met him, and she felt immensely grateful.

After lunch, before her anguish sank her to the very

depths, an ageless, beautiful Argentine woman she'd met in the sauna one afternoon, a satisfied client of Radámes's, lured Anne into a fast-paced, competitive round robin of checkers. Clanging timers and irrepressible jokers left everyone holding their sides.

Surrounded by a safety fence of laughter, Anne watched Tavo enter the crowded salon. She was a dispassionate observer, more or less. She grimaced inside and tried to make light of it to herself. *Ma o meno dispassionate,* as the Chileans would say, dropping their S's. *Más o menos.*

Tavo's navy slacks hung just so, the long sharp crease continuing without fail from his hips to his polished black loafers. The slacks had obviously been tailored for him. Off-the-hanger selections, sized to fit his narrow waist and hips, would have stretched too tightly over his strong thighs.

He was carrying a soft drink in his right hand. He must have just come from the bar, Anne thought, wondering why she was confident he didn't have bourbon in his drink, or Chilean *pisco*, for "piscola," as they called their rum and Coke.

She pondered the thought a while, deaf to the loud political discussion on her left. Then she realized no one around her was drinking. It was five-thirty in the afternoon. They had been snowbound for seven days, and the glasses were filled with carbonated drinks or orange juices.

That was a sharp cultural difference, especially to an Irish American. Another was the heated, arm-waving, friendly political discussion going on.

She tested the trend of her analysis on the person to her left. "In the United States we're taught it's rude to talk about politics or religion at a party, because everyone has a difference of opinion.''

"What do you talk about?"

Anne forgot to answer. Her mind churned. Her piece on the oxen was a test run. She now knew what she wanted to write. Slice-of-life stories, true events that, when described in artful detail, told truths extending beyond the occurrence.

The oxen article needed people. It needed a farmer who never wanted a tractor. It needed a struggle to pull out the biggest tree in a roadless forest, an *Old Man and the Sea* challenge for a farmer turned summertime logger after the spring crops were sown, using equipment from the factories that specialized in machinery for teams of bullocks....

When they'd strolled the fertile land of his grandmother's farm in the south, Tavo had assured her that the answer to what kind of writing she could do after they were married would come in an unexpected way. Now she knew, and now she wouldn't as his wife. That hadn't been part of his prediction.

Anne's eyes riveted on Tavo. He had pushed up the sleeves on his white cashmere sweater. He sipped his drink, listening thoughtfully to something Radámes was saying. The copper bracelet was gone.

Instinctively she smoothed her hand over her naked neck. She had wept when she'd removed her necklace the previous night. For Anne, the gesture symbolized her final acceptance of the end. She glanced back up and saw his eyes follow her hand. He glowered, and she shot him a look of pure venom.

He saw it. She could sense the cords in his neck tensing, could read the hostile set of his jaw. Anne had seen

that look before when Liliana had caressed his chest
with her unwelcome hand. She hated him for repeating
the look for her.

Anne tossed her freshly washed hair, longer now than
when she'd left Los Angeles a month earlier. He raised
his glass to her in mockery. She laughed. Hollows under
Tavo's eyes betrayed his restless nights, his rangy body
was thinner. She was glad she had taken time, thanks to
Pascal's patient encouragement, to cover her discontent
with makeup.

"If you can't take the heat, stay out of the kitchen,"
Anne said aloud.

"What did you say?" asked the perplexed Brazilian
to her left.

Anne was startled. She hadn't realized she'd spoken
aloud. "It's an old American political philosophy," she
explained, turning her full attention on the man. "If you
can't take the heat, stay out of the kitchen," she repeated.

"Curious statement. How is it generally inter-
preted?"

Anne looked up to see Tavo striding out of the room.

"It means don't promise what you can't deliver."
And she went upstairs and began writing.

THE CLOUDS BLEW OVER THE ANDES on September 9,
leaving the Friday-afternoon sun blazing as if nothing
had interrupted the perfect climate of the resort.

Portillo guests crowded around the barometer in the
lobby. It was rising, but most of them were afraid to
count on science for assurance that their hopes wouldn't
be buried in another six feet of snow. Yet they hoped.
After nine days of confinement, there was nothing left
to talk about.

The large balcony outside the salon filled with bikinied skiers. Fresh-fallen snow was piled nearly level with the second-story balcony. Attendants were shoveling out the pool and decks below. Snow could be heard dropping from rock precipices in every direction, from chimney faces too sheer to hold snow for long. The avalanches were muffled roars, smoke grenades blowing hundreds of feet high, whispering the way for weighty slabs of snow flying down the rocks.

The crowded balcony was the outer limit for the guests until the avalanches had slipped down their traditional riverbeds, collapsing hundreds of thousands of tons of snowpack into the base. Two days, said Portillo's management, maybe three, and skiers could return to the slopes.

Anne hadn't paid much attention. She was returning to the desert mountains of Los Angeles, burning mountains in the scorching, dry air of autumn, just as soon as rescue helicopters could land. Two days, maybe three. Four Brazilians from her dinner table planned to share the flight and the bill with her.

Anne basked in the renewing rays of the sun that first clear afternoon until her paling skin was crisped pink and her mind was loggy. She would return to Los Angeles, far more changed than William A. Snider had ever anticipated. He had lost a tragedy writer. Hopefully, in her extended absence, Snider had discovered some other ambitious reporter's forte was other people's sorrow.

Anne was ready for happy endings of her own. It would be easier back home, she knew, when her stretched vacation was over and her reality in place.

By ten o'clock Saturday morning, Anne was on the deck again, stretched out on one of the padded chaise longues. Pascal, at her side, restlessly waited to sample the fresh snow before it gave way to spring corn under the heat of the approaching summer.

Their sunbathing stupor was surrounded by a noisy war. Ski instructors were pounding explosives on the high ridges, knocking avalanches at their will, not nature's, looking to reopen the runs.

It was close to noon when the bad news became general knowledge. Rivers in the northern end of the Central Valley were flooding, and the Mapocho River through Santiago had risen above its high-sandbagged banks for the second year in a row.

Although Anne pitied victims of the floods, she was professionally detached. Fire victims were on her mind. She would cover the September fires for Snider, but he had to get her off the bloody end of general assignment before the winter floods started in L.A. She wouldn't talk to one more sandbagger at Malibu Colony, screaming her questions over the terrifying roar of the invading February ocean.

A yellow helicopter buzzed around the hotel and departed down the mountain, loosening avalanches in the wake of its rotor.

"It doesn't take much noise to trigger one," said Pascal, propping himself up on his elbow and squinting at the snow dust booming not more than fifty feet from the Plateau run. Sweat glistened on his dark skin. "The sound of a cross-country skier, or a laugh, can set off a slide."

No one was in the mood for laughter. "Didn't that

helicopter look like Tavo's?" she said, settling back into the cushions. "Or are all helicopters yellow?"

Before Pascal could answer, Radámes found them. "That's the last helicopter we'll see for days," he said, sitting on Pascal's longue. His grandson made room for him with welcoming friendliness. "All the helicopters are making emergency evacuations and carrying supplies. Tavo didn't have time to wait for a platform to be flattened. He had to get to his farms."

"If the chopper couldn't land, how did he leave?" Anne sat up, alert.

"Climbed a rope ladder."

"Flooding wouldn't hurt orchards, would it?" she asked. "Unless the water is over the tops. But that seems improbable, except in the bottomlands."

"Trees need oxygen to breath. When the ground is covered for a week, ten days, their roots drown and they die. All it takes is standing water. It doesn't have to be deep."

Suddenly the flood victims were in her personal circle of concern. Naturally, Tavo hadn't shared his fears with her. He hadn't even said goodbye. Why should he? She hadn't made up her mind whether to politely shake his hand when she left or dash over to her helicopter and leave him with a little smile and a littler wave. A royal wave, a Queen Elizabeth II wave.

He hadn't even attempted a goodbye. She desperately wanted to return home and never think about the man again.

"When did you say the helicopters can take us to the airport?"

"No one knows. It depends what happens when this snow hits the rivers. It was late for a storm this strong, and they had had a one-hundred-year record by mid-August...." Radámes was on his fact kick again. "I'd anticipate a week minimum and ten days maximum, unless you can claim grave medical emergency, Ana."

"Ten days more! That's September 20." Anne blanched. "I can't stand it," she admitted in a tight voice. If she'd taken off her sunglasses, the Argentines could have seen her eyes were wild. "I can drive out of here by then."

"No, Ana. People waiting for cars won't be out of here until sometime around the twenty-fourth," said Pascal. "That is," he added, "if it doesn't start snowing again."

Anne anxiously stood up and leaned over the railing, looking down the mountain in the direction of the Pacific, mother of the juggernauts. The sky was as blue as the day she arrived.

"How's the barometer?" She turned to the two.

"Up." That was Radámes. "And Tavo's pilot told him the five-day forecast was for good weather."

"I'd better go down to the desk and have them short-wave a new message to the *Chronicle*," she said, picking up her towels, cover-up and stationery. In her distraction she dropped a pen. It rolled off the deck and disappeared in the deep snow.

"Oh, well," she sighed. "It's not important. Nothing much seems to be when you're a prisoner."

CHAPTER ELEVEN

THE CONFINEMENT DRAGGED, yet by Saturday afternoon, the seventeenth day of September and the seventeenth snowbound day, as Anne was snapping on her skis, she was nostalgic. Five weeks in Chile were a bullet train in her memory. The vista had passed in a normal clear fashion until she had a point of comparison, like a speeding car on a highway alongside railroad tracks that seemed to be stationary.

Anne's point of reference were two notebooks filled with large loopy scrawls. Her stories of luxurious imprisonment were not fiction; she had scoured all embellishments from her writing. These were not "Chile: Land of Contrasts" pieces, neither had she opened with the typical travelogue: "It was sunset in Santiago.... We sat at our charming table for two, sipping a marvelously bouqueted 1978...."

Anne wrote each morning after breakfast with Pascal and Radámes for company. At lunchtime she put down her pencil and went out on the slopes. Skiable regions were limited for the first few days to the upper area around the hotel. Below, on Juncalillo, the boom of explosives continued. Then some of the lower runs opened, and skiers merely maneuvered around rough mounds of snow where the avalanche slides had slammed into flat ground and shuddered to a stop.

Even eight days after the second September storm blew over the Andes, an occasional swoosh like a distant jet sounded. Anne would go down the valley and see a cascade of white power drop from the highest ridges. Avalanches were seldom discussed in the shimmering heat of lunch on the Plateau, nor at dinner. Unfailingly, the subject remained the same—namely, when would the guests be released.

Disaster reports were being transmitted to Portillo by shortwave radio. Floods raged in the valleys, the guests heard. Some wealthy residents of Santiago had been evacuated from their brick homes bordering the boulevards and wooded strips of parks along the Mapocho River. Helicopters couldn't be spared. They were hovering over mountain canyons watching for logjams. Every pileup was a dangerous dam ready to burst with accelerated fury into the valleys.

Bulldozers, however, were scraping their way up the Pan American highway toward the stranded hotel and the Argentine border. Their daily progress was posted by nightfall.

Anne swung from a desperate impatience for freedom to an illogical wish that the time would never pass. She was swaddled in a silken world of bright uncritical friends, creative work, exhilarating exercise, sunshine, cool air and exceptional food and wines. The only thing missing was love, but that would be missing in Los Angeles, too. At least here the hotel manager kindly kept track, as best he could, of the flood damage to Tavo's orchards.

It was a tragic link to him, her only link. Her last one. In the enforced contemplative quiet of her life, that ironic twist didn't escape her. She knew full well that if the same "killer floods," as the *Chronicle* would have headlined them, had occurred in Los Angeles, Anne would have convinced the region's preeminent fruit man—in her scenario, a man very like Tavo—to let her ride along in his helicopter while he surveyed the damage.

To personalize the disaster, she would have blended the precision of the statistics the man would cite with his distressed reactions. Because Tavo himself was so subtle, this would have been effective. Pupils as swollen as the rivers made good copy; tiny, rigid lines around his mouth; an impatient drumming of his index finger on his knee. She knew the signs so well.

She thought she knew him, and she did—two sides of him. No, three: the cheerful hunter, the tender man who mothered his loved ones, the efficient, ambitious executive. And there was a fourth, the one she had accused him of being, her charge accurate, so stupidly ill-timed, but true: the scared, angry, orphaned twelve-year-old.

Nevertheless, she was obsessed with Tavo's problems, worrying with him, although he'd never know. At least she hoped he wouldn't learn later of her interest.

Vineyards and orchards in the Aconcagua Valley had been covered with water five days, then six...and finally, the death sentence. The critical week had passed, and the water hadn't receded. Which acreage was Tavo's and which wasn't was not relevant. They had talked often enough of the contracts he had with other growers.

South of Santiago, the swollen Maipu and Las Lirios rivers were rampaging over farmers and townspeople alike. Tavo had built the majority of his warehouses in that region of the Central Valley. Storage facilities had been refrigerated at great expense to handle the perishable fruit. His new freezing operation for peaches and bing cherries was in.... Anne had to study a map to recall the specific site of the plant. Rancagua. The cartographer had widened the Las Lirios on the outskirts of the city. How severe was the damage, or was the plant located a safe distance away?

A shortwave call the afternoon before to the Santiago headquarters of Industrias Mohr, S.A. brought no response. Considering Tavo's need for privacy, Anne wasn't surprised that his employees were even more cautious than their demanding boss. A plea that Dr. Ebert Gamen, a personal friend of the *señor*, wanted the information brought no additional help.

And there Anne's information had stalled.

Rumors were rife on the Plateau during lunch on the seventeenth. One group of informants had heard that a few helicopters would begin carrying guests to the airport the next day, a Sunday. Pessimists claimed the barometer was dropping.

Hope and despair pulled with equal force, and claustrophobia pressed Anne's lungs until she, like the drowning trees, couldn't breathe. She didn't finish the food on her plate; her stomach was knotted and her temples throbbed. Finally unable to tolerate any more speculation, she returned to the hotel to pack.

The same clothes that had fit in the suitcases so tidily when she first arrived in Chile now filled the same spaces nearly to bursting. She was ramming the contents in carelessly, blisters rising on the sides of her fingers from forcing the cases closed, when Pascal called her name.

His voice was urgent. "Ana, are you there?"

"My grandmother's had a heart attack," Pascal told her when she hurriedly opened the door. His face was grayish, his mischievous brown eyes damp. Anne guessed he had run up the stairs, too impatient to wait for the elevator.

"How bad is it?" she asked.

"We don't know. Mother's message said they've stabilized her in intensive care at British Hospital. Grandfather says no one will know anything certain for three days."

"How much longer do we have to wait?" Anne felt she knew the generous Sophia. Radámes carried several photos of the slim, elegant woman who wore her gleaming silver hair in a soft chignon. As their entrapment had worn on, the surgeon had spoken more and more often of his wife. He was homesick. Anne had accepted his invitation to come visit on her next vacation. Buenos Aires was sufficiently removed from Santiago to enjoy without ruinous memories.

"The message we got said she had the attack early this morning...."

"We're going to be in agony until Monday morning; then." Anne pitied Pascal. He had never experienced death within his family. He might have to learn a different courage than it had taken to defy death himself.

"We have got to get out of here," Pascal said. "Grandfather's on the shortwave now trying to contact Tavo. We need his helicopter—"

"Quick, let's get down there and find out what's happening." Anne grabbed her room key. "Up at the *asado* people were saying the barometer is dropping. If they're right, another storm's on the way. Tavo needs to get his chopper up here fast."

They ran down the hall, took the steps two at a time and rushed breathlessly into the hotel office. Radámes sat immobile, the shortwave radioist beside him, his eyes intent on the silent microphone, as though if he stared long enough, it would speak.

He looked up when Anne and Pascal entered and smiled, a sad, weary smile. His helpless shrug gave the younger ones the answer to their first question. "His people are searching for him now. The last they knew he was in Rancagua working with sandbagging crews."

"Where's the helicopter?" asked Anne.

"San Felipe. They don't want to send it down for Tavo until he gives them the orders."

"Once he tells them, how long would it take the pilot to pick him up and get up here?" Distances were a muddle in her mind. All she knew was that San Felipe was north of the capital and Rancagua to the south.

"I do not know time with a helicopter, but by car, the two cities are two or three hours apart, depending on the traffic in Santiago," said the shortwave radioist.

Radámes looked at his watch and sighed. "It is 3:15. About three more hours of daylight."

The anxious group sat restlessly by the radio. Waiting. Waiting. Anne shifted in her hard chair, then paced. Radámes radioed for two seats on a flight to Buenos Aires. "We might as well be optimistic," he said to no one in particular.

The call came back that there were only two first-class seats left on the 10:00 P.M. flight. "Book them," the surgeon said.

Anne sat back down. It was 3:42. Where was Tavo? She knew he would come to the rescue as soon as he knew he was needed. Despite his other faults, he always had.

Suddenly it seemed ludicrous for the three of them to be wasting time. When Tavo flew to the rescue, the Argentines needed to be ready to step on the helicopter with no delays. Radámes voiced the same thought.

"We'd better get packed fast. You have that pile of speed-racing gear, Pascal. I don't know where we're going to put it. The bellboy needs to find a big box and a sturdy rope.... Can you explain our dilemma, Ana?" Radámes asked, distracted. His voice was shaky. "I know—"

"Of course. As soon as I've heard something here," Anne interjected. "We're adults." She didn't add, "sometimes."

"I intended to wait until I heard from Tavo before calling Buenos Aires again to find out what is happening with Sophia, but...well, maybe Tavo will get to a phone shortly."

Radámes walked out slowly, despite the need for haste, his arm around his grandson's shoulders, leaning on the young man for support. Anne watched the frightened pair until they were out of sight, then resumed Radámes's desperate staring at the microphone.

The radio operator from the Hotel Portillo's office in the Santiago suburbs broke the nervous silence. The only Spanish word Anne understood was *tormenta*. The negative weather watchers had been accurate.

"What did he say?" she asked the bilingual radioist at her side. He answered Anne briefly and replied to the message.

The helicopter couldn't reach them before it was too late to land. Tomorrow was too late; a storm was blowing in. Tavo was en route to Santiago. He was radioing to airport tower, where a controller had cooperated by telephoning Portillo's Santiago office.

This five-way communication is like a game of gossip,
Anne thought, wondering how accurate the translations
were by the time she heard them.

"What time did Dr. Ebert Gamen say his plane
leaves?"

"Ten."

"Diez."

The silence was endless. During the delay, Anne agitated over the upcoming storm. She couldn't stay in
Portillo another two weeks. Emotionally, she had to get
back to her life, and financially she couldn't afford the
rates, not even if the credit union loaned her money.

The *Chronicle* wouldn't pick up the tab. They'd insist
she should have had the ingenuity to get out of the
mountains. "A *tormenta*?" She could see Snider's per-
petually skeptical expression. "You're the torment,
Lady Jane. We've had to double up on staff to cover
your life as a lady of leisure...." Snider always exaggerated until she hit him for merit raises; then he immediately downplayed her worth.

"Mr. Mohr has ordered a car to be left for him at Los
Andes. He says to ski down to the first tunnel. The highway is cleared to that point. He will meet them at
seven."

"How—"

The radioist signaled her quiet as a rapid Spanish
postscript came on.

"Tell them to keep Señor Mohr on the line," Anne
ordered, nervousness making her blunt.

The radio operator obeyed, then repeated the additional message. "Mr. Mohr is having his office call the
British Hospital right now. It will be back with the latest
update. When he heard you were relaying the messages

for Dr. Ebert Gamen, Miss Mahoney, he asked how Dr. Ebert is. Should the airline make emergency provision with medical oxygen?''

Anne considered. She shirked the final decision, settling instead for listing her observations: the surgeon's color was good, his breathing was normal, his walk, however, was slightly shuffling. In her judgement he would make it through the emergency for the sake of his wife, if for no other reason.

Silence. Then, ''And Pascal?''

''Immensely supportive.'' The teenager's matured, changed behavior brought tears to her eyes. She rubbed them away with a fist. ''Ask Señor Mohr, please, if he could call Carlos Luzzini and ask him to meet me at the tunnel, too. I must return. . . home.'' Even now it hurt to say the word.

Silence.

''Diez-cuatro.''

Anne had already taken the room key from her pocket and was on her way out the door when she heard the official translation. ''Ten-four.''

''I need to settle my bill immediately,'' she told the receptionist at the main desk. ''Can I rent skis to get to the tunnel? My driver, Carlos Luzzini, will return them as soon as it's possible to reach the hotel by car. Who do I talk to about that?''

''It's five o'clock. Hank Purdoe is probably in the bar. He can give you suitable skis.''

Anne gave Tavo's message to Radámes and worried her way back to her room. She put on the long underwear she'd never worn, jeans and a tank top and covered that with a flannel shirt and shetland sweater, then ran downstairs to the boutique. Plastic money bought a chic European one-piece suit, two sizes too big and very expensive. The sunny yellow, lightweight material was windproof and waterproof. She had to be able to unlayer herself for the one-hundred-degree temperatures of Los Angeles in September.

Hank wasn't in the bar. Neither was Lunch. The bartender spoke no English to tell her if they had been there.

Anne ran downstairs to the rental shop. The light shone under the closed door. She knocked impatiently.

"Say, hey, Annie." Hank looked up from the work-table, where he was roughing up the silver wax on a pair of long skis. His straw-blond hair was as unruly as usual.

"Hear you're going down to the tunnel with us," said Lunch, at the door. "Hank's working over the skis we'll need. Yours are in the corner. The red Rossis."

"I didn't know you were coming."

"Señora Marcellini broke her leg this afternoon, so we're sledding her down. Besides, the bossman says it's too dangerous for you guys to go alone."

"Dangerous?"

That had never occurred to Anne.

"Juncalillo gets the afternoon sun. When that skied-up mush freezes tonight, you're talking about I-C-E, lady."

"We'll be down by then, won't we?" Anne's eyes widened with fear. She handled the steep section on Jun-calillo easily now. Still, she only ventured out in midmor-ning, when the snow softened. "Is Hank putting on special wax to keep us from skidding on the ice?"

"No such thing as no-skid tires in this sport, Annie," he said. "I'm just scratching up your basic daytime, spring-ski wax to break up suction on the bottoms. That layer of water on snow's worse than snakes for grabbing at you." Hank finished the final ski and put his equipment away. "Best we can hope for is to take off in the next few minutes before dark, and be grateful that storm's blowing in."

"The storm—"

"Warms up the wind," said Lunch. "You ready? Grab that expedition parka on the hook in the corner. Too much goose down never hurts. Where're the kid and the grandfather?" Lunch settled both his skis and the red ones on his shoulder and was out the door. "We've got the toboggan by the door. The doc has the *señhora* across the hall in the infirmary."

"Right," said Anne, putting on the brilliant orange parka. It hung to her knees. "I'll run get Radámes and Pascal." Her voice trembled slightly as she envisioned the physical ordeal ahead. Gone were ambivalent feelings about leaving Portillo and returning to work. Her anxiety about facing Tavo for the last time disappeared. The alpine glow that follows sunset was dangerously near....

THE GROUP HERRINGBONED UP the gradual slope to the lift, following alongside the caterpillar tracks of Portillo's skimobile. Their luggage was strapped to the Snowcat's loading platform. One of the maintenance experts was driving.

Hank and Lunch hauled the Brazilian woman up the hill effortlessly. Although her face was familiar, Anne didn't know her personally. The middle-aged woman lay in the toboggan, a horizontal papoose, wrapped and strapped, her eyes closed. Whether in understandable terror or doped with painkillers, Anne didn't know. Probably both.

Pascal slowed his pace to bring up the rear, pretending it was his natural speed. Anne heard Radámes panting behind her, an anxious reaction, she knew, because the surgeon was in superb condition. The ski instructors ahead of her had large flashlights poking out of backpacks. Distress radios had been stowed along with emergency medical equipment.

An attendant was waiting for them at the Poma. As soon as the group exited at the top, another attendant radioed down, and the poles with their gray saucers stopped. For how long, Anne wondered. If the new storm was as ferocious as the last two, it might be another week before the guests reemerged from the hotel. She shivered. A blast of wind fired needles of piercing snow into her cheeks, and they burned. The wind died down, but light snow continued falling. The storm had arrived.

"How long do we have before it gets bad?" she hollered up to the instructors in the lead.

"Shh." Pascal was at her side. Hank had turned back and was waving her silent.

"Don't waste your breath," the teenager whispered very close to her ear. "Hurry."

Anne nodded. She understood, her heart racing. The eerie, darkening silence was more nerve-racking than the most clever sound track in a horror movie.

The wind returned, as warm as red-faced Hank had predicted. It stirred old snow and new, blowing it up the mountain into their faces, into their noses and eyes—

burning, blinding. Goggles would shut out the last light of day; no one put them on. They simply suffered and skied into the painful onslaught.

Perhaps five minutes later, perhaps ten, for time had no landmark, Anne stumbled on the rubble of a previous avalanche. Her skis squeaked sharply on the chunks of snow; the mush was beginning to harden. She headed farther away from the sides of the mountain, away from halted rivers of far-flung snow, closer to the edge of the run. There was no choice.

They pressed on.

A moan from the toboggan brought the party to a sharp halt. Pascal nearly collided with his grandfather, who in turn almost struck Anne. Radámes skied around Anne and down to the patient while Lunch held the flashlight on her. The surgeon searched through Hank's pack until he found what he wanted. The injection took a few long minutes to take effect.

No one spoke. Radámes kept his fingers on the woman's pulse until he was satisfied. Then they continued, Pascal directly behind Anne.

Her thick lashes were icing now as blown snow melted on her body and froze. With every inhalation, the membranes in her nostrils pinched together until her hot, moist breathing thawed the tender skin. With each labored exhalation, the thaw came more slowly. She refastened the wide neckband on her parka tighter under her nose and breathed through her covered mouth.

Snow began to fall heavily, muffling the scream of the rising wind. Although it wasn't gale force, the bitter draft held the promise of another snowy hurricane.

By the steepness of the incline, Anne judged they were close to the tunnel now, and she was appreciative of the uphill wind. It pushed her back up, even as her gravity-drawn skis tried to slip down faster than she wanted.

Silently they crossed the highest tunnel. The Snowcat ahead cut its motor. Below towering bulldozed banks, they could see car lights. The problem was how to reach them.

"Let's get the toboggan down first," The deep voice was Tavo's.

Pascal was out of his skis in a flash. He rocketed them down the fifteen-foot-high canyon to the highway.

"*¡Está bien!*" That was Luzzini's voice.

Pascal slid down on his seat, while Hank and Lunch angled the toboggan into place and lowered it slowly. Even under the puffy camouflage of their fat goose-down jackets, despite the snow, Anne could gauge the strain of lowering the injured Brazilian.

"Stash my stuff in the tunnel, will you, Pascalito." Lunch shoved down his skis and poles, and Hank followed suit. While Radámes slid down, Lunch, Hank and the Snowcat driver handed down luggage and skis. They worked quickly. The three men had to get back to the hotel in a hurry. Juncalillo's vertical walls were treacherous when packed with new snow.

"C'mon, Annie, get crackin'." Lunch motioned her over to the edge.

She swayed with vertigo. A story-and-a-half descent faced her, straight down, and there was no path. The men had loaded the patient into the end of a station wagon whose back seat Tavo had lowered. His bare head was dusted with white. Snow clung to the green, windproofed shelf of his broad shoulders.

Anne bent over to unfasten her skis, groaning softly at the tight layers of clothing.

"I am here," Tavo called from below, startling her. Luzzini climbed behind the wheel of the station wagon. Radámes and Pascal settled the last of their luggage in the trunk of the second car, then hurried into the front seat beside Luzzini. They headed down the highway. Tavo stood there alone, holding up his arms to help her.

"I am here." Anne was insulted by his words, and comforted at the same time. Yet apart from her contradictory reactions, she remained terrified of the slide she had to make.

She clenched her teeth and slid, quivering at the cold snow on her seat, a burning sensation that flushed her whole body hot and cold when Tavo caught her in his arms and lowered her carefully to the ground.

He gathered up her skis as easily as pick-up sticks and carried them inside the tunnel, where he laid them with the others. After the storm Portillo employees would fetch them.

Anne trotted into the tunnel after him, her head bowed into the fierce wind. Tavo went back outside, climbed into the parked car and drove to the end of the tunnel, about fifty feet from where she stood at the upper end of the concrete structure. The lights from the car ricocheted off the snow, falling in the final dullness of dusk.

"Luzzini and I only had time to put chains on the bank's station wagon," he explained, opening the trunk, taking all the Argentine's gear out to reach the box of chains.

"Do you need help?" Anne's polite offer almost stuck in her throat. She hadn't spoken to him since his unforgivable attack after the musical show. She dreaded the drive down with him. Why had he stayed?

"You can drive forward as soon as I lay these straight." He arranged the strong steel links in front of the tires. Anne unzipped the orange expedition parka and threw it in the back of the car. She was tired of its bulky interference, and inside the shelter, away from the wind, the temperature wasn't bitter.

She moved the seat forward so she could reach the pedals. With time to waste, she watched Tavo straighten the cross-links from the driver's seat. For the first time she noticed he was wearing old-fashioned black rubber boots, caked with mud. Above the tops, almost to his knees, the jeans were splashed with scummy streaks of dried river water. His eyes were dark holes in an exhausted face. A powerful urge to run a hot tub for him and tuck in the covers when he went to bed made her heart pound. Never again.

Anne gripped the steering wheel to steady her hands. The remembrance of their last two encounters curbed her instincts. She had renounced her pride and begged, and he had walked away. Humiliation set a rigid tone to her voice, rigid as the back he had turned on her.

"Too bad—" *for you and me,* she thought "—that Radámes had to accompany the woman with the broken leg down the mountain." She spoke out of the rolled-down window, not looking at him.

"He didn't."

"Then why—"

"I wanted to talk to you." He sounded weary. "I had hoped I would have more time before you left...." He got way down on his hands and knees in front of the chains and signaled Anne forward. She stepped on the brake and the clutch. The distant whistle of a jet fractured the calm as she shifted into first gear.

Then suddenly the ground quaked violently. Her feet automatically glued both the brake and the clutch to the floorboard. A screaming snow-laden wind crashed with a deafening roar. The entrance was plugged closed. Anne choked in the smoking snow dust.

The earth quaked again, rocking the small car, slamming Anne's head into the steering wheel. A protective subconscious force kept her feet flat on the floor. Holding her head, crying in pain, she turned off the motor and yanked the handbrake to secure the car. Her hand felt bruised. No matter. She slowly climbed out of the car, dazed and fighting nausea from her headache.

A wall of white reflected the headlights, a solid screen, a movie acted for real. Where the wall met the pavement, one arm lay. Perfectly still.

Screams ripped from Anne; she felt them tear her throat, but heard nothing. Frantically she dug at the snow like a helpless dog. "Tavo! Tavo! Tavo! Are you alive?" she yelled until she realized her words thudded in a deadly vault.

Anne walked back to the other entrance, feeling her way through black. It was completely blocked, too. She ran back to the car, her brain working rapidly now. Their survival was up to her. With all her strength, she willed rational thinking back into her hysterical brain.

First things first. Was Tavo alive?

She knelt by his arm. His hand was warm. Good, good. Blisters had broken on his firmly fleshed palms; the dead flesh had callused under the pressure of unstinting manual labor. She slipped her thumb down his wrist, under the warm copper bracelet. The pulse held steady and strong.

"Are you all right? Wiggle your fingers."

They lay still in her hand.

"I'm trying to find something to dig you out with," she shouted as loud as she could. Already her throat was raw.

Anne fumbled for the trunk key, then opened the trunk. Under the floor, with the flat-tire equipment, she found a short-handled shovel. She grabbed it on a dead run, then hesitated. She needed the light, but when—she forced herself to say—when they dug out of the tunnel, they needed a car that would run. Lights would quickly drain the battery.

She turned out the lights and impatiently waited for her eyes to adjust to the dark. They didn't, for there was not one glimmer of light. She inched her way back to Tavo. "I'm coming with a shovel. I'm coming with a shovel...."

Anne felt along the concrete road until she found his arm. His hand was colder. His pulse...slower but steady. Crouching alongside, she put his arm between her kneeling thighs, clamping them as best she could, trying to infuse warmth into his bloodstream.

She plunged the short shovel into the interminable mound, and a mass of snow sprayed in her face.

Blindly she dug on, tossing shovelsful over her shoulder. She felt for his shoulder; it was still buried. She'd made no progress at all, and her knees hurt unbearably. She shifted to a more comfortable position, but Tavo's arm didn't bend adequately. She returned to her original stance. Afraid to check his pulse, she fought on.

It was like hollowing out the bottom of a sugar mountain. Her forehead was wet. Her hair stuck to her face. She unzipped the yellow coveralls to the belted waist and dug on.

"I'm here!" she kept yelling. Her voice cracked with hoarseness. Her throat was dry beyond imagination.

The lower half of Tavo's right leg broke free. "Hooray!" The exclamation came out a scratched whisper. She leaned down as far as she could. Part of his hip was out...the hard corded thighs. She couldn't reach farther. The leg was motionless.

"Have courage." Did she say it or think it?

Weakly he wiggled his fingers into the layers of clothing covering her legs. Only sensitized skin, eager for some sign, any sign of life, would have noticed the faint movement. Joyfully she dug deep, sending a giant cascade of snow down on her shoulders.

The stiff thud of a rubber boot sounded on the concrete.

"Did I hit you?" she croaked painfully, but he didn't respond. Anne was afraid to keep spearing into the mound, for the edges of the shovel were sharp when she tested her goose-downed thumb against the steel.

"Help me, Tavo!" She mustered all her vocal resources into a rasping shout. "I'll pull." The long fingers wiggled their assent.

She took his hand in her gloved ones and squeezed encouragement. She felt down the snowbank until she found the few inches of exposed hip.

There she sat, ignoring the shock of the freezing-cold concrete on her buttocks. No fabric, no matter how many layers, protected her from the direct chill of the road. Anne slipped her hands underneath his hips and grabbed hold.

It was impossible to get a good tight grip with her bulky gloves. She stripped out of them in an instant and grabbed his wet jeans. Finally she braced her legs up on the bank.

"Ready!" she yelled. Pain seared her throat.

She pulled until she thought her arms would pull from the sockets. The rubber boot thumped and scraped behind her. "Rest!" she warned him, rolling back up to a sitting position. Once released from the strain, her legs quivered uncontrollably. She had no time to still them. She felt along the bottom of the mound, her exposed fingers seeking information on their success. His waist was partially free. She could feel the leather belt. Then snow. Only snow, only snow, then his shoulder was partially exposed. Anne traced her fingers up the stout windbreaker until they met the wall of broken snow.

She sat down, blew on her fingers to thaw them, gripped the underside of his shoulder and rocked back to brace her legs once again.

"Ready? Go!" The words rattled in her chest. Anne could only hope his ear was close enough to hear. She pulled and pulled. The shoulder wrenched and twisted, and she pulled. The boot thumped and thumped.

Suddenly snow showered in her face. She dug her fingers farther under his shoulder, sputtering for breath under a noseful of snow—and Tavo bellycrawled free.

His head knocked hard into Anne's braced leg, knocking her off the snowbank. She couldn't see where he was. She somersaulted backward, keeping her legs high in order to miss his face, landing with a thud.

Anne snatched her bruised fingers off the icy pavement and put them in her mouth, first the right fingers and then the left, then the right. They stung badly at the touch of warmth, yet burned at the onslaught of cold air.

"Ana. Where are you?" Tavo's voice was groggy. Anne felt the wind of his arm waving, searching the darkness.

"Here." The ragged whisper was all she could manage. She was drained of all sentiment—relief, joy at Tavo's survival—of everything.

His groping hand found her foot, then calf, and Tavo dragged himself up beside her. "Where is the car?"

Anne fumbled for his hand, drew it to her cheek and held it there while she nodded vaguely. "Back there." It hurt too much to speak.

He sat still for a time. "We would be better off in the car," he said finally. His voice lacked its usual vigor. The possibility of further danger penetrated Anne's delayed shock.

"Yes." She swallowed. "Wait." Standing up, painfully and carefully she walked into the black void, her hands extended, held about waist height, feeling for safety. The fender, thankfully, was close.

"Found it." Tavo spoke then, relieving her of a reply. He had recognized her laryngitis. That concrete sign of his recovery propelled Anne forward. She needed to see the extent of his injuries. She touched the frigid metal of the car with rapid jumps of her fingers, searching for the door. When she found it, she bit her lip at the agony of flesh against the freezing chrome handle.

Tavo was boosting himself to his feet when the headlights caught him full glare, a wounded giant, Samson without his hair. He blinked, unseeing, and turned to face the mountain that might have been his tomb.

Anne squawked a couple of unintelligible words and ran to him.

"I am okay." He answered her question, flexing his shoulders and rotating his head one way, and the other. "I am a little—no, truthfully, I am very stiff."

Slowly he bent over and picked up the filthy gloves she had discarded. "Give me your hands." He reached for them and held them until they passed the burning threshold and eased into secondary aching. "Now you can slip your gloves on."

"When did you get that outfit?" Tavo asked, then remembered. "Shh, do not answer, sweetheart. In the boutique on your way out the door, no? But it is huge on you."

The idea occurred to them both at the same moment.

"It would not fit me," he said, "but I do not need my arms through the top. I have to get out of these drenched jeans. Wool sweaters trap body heat and hold it inside, no matter whether wet or not."

Anne had already unzipped the grimy, stained jumpsuit and was stepping out of it by the time he finished speaking. "Hurry," she croaked.

"How stupid of me. . . ." he cursed himself, even as he unbuckled his belt and unzipped his pants. Anne forgot to lower her eyes. He kicked off the rubber boots. Underneath he had on his running shoes and muddy socks. Goose bumps prickled his bare legs. Hard muscles quivered in the damp air. Then he slipped out of his soaked briefs, and Anne, drawn by a need to be united with him, moved to his side. He leaned on her makeshift shelf, stepping quickly into the expensive woman's ski suit and tying the arms around his waist.

"Into the back seat," he ordered. "First we must

warm ourselves. Then we will commence our rescue."

He killed the lights while Anne snuggled in the back, holding the huge goosedown parka to receive him. The door was open on his side to make room for his long legs. Anne curled into him, and soon her breathing deepened.

Tavo shook her gently. "We must stay awake."

"Hmm?" Anne nestled closer. His concern didn't pierce her drowsy contentment.

"Sit up. It will be easier for you to stay awake." He pried her from him.

"Don't—"

"Stop straining your throat," he ordered. Worry made his tone sterner than he apparently intended, for when she drew back, he began chatting about this and that, working to keep her awake.

"Radámes looked like the trip down to the tunnel was no strain...Sophia was resting comfortably the last I heard...and Pascal seemed full of *frijoles*. Hard to remember how lazy he was when they first arrived...." Tavo's sentences were short. He hesitated between subjects. "I did not recognize the woman with the broken leg. Anyone I know? Shh...."

He felt for her mouth to hush her, his scratched finger raising a response. The bad times blurred in her confused memory. "Sorry. I forgot, Ana. Her identity is not important. It is very difficult to think. I had many things I wanted...ideas I was thinking about you...."

Anne stirred. *Couldn't he say us?* But Tavo had stopped talking. After a brief time she heard him step out of the car. The synthetic of the yellow ski outfit rustled. He must be stretching.

"Pucha!" he groaned. "I ache everywhere. Do not

say anything, Ana. Come on. We need to set about our rescue." His questing hand found her leg. "Where is your hand? Let us get busy. Where is the shovel? Do you remember? Damn, I never realized a monologue was so difficult."

Anne giggled. The strain to her respiratory system sent her into a spasm of coughs.

"Ridiculous. A bloody serious monologue at a time like this? Never mind. Where are the lights? I am assuming you are strong enough to run around the front of the car and find the shovel."

Anne's eyes, unaccustomed to illumination, were dazzled blind when he switched on the headlights. She didn't coddle them. She hurried, sightless, to the source of light at the front of the car and found the shovel where she'd laid it.

"Do you see my gloves anywhere around?"

She searched without success.

"I took them off to hook up the chains. They must be buried. *¡Carajo!* I guess that means I shovel barehanded." He got out of the car. "When you damned me to hell, Anne Mahoney, you must have had a direct connection."

He walked stiffly over to the wall. After studying it, he took the shovel and chipped out an area about a yard wide. "Okay. Here is where our tunnel begins. Douse the lights, please."

Tavo began shoveling steadily. His curses led Anne back to his side in the dark. She touched his ribs to let him know she was there. He grunted a response and kept working.

"Puncha." The sound of the shovel scraping rough chunks of snow ceased.

"Where are you, sweetheart?" This time the old endearment offended Anne. She had temporarily forgotten his unforgivably mean behavior until now.

Tavo groped for her and drew her to him. She could hear his teeth chattering, and in kindness could not refuse him aid. "I need defrosting." He lifted her Shetland sweater, his hurry revealing the degree of his chill. Impatiently he yanked her flannel shirt out and lifted her tank top. Anne shuddered at the feel of wet cold skin clamping her body from her breasts to her bare waist.

"Damn, it stings.... You sure never know what fate is going to dump on you next, *no cierto!* My grandfather knew a man who had a rich productive farm near Valdivia. An earthquake came, and instantly his farm was the bottom of a new deep lake. His cattle were drowned. Everything he owned was gone...."

What was the point of Tavo's story? A quake that great might have been the same one that killed his family....

"What happened to—"

Her squawk was cut off by a kiss, placed with the unerring marksmanship of a starving man. His lips sought a response from her; his tongue pleaded for attention. She capitulated with a surge of blind need as great as his own. Finally, wrenching away, Tavo muttered distractedly to himself, "There is that answer."

"No." Her monosyllable scratched out painfully.

Tavo took the shovel from her and set back to work.

"My grandfather's friend and his wife, by chance, had taken their children shopping in Santiago. They lost everything...but they lived." His voice was more muffled now as he dug deeper into the barrier. Anne ducked in behind him, pushing the shoveled snow out into the highway tunnel.

"The floods are terrible. Some of our contract farmers may lose all their orchards. It depends how hot this summer is. We can cnly conjecture the extent of root damage. High temperatures stress the roots. If we have warm winds, too, as you did last year in northern California, then...."

The only sound was the shovel biting into the icy snow.

"Wind sucks moisture out of the leaves. More stress. At last count, when I flew up to Los Andes this afternoon, I had 2,500 hectares under water...."

Anne noticed Tavo hadn't bothered translating Chilean measures for her. She converted to acreage in her mind...1,500 times 2.5...3,750 acres.

"That might effectively take care of my dilemma of how many Jonathan apple orchards to replace, *Bueno, Ana.* Your turn with the shovel. My hands are wet. The blisters are probably bleeding again— Now do not gasp. I am just stating facts. Can you take a turn?"

Grabbing the shovel, Anne ducked into the tunnel and began working.

Tavo continued talking, the flatness of his observations becoming increasingly emotional. A jumble of scenes spilled out. Families with their meager possessions packed into rickety wooden wagons crowding the highways. Rampaging creeks rushing out of high mountain passes, sweeping homes off banks. Foaming, treacherous rivers ripping trees out in their terrifying route to the ocean, trees that became gigantic cudgels downstream, battering the helpless in their swollen path. Dead cattle. Dead horses.

"People?" she croaked.

"Two dead. Several dozen missing."

He had spent the past two days and nights sandbagging his freezer facility. The task wasn't quite completed when the distress call came from Radámes.

Anne's arms ached so badly that tears flooded her eyes. Inside the gloves her hands felt wet and sticky. Blood? She couldn't see in the dark, even if she pulled them off. She removed the gloves, anyway and wiped her hands on the pulverized snow behind her.

Tavo, at her rear, heard the pause. "My turn with the torture shovel." He crawled out. Anne crawled backward. It was good to set her feet on the ground again.

Tavo fumbled for her shoulder and grasped it firmly. "You are a Wonderwoman."

"Need Lois Lane," she gasped.

He chuckled. She heard him crawling into their excavation. She twisted and flexed her neck. Exhaustion debilatated her. The sweat on her body was freezing cold in her inactivity. The narrow icy escape gave her claustrophobia. She lingered outside, using the excuse of looking at the luminous digits on her watch.

"Two-thirty," she rasped. Chilean time.

"Eat some snow. You need to lubricate your throat. And stop talking, dammit. Can you not follow orders?"

Anne scooped up a handful, and the icy water did soothe her parched throat. She let it trickle down, wishing it was liquid novocaine to numb the pain, or a malted milk, a thick chocolate malted milk.... Her mouth watered; she was hungry. She grabbed another handful of snow.

They were going to die on Chilean time. Someone would dig her frozen arm out and look at the time, and it would mean nothing. The batteries were waterproof. No one would know the exact time she and Tavo had frozen to death. Rigor mortis couldn't set in until their bodies thawed from nature's deep freeze. Or could it?

What followed was an emotional sensation so intense Anne felt it physically. Almost in slow motion, her spirits sank, down, down, down into the deepest despair. She trembled, shaken by her sagging will to survive, until like the poplars upriver from Vienna torn by November gales, no leaves, no hope remained.

"Why bother? Storm," she cried, quietly at first. Then she was shrieking in a high-pitched eerie voice that wasn't her own. "Storms last three or four or five days." The sobs burst out, tremendous croaking cries.

Tavo's hands felt for her, a blind man touching his path to her waist. "Let me hold you close, Ana," he said. "You are safe, believe me. We are nowhere near the end. But I need help, too."

Anne flinched when the large dripping ice cubes, his hands, slipped under her shirt, wetting her already damp tank top. Eventually her breath slowed, and she stood quietly, her spine rigid. From time to time a tremor passed the length of her body. She didn't want to die.

"Do you remember the avalanche at Alpine Meadows in the Sierras, Ana?" He tightened his grip slightly, and Anne heard his heartbeat quicken against her ear. "A girl was trapped in a five-foot-long, two-foot-high space under a row of lockers that fell across a wooden bench. She lived in that coffin of snow for five days before rescuers dug her out. We have been here less than eight hours. My thought is...."

Anne took off one of her gloves and lightly touched his face. Sonar fingers to help her detect the situation.

"We tunnel to the top of the mound. Record storms drop three or four meters...yards...."

The muscles of his face belied his reassuring tone. They felt taut under the warm sheath of skin. Whiskers tickled her fingers. A day's growth? No, at least two days', or three. She felt his cheek stretch into a smile.

"Do not fear the storm. We are not going to pop out of our snowhill into a white hurricane, like Mexican jumping ants—"

"Beans." The correction was a crackling squeak.

Tavo's laughter was cheery, and the muscles in his jaw relaxed. His reaction puzzled her. He'd been secure in his escape plan all along. But she liked the fact that he'd been worried. Years of experience had taught her to distrust iron control. You never knew at what dangerous moment the iron would crack.

"Back to the snow mines."

Anne put her glove on again, tugging the leather wrist with her teeth to fit the stubborn ski gear completely over her fingers.

"Here is the shovel. As our tunnel gets longer, it makes more sense for me to haul the snow back down."

"Pucha...Tonto." A moment later, Anne heard the muffled thump of fist against bone. Probably his forehead. "I have been suffering stupidly. We left the expedition parka in the car, *no cierto*? I can use it to haul snow without frostbiting my hands."

The snow tunnel they were digging was narrower and colder and darker than Anne remembered. Truly dark. Darker than the total darkness of the large highway tunnel, because every sense was trapped in the tight frozen cocoon.

Anne inched her way up the gradual incline, one hand outstretched, waiting to feel a solid impact. The only smell in her nostrils was her own nervous sweat. She tasted fear in her mouth, mild, salty, sour. Her heartbeat resonated in a silence so deep that the beat could as easily have been the jarring blast of a jackhammer.

When she found an obstacle, Anne attacked it fiercely. Chips of ice and snow splattered her face. She shut her eyes against the blitz and worked steadily forward, carefully carving out a space she estimated would be wide enough and high enough for Tavo to enter. She could hear him working several yards behind her. A couple of times he started to talk, then stopped.

Treacherous thoughts were firmly squashed into place. Thus far, none of the storms had lasted more than three-and-a-half days. If she was angling the tunnel too flat, so what. They had days to dig, and she would only be a matter of yards off. If the angle was too steep, she'd slide back into Tavo. He'd pushed her forward. How were his hands? Maybe she should slip back....

She paused to look at the bright numbers on her watch. 3:36. He'd been hauling snow for forty-five minutes.

"Hands?" Concern forced the question from her sore throat. She grabbed a handful of snow and sucked on it.

"They are okay. This parka makes a big difference. Sorry, I forgot to tell you. I was distracted.... I was thinking...."

Would he stop talking again?

Anne waited mutely, her shoulders throbbing now that she was still. What was he trying to say? She resumed hacking at the snow, hoping....

Then some decision was made. A floodgate of battered reactions lifted, and ideas surged forth. Partial images, half-finished thoughts, drowned dreams.

If Anne could have spoken easily, she would have impatiently moved him toward the point. But she couldn't utter painful garbled sounds loudly enough to interrupt the tormented man behind her.

Tavo rambled for what seemed like hours. He raged at himself for not foreseeing the extent of the floods— he should have spent the summer constructing higher dikes and more levees. There was no excuse for surprise. "California's winters are a prologue for us," he said. "It is all hooked up to the El Niño current off the Galápagos."

He agonized over the swirling waters rampaging through Santiago's slums and mansions, and the bewildered faces of rich and poor alike. Bewildered, beaten expressions visible from the air. Men and women standing side by side, holding crying children in their arms.

Forever, seemingly, he talked about his friend, the Frenchman's vineyards, scratched from a farm to the north the man bought thirty years earlier. Worthless desert land, the Frenchman was clever. He'd studied irrigation in South Africa and Israel, and now, a mess. Maybe nothing left.

Nothing but his sons, dapper, urbanized young men, standing by his side with the farm workers, sandbagging the land. His Chilean wife had organized the workers' wives. The women had carried endless sandwiches and coffee to the men. "Probably they are still carrying picnic thermoses of coffee."

Anne glanced at the glowing digits of her watch. It was well past dawn at the Frenchman's farm.

"We Mohrs do not seem to have many children, no matter how many we have." Thirteen children, she remembered. Three survivors? His voice was too muffled to hear the rest. He was hauling trash snow out to the highway tunnel.

Anne shoveled doggedly. Her eyes burned from squeezing her lids shut too long. Her nose constantly tickled from the chipped snow. Scratching the itch took too much time. Her back ached ceaselessly from her waist to the top of her head. What was it the exercise instructor called the position when you lay on your stomach and arched your head back? The cobra. The deadly cobra. Was she angling too high?

Anne lowered the path, enough for minimal comfort. She was eager to break through to fresh air, no matter how brutal the storm was. Just one clear breath.

She heard Tavo behind her. An electric charge pulsated throughout her tired body. His strength was hers; his thoughts were hers. She felt only the power of the questing, strangely passionate mood in which he enveloped them.

"My grandfather's dream was to take Chile's agricultural wealth out to the world. Our copper was already owned by the multinationals. Chilean plywood rebuilt Europe after the Second World War, but the lumber industry was already fully occupied by other Chilean families.

"His grandfather and his father made money—they made fortunes, Ana—shipping the copper and wood. Yet grandfather wanted to do more than carry Chile's wealth to the industrial countries. He wanted to produce valuables that gave back to the country. Jobs, *bueno*. Teaching marginal grass farmers how to make more profitable use of their land...generating taxes to pay for schools, hospitals, roads...yes. But he wanted to sell goods that lived and did not die after the mining or lumbering. He did not carry this idea when he was a young man. I think it came later, with my grandmother's influence.

"My father was a businessman. He did not have the love of the soil my grandfather had developed within himself, but my father was clever with our shipping work.

"My grandparents endured the loss of their only child, because I needed a solid home...I think. They were very old-school German, Ana, stoics. We never discussed feelings and motivations. European girls were a shock to me—all that blah-blah-blah about things that were none of their concern, fruitless speculation about things no one can know.

"Reading your folk philosopher, Dale Carnegie, gave me the idea how to avoid the pressure. I learned to ask them about their feelings, and with few exceptions, Ana, they were too busy describing their psyches to worry about mine."

Anne was alert to the nuances. The discouraged pauses, a rush of pride and dismayed silences. She knew with a certainty forged from love that he would never again expose himself so completely; it wasn't in his nature. But exhaustion, burial, the very tomb they were escaping had shattered his defenses. And maybe—her shovel scraped sharply against his latest silence—maybe losing her had affected him, too.

"My grandfather planted the seed of his dream in me—" Tavo halted to drag another bundle of snow out.

His pained tone completed the unspoken thought: *I failed my grandfather.*

He was speaking again, rambling.

"My grandmother had fancies more so than dreams, you know.

"Two weeping birch trees grew outside her bedroom window. Their branches danced in the wind. With the coming of spring the trees budded, and their leaves touched in the breezes. The trees were kissing, she told grandfather. . . .

"In August, the day after I arrived home, he had a phone call from the south. His tenant mentioned in passing that the trees had fallen over during a bad winter storm.

"I came home from Munich for my grandmother's funeral in early November. . . ." His voice drifted away and returned, ironically humorous in a feeble attempt to protect his sentiments. Anne heard his sorrow and suffered with him.

"Her death was conveniently timed. It came at the beginning of our fall break. My grandfather was valiant, strong-minded enough for the two of us. He ordered me back to finish my graduate work. My examinations ended as that winter began. It was a dormant time here. Grandfather wanted me to take a few months off and go traveling. . . .

"She had suffered with cancer for quite a while. . . . It was ugly, I heard later from her friends. She refused to let anyone warn me. My education was very important to her. The final few months, she insisted on moving back to the farm at Lake Llanquihue."

Anne could visualize again the green pastures and

wind-stirred white clouds. She and Tavo had talked of children then, their children and a life together. She had trusted him, and he had turned on her.

Behind her closed lids, Anne was weeping. She must have been weeping for some time—for his grandmother, for him. For herself. She stopped shoveling to wipe the tears away, and blinked.

The darkness didn't seem as intense. The tunnel was black, but a gray black. Maybe they were close to the top. Anne attacked the snow. *Don't tell him you're sorry,* she mourned, convinced now only the threat of her death had jarred his memories into the open. Yet she loved him. She gripped the shovel with new determination, trying to call out the news. Instead of words, a faint, racking cough sputtered, unheard in the flow of his story, a new story, an important one, she could hear.

"My grandfather cried that afternoon. It was shocking for me. And then we began to work. We were demons. We worked day and night. All the concentration I had put into racing, all the study I made at the university was nothing to our effort. I was the son he never had. I was the seed that in time would plant more seeds...."

She could see dimly now. Jagged rubble of gray. *No time to waste socializing. Tell me. Me, Tavo. Don't confess to an anonymous set of priest's ears in this dark hole.*

In the intimacy of their frozen cocoon, he responded. "A wife would come later, Ana. And when later came and my grandfather was long dead, his great-nephews were developing nicely, doing well in their studies, showing a strong character. A wife was unimportant to me. The important factor was that I had completed his dream. No, in fact, it was my dream, too, Ana...and I was comfortable in it. I did not want to mourn again. Everyone I ever loved was dead. You miss dead friends. You have to replace employees when they die. But none of them are the core of your life. When my core was empty, I refused to permit anyone to enter." There, his confession was complete.

"Then I met you," he continued without hesitation, which was everything Anne needed to hear. "This, after hours of talking, is still not easy for me, Ana," he said, ordering her not to answer, since her throat was too raw. "The floods did not destroy Industrias Mohr. Our foundations are very firm. What they did was rip off the shell I had built around myself. What a fool I was to believe I would rather live without you than risk losing you. It came to me in Rancaucaga, with the river cresting over the sandbags, that if I lost everything, I would have nothing.

"Others who lost everything still had their families. But it was not having children to carry on through the generations that gave them the surviving power. The force came as it does to teams of oxen, with two pulling the load.

"And only then—only now—I understand grandfather. When grandmothers' two kissing trees died, he was shocked, for only then, I believe, he realized that he would not die immediately, too, and join her. That he lived and had no choice but to continue living with nothing. For without her, his life had ended." He laughed ruefully. "Grandfather used me to charge forth with *her* dream. We were working for the past. He had no other outlet for love...and I...I never realized it was my only outlet. Hectares of bushels and strategic prodding of the Japanese."

Anne opened her eyes and blinked. She had to squint against the brilliant, translucent light ahead. Sun! No storm could cast such light.

Her joy died. She had to hear the end. If they escaped, Tavo might not have the conviction to finish. He had paused so often. . . . Anne lacked the courage to risk another withdrawal. She crawled sideways in the tunnel, chipping at the sides, confident her body blocked most of the light below.

"I have never known a woman like you, Ana. I have never lied to you. . . except when I did not deny I was an Austrian ski instructor." He laughed easily.

Anne realized then that there would be no holding back. He was clear on his goal, and she shoveled forward. She had to see his face. He had to witness her emotions. She could only show them. She could not say her heart.

"I wanted you. I loved. . . I love you, Ana. . . . All week I have been afraid that you no longer loved me. That after I spoke so cruelly to you, you would never forgive me. That you had set the date for a senatorial wedding by shortwave, and I could say nothing to return your heart. The floods had banished me from you."

Anne shoveled automatically, driven by passion. The metal broke through the crust. There was a brilliant patch of peacock blue.

His laugh was grim this time. "Imagine that great twist of fate you Irish are forevermore going on about. I nearly lost you tonight, but by my death, not yours. I do not know why I thought I was invincible—"

Anne impatiently rammed her head and shoulders through the final layer of avalanche.

"What the hell?" came the grunt of surprise from below.

With a twisting, kicking motion, she hoisted herself up onto the summit. The highway ribboned out from the base of the snow, perhaps thirty feet below. Only a few inches of snow covered the concrete. Bulldozers were already clearing their way to the roadblock.

Anne bent down and grinned, a delirious, happy grin. Tavo's unshaven face was haggard. Bruises showed on his forehead where the avalanche had knocked him to the pavement. His dark green windbreaker was wet and muddy. Her butter-yellow Italian chic was ridiculous tied on at the waist.

And he looked wonderful when she looked down on his face, all he had told her was there to see: vulnerable, sensitive, intelligent, disciplined. Loving.

Anne reached for his hand with hers to help pull him through the narrow gap to freedom. Her thumb brushed the copper bracelet. Love could be freely given, she finally understood, and accepted.

"Oh, please. Yes." With those words she finally proposed, and cried at the pain in her throat. Her scratched raw words were deliberate. She never took her eyes from his.

And Tavo smiled at her with such tenderness, and wisdom, such secure love, that Anne never doubted the rightness of her faith.

ABOUT THE AUTHOR

When Catherine Healy described her Super-romance to several journalist colleagues, they were convinced it was the story of her life. "What could I tell them? I happen to have developed a lovely habit of skiing Argentina in August and September when the California sun loses its appeal. But apart from that my experiences have been quite different."

Catherine had acquired her bachelor's degree in Latin American Politics, and other impressive credentials, when her life changed course. She began work as a newspaper reporter and full-time freelancer for various travel publications. *Private Corners* marks her entry into romance fiction; the vibrant writer hopes it's just the beginning of life on location, researching her stories in fascinating locales.

Getting the facts is one of her fortes. She is grateful to the fruit exporters, speed-ski champions, plastic surgeons and ranchers whose knowledge contributed to this vivid tale of love in the Andes. Her next Superromance will feature naturalists and urban sophisticates in the Galápagos islands, observing ancient tortoises "who may have seen Darwin."

Yours FREE, with a home subscription to

SUPERROMANCE ™

Complete and mail
the coupon below today!

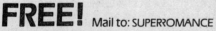

- -

FREE! Mail to: SUPERROMANCE

In the U.S.
2504 West Southern Avenue
Tempe, AZ 85282

In Canada
649 Ontario St.
Stratford, Ontario N5A 6W2

YES, please send me FREE and without any obligation, my
SUPERROMANCE novel, LOVE BEYOND DESIRE. If you do not hear
from me after I have examined my FREE book, please send me the
4 new **SUPERROMANCE** books every month as soon as they come
off the press. I understand that I will be billed only $2.50 for each book
(total $10.00). There are no shipping and handling or any other hidden
charges. There is no minimum number of books that I have to
purchase. In fact, I may cancel this arrangement at any time.
LOVE BEYOND DESIRE is mine to keep as a FREE gift, even if
I do not buy any additional books.

NAME _____ (Please Print)

ADDRESS _____ APT. NO.

CITY _____

STATE/PROV. _____ ZIP/POSTAL CODE _____

SIGNATURE (If under 18, parent or guardian must sign.)

134-BPS-KAPJ
SUP-SUB-1

This offer is limited to one order per household and not valid to present
subscribers. Prices subject to change without notice.
Offer expires September 30, 1984

Just what the woman on the go needs!

BOOKMATE

The perfect "mate" for all Harlequin paperbacks!

Holds paperbacks open for hands-free reading!

- TRAVELING
- VACATIONING
- AT WORK • IN BED
- COOKING • EATING
- STUDYING

Perfect size for all standard paperbacks, this wonderful invention makes reading a pure pleasure! Ingenious design holds paperback books OPEN and FLAT so even wind can't ruffle pages—leaves your hands free to do other things. Reinforced, wipe-clean vinyl-covered holder flexes to let you turn pages without undoing the strap...supports paperbacks so well, they have the strength of hardcovers!

Snaps closed for easy carrying.

Available now. Send your name, address, and zip or postal code, along with a check or money order for just $4.99 + .75¢ for postage & handling (for a total of $5.74) payable to Harlequin Reader Service to:

Harlequin Reader Service

In U.S.:
P.O. Box 52040
Phoenix, AZ 85072-2040

In Canada:
649 Ontario Street
Stratford, Ont. N5A 6W2

MATE-1

TAKE THESE 4 Harlequin Romances FREE

as advertised on TV

Delight in **Mary Wibberley's** warm romance MAN OF POWER, the story of a girl whose life changes from drudgery to glamour overnight....Let THE WINDS OF WINTER by **Sandra Field** take you on a journey of love to Canada's beautiful Maritimes....Thrill to a cruise in the tropics—and a devastating love affair in the aftermath of a shipwreck—in **Rebecca Stratton's** THE LEO MAN....Travel to the wilds of Kenya in a quest for love with the determined heroine in **Karen van der Zee's** LOVE BEYOND REASON.

Harlequin Romances . . . 6 exciting novels published each month! Each month you will get to know interesting, appealing, true-to-life people . You'll be swept to distant lands you've dreamed of visiting . . . Intrigue, adventure, romance, and the destiny of many lives will thrill you through each Harlequin Romance novel.

Get all the latest books before they're sold out!

As a Harlequin subscriber you actually receive your personal copies of the latest Romances immediately after they come off the press, so you're sure of getting all 6 each month.

Cancel your subscription whenever you wish!

You don't have to buy any minimum number of books. Whenever you decide to stop your subscription just let us know and we'll cancel all further shipments.

Your FREE gift includes
- MAN OF POWER by **Mary Wibberley**
- THE WINDS OF WINTER by **Sandra Field**
- THE LEO MAN by **Rebecca Stratton**
- LOVE BEYOND REASON by **Karen van der Zee**

FREE GIFT CERTIFICATE

and Subscription Reservation

Mail this coupon today!

Harlequin Reader Service

In the U.S.A.	In Canada
1440 South Priest Drive	649 Ontario Street
Tempe, AZ 85281	Stratford, Ontario N5A 6W2

Please send me my 4 Harlequin Romance novels FREE. Also, reserve a subscription to the 6 NEW Harlequin Romance novels published each month. Each month I will receive 6 NEW Romance novels at the low price of $1.50 each (*Total–$9.00 a month*). There are no shipping and handling or any other hidden charges. I may cancel this arrangement at any time, but even if I do, these first 4 books are still mine to keep.   Offer expires September 30, 1984

NAME   (PLEASE PRINT)

ADDRESS   APT. NO.

CITY

STATE/PROV.   ZIP/POSTAL CODE

116-BPR-EASJ

Offer not valid to present subscribers

If price changes are necessary you will be notified.